Matt didn't want to look back, because he knew it was gaining. "Faster," he said.

Jill took long, quick strides, unfazed by running on a catwalk ten feet in the air. Compared with her fluid movements, Matt thought he must have looked like an arthritic rhinoceros.

He heard the thing shriek again, and the noise shot through him, cold fingers tickling his spine.

Matt spied a window ahead and he thought they could reach it in time. He had no idea what was on the other side of the window.

The catwalk rocked and Matt nearly teetered sideways. Their attacker had reached the platform.

"Don't look back," he told Jill.

She was already way ahead of him, under the window and drawing the crowbar back to smash it out. She busted the window, the glass cracking into jagged splinters. Winding up again, she busted out the shards and then poked out the remaining glass in the frame. She stuck her head out the window, peeked back in and said, "There's another roof about five feet below the window. I'll go first."

"Wait—"

In one smooth movement, she pushed herself up on the sill and swung her legs outside. Her butt on the sill, she pushed off and slipped out of view.

He heard her hit a solid surface with a soft thud and looked out to see if she was okay. She stood on the rooftop and waved him on.

"Your turn," she said.

Not much time left. Behind him, metal bucked and shook.

He threw one leg over the sill, straddling it. That's when it grabbed him . . .

JUN 13 2007.   HORROR

EVIL HARVEST

ANTHONY IZZO

PINNACLE BOOKS
Kensington Publishing Corp.
www.kensingtonbooks.com

PINNACLE BOOKS are published by

Kensington Publishing Corp.
850 Third Avenue
New York, NY 10022

All Kensington titles, imprints, and distributed lines are
available at special quantity discounts for bulk purchases for
sales promotions, premiums, fund-raising, educational, or
institutional use. Special book excerpts or customized print-
ings can also be created to fit specific needs. For details, write
or phone the office of the Kensington special sales manager:
Kensington Publishing Corp., 850 Third Avenue, New York,
NY 10022, attn: Special Sales Department; phone 1-800-221-
2647.

This book is a work of fiction. Names, characters, businesses,
organizations, places, events, and incidents are the product
of the author's imagination, or are used fictitiously. Any re-
semblance to actual persons, living or dead, events, or lo-
cales is entirely coincidental.

PINNACLE BOOKS and the Pinnacle logo are Reg. U.S.
Pat. & TM Off.

ISBN-13: 978-0-7860-1875-4
ISBN-10: 0-7860-1875-5

First printing: June 2007

10 9 8 7 6 5 4 3 2 1

Printed in the United States of America

For Anthony "Big Jim" Izzo

ACKNOWLEDGMENTS

It's difficult, if not impossible, to make it down this road by yourself. I'd be remiss if I didn't thank the following people: Audrey Sander, Cheryl Wasson, and Lee Jones for their help with promotion; Miles Lott for his keen editorial eye; Scott Miller for getting the deal done. And as always to my wife, Jenn, for helping me live the dream.

Special thanks also to the Heaton family, owners of the Bookworm in East Aurora. You guys and your staff are terrific.

And last but not least, Pat Izzo. Mom, those Saturday afternoon creature features did some good, after all.

BOOK ONE

Coming
Home

CHAPTER 1

Matthew Crowe was stopped at a red light when he heard the woman scream.

The scream came from his left, and he glanced out the open driver's-side window at the Folsom Furniture plant. The main warehouse looked the same as it did in his youth, a pile of rust and bricks that resembled a long-dead industrial relic. He would have thought it abandoned. A spotlight shining on an open door at the front of the building and a tractor trailer with FOLSOM in blue letters parked at a loading door told him they were still in business.

He checked the light again; it was still red. He looked back at the open warehouse door. That was bad news. Business owners didn't make a habit of leaving doors open, especially with thousands of dollars' worth of merchandise sitting behind them. Did something break in, or out? That was the question.

The woman cried out again, this time a hoarse groan. No mistaking it, someone in trouble. He checked—no oncoming cars—and turned left against the light.

As he turned, he heard a second shriek, a low growl

that rose in pitch to a keening wail. He felt the shriek reverberate through his guts, felt his stomach and bowels get liquidy. The last time he had heard that sound, there had been blood and pain and cries for mercy. Leaving now was not an option. One of the bastards was after someone.

He gunned the Cavalier's engine and rolled up the driveway, gravel crunching and popping under the tires. He swung the car into a diagonal parking spot in front of the warehouse. *Hope nothing happens to the car. Rental company will be pissed.*

When he boarded his plane, he never counted on something like this happening so soon. *Ten years out of Lincoln and I run into Them the first night back.*

Ten years away, first in the Army Rangers and then in cramped apartments and Motel 6s around the country. Hell of a way to live, collecting newspaper clippings, Internet printouts and interviews about creatures that shouldn't exist.

But they did exist, and from the sound of it, one of them was on the hunt.

Throwing the car in park, he got out, unlocked the trunk and pulled out the tire iron. If he had an automatic weapon handy, it might be a fair fight, but the tire iron would have to suffice.

The warehouse was separated from a four-story factory building by an alley. At the end of the alley, another spotlight shone like sunlight at the end of a train tunnel. Matt watched for any sign of movement, any shift in the shadows. When nothing rushed from the alley, he moved ahead, tire iron in hand.

The woman cried out again and he heard footsteps flop on the concrete floor of the warehouse. Had she managed to slip away? It sounded that way.

Creeping up on the door, he peered inside the warehouse, half expecting the thing inside to pop out and grab him. *Here goes*, he thought.

He ducked inside and looked up at the three-tiered steel racks, the highest of which ran twenty feet in the air. Crates, pallets and rows of shrink-wrapped furniture went on for what seemed like a mile. It also created hundreds of hiding spots. Moonlight filtered in through the high windows, but instead of providing welcome illumination, it seemed to create more shadows.

He glanced at the door. The bolt was a mangled lump of metal. Likewise for the rings that held the door's security bar in place. Something wanted to open the doors, and had done so from *inside* the warehouse.

He ventured a soft, "Hello?"

The woman darted out from under the storage bays and into the center of the aisle. She ducked and scrambled underneath one of the lower racks. The darkness swallowed her up. *Dammit*, he thought.

He started down the aisle, aware that he could be ambushed from any angle.

A thundering crash behind him. Matt spun around to see a pallet of kitchen chairs piled on the floor. The plastic shrink-wrap had busted, and the chairs' legs had snapped like kindling.

A second pallet of chairs tumbled down from the third tier and landed on the first pile. Matt realized the assailant was attempting to block the exit. It would not be impossible to leave through the door, but anyone who tried moving the chairs would be an easy target as they attempted to clear the exit.

Now he heard it move, thudding along the top racks, its breath coming in heavy, wet grunts.

Matt searched the racks, trying to get a glimpse of the woman. He crouched down, scanning the crates under the racks. "You in there?"

No answer came, so he continued to the end of the aisle. As he turned left, he heard footsteps, someone in a hurry. He turned quickly, but before he could square his shoulders, something hard and metal smacked his ankle.

Shit, that hurts! he thought, hopping in pain.

The attacker followed up with a shove; already off-balance, Matt toppled over and smacked the concrete. The tire iron clanged to the floor beside him. Being a Good Samaritan hurt like hell.

"You son of a bitch!" the woman said, and pounced on top of him. She raised the crowbar over her head and brought it down like a lumberjack. He blocked the blow, his arm smacking her forearms. The crowbar flew out of her hands and tumbled under a pallet.

Her primary weapon gone, the woman dug her nails into his cheek. He winced but managed to grab her wrists and hold them. "I'm trying to help you, dammit!"

She tried to pull away, but then it dawned on her she couldn't get loose her shoulders slumped in defeat.

I'm not what dragged you in here, he thought.

"My God," she said. "I'm sorry." A tear dribbled down her cheek. He wanted to wipe it away for her but thought better of it.

She was straddling him, and he glanced at her Nike T-shirt. It had been torn across the belly; blood stained the white fabric and had dribbled onto her running shorts. Something had clawed her before she slipped away.

"Thank you," she said. "For coming in after me."

In the dim warehouse, her eyes stood out. Pale green, they looked like they could be sniper's eyes under the right (or wrong) circumstances. She was compact and had the lean, smooth legs of a runner. Her curly black hair was pulled into a ponytail. He took her for about twenty-eight or twenty-nine.

Matt said, "We need to get out of here fast. We're in here with someone very dangerous."

"You've got my vote." She stood up and brushed off her shorts.

Matt got to his feet as well. His cheek stung from the scratch, a low throb pulsed through his ankle. A gimp leg wasn't going to help them get out of Folsom's warehouse.

He lowered his voice to a whisper. "That was pretty smart, hiding out and whacking me with the crowbar like that."

"I found it under one of the racks." She looked down at his foot. "I didn't hit you full force, but you're lucky your ankle's not broken."

He hoped there was an ice pack at his aunt's house with his name on it. "Could've fooled me," he said. "And now that you've nearly maimed me, I'm Matt Crowe."

"Jill Adams," she said. "Nice to meet you, Mr. Crowe—let's get the hell out of here."

She retrieved the crowbar and he picked up the tire iron. They turned the corner to the next aisle, heading toward the front of the building, nearest the street.

Glass crashed and wood cracked in the aisle behind them. The attacker had pushed another pallet full of goods off of one of the top bays, hoping to crush them. One of these times he wasn't going to miss.

Matt looked at the far wall and noticed an elevated platform running along the walls. There was a small office, with plywood walls and a picture window. Thick steel posts rose from the ground, supporting the office and the catwalk. Matt imagined a stogie-chewing, bull-necked boss in a shirt and tie looking out the window, making sure that the employees hauled ass during working hours.

A metal staircase led up to the catwalk, which seemed like their best chance for escape. He guessed the ware-

house would have large doors somewhere to accommo-
date trucks. But could they open them?

If they could get on the catwalk, it would allow them
to move around the warehouse and find a window to
climb out of.

"Let's make a move for the stairs," he said.

"What about the door?"

"Blocked off by a pallet."

"Then what are we waiting for?" She brushed a lock
of hair off her forehead. "The walkway it is."

They crept down the aisle, watching every direction
for any sign of movement. As they neared the stairway,
Jill shouted, "Look out!"

She clamped down on his arm and yanked him toward her. A pallet with a recliner on it smashed against
the concrete where Matt had stood a second ago. He
put his arm up, as if to ward off the already fallen pallet.
It was purely reflex and he realized if Jill hadn't pulled
him away, he would have been crushed like an ant
under a boot.

"Whoever he is has rotten aim," she said.

Matt's heart beat a rhythm in his chest John Bonham
would have envied. His hands trembled and cool sweat
trickled down his back. "Now it's my turn to thank you."

"Keep moving," she said.

As they started up the stairs Matt glanced up at the
third tier of racks. A cold lump of ice formed in his
belly when he saw their attacker climb over a crate and
stand upright. It wrapped its too-long arms around a
support beam and swung itself around the pole. He saw
a row of spiky quills running down its back, got a look at
the oversize skull. It lowered itself like a man descending a rope, hand over hand. It had decided to finish the
hunt.

They hurried up the stairs.

* * *

Chief Ed Rafferty watched Billy Hamil crawl across the floor of the cell block. He'd slammed his nightstick into Hamil's knee, driving him to the ground. He looked down at the crawling worm, right between the 1 and the 8 on Hamil's Lincoln High Football jersey. It made a perfect target. He swung and connected.

Hamil let out a grunt and flopped on his belly. His breath came in shallow gasps. Hamil was learning quickly that you didn't mess with the Chief of Police. When he rolled over Rafferty saw blood dripping from his lower lip where Rafferty had smacked him earlier.

"Don't get blood on my floor. You'll be licking it clean if you do."

Hamil curled up in a ball, as if expecting more punishment, and Rafferty liked that. The scumbag looked like a dog that had taken a good beating from its master for pissing on the rug.

"Gonna get drunk again, Hamil?"

"Uhhhh."

Rafferty nudged him with his foot. "Gonna spray any more of your shitty-ass graffiti again? Better answer me, 'cause the next one's not gonna be a love tap."

"No."

"No, what?"

"Sir."

"Good, now get your ass up and into that cell."

The Hamil boy, all of eighteen, propped himself up and staggered through the open cell door. The Chief slammed the door shut and it echoed in the hallway. He liked it down here, the hot light from the naked bulb overhead, the moldy smell, the spiders that dwelled in the corners. Doing business in the cell block was the best. The only thing that could have improved it was a rack and a set of hot irons, Inquisition style.

He looked at Hamil, who lay on the cot. "If you're good, you go home tomorrow. After the fine, of course."

"And if I'm not?"

"You don't want to know."

Rafferty turned and left the cell block, smiling the whole way, glad to have taught another one of Lincoln's little punks a lesson. After all, he had been Chief here for thirteen years and it was his town; if he had to dish out some pain to keep the peace, then so be it.

It was good to be the king when the subjects were all terrified of you.

Rafferty ascended the three steps that led back into the main office. Linda Mulvaney, his secretary and dispatcher, sat at her desk near the front door, typing away on her Dell. He noticed her shudder a little as he entered the room and he liked that. It kept her in line.

He crossed the room, squinting from the glare of the fluorescents overhead.

Rafferty sat down at his desk, his considerable bulk making the swivel chair squeal. His knees felt jammed under the county-issue desk and he had to hunch over to properly write anything. The air conditioner rattled behind him; across the room one of his officers, a milky-skinned redhead named Clarence Grey, sat at one of the desks, scribbling on a legal pad.

Head down, Clarence said, "Call for you on One, Chief. It's been holding."

"You gonna tell me who it is?"

"I dunno who it is."

Rafferty rolled his eyes and picked up the receiver. "Rafferty. Speak."

An elderly female voice said, "Chief Rafferty?"

"That's what I said."

The caller identified herself as Agnes Leary, from 112 Wharton Street. "I have some information you might like."

"Go."

"We've got a new person on our street."

"An Outsider?"

"I think so."

Rafferty felt like he just won the lottery. "Name?"

"I know the last name's Adams. There's a piece of masking tape on her mailbox with the name on it. I heard one of the movers call her Jan. Or maybe it was Jill."

"You live next door?"

"That's right."

"Thank you, Agnes. You're a good citizen. Next time don't call so goddam late, though."

"Well, I was up anyway watching the news and . . ."

Rafferty hung up on her. The news of a new Outsider living in town got his juices flowing. He slapped the top of the desk, a grin on his face. Clarence looked up from his paperwork.

"What's up, Chief?"

"Gonna roll out the red carpet for someone."

"Outsider?" Clarence asked.

"Keep your voice down. I don't want *her* hearing." He nodded in Linda's direction. She couldn't hear a bulldozer dropping off a cliff, but it didn't hurt to be careful.

There was always something to be typed or filed at the station, for even though Lincoln only had five thousand residents there was plenty of police work. If there was no one to arrest, he always found ways for someone to violate the law, especially Outsiders. Rafferty kept the traffic tickets, fines and citations flowing, most of them legitimate, some of them more imaginative.

Clarence scratched his ear with the pen. "That new one a woman, Chief?"

"Yeah. And don't go getting any ideas. I want to check her out first."

"You ruin all my fun."

"My heart really bleeds for you."

The phone on Linda's desk rang and she picked it up. Rafferty heard her say, "Lincoln Police, can I help you?"

Rafferty's ears perked up. Linda wrote down the information, then told the caller an officer would be out to investigate. She thanked the caller and hung up the phone.

"What's up?" Rafferty said.

She pushed her glasses up on her nose and held the note she had scribbled at arm's length. "Call from a Richard Havermeir."

"And?"

"Disturbance reported over by Folsom Furniture."

"What kind of disturbance?"

"Noises. A woman screaming, and an animal howling. Mr. Havermeir said he also heard glass breaking."

"Okay."

"Need any backup, Chief?" Clarence said.

"Is the Pope going to hell?"

"Probably not. Well, no."

"Then there's your answer." Clarence was a good cop, having cracked a few heads at Rafferty's side over the years, but sometimes he asked too many damn questions. "Check on the kid in the cell. If he gets out of line again, you know what to do."

"Got it."

Rafferty headed for the front door. As he passed Linda's desk, she shifted in her seat. Nervous. That never failed to amuse him.

CHAPTER 2

Matt's ankle throbbed and the flesh felt hot and swollen, but he pushed himself up the stairs until he reached the platform.

The office with the plywood walls was ten feet in front of them. It looked like a makeshift construction job, with rusty nails jutting out of the boards and an unfinished wood door with rough-looking grain. A white piece of paper with black magic marker read Carl Jablonski, Warehouse Supervisor. Either Jablonski didn't warrant an engraved sign or Folsom was too cheap to spring for one.

Pressing their backs against the office wall, they shuffled around the office on the two-foot ledge. A waist-high railing ran around the catwalk, but even with that safety measure, one slip could mean a fall to the concrete floor.

They'd just rounded the corner when Matt heard it. A clicking sound, which grew faster, like beats of a metronome, as its claws grabbed at the floor. Matt didn't want to look back, because he knew it was gaining. "Faster," he said.

Jill took long, quick strides, unfazed by running on a catwalk ten feet in the air. Compared with her fluid movements, Matt thought he must have looked like an arthritic rhinoceros.

He heard the thing shriek again, and the noise shot through him, cold fingers tickling his spine.

Matt spied a window ahead and thought they could reach it in time. He had no idea what was on the other side of the window. He hoped for a ladder, but he didn't expect that any more than he expected their pursuer to give up and go home for the night.

The catwalk rocked and teetered sideways. Their attacker had reached the platform.

"Don't look back," he told Jill.

She was already way ahead of him, under the window and drawing the crowbar back to smash it out. She busted the window, the glass cracking into jagged splinters. Winding up again, she busted out the shards and then poked out the remaining glass in the frame. She stuck her head out the window, peeked back in and said, "There's another roof about five feet below the window. I'll go first."

"Wait—"

In one smooth movement, she pushed herself up on the sill and swung her legs outside. Her butt on the sill, she pushed off and slipped out of view.

He heard her hit a solid surface with a soft thud and looked out to see if she was okay. She stood on the rooftop and waved him on.

"Your turn," she said.

He set the tire iron on the windowsill and pushed himself up. Not much time left. Behind him, metal bucked and shook.

He threw one leg over the sill, straddling it. That was when it grabbed him.

The clawed hand clamped onto his thigh. Pain shot

up his leg. The thing tugged on him, and for one awful moment he thought he would be dragged back into the warehouse. His ankle was already killing him. Matt didn't need the other leg ruined.

He pulled the tire iron out from underneath him, the metal cool and heavy in his hand. He brought it over his head, then smashed it into the thing's hand. It screeched in pain but held firm, yanking at his leg.

He brought the iron down on the hand once, twice, a third time. The grip loosened slightly and he jerked his leg free. It set him off balance, and he fell sideways, his shoulder smacking the rooftop first. Pain shot up the side of his neck and down through his arm.

His shoulder was numb, which was somehow more troubling than excruciating pain. Add that to the now-stiffening ankle, and he was really a mess. The creature's hand had nearly fit around his thigh. Luckily it hadn't clawed his leg.

"Let's go. Are you okay?" she asked.

He rose to his feet. "For now. I don't think it can fit through the window."

"Do you really want to find out?"

"No."

He heard thuds against the brick. Mortar puffed and flaked as the creature pounded on the wall. A steady stream of hisses and grunts came from inside the warehouse. On its third attempt, a brick popped out and hit the ground, and it shrieked as if in triumph.

Matt knew they were strong, but pounding through a brick wall? It was time to bail.

They scurried across the roof to a ladder bolted to the building. He looked over the side, saw they were only one story off the ground and started down the ladder. Jill asked if he wanted a safety harness this time. *That* was just what he needed, someone with a sense of humor.

He hit the bottom and she followed.

A crash thundered as brick scattered onto the roof, and they looked at each other, knowing that the assailant was out of the building and coming after them.

To their right was the warehouse. To the left was the end of the property, where a hill covered in brown weeds led to railroad tracks.

If they went up the hill, they could cut back around the front of the complex to where Matt had parked his car. If they went right, around the back of the warehouse, they would have to cut through the alley to get back to the car. The thing in the warehouse was not something he wanted to confront in a dark alley.

"Let's go up the hill," he said.

"Wouldn't it be quicker the other way?"

"I don't want to get caught in the alley."

She pursed her lips for a moment, thinking it over. "Okay."

He scrambled up the hill, the weeds ruffling under his feet, Jill behind him. With every step, the pain in his ankle grew; the numbness in his shoulder had turned into icy pain that ran the length of his arm.

"I'm sorry I got you into this," she said.

"Don't be."

He heard the thing coming, its claws scrabbling on the pavement. It must have leapt off the building and onto the ground near the bottom of the ladder.

They came to a gravel path that wound down the hill. It was dotted with broken glass, Styrofoam cups and cigarette butts. Matt watched the path, but looked over his shoulder every few seconds for any sign of the creature. They reached the bottom, where a buckled sidewalk led back to the parking lot.

They started up the sidewalk, both of them breathing heavily, hearing the creature crashing through the weeds behind them. Reaching the car, Matt fumbled for his keys, dropped them and then picked them up. He opened the door, threw himself in, then reached over and unlocked the passenger side door.

Jill got in and Matt stuck the key in the ignition. He had a horrible second where he thought that the car wouldn't start, like in every slasher film—when the killer was about to bear down on the heroine, cars that ran fine the entire movie decided to crap out at the moment of truth. But he turned the key and the engine rumbled to life.

Matt put it in reverse and stepped on the gas. The car whipped backward and the tires kicked up gravel and dust.

Out of the corner of his eye, he saw a shape coming at the car and he gunned the engine, swerving onto Elmwood, the tires squealing. He cut off a red Mazda and the driver blatted the horn, shouting, "Asshole!"

He got the car under control and the two of them sped away at fifty miles an hour. He passed a speed-limit sign that said thirty.

The beast howled as they drove away, and the goose bumps returned to Matt's arms.

Rafferty walked out the door and down the police station's concrete steps. He passed the flower garden, took a whiff of the roses and daylilies. Man, did they stink. He might have to let Rolf, Bob Fidori's German shepherd, dig them up. How did people stomach the smell of flowers?

He went around the back of the station, already sweating and wiping his brow. The temperature had been in the nineties all of August and the humidity at God knows what. Even at night it was seventy-five or eighty with no letup to the humidity. All that sweat made him feel like he had sprung a leak.

He walked over to his cruiser in the parking lot and opened the door. He was happy to see the riot gun secure in its holster, and he relished the thought of using it on an Outsider someday. He bet their eyes would get real big right before he pulled the trigger.

After rolling down his window, he started up the Caprice Classic and pulled out of the lot onto Elmwood. He accelerated to fifty, the engine humming under the hood.

Rafferty pushed the car through two yellow lights but got caught at the next one. Slowing down, he pulled up next to a black Dodge pickup stopped at the light.

Pennsylvania plates. Outsiders for sure.

The kid driving the Ram had on a denim baseball cap turned around catcher-style and wore a pair of mirrored sunglasses. Not particularly bright, wearing sunglasses for night driving. A girl of about seventeen sat in the passenger seat. She had short, curly hair and wore a pink tank top.

He scanned the pickup's bed. Three guys and three girls sat in the back of the truck, the girls scantily clad. One had on a thin white tank top; her nipples poked through the fabric. The other two girls had on bikini tops and short-shorts. The guys in the back were shirtless, no doubt trying to impress their girlfriends with their puny physiques.

I'll show you a real man, ladies, he thought.

He pressed a button on the door and lowered the passenger window.

One of the guys in back, a kid with sandy brown hair and a deep tan, picked up a bottle of Rolling Rock and chugged heartily.

Rafferty glared at the driver and said, "Evening."

"Hey," the driver said. The girl in the passenger seat giggled.

"Think it's a good idea to drive with those shades on at night?"

"Probably not."

"Wanna take them off?"

"Okay." He pulled the glasses off, folded the arms and hung them on his shirt collar.

"Now how about your buddy in the back with the Rolling Rock?"

The light turned green and the driver looked anxiously at the light, then back at Rafferty.

"Stay put. There's no one coming. Now what about the beer?"

The driver stuck his head out the window and looked back. "Aw shit, Randy. I told you not to go into the cooler yet."

Randy, the sandy-haired kid, took another pull off of the bottle and let out a loud belch. The girl in the white tank top rolled her eyes and said, "Jeez, Randy, that's gross."

"Where you from?" Rafferty said.

"Bradford, Pennsylvania," the driver said.

"And I suppose you're all twenty-one?"

"Uh, yeah."

"What are you doing in Lincoln?"

"We're on our way to Niagara Falls."

"You staying in town?"

"Just for tonight. We're going back to our hotel."

"What hotel?"

"The Sun Motor Lodge."

"If you say so."

Rafferty looked at Randy in the back of the truck. The kid had a crooked smile on his face, as if he were waiting to deliver the perfect retort to Rafferty if called upon to do so.

"Hey, sport."

"Me?"

"No, your fairy fucking godmother. Yes, you."

That got his attention.

"Dump the beer out. Now."

"I ain't driving."

"Dump it."

"This is bullshit."

Rafferty felt the heat start to flush under his skin and he took a deep breath to get it under control.

"Pour the beer out or you'll all spend the night in jail."

Randy rolled his eyes in disgust. Rafferty had to be careful, because he could feel the Change rising inside of him, the prickly heat under his skin and the redness that seeped into the corner of his vision like a spilled bottle of ink.

He could change forms, rip open their throats, slash their bellies open and eat their guts, claw their eyes out. . . .

Get ahold of yourself. No kills before Harvest.

He closed his eyes, kept them shut for a second. The redness dissolved, the flushed sensation melted away. That was better. "Do I have to pull you over?"

"Just dump it, Randy," the driver said.

Randy blew air out his nostrils in disgust and poured out the Rolling Rock, the beer lapping against the pavement.

Rafferty leaned over the passenger seat and pointed at the driver. "Your pal Randy's not too bright. You're all lucky I'm on my way to a call or I'd bust all your asses. For one thing, I don't think any of you are twenty-one. Now get where you're going, and if I see you little shits on my way back you're all gonna spend the night in *my* hotel. Got it?"

"Yeah man, we got it," the driver said.

"We got it, all right. And if we're lucky we'll get it

some more at the hotel," Randy proclaimed. This time all three girls in the back giggled.

It was time to teach these smart asses a lesson. "Don't go anywhere."

Rafferty put the car in park, turned on the flashers; the lights strobed red and blue against the black Dodge Ram. He got out of the car and went to the driver's side door of the pickup. He reached in his pocket and pulled out a Swiss Army knife, then clicked it open. The kid who was driving looked like he had just seen the Ghosts of Christmas Past, Present, and Future all at once.

"This is for your smart-ass fucking friend."

Rafferty pressed the tip of the knife against the side of the truck, dug it in and ran the blade down the driver's side. It left a thin white scratch the entire length of the truck.

"Aw, man," the driver said.

Rafferty walked to the driver's side door and looked at the kid behind the wheel. "Stay off of my road."

Rafferty stomped back to his car and got in. Turning the gumballs off, he pulled away from the truck. He took a look in the rearview mirror and saw the driver standing on the road, yelling and pointing at the kids in the back. No doubt he was chewing out his friend for causing so many problems.

Two minutes later, Rafferty pulled up in front of Folsom.

Grabbing his flashlight, he got out of the cruiser and walked to the doorway. The steel door was open, and the inside lock was busted. He pulled his revolver from his holster, shone the light inside and saw a pile of kitchen chairs and a splintered pallet blocking the entrance. The chairs' legs had snapped like toothpicks and the pallet lay busted in half, the wood all jagged shards.

There came a thud and a clang from around the

back of the building, the sound of metal hitting metal. Was somebody hiding on him?

He shone his light down the alley between the two buildings and saw only murky brown shadows. Revolver in one hand and flashlight in the other, he crept down the alley until he reached the rear of the buildings.

He was in a courtyard. The rest of the buildings in the complex butted up against the concrete slab on which he stood. To his left was the warehouse, a green-and-white sign reaching BUILDING 57 hanging on the wall. Behind the warehouse was a blue Dumpster with the name BROWN RECYCLING painted on the side. A cloud of flies buzzed over the container.

He lifted the Dumpster lid with the barrel of the revolver and found only maggots squirming on a grease-covered piece of cardboard. Apparently he had missed whatever happened at Folsom. He was ready to go back to the car and tell Clarence to get down here. Put old Red to work, have him haul some chairs out of the way.

When he turned to leave the alley he heard shuffling coming from the other side of the Dumpster. Shining the beam, he hunkered down and moved to the front of the container.

He pointed the revolver in the direction of the noise. "Come out of there. Put your hands where I can see them."

A man stepped out from behind the Dumpster and Rafferty's flashlight beam lit up his face. He was thin and pale with white-blond hair and had full, almost feminine lips. The lips were an unusual feature, but not his most unusual. The man was naked except for a collapsed cardboard box wrapped around him like a towel.

"Nice outfit. What are you doing here?"

"I don't know."

"You don't know why you're standing naked with a

cardboard box around you at a furniture factory in the middle of the night?"

"Well—"

"What's your name?"

"Charles Dietrich." The guy lifted the box a little, as it had begun to slip down further on his body.

"Hold still," Rafferty said.

Rafferty stepped toward him until they were standing nose-to-nose. He sniffed, taking in the rotten fruit smell of the trash, Dietrich's underlying body odor, and underneath that, underneath his skin, the smell of Rafferty's own kind. A hint of sulfur. It would smell like skunk or rotten eggs to most people. But you had to get up close, within kissing distance, and really take a good sniff to notice it.

Rafferty took a step back. "I'm taking you back to the station, Charles. I want to hear your story, and I mean all of it. If I don't think you've told me everything, I have a Tazer in my office and I can use it on some very unpleasant places on your body. Tell me the truth and we won't have a problem. Got it?"

Dietrich nodded.

Rafferty motioned him ahead with the revolver, and they headed down the alley.

CHAPTER 3

Jill glanced at Matt as they sped down Elmwood. He narrowed his clear blue eyes and seemed to take aim, as if the car were a torpedo and there was a ship to sink in the road. What if he was a psycho? Nah, he was just wound like a jack-in-the-box after their encounter. So was Jill, the muscles in her neck feeling like tangled barbwire.

Her hand crept down to her belly. The blood had gone sticky in spots and although there was a lot of it, the wound would amount to nothing more than a bad scratch. The shirt, however, was a loss, unless she clipped it and brought it back as a crop top. Or a dust rag.

She took another glance at him. Good-looking in a college boy sort of way. Close-cropped hair, nice flat stomach and a fine set of blue eyes. Looked like a guy who might bag your groceries, help you to the car and say, "Have a good day, ma'am." Looked innocent enough at first glance.

He peeked in the rearview mirror and braked. She watched the speedometer needle drop from fifty-five to thirty-five. The engine rattled and knocked. The only sound in the car was Jill's breathing.

"We were a pretty good team back there," she said.

"I'd say we'd get the gold in the run-for-your-life Olympics." He wiped his brow with the back of his hand. "What were you doing out at that hour?"

"Jogging," she said. "I usually do it in the morning, but today I overslept."

"It almost cost you your life."

She couldn't disagree with him. If he hadn't shown up when he did, there was no telling what would've happened. She had been jogging on Elmwood when she heard the metal door screech and fly open with a bang. A man darted toward her, quicker than she had ever seen someone move. Jill was no slowpoke, but before she knew it, he had his arm across her throat and dragged her into the warehouse. Her throat still felt raw from the attacker's grip.

"So what happened?"

She told Matt the story, adding, "And when you got there, things started getting weird."

He looked at her belly. "Do you want me to take you to the hospital for that?"

"Eight hours there was enough."

He looked at her quizzically and then looked back at the road.

"I'm an R.N. at Lincoln Mercy. We should be taking *you* there for that ankle. I banged you pretty good with that crowbar."

A smile curled up at the corner of his mouth. "Nothing that crutches and hours of painful physical therapy won't cure."

"That's rotten," she said, but laughed anyway. It felt good, drained some of the tension. "You should have yourself checked out. I can go with you and have one of the docs look you over."

He shook his head. "Hospitals give me the willies."

"Typical man."

She gave him directions to her house on Wharton Street.

Normally she would never invite a stranger into her house, but he *had* helped her out of the worst jam of her life, and he looked like he needed some repair work. A purple-yellow bruise was beginning to swell on his cheek, and she knew his ankle must have been killing him. "At least come upstairs and let me have a look at you. Maybe do a little first aid."

He shook his head again.

"You sure you won't let me pay you back? Dressing your wounds is the least I can do for you."

Matt blew out a stream of air. "I *should* call my aunt and let her know I'm still alive. Would a free phone call be included in the deal?"

"I think I could manage that. And after you call your aunt, I should call the police. We really should have called already, but—"

"No police," he said. "Not in this town."

"What's that supposed to mean?" She brushed hair off of her forehead.

"They're crooked. The chief's the worst one."

"I take it you've dealt with them before."

"Yeah. Just let's leave them out of this, okay? Maybe I can explain it to you some other time."

That was weird. She hoped that he didn't have some sort of record, maybe for kidnapping and raping joggers. Looking at him, she dismissed the thought. He looked weary, and incapable of doing her any harm at this moment. There were purple bags under his blood-shot eyes, as if he hadn't slept well. Maybe he hadn't.

She decided to drop the matter of calling the police for now.

"Can I ask you something? Something weird?"

This night couldn't get any weirder, she thought.

"Were you dragged into that building by a man?"

"Actually, it was an Ethel Merman impersonator."

"I'm serious."

"Yeah. It was a guy." Despite her joking, her heart thudded and she could almost feel the guy's arm tightening across her windpipe. His forearm had been sweaty, and she remembered the slimy dampness of his skin pressed against her throat. "Why do you ask that?"

"Did you see what was chasing us? You had to have heard it."

"I didn't get a good look at it, but yeah, I heard it." She just didn't want to be the one to bring it up. Things like that could blow holes in the fabric of your sanity. She'd always had a healthy appetite for all kinds of novels, science fiction and horror included. But to think they had been chased by something that should exist only in a movie or a book blew her mind.

"Where are you going with this?" she asked.

"I can't explain it all right now, just like not calling the cops, but I have my reasons. I want to tell them to you. But not right now. I hope you don't think I'm nuts," Matt said.

"A little odd, but not nuts."

"Did you get a look at the guy?"

"He was tall, blond and pale. For some reason I noticed he had thick lips. Don't ask me why."

"It's funny the things you remember."

"There was something else about him."

"What's that?"

Jill thought about not telling him, thinking that maybe she had imagined it. "He smelled funny. It was almost like, I don't know—I can't put my finger on it." She frowned, frustrated at her inability to describe the odor accurately.

"Like rotten eggs, maybe sulfur?"

"Yeah! When he had me in that armlock, the smell was so strong that my eyes started to water. How did you know that?"

He watched the road.

They approached the corner of Wharton and Elmwood. It was nearly midnight and the pizzeria on the corner was still open. A white sign with purple letters proclaimed PIZZA MAGIC: WHEN ORDINARY PIZZA ISN'T GOOD ENOUGH. Next to the lettering was a cartoon chef complete with a floppy hat and curly mustache drawn over his lip. A few teenagers stood at the pinball machines, swerving and juking as if body English would influence the little silver ball.

Matt still wasn't talking. He had insider knowledge and didn't want to give it up. He would, Jill vowed silently.

"You know something about what was in that warehouse, and I wish you'd tell me. I'm having trouble accepting the fact that we might have been chased by the bogeyman—I think if I admit it to myself I might go a little bonkers. At least if you admit it too then maybe I'm only half a crackpot."

"Not right now," he repeated.

"When?"

"Soon."

"Promise? I know we barely know each other, but we need to talk about this," she said.

"I promise."

They turned down Wharton, drove under the canopy of leaves created by the maples that lined the street. She told him to start slowing down and pointed out her house. Like most of the houses on the street, Jill's was a double, with a large porch upstairs and down. He turned into her driveway.

Faintly, in the distance, she heard a howl. Maybe just a neighborhood dog, but maybe not.

"Let's hurry and get upstairs," Jill said.

"I heard it too."

The two of them got out of the car; Matt went around the rear of the Cavalier and opened the trunk.

"What're you doing?" she said.

"Do you mind if I change clothes? I can't go to my aunt's looking like this."

She said she didn't mind, because he looked like he had just fought the Third World War and lost single-handedly. His T-shirt was torn and smeared with dirt; his hands were covered with dust and grime.

After pulling his suitcase out of the rental, he slammed the trunk and followed Jill up the front steps. She produced a single key from the pocket of her running shorts, opened the door, and flicked on the foyer light. There were two doors in front of them; Jill explained that the one on the right led to the downstairs apartment, which was vacant right now.

He followed her through the door on the left and went upstairs to her apartment.

Jill went around and turned on the lights. There were cardboard boxes lying around, some marked BOOKS and others KITCHEN. A laundry bag with a white shirt poking out of it lay slumped in the corner of the dining room.

"Excuse the mess. I'm still in the middle of unpacking, as if you couldn't tell."

She went over to the answering machine and pressed the Play button. Matt didn't listen to the content of the message but the woman had a shrill, nasally voice. Jill explained with a sigh, "It's my mother calling to check up on me. "Sit down. Want a Coke or something?"

"Coke sounds good."

He limped into the living room and sat on the couch, his ankle throbbing the whole time. Jill had three big oak bookcases in the living room, two flanking the fireplace and one on the wall near the door to the upstairs porch. He scanned the titles and saw a who's who of popular fiction: Dean Koontz, Janet Evanovich, James Patterson, and a few Stephen King titles. There was also a book of poetry by Robert Frost and a collection of short stories by Edgar Allen Poe.

"Nice collection of books," he said, raising his voice so she could hear.

"Surprised?" she asked from the kitchen.

"Not really."

"Most guys assume because you're a woman that all you read is Danielle Steele and Judith Krantz."

He heard an ice cube tray being bent and cracked. Then he heard her digging in the cupboard for something and heard it clang as she pulled it out.

She walked into the living room carrying a tray with two cans of Coca-Cola and two glasses filled with ice. There were also two folded dishrags that looked suspiciously lumpy, and he knew she had made makeshift ice packs.

"Be right back." She disappeared through a hallway that ran off the dining room.

While he waited, he surveyed the living room and noticed a picture on the mantle. It was a young Jill flanked by a man and rather dour-looking woman. The man was tall with thick chestnut hair and was handsome enough to be in the movies.

The woman was dark-haired, with an Elmer's glue complexion and puffy purple circles under her eyes.

She looked like she'd been pretty at one time and either time or a hard life had caught up with her.

He didn't see a picture of a boyfriend, and that was a good thing. Jumping from city to city didn't make for long-term relationships with women. But if he got to know Jill, who knew what could happen?

She reappeared from the hallway, carrying a box of gauze, Band-Aids, a bowl of water and a tube of Neosporin. A washcloth completed her homemade first-aid kit.

"Take your shoe off."

Matt leaned forward, untied the sneaker and pulled it off slowly. Then he pulled his sock off and rested his foot on the table. "I feel sorry for your table."

"Don't worry about being embarrassed. I'm a nurse. Besides, right now I don't smell like a peach tree either. Now off with the sneaker."

He looked at the ankle and saw it hadn't swollen. He had expected it to look like someone had stuck a balloon under the skin and inflated it.

"We should really get you some X-rays," Jill mused.

"No hospital."

She frowned at him, giving him the same look that a mother might give a petulant child who refuses to take medicine. Shaking her head, she took an ice pack off of the tray, sat on the table and put the pack on his ankle. He flinched a little at the cold, but then it felt mercifully cool on top of the pain.

She poured the Cokes, handed him one and joined him on the couch. While he drank, she tended to his wounds, washing out the cut on his face and applying a Band-Aid. He sipped his Coke and it felt icy cold to his parched throat. Matt was surprised she had let him up here considering she'd almost been killed by a stranger. It had been a long time since he had felt a woman's touch and it felt good. At the moment, it wasn't erotic or sexual, but comforting. Her hands were soft, the skin cool, and she touched him with the delicacy only a woman possessed.

Jill asked him a few questions (how many fingers am I holding up, what day is it, do you know where you are?) and concluded that he probably didn't have a concussion but told him he should go to the ER anyway. Again he refused. He noticed she had tended to her own wound while in the bathroom with a piece of gauze and some tape. The torn shirt remained.

"Why are you doing all this for me?" he asked.

"You saved my life."

"Something tells me you can handle yourself pretty well. Maybe you wouldn't have needed my help."

"Trust me, that guy was quick. I didn't stand a chance without a helping hand," she said. "And you gave it to me."

"But you don't even know me. What if I'm really a serial killer or a rapist or some other kind of freak?"

"I don't think many serial killers have rushed into dark warehouses and tried to stop a woman from being assaulted. Besides, it's my nature to help people.

"Take these," she said, producing two Motrin. "They're not as good as the prescription kind, but they'll help. I imagine you're going to be one hurting puppy in the morning."

"Don't remind me."

For a moment, he thought about what happened in the warehouse and whether he should tell her what he knew and how much danger she might be in, but decided against it. If he spilled his guts right away to her about Lincoln's secret, she would think him a crackpot for sure.

"That thing in the warehouse gave me the creeps. Must've been some sort of animal that got loose."

He agreed with her for the sake of argument, but he didn't think that she believed her own statement. He didn't know any animal that frequented warehouses and made shrieking noises like the thing at Folsom did.

"Do you mind if I use the phone?"

"Be my guest. I'll bring you the cordless from the dining room."

She got up off the couch a little gingerly and went into the dining room to retrieve the phone. As he waited for her to come back, he pondered how to explain his tardiness to his aunt.

It turned out Dietrich was being a good little suspect after all.

After arriving at headquarters, Rafferty led him into the back entrance to the police station and down into the holding cell area. As he passed the holding cells, he saw Hamil flat on his back, snoring. That was good.

Now they were in a small room at the far end of the cell block. It had a thick steel door and Rafferty had lined the walls with foam rubber to dampen the sound. A rectangular table and two chairs sat in the center of the room. Dietrich sat in one of the chairs, naked and handcuffed.

Rafferty left him that way because it made a man feel more vulnerable, less likely to give him any shit when he wanted questions answered.

So far, Dietrich had told him he had broken into the Folsom warehouse looking to boost something to sell for smack. He had smelled the woman coming down the road, her scent carried by the hot breeze. Becoming excited, he smashed the locks on the door, cracked it open and waited for her to pass the warehouse.

"So you grabbed this woman and decided to have a little fun with her, am I right?"

"Yeah."

"What'd she look like?"

"About five-six, curly dark hair, light eyes. Killer body. Made her tell me her name. I think it was Jill." Dietrich wriggled and his moist skin squeaked against the chair.

"You got her in the warehouse, right?"

"Right."

"And then what?"

"I got her inside and started to get, you know, more aroused. And then the Change happens. While I'm going through that shit, she breaks free and runs."

"And?"

"I climbed up on the racks. I wanted to have a little fun with her, you know, hunt her without her seeing me."

"Draw it out, in other words. A little cat and mouse."

"Yeah. You got it. Pretty good, huh?"

Rafferty stood up, pushed his chair away and back-handed Dietrich across the face.

"Ow, what the fuck!"

"I'll tell you what the fuck. The Harvest is in two months and everyone knows the rules. No kills four months before the Harvest."

"I wasn't going to kill her," Dietrich protested.

"Bullshit. You were out of control—once you got the scent of her you knew what would've happened."

Dietrich pouted, blood dribbling from his swollen lower lip.

"Any idea who this girl was?"

"No. Never seen her before. Why?"

"Because I'm gonna pay her a visit if I can find out who she is. Check her out. Maybe save her for myself when Harvest time comes. You said her name was Jill?"

Maybe the new girl in town that the old woman called about.

"Yeah. Can I go now?"

"Yeah. But you spread the word among your lowlife friends that I want no hunting or killing before Harvest. Anyone that does will deal with me. Got it?"

Dietrich nodded.

Rafferty unlocked his cuffs and the naked man stood up.

"There's a mechanic's coveralls in the garage. Take them and put them on. You're making me sick looking at you."

Dietrich slunk out of the room, head bowed, hands cupped over his crotch to protect what little dignity he had left. Rafferty followed him to the garage, where Lincoln's other two patrol cars were parked.

Rafferty let him into the garage and flipped on the lights. The garage smelled of oil and fresh gasoline. Dietrich took a pair of grease-splattered coveralls off of a hook on the wall and stepped into them.

Rafferty led him to the back door and issued him one more warning.

"Remember, no more hunting. And tonight never happened. Not the warehouse, not me bringing you back here, nothing."

Dietrich nodded and walked away, disappearing around the corner of the station house. *Good riddance*, Rafferty thought. He stepped out of the humidity and back into the police station.

CHAPTER 4

"My God, Matthew, are you all right? I've been worried sick."

"Really, Aunt Bernie, I'm fine. I'm sorry I couldn't call sooner. I was busy changing that flat," he said.

"Well, you come on over now, Matthew. I'll cook you something right away."

His Aunt Bernie was five-three, weighed maybe one hundred five in two layers of clothes and constantly cooked. She ate like a white shark and Matt could never figure out exactly where she put it all.

She was a second mother to him, and he loved her like one, but she had always called him Matthew and never Matt. That was really the only thing that bothered him about her. Other than that, he didn't think there was a sweeter person on earth.

"Give me about twenty minutes, okay? I stopped outside town to use a phone."

"All right, but you be careful. See you soon."

He said good-bye and hit the End button on the cordless, cutting the connection.

"Everything okay with your aunt?" Jill asked.

"I worry about her. When my uncle's been into the beer, he can be pretty mean."

"You should get going and see her."

He asked her if he could use the bathroom to change and she said that was fine. Carrying his suitcase, he went into the bathroom and caught the smell of roses in the air. Jill's soap or perfume. He inhaled the scent, wondering if her neck would smell like that if he were to nuzzle it.

Take it easy there, cowboy. You've known her a grand total of an hour.

He pulled his shirt off, his muscles screaming in protest as he did so, rinsed off his face and chest and changed into a fresh T-shirt.

Jill came to the door and knocked to see if he was okay and he told her he was fine. In reality, he felt like Ken Griffey Jr. had used his head for batting practice.

Stuffing his dirty clothes in his suitcase, he returned to the living room where Jill sat on the couch. She rose and handed him a piece of paper with her phone number scribbled on it in blue ink. Then she handed him a paper and a pen and instructed him to do the same.

He wrote down his aunt's number and gave it to her.

"Will you give me a call so we can talk? This whole thing is blowing my mind," Jill said.

"We'll make a date."

As he turned to leave, she reached out, squeezed his arm and thanked him. Tears welled in her eyes and he wanted to hug her, but decided against it. He smiled and told her she was welcome.

He told her good night and went down the stairs, his ankle killing him.

Jill watched Matt limp down her stairway. Her heart finally stopped hammering and was back to a normal rhythm. The incident in the warehouse had spooked her: when the perpetrator grabbed her around the neck and cut off her air, she thought she was a goner. She wasn't one to back down or scare easily, but the attack left her genuinely frightened.

She supposed that her tough attitude arose from living with a mother who had tried to plot every course of her life.

She had skipped two grades in school, partially because of her intelligence and partially because school came easy to her. She devoured books, made the most difficult equations in algebra seem simple and could recite chemistry formulas faster than most people could tell you their phone number. On top of it, she drove herself hard, one time crying when she received a B and not her standard A on a Revolutionary War essay.

High school was a breeze, and she became the first valedictorian at Sacred Heart Academy to have a 4.0 all through school. Scholarship offers poured in: Berkley, Stanford and Duke were among the many. But she had settled on the nursing program at the University of Buffalo, instantly disappointing her mother.

She took her first real job at Buffalo General as an R.N. in the emergency room. It had been tough and messy, and during the first week on the job, she had been bled on and puked on. Despite the unpleasant aspects, she found it rewarding. That was something that her mother could never understand. Mom had always told her she should go to Harvard or MIT.

She thought of the message on the machine.

It was a little past one in the morning, and she knew Harriet Adams would still be awake, watching Turner Classic Movies. Reluctantly, she picked up the phone and dialed her mother's number.

"I was worried about you, dear. I left that message at ten o'clock."

"I was out jogging, Mom."

"So late?"

"I didn't have a chance this morning."

"You shouldn't do that, dear. It's dangerous out there."

Harriet Adams rarely left her house, so anything further than her front porch was considered "out there" and therefore dangerous.

"Gotta stay in shape, Mom."

"Why don't you join a health club? Don't you have the money?"

"Plenty of money. I just like jogging outdoors."

"How is the new job, anyway?"

"Going great."

"Better than the General?"

"Much better."

"That's good, dear. I still wish you'd consider being a doctor. Nursing is so lowly, you know, cleaning up vomit and blood and other things."

Jill's grip on the phone tightened. "There's more to it than that, Mom."

"I can see I've ruffled your feathers a little. Didn't mean to. Just giving you something to think about. I'll let you get going now."

"Good-bye, Mom."

"Good-bye, dear."

Jill slammed the receiver onto the base. Her mother could never understand why Jill wanted to be a nurse. Her father's death had a lot to do with it.

The memory of her father and the anger at her mother made Jill's throat tighten. It seemed an eternity since he had been killed, but Jill could remember that night with no problem. Sometimes the memory could be a curse.

Jim Adams had been returning home at night after a long day at his law firm when he stopped at Wilson

Farms to pick up a loaf of bread. A guy in a ski mask entered, robbed the cash register and then for no apparent reason, shot the cashier and her father. The staff at the ER worked feverishly to try and save him, but he couldn't hang on; the wounds to his liver and heart proved too severe.

Jill had been eight at the time and remembered her mother coming home from the hospital to tell her the doctors and nurses couldn't save her daddy. She had broken into tears and gone to her mother for a hug, but her mother turned her away with a pat on the head, telling her she needed to be alone.

Jill had soaked her pillow that night crying herself to sleep, alone in her bedroom with the moonlight spilling onto her bed. It was one of the loneliest, most awful nights of her life. The sun seemed like it would never come up again and she felt like she had been sentenced to live with eternal night.

Could she make up for Dad's death by saving others? She didn't know, but she loved her job. That was good enough.

Now, she brought the tray with the medical supplies on it to the kitchen and then went into the bathroom. She turned the shower on, making the water lukewarm, and stripped off her clothes, careful to avoid the bandage on her abdomen. Peeling off the bandage, she got into the shower and found her thoughts drifting back to Matthew Crowe.

The comments he made about the police being crooked were strange. Hell, *he* was strange. But there was something appealing about him, maybe the whole knight in shining armor thing. Hopefully her knight would call back and tell her what the hell was going on in this town. Should she call the cops? Right now all she wanted to do was hit the pillow and sleep.

She lathered up with the soap, rinsed off and got out of the shower. After toweling off, she went into her bedroom and slipped on a pair of panties and a T-shirt. Then she climbed into bed, thinking that she might give Matt Crowe a call after work tomorrow.

It was one hell of a way to meet a guy.

Matt pulled in his Aunt Bernie's driveway, got out of the car, and dragged his suitcase from the backseat.

He approached the house, a white Cape Cod with black shutters and a large picture window overlooking a rose garden in front. There was a set of copper wind chimes hanging over the door and a large pot of herbs on the porch. From the outside, it looked like a typical suburban home, but it carried a lot of bad memories for Matt. Memories of a black eye from his uncle, and the night when he'd left Lincoln for good.

This was supposed to be a new beginning for him, coming home to make things right, and dwelling on his drunken uncle would only soil his homecoming. *Leave it in the past*, he thought.

He rang the bell and Aunt Bernie opened the side door. She was a slim, dark-haired woman with a narrow waist. She gave him a little wave. For some reason, he always thought of her hands as her most distinguishing feature. They were thin and small, but always capable of threading a needle on the first try or untying a stubborn knot with little effort.

As he stepped inside she hugged him, and he put an arm around her, returning it. She stood on her tiptoes, kissed his cheek and then led him by the hand into the kitchen.

"I was up waiting for you, as if you couldn't tell. You want something to eat?"

As they stood in the kitchen Matt smelled the aromas of garlic and onion. "No thanks. I just want to hit the hay."

"Matthew, it's so good to see you after all these years. Your uncle is sorry for what happened, and that you left. He's really changed, you'll see."

"He's sleeping now, I assume."

"That's right."

Good. If he didn't see Uncle Rex the whole time he was back in Lincoln, it would not break his heart.

"I really should get to my room. I hate to be rude, but I'm bushed."

"That's okay. We can talk in the morning. Over blueberry pancakes."

"Sounds good."

She said he could stay in the loft over the garage, newly remodeled. There was even an air conditioner to keep him from roasting in the heat.

As he bent over to kiss her good night, she touched the Band-Aid on his cheek and said, "What's this?"

He shrugged. "Canary attack?"

She stood with her hands on her hips, weight on one leg, hip stuck out to the side.

"You look just like my mom when you stand like that."

"I do?"

"Yeah, exactly like her."

"That's a nice thought, Matthew, but you shouldn't change the subject."

His hand went to the Band-Aid. "I took a spill getting out of the car and landed flat on my face. Tripped over my own feet, basically."

Her eyes narrowed in suspicion. "Are you sure that's what happened?"

"Positive."

"I'm still not sure I buy it, but it's late and I know you're tired, so I'll let it slide. This time."

She gave him a friendly punch in the arm and he smiled wearily.

"Good night, Aunt Bernie."

She went over to the door with him and took a leather key ring marked GARAGE off of a key rack.

"Remember, blueberry pancakes."

"You got it."

He trudged out of the house, relishing the thought of collapsing into bed in his air-conditioned loft.

The garage was a two-car, white like the house, with a busted window in one of the door panels. Matt opened the door to the right of the garage door and entered.

Moonlight shone through the window, illuminating a splotch of oil on the floor beside his uncle's Chevy pickup. The garage smelled dusty and Uncle Rex had several boxes stacked on shelves, no doubt containing tools, rags and other implements of the American Male Repairman.

Matt climbed the stairs to the loft and flipped on the light switch. There was a single bed, a scarred pine night-stand (with a black phone) and a thirteen-inch television on a TV stand. There was also a card table with a folding chair and a small refrigerator plugged into the wall, the kind college kids used in the dorms. There was no bathroom, but that was okay; it wouldn't kill him to use the one in the house.

Matt set his suitcase on the floor at the foot of the bed and switched on the air conditioner in the window. It hummed to life and within ten minutes, the place was as cold as Alaska. The cool air felt great.

After stripping off his clothes and folding them, he put on a pair of sweatpants and nothing else. Then he took out one of his keepsakes from the suitcase and sat on the bed. *Time to pick at the scabs again, maybe draw blood and have it run again. Why do I do this to myself?*

He held a New York Yankees cap in his hands. It was wool, just like the Major Leaguers wore. Its brim had been folded in half and properly "duck billed" and the liner inside was yellowed with sweat. It had belonged to his little brother, Mike, and he had been wearing it the day he was killed.

Mikey had bugged their dad for a month to get him an authentic New York Yankees cap, just like Don Mattingly wore. His father had surprised Mikey one night by bringing it home from work, and for the next two months, Mikey had kept that hat glued to his head.

It still had mud caked on the brim. Matt sniffed it to see if he could conjure up a memory of his little brother. He smelled the faint odor of sweat, a child's sweat, but no bubble gum. Mikey had constantly chewed Double Bubble, stuffing four or five pieces in his mouth at a time. Their mother always worried that he would either choke himself or rot out all his teeth.

Mikey had only been five when They chased him down to the ravine, where he lost his balance and went over the edge. Matt could still hear the high-pitched scream as his brother tumbled over the edge and fell eighty feet to his death on the rocks below. He had screamed for their mother the whole time.

Matt had been fourteen when that happened. Mikey and his parents murdered on the same day, Matt helpless to stop it. He wished for the three of them back. In the next four years after the murders, Aunt Bernie had done well filling in for his mother. Then came the blow up with Uncle Rex and Matt's departure. After leaving his aunt and uncle's home, he'd thought long and hard about his future and decided on the Army Rangers. He'd learn to fight, handle weapons. And then he'd return.

Matt felt himself start to tear up; his throat felt as if he were trying to swallow a chestnut, and he thought again that it probably wasn't healthy to carry around the dead's clothes. It was even a little morbid, he supposed. But it was also fuel that fed the fire that burned inside of him. Every time he took out that hat, it cut him open again, pissed him off. Like poking a cut just to feel the pain and remember what it was like the moment the skin tore open.

Someone would pay. That phrase had echoed in his mind while he endured marches with sixty-pound packs, freezing cold mud and water and drill sergeants screaming in his ear. That was why he had almost relished it, the sizzling sand and heat and walking through a minefield during Desert Storm. It all led back to Lincoln, getting ready for his own war.

He put the hat back in his suitcase and lay back on the bed, his hands twined behind his head.

"I miss you guys," he said.

Remembering the light, he got up, switched it off and flopped back on the bed. As he drifted off to sleep, he prayed for no dreams of a little boy plunging over a cliff.

CHAPTER 5

The sun creeping through the blinds awoke Matt at six o'clock the next morning. He sat up on the bed and stretched. Six o'clock, the same as every other morning. He swung his legs around, put some weight on his ankle. It smarted, but not as badly as he thought it would. Just a twist, no sprain.

He managed fifty push-ups and two hundred crunches. Normally, he also would have run a few miles, but Jill Adams and her crowbar put that on hold.

Matt went downstairs, opened the door and peered at the house. There were lights on, and Aunt Bernie walked past the dining room window in a fuzzy red bathrobe. He wondered if Uncle Rex was still asleep.

Uncle Rex was the reason Matt left Lincoln in the first place. After the death of Mikey and his parents, he went to live with Uncle Rex and Aunt Bernie. Aunt Bernie cooked him huge meals, trying to fatten him up, always telling him he needed to eat more.

Uncle Rex was another story.

Rex Lapchek was ill-tempered, ignorant and in Matt's

eyes an all-around gorilla. He even looked a little apish, what with his hairy knuckles and jutting forehead. He'd been working at the Ford plant since he was eighteen, starting off in the foundry and still putting together engine blocks after thirty years on the job. In his mind, he was always getting screwed.

The UAW wasn't fighting hard enough for him, GM was trying to take away his pension, the other workers were "lazy sonzabitches" and he still had to work with too many minorities.

The world was never right with Rex Lapchek, despite the fact that he had a highly coveted manufacturing job and brought home nearly sixty thousand dollars a year with overtime.

When Matt had lived there during his teen years, he made every attempt to stay away from his uncle. It was relatively easy, because Uncle Rex worked second shift—even after thirty years at the plant, he never exercised his option to take a position on the first shift. Matt suspected he worked second shift so he wouldn't have to spend time with his wife. He would come home at twelve thirty or one in the morning, reheat the leftovers Aunt Bernie left him and slam down a few Budweisers. Then it was off to bed until noon the next day. When he'd been into the Budweiser a little too much, he referred to Matt exclusively as "shithead." Charming man.

The big blowup had come the summer Matt turned eighteen. Matt had finally gotten Tammy Varga to go out with him after two months of asking. It was a Saturday night, and Uncle Rex had set his curfew at eleven o'clock. Matt and Tammy had gone to the Transit Drive-In, and after about half and hour, they decided they were more interested in each other than the movie.

After some making out, Tammy had let Matt feel her breasts and then took his hand and slid it down into her shorts. He had fumbled around until she asked him if he wanted to see what was "up there." He happened to catch a glimpse at Tammy's watch. It was eleven ten.

Disappointed because he couldn't do any more back-seat exploring, but more afraid of Uncle Rex, he dropped Tammy at her door. Tammy called him chickenshit for listening to his auntie and uncle too much, then gave him the finger as he sped away. So much for that date.

He had come home to find the door unlocked. Thank heavens for small miracles, he remembered thinking. Uncle Rex's truck was not in the yard or the open garage. Matt began to slink into the door when headlights lit him up. It was Uncle Rex coming home from work.

Rex Lapchek didn't even bother to turn the car or the lights off. Like an angry grizzly, he charged at Matt and caught him in the doorway. He slammed Matt into the wall, making Matt's teeth rattle in his mouth. Matt could smell cigarettes and stale Jim Beam on his uncle. There had been some yelling, some protesting by his Aunt Bernie for Rex not to hurt him. Uncle Rex cuffed him across the cheek, his high school ring slicing Matt's cheek open.

He got up, holding his face and muttering "bastard" under his breath as he went to his room. The next morning, he packed his bags and left. He scrawled an apology on a napkin to his aunt for causing so much trouble, withdrew his savings from the bank and took the first Greyhound out of town.

Now he was back, a little older and a lot less apt to put up with any of his uncle's bullshit. *Screw him*, Matt thought, and went outside.

He walked over to the house and rang the bell. Aunt Bernie opened the door.

"Come on in, Matthew. You look famished!"

* * *

"Damn fool had the blunt end of a Phillips head screwdriver up his ass. No lie." Cora Matthews let out a shriek of a laugh. Folds of fat strained against her blouse and jiggled like a renegade piece of Jell-O.

"How did you get it out?" Jill asked her.

"Very carefully. You shoulda heard that man squeal! We almost tore the ass out of him getting that thing out."

Jill Adams and the other nurse, Julie Maretto, both burst into laughter, drawing a dirty look from a shrunken old woman seated in the waiting room.

The ER had been quiet all day. An elderly man had been in Room 4 with intestinal discomfort, but he was up having an ultrasound. The other patient was eleven-year-old Danny Lopez, who had come in with a stomach bug.

Jill sat on the desktop among a pile of file folders and someone's red-and-white 7-Eleven coffee mug. Cora sat in a swivel chair, her bulk making the chair look like a child's toy. It wasn't that she was just heavy, she was a large woman, standing at what Jill guessed to be about six-two.

"I've never seen it, but I've heard stories about small rodents being stuffed up there," Julie replied.

"That's a one-way street as far as I'm concerned," Jill replied.

"You don't know the half of it." Julie gave her a grin, showing off neat, square teeth. The woman had a terrific smile except for one yellowed incisor that always reminded Jill of a wolf's tooth.

"I don't know what little Miss Jilly's doing here anyway, Jules. She could've had a scholarship to Duke," Cora said.

"What *are* you doing here?" Julie asked.

"I've always wanted to be a nurse."

"That attitude will change." Julie snorted.

Cora placed a hand on Jill's leg. "Seriously, Jill. You're bright and pretty and I'd kill to have that cute little figure. Why don't you get a job making some real money, find yourself a nice man?"

Cora was starting to sound like her mother. "Like I said, my dad died when I was young. Shot in a robbery. When my mother told me, it hit me like you wouldn't believe."

"I'll bet." Cora nodded somberly.

"I thought it was awful that he had a chance to live and couldn't be saved. So I decided I would get into medicine. Maybe I can stop that from happening to someone else. Save a few lives."

"You're too idealistic," Julie said.

"Or it could be you're too jaded," Jill retorted.

Julie sighed. "It's a way to earn a living, that's it."

"Don't you think it should be more than that?"

"It pays the bills," said Julie.

"Uh-oh. Here she comes," Cora said, rolling her eyes.

"She" was Dorothy Gaines, their supervisor. She walked down the hallway toward the nurses' station with long, purposeful strides, a clipboard tucked under her left arm. Reaching the nurses' station, she stood board-straight and drummed her fingers on the counter.

Dorothy wore horn-rimmed glasses on the end of her pointy nose. She was rope-thin, knotted her hair in a tight bun, favored solid brown or gray tops and pants. Jill heard she was around forty-five, but she looked sixty, and that was on a good day.

"How are we doing, girls?" she asked.

"Things're just a little slow, Dorothy," Cora replied.

"How is Mr. Fleisher?"

"Still having his ultrasound."

She frowned and checked her clipboard. "Jill, what about the Lopez boy? Have you checked his IV? I don't want him getting dehydrated."

"He's got almost a full bag. I just sent one of the aides in to get his temp and BP," Jill said.

Dorothy pushed her glasses up and gave Jill a look designed to freeze. "This place is going down the tubes. They'll hire anybody these days." She stalked away, parting two nurses' aides as she went.

"Boy, she sure don't like you," Cora said.

"I guess not."

"It's because you're smarter than her. Old witch," Julie muttered.

"There's just one thing I'd like to know," Jill said.

Cora and Julie both looked at her.

"When she's having her operation."

"What operation?" Cora and Julie said in unison.

"The one to have the two-by-four removed from her ass."

Cora and Julie broke into a fit of laughter.

Matt sopped up the last of the syrup on his plate with a piece of pancake and popped it in his mouth, relishing the tangy blueberries. He had polished off seven pancakes and now his belly felt like it would burst.

Aunt Bernie leaned across the table, studied him. "Are you sure you don't want more?"

"If you want me to explode, I'll eat more."

Aunt Bernie smiled at him, satisfied that he had eaten enough, then sat back. She had eaten four pancakes, five strips of bacon and half a cheese omelet. The remains of their breakfast sat on the table: sticky plates, an empty coffee cup and a juice glass. He leaned back in his chair and patted his swollen belly, thinking he would have to step up his exercise program to work off this meal.

Aunt Bernie had asked him where he'd been over

the past ten years and he rattled off a list of cities: San Francisco, Seattle, Las Vegas.

They talked about Matt's mother, what a kind woman she was and how they both missed her. Was he going to stay long in Lincoln? For a while at least. Did he have a job lined up? Not yet, but he was working on it. He was going job hunting this morning, but before that he had a few errands to run.

Thanking Aunt Bernie for the breakfast, he kissed her on the cheek, promising that they would talk more when he got back, and headed for the side door.

Aunt Bernie followed him, asking, "What kind of errands are you running, Matthew?"

"Going to do some clothes shopping and pick up a few groceries."

She scowled. "You're a guest here, remember."

He'd forgotten rule number one: no guest pays for food in Bernadette Lapchek's house. "I know, I know, but at least let me pick up a few things."

"Why don't you take the truck out on your errands? You can fit more in it and it needs a good running anyway."

"Uncle Rex won't mind?"

"He barely uses it. One of his buddies drives him to work." She took the key ring off a wooden holder and handed it to him.

He walked outside, the sun glaring in his eyes even at this early hour. He appreciated the truck, but if anything happened, his uncle would flip out. Matt wasn't afraid of Rex Lapchek, not anymore, but he was afraid of what he might do to Rex Lapchek if things turned violent.

He felt a little sluggish after the huge breakfast and went back to his room for a morning nap. When he awoke, the digital clock read 9:36 and he decided it was time to get the day moving along.

After a quick shower and shave inside the house (still no Uncle Rex), he borrowed the phone book from Aunt Bernie and looked up Lincoln Firearms, the local gunshop. It had been in Lincoln for years, but he could never remember whether it was on Elmwood or Delevan. The address was 4231 Delevan Street.

He picked up the receiver, dialed the number for Lincoln Firearms. A gruff-sounding male voice on the other end told him that their hours were from ten A.M. until five P.M.

He toyed with the idea of calling Jill Adams but decided it was too early, even though he was dying to talk to her. Besides, she was most likely tending to patients.

Patients at a hospital he wanted to avoid. You couldn't get him inside Lincoln Mercy if he had blood coming out of every major orifice in his body. As a kid, he and his friends had passed around stories, mostly overheard from grown-ups. Patients mysteriously dying. Botched surgeries. A nurse named Helen Devereaux vanished from the parking deck back in the eighties. Police from three surrounding towns searched for her for a week before finding her dismembered corpse in a wooded area two towns away.

The papers said that the body looked like it had been mangled and there were rumors that the body had claw and bite marks on it, but they were never confirmed or denied by the police department or the county coroner.

God only knew what would happen to anyone who checked into Lincoln Mercy. *I want no part of that place, thank you very much.*

He pulled out his wallet and flipped it open, double-checking to make sure his ATM card was in place. The green-and-white M&T logo poked out at him.

Once in the garage, he climbed into the big Chevy and started up the motor. It rumbled, gave a few coughs and then smoothed out. He took the garage door opener from the sun visor and clicked it. The door opened and he heard the buzz of cicadas raise and kids riding past on bikes, whooping as they cruised along.

As Matt walked up a wheelchair ramp to the glass-enclosed automatic teller machine, a bead of sweat dribbled down his nose. He wiped it away, lamenting the fact that it was going to be another scorcher. It was only ten o'clock and already it felt like ninety degrees outside.

A guy with frizzy hair and a bald spot the size of Australia was using the ATM. His gut hung over his shorts, stretching the faded yellow T-shirt that said MAUI on the front in bright red letters. To complete his look, he had on a pair of sandals with black nylon socks and a fanny pack around his waist. *That outfit should be banned in all fifty states,* Matt thought.

Head down, the man stepped out of the booth, letting the door slam as Matt reached for it.

His ponderous belly knocked Matt back a step and he looked up, a snarl on his face. "Watch where you're going."

Matt looked him up and down. "You actually own a mirror?"

The guy gave Matt a puzzled look, then shoved past, muttering, "Jerk-off."

Matt inserted his card, entered the ATM booth and withdrew a thousand in cash.

CHAPTER 6

Ten minutes later, he arrived at Lincoln Firearms and walked in the door. The bell over the door jingled as he did. As expected, there were racks of guns, knives and bows. In one section stood two mannequins outfitted in fluorescent orange hunting gear. They were set up in front of a pitched tent. Sleeping bags and a mock campfire on green outdoor carpet completed the scene.

It was rumored that Lincoln Firearms stocked more than just your garden-variety rifles, shotguns and pistols. When Matt was thirteen, he heard his father and one of his golfing buddies, Robert Brennan, discussing the store. Robert was also an avid hunter and had told Matt's dad that Harry, the owner, had a small arsenal hidden away. If you were willing to pay the right price, he could hook you up with automatic weapons or even explosives. Matt hoped the rumor was true, for he would need special weaponry to suit his purposes.

The counter was a clear glass case with some of the largest knives Matt had ever seen. *You could gut Moby-Dick with one of those.*

There was a bell on the counter. Matt rang it.

A man stepped out from a doorway behind the counter and asked in a hard voice, "What can I do ya for?" Head-on, he reminded Matt of a bulldog: he was short and squat, with heavy jowls and a thick jaw.

The clerk stepped up to the glass counter and leaned on it, his knuckles pressed on the top of the case. His flannel shirt rode up and Matt saw a faded Marine Corps tattoo on his forearm.

Matt scanned the case and pointed to a knife with a polished walnut handle and a shiny blade that looked sharp enough to split a piece of paper in half. "One of those, for starters."

The clerk unlocked the case and took out the knife. He set in on the counter.

Matt picked up the knife and held it at eye level, tilting the blade back and forth slowly. When the moment of truth came, could he really stick this lethal object into a beating heart, or cut a throat, spilling his enemy's blood? As he tilted the blade again, he caught a glimpse of his eyes in the polished surface. He stared at it for a long second, his gaze flat. Would this tear through one of Their hides?

"You all right there, Chief?" the clerk asked.

"Just thinking," Matt said. "I'll take this."

"Let me get the sheath for you." He bent down to retrieve it.

Matt pretended to be admiring the rest of the knives in the case and leaned as close to the clerk as he could without it seeming like he wanted a kiss from the guy.

He inhaled and smelled Dial soap mixed with cheap cologne, maybe English Leather or Brut. There was no sulfur smell; a good sign.

Looking around, Matt saw the store was empty. *Perfect time to ask about doing a little extra business,* he thought.

"I might be looking for something a little heavier. Some automatics, maybe some explosives."

The clerk eyed him with suspicion. If the guy *were* a bulldog, he might have bitten Matt. "Buddy, just who the hell are you anyway?"

"What do you mean?"

"I mean what kind of question is that? Do I look like I deal arms to third world countries? Do you see any heavy armaments on the walls here?" He waved his arms around, indicating the store.

"I don't know—do you? Deal heavy arms?" Matt retorted.

"Just what does someone like you want with automatics and explosives?" The clerk stepped forward so his belly rested on the glass case. "Come here."

Matt stood still.

"Will ya come here? I don't bite."

Matt stepped closer to the counter, his right hand curled into a fist, ready to pop the guy.

To his surprise, the clerk grabbed him by the front of his shirt and jerked him forward until they were nose to nose. Matt raised his hand to punch him. The guy whipped out a revolver from behind his back and jabbed it into Matt's belly. The cold steel dug into him hard, seeming to press against his backbone.

"Let's see about you," the clerk said.

Panic struck Matt, and his mouth felt as if it were full of paste. His bladder felt like an overinflated water balloon. Two ways to lose your dignity in one day: get gut shot and piss all over the floor in the process. At least it would make for a gripping obituary.

The clerk sniffed, his eyes narrowed, and his hold on Matt's shirt tightened. He looked into Matt's eyes.

"Hmmm," the clerk said. He released his hold and Matt breathed a sigh of relief. The clerk tucked the revolver away and into his belt as casually as a man tucking in his shirt. Matt backed away from the counter.

"Are you sure you're not a cop?"

"I left my badge at home," Matt said sarcastically.

"Then why in blue blazes did you ask me about heavy weapons? Rafferty send you in?"

"Hell no," Matt said. "I'm doing some hunting."

Now the clerk leaned on the rear counter, below the racks of rifles on the wall. "Hunting what?"

"Some things here in town."

He rubbed his chin, then stared at Matt for a good minute. "Come around here."

"You're not going to pull another Jesse James on me, are you?"

"Just come on." The clerk ran a hand through his spiky flattop and disappeared through the door behind the counter.

Matt followed him into a small room that held a kitchen table, chairs and a portable television. There was also another door, this one padlocked. There was also a mini fridge; the clerk hunkered down (Matt heard his knees groan like a sinking ship) and took out a Pabst Blue Ribbon.

He held up the beer. "You care for one?"

"You always invite someone in for beer after you nearly scare them to death?"

"Shit, I'm sorry about that. That's why I brought you back here, to explain."

Matt took the beer from the clerk. Little beads of moisture dotted the side of the can. It seemed surreal to be standing here with a beer in his hand right after almost getting killed by a nutty gun store clerk, but nothing had ever been normal in Lincoln.

The clerk stood up, wiped his hand on his jeans, then offered it to Matt. "Harry Pierce."

Matt introduced himself and shook Harry Pierce's hand. The man's grip felt like he could squeeze iron and make it bend with no problem. It was deceiving, because Harry looked like a mound of flab.

"I had to check you out. You come in here and ask for heavy weapons, I get nervous. There are some strange folks in this town, folks I wouldn't sell anything larger than a peashooter to. Got me?"

"I think so." Matt took a swig off the beer and Harry did the same, and it finally occurred to Matt that he was drinking a beer at eleven o'clock in the morning. Probably too early, but it tasted good—and after the scare he just had, it calmed his frayed nerves.

"Did you say you're from around here?"

"Born in Lincoln and lived here until I was eighteen," Matt replied. "Then I headed out west."

"Why'd you leave?"

"It's a long story."

Harry turned one of the chairs around backward and sat in it, his elbows resting on the back of the chair. "You ever notice anything strange about this town?"

There was no point in beating around the bush, because it was obvious to Matt they both knew about the town's secrets and just how dangerous it was here for anyone who was an outsider. "You mean the creatures, the monsters, whatever it is you want to call them? Yeah, I'd guess I'd call that strange," Matt said.

"So you know about Them."

"More than I would like."

"And you know why I was sniffing, checking."

"Checking for the scent."

Harry slurped his beer. "Yeah. If you were one of Them I would have had to done some shootin'."

Matt didn't doubt that.

"That's my reason for needing the guns," he said aloud, and took a sip of beer. "And I want to make sure that what happened to me doesn't happen to anyone else."

"What exactly happened to you?" Harry said.

"It's a long story."

"My wife whips up a mean pot roast. Why don't you stop by for dinner sometime. Of course I'll need to clear it with her. May take some convincing."

"We can compare notes. Would you mind if I brought a guest?" Matt asked.

"Is he okay? You know."

"Yes, *she* is. She knows about them too, but I don't think she's convinced herself yet."

"Now about those weapons. Let's see what we can do. Follow me."

Harry got up, took another sip of beer and walked over to the door with the padlock on it. He fished a key out of his pocket and undid the lock, then opened the door and flicked a switch on the wall.

"C'mon!"

A stack of mannequins stood in the corner, one of them naked save for a camouflage baseball cap. A large box marked COLUMBIA SPORTSWEAR sat against the wall, the sleeve of a blue winter jacket poking out of the box. Across the room, a red-and-yellow banner with the Marine Corps anchor, eagle and globe hung on the wall.

"Over here."

Matt followed Harry across the room, where a row of shiny black gun safes lined the wall beneath the banner. Harry turned the combination on one of them, then pulled it open, revealing half a dozen M-16 rifles standing on end. They had cylindrical grenade launchers mounted under the barrels.

"Pretty impressive, huh?"

"Where in the hell do you get this stuff?"

"Friends in low places," Harry said, and gave him a conspiratorial wink. "That's all you need to know."

"I won't ask."

"Good. Now let's get you set up with some weaponry. It'll be better if you buy from my private stash here. That way you don't have to fuck around with pistol permits and waiting periods. And the serial numbers have been filed off of these babies. Difficult to trace."

After browsing the rest of the safes, Matt selected a Browning M951R handgun, capable of firing in auto or semi automatic modes, and a pistol-grip Mossberg twelve-gauge for some extra punch. These would be good for a start.

"Rafferty know about this place?"

"I think so. He's just too busy going around busting people's ribs and throwing them in his jail to care. I paid his predecessor a pretty nice sum—bought him a summer home, in fact—to keep quiet about this place. Although I got an extra-special present for Rafferty and his boys if they ever come for me."

Matt wondered about Harry's clientele—how much white powder they sold, how many of their enemies were now encased in concrete.

As if reading his mind, Harry said, "Case you're wondering, I sell to guys who target shoot, maybe want to go off to a mountain cabin and drink Budweiser and blast targets with a little bit more than your garden variety thirty ought six. No drug dealers, any of that shit."

Matt didn't know if he entirely believed that statement. "No other reason you got this stash?"

Harry gave a laugh, his belly jiggling. "You see where I live, don't you?"

Good point. If you were foolish or crazy enough to stay in Lincoln, then having some firepower at your disposal wasn't a bad idea.

After paying for his weapons, Matt shook hands with Harry and left.

Vomit stood between Jill and punching out at three o'clock.

At two-thirty, Dorothy Gaines approached her, smil-

ing a thin-lipped smile, announcing that the Lopez boy
had thrown up all over himself and Jill was to clean it
up.

Jill accepted the assignment with feigned enthusi-
asm, not wanting her supervisor to get the satisfaction
of humiliating her. She tended to the boy with patience,
asking him what his favorite sports teams and television
shows were, trying to keep his wounded dignity in tact.
The boy's mother had gone outside for a cigarette—the
poor kid had been in the emergency room all day waiting for a bed.

At eleven, the last thing most boys wanted was for a
strange woman to see them in their jockey shorts. Jill
felt for the kid, and felt even sorrier for him when he
apologized for making such a mess. She assured him it
was no big deal, ruffled his hair and was on her way.

After gathering her purse from her locker and punching out, she left the main hospital building and stepped
into the sunshine. It was the middle of August and summer was baring its teeth, the sun blinding her for a moment until she could dig out a pair of sunglasses from
her purse and get them on her face. The air felt thick
and sticky; it was ninety-five, easy.

She entered the parking garage, her footsteps clacking on the pavement and echoing through the cavernous
structure. It always amazed her how silent these ramps
were, and she found it a little unsettling. She hurriedly
took the stairway to the second level and found her Toyota.

After paying the attendant in the booth, she turned
right onto Elmwood Avenue and headed toward home.
The encounter with Dorothy Gaines had gotten her
pipes warm, but she had kept from overheating. No
reason to give Gaines justification for writing her up.

Her street was a little more than two miles away from
the hospital. The houses on Wharton were mainly du-

plexes, built after the Second World War. Gnarled maple trees, some a hundred years old or more, provided shade for the entire street and created an effect not unlike entering a cave. Jill supposed it was good to have them because they provided at least some relief from the heat.

She saw the cop car in her driveway and immediately thought, a cop car in the driveway could not be a good sign. It was like getting a phone call at two in the morning. It was always bad news, like someone had a heart attack, or there was a horrible car crash and a family member was lying mangled on a highway.

Jill pulled the Corolla up behind the silver-and-blue patrol car, threw it in park and climbed out. The police car's left rear tire sagged, low on air. The driver's side window was open and voices buzzed on the radio. There was no sign of an officer.

She approached the house, which was painted yellow with black trim and always made her think of a bumblebee. The front porch ran the entire width of the house and on it was a glider that creaked with the slightest breeze. Jill kept promising herself she was going to park herself in that glider and read a good novel, but she'd been too busy.

She opened the screen door, took her keys out of her purse and inserted the house key into the lock.

The door creaked open. She would swear on her mother's name that she'd locked it that morning. Jill looked up to see a cop taking up the doorway and gasped.

"I'm sorry, Miss Adams. Didn't mean to startle you."

"Is there something wrong, Officer?"

"Nothing wrong. And you can call me Ed. Everyone else does."

"He gave her a big smile, but it lacked any sign of warmth. The fact that the cop had been shorted in the looks department didn't add anything to the smile. His head was shaved bald, the forehead lined and cracked like a dried riverbed. His face looked as if it had been carved by an angry sculptor: sharp cheekbones, a pointed chin. And the eyes, seemingly locked in a permanent squint.

"How do you know my name? Are you sure I'm not in trouble?"

The cop threw his head back and laughed, revealing big, yellowed teeth. "No trouble. I make a point of having the townspeople let me know when someone new moves in. I like to come out and personally greet folks like yourself."

Something about him made her uneasy, but if asked she could not put her finger on the exact reason. Maybe it was the fact that she knew she'd locked the door before leaving. Had "Ed" somehow jimmied the lock? Surely she was being crazy, maybe reacting to what Matt Crowe said about the cops being crooked.

"Mind if I come upstairs for a minute?"

She wanted to come up with an excuse why he couldn't, but none came to her and after all, he was an officer of the law. What harm could come to her in the company of a police officer? "I suppose not."

He moved out of her way and she entered the vestibule. Jill fumbled with her keys for a moment and dropped them on the mosaic tile floor. She bent over to pick them up and suddenly wished she had stooped instead. She could feel his gaze affixed to her backside, probably checking out her panty line through her white uniform pants.

Unlocking the door, she climbed the stairs and opened the big wooden door that accessed her apartment.

"I'm Ed Rafferty, by the way. I'm the police chief in Lincoln."

Oh, great. She was dealing with the head honcho.

Jill passed through the dining room; the chief followed her.

"You're a nurse, huh?" Rafferty hooked his thumbs in his belt loops and scanned the ceiling, as if checking the structural integrity of the house.

"Yeah."

"I always loved nurses. Something about the uniforms."

Maybe because you can see through the pants if you look long and hard.

"How long at the hospital?"

"A month. I lived in Buffalo before I moved to Lincoln."

He flashed the yellowed grin again. "Well, it's nice to have such a lovely lady gracing our community. Pretty girl like you *must* have a boyfriend."

Jesus, he was getting personal. She wished he would leave. "Not at the moment," she replied.

"Recently separated?"

"You could say that."

Her fiancé, Jerry, had called off their year-and-a-half engagement this past January, saying he wasn't ready for marriage. She found that odd because buying the ring and getting engaged was his idea in the first place. It was even stranger that a month after the breakup she saw him at the movies with an overweight blonde in stretch pants and a tropical shirt. The woman looked ten years older than him.

She hadn't said anything to them, but had watched while they held hands and kissed throughout the movie like horny teenagers.

After that incident, she decided to get a job in another town. She had enough of Buffalo; it held too many bad memories. A fresh start was what she needed and she hoped to find it living and working in Lincoln.

But to her dismay, she already had to deal with a leering creep, who turned out to be the Chief of Police, of all people.

"That's a shame," he said. "Somebody break your heart?"

"Unfortunately."

"Tsk, tsk. With that beautiful black hair and those killer eyes, I don't see how anyone could resist you."

"I really have a lot of unpacking to do. If you'll excuse me," she said pointedly.

He smacked his lips together. "Yes sir, irresistible."

"I have to unpack."

"No problem, hon."

"Don't call me hon." She felt a hot flush of anger rise in her but quickly suppressed it. She was dealing with the Chief of Police, not some pickup artist on the prowl at happy hour. She didn't want to wind up in jail.

"As long as I don't call you late for dinner, right?" He smiled again and she thought it might be the same way a hyena smiles before tearing into its prey. His friendly small-town-cop act was wearing thin.

"Thank you for stopping by, Chief," she said. "That door off the kitchen leads to the steps and the side entrance. You can use that."

He winked at her. "I'll be seeing you around." Hands in his pockets, he ambled through the kitchen and went through the door.

Jill padded through the kitchen. She shut the door that lead to the steps. When she heard his lumbering steps hit the bottom landing, she slid the security chain in place.

CHAPTER 7

Rafferty looked up at Jill Adams' house from the driveway. What was she doing up there right now?

Picking her lock had been a brilliant idea. He had watched her car pull in behind his, enjoyed the look on her face when she saw the squad car in the driveway. She was the same girl Dietrich had pulled into the warehouse, no doubt. Half of him wanted to rip off those white pants and have his way with her. The other half wanted to sink his teeth into her flesh, maybe tear off a piece from her buttocks while she screamed. That would come later, at Harvest time. Then she would be his. Human lust versus the need to hunt. That was pretty much what he felt toward human females.

He pulled out of Jill's driveway and turned right, pushing the cruiser up to forty-five and cutting off a guy in a red Saab. The guy had the balls to honk his horn at him. Rafferty checked the rearview. The Saab's front end swerved over the double yellow. *I'd stop his ass if I had time*, he thought.

When he pulled into the lot behind the station house, Clarence was standing at the gas pump. With one hand, he held the nozzle in his cruiser's tank, and with the other, he idly scratched the back of his neck. That pump was another source of joy for Rafferty. Maybe once a year he caught someone trying to steal gas from it. They didn't try to steal a second time.

Rafferty parked the car and climbed out. It was close to four P.M. and the sun was beating down on the blacktop. As he walked across the lot, the chemical smell of tar rose up and his feet smooched against the softened asphalt. He approached Clarence at the pump.

"Afternoon, Ed," Clarence said.

"How's Hamil doing?"

"He's been pretty quiet. Haven't had to beat him."

"Too bad for you," Rafferty said. "Release him. And tell him if he pulls that shit again he'll get it worse."

"Right, Chief." Clarence shut the pump off and returned the nozzle to the holder.

Rafferty went inside. He had phone calls to make.

Inside, Linda stood at a file cabinet, its top drawer open. She jammed a report in the top drawer and slid it shut as he passed her on his way to his desk.

He dialed the number for Jimbo's garage. The phone rang three times and Carl Downey, the other mechanic, answered.

"Get me Jimbo," Rafferty said.

"Is this the Chief?"

"You got it. Where's Jimbo?"

"Hang on."

Carl hollered for Jimbo, his yell squawking in the receiver. *Damned moron*, Rafferty thought. He held the receiver at arm's length.

When he returned the receiver to his ear, Rafferty heard the clink of metal on metal, the whiz of an impact wrench and then Jimbo telling Carl to go check the rotors on the Ford in bay two.

"Jimbo here." Old Jimbo's voice always sounded like

he had gargled with razor blades. Jimbo was the best source in town for information on Outsiders. He owned the town's only gas station, and he saw all kinds go past his rusted pumps.

"Rafferty. Seen any action in town lately?"

"Had a young piece of tail come through here for gas a few times. Fine, she was. Said something about just moving into town. Other than that, not much."

"I knew about her already."

"Oh?" Jimbo hawked and spat, presumably on the floor of the garage.

"Keep your eyes open for any more newcomers. And remember, anything good you call me, got it?"

"I suppose. If I gotta share, then I gotta."

Rafferty lowered his voice to a whisper. "No kills before Harvest. Unless I say so."

Jimbo coughed, harsh and raspy. Then Rafferty heard the wet *twhock* of him spitting.

Maybe the old bastard will just keel over and die someday, choke on all that crap in his lungs. Serves him right for sucking down Pall Malls all day.

"Sure wouldn't of minded stickin' it to that little girlie who came through here. What's her name, anyway?"

"Don't get any ideas," Rafferty warned. "I'm saving her."

Jimbo cackled. "Well, if you want to share, Ed, you just give me a holler. My old pecker ain't seen a beaver in years."

"Keep it in your pants, you old pervert."

Jimbo started coughing again and Rafferty hung up.

This town sucks, thought Bill Jergens as he sat in the waiting area at Jimbo's garage. He had come all the way out to this pissant little town to sell a new pager account at Drover Industrial Supply. When he got there, the guy told him that Drover had already gone with Mobile Comm, Bill's main competitor. And the asshole had told him over the phone that if Bill came out personally, they would sign with Rapid Communications, Bill's company. He felt like threatening the guy with a lawsuit.

To top it off, AAA had brought him to this stinking garage because his Lexus had refused to start. Forty thousand dollars for the car and it quit on him.

He sat in the area of the garage that doubled as an office and waiting room for the customers. There was a scuffed metal desk and an office chair with the stuffing poking out of the seat, three plastic chairs and a magazine rack. The rack held a copy of *Life* with a picture of Ronald Reagan on the cover. To top it off the place smelled like a cross between gasoline and a sweat sock.

The sun beat on the back of his neck. The collar of his shirt scratched his neck, and sweat beads formed on his forehead. He wished for a pair of Bermudas and sandals instead of a suit.

He had sold Chryslers, life insurance and even pawned off thousand-dollar vacuums on gullible housewives. Now it was pagers and cell phones, mostly sold to corporate customers.

He was pretty damn good at selling—been top salesman three years running—and he had the Lexus to prove it. He liked thinking the other salesmen drooled over it when he pulled in the lot.

Now, sitting in the garage, he began to get nervous, wondering what these small-town yokels would do to his prized automobile.

The geezer named Jimbo entered the waiting room. He was George Burns old, with a scraggly white beard and an off-center eyeball. The guy could probably see his left ear with that eye, Bill thought. Jimbo wiped his hands on the front of his coveralls, smearing them with grease. He approached Bill and stopped.

"That's a pretty fancy car."

Scratchy voice, probably a heavy smoker.

"What's the damage?"

"Fella like you must make a lotta money."

"I do all right," Bill said. "What's wrong with it?"

Instead of answering, Jimbo hawked and spat a wad of phlegm on the floor. Bill recoiled in disgust.

"Well, I believe it's your alternator."

"That car's only a year old!"

Jimbo scratched his beard. "Yeah, but it's a Jap car. Never did trust them to make cars, not after the War, that is."

"What exactly is wrong with the alternator?"

"It's just shot."

"I want to see it."

"Sorry, can't let you in the garage," he said and shrugged. "Insurance reasons."

"If you don't let me in there, I'll call the cops."

"Be my guest. Call 'em."

This guy is a number-one jackass. "All right, suit yourself,"

Bill took out his cell phone, flipped it open. "I'm calling 911."

Jimbo reached out and grabbed Bill's arm. "Well, maybe I *should* let you take a look. I'm getting a little crabby in my old age."

Bill gave him a speculative look; after a moment, he put the phone back in his pocket.

"But it'll cost you. Twenty-dollar consulting fee. That's on top of parts and labor."

"And what's that going to cost me?"

"Oh, in the neighborhood of a thousand."

"You're out of your mind if you think I'm paying that

much. I'm getting my car out of here if I have to put it in neutral and push it out myself."

Bill stood and stomped into the garage.

A skinny, acne-faced kid with "Carl" sewn on his coveralls looked over at him. There was a Ford up on the lift and Carl was monkeying with the front brakes.

Bill's Lexus, black and gleaming, waited in the bay next to the Ford. Jimbo followed Bill into the garage and slid up next to him. The hood of the Lexus was propped open; Bill leaned over the engine pretending to inspect the car's components very carefully. He furrowed his brow, hoping the geezer wouldn't catch on that Bill had no idea what to look for. "There doesn't look like there's anything wrong under here."

"Well, you got no juice. And I say it's your alternator."

"Are you telling me you're guessing?"

"Not guessing," Jimbo said, and tapped his finger against his temple. "Instinct."

That was it. Bill would go outside and call a tow truck on the cell. He had to get out of this place. It stunk.

Bill started to move for the door, but Jimbo put a hand on his chest. Bill shoved forward, but Jimbo held him in place. He was surprisingly strong for an old man.

"Maybe I misjudged you. You seem like a decent guy, and you sure don't take any bullshit."

Bill beamed a little, happy with himself for getting the old man to back down. With any luck he'd be out of this Podunk town in a hurry. Bill glanced at the other mechanic, who had stopped working on the brake job and now stood at the overhead doors. He pressed a red button and the doors hummed and clacked before closing. That was weird. Why the hell would he do that?

"Let's sit down and talk about this and I'll level with you. It's just going to be more of a hassle for you to have this towed again anyway. Sound fair?"

"All right. But you'd better not try and screw me."
Bill wagged his finger at Jimbo. "Got it?"

"Hey, I know a tough customer when I see one. Let's
go into my office and talk."

As Bill stepped forward, something solid thudded
against the back of his head. The ground rose up at terrifying speed, and a second later, everything went black.

The fat guy in the expensive suit twitched and flopped
like a snagged trout. After a few seconds, he stopped. The
back of his skull now had a divot in it. Jimbo looked at
Carl, who held the tire iron, now specked with blood and
hair. A big grin crossed his face, and his breathing had
quickened.

Jimbo wound up and punched Carl square in the
chest. Carl rocked back a step.

"Now I'm gonna have to deal with Rafferty, you
numb fuck!"

Carl continued to stare at the body, an idiot grin on
his face.

"Carl!"

Carl looked at Jimbo.

"If you had to hit him, why did you hit him in the
noggin?"

"He was giving you trouble," Carl said, wiping the
blood from his face with his sleeve.

Half-wit, Jimbo thought. He didn't have a problem
with teaching the fat salesman a little lesson, but now
Fatty was dead and if Rafferty found out, Jimbo might
be joining him in the afterlife.

They had to get rid of the body, and quick.

Jimbo looked down at Fatty, guessed him to weigh
two-fifty, maybe even two-eighty. He squatted down and
rolled Jergens over, then stepped over the dead man,
hooked his arms under the body's armpits and heaved.

One of Fatty's tassled loafers slipped off, and the smell of shit was overwhelming. Apparently, Fatty had let loose when Carl caved in his skull.

He thought for a moment about canning Carl, and then dismissed the thought because he needed the help at the garage.

"Where you going with him, Jimbo?"

"To the local barn dance, asshole. We're gonna do the do-si-do together." Jimbo shook his head. "Where the fuck do ya think I'm going with him?"

"Uh, I dunno?"

Jimbo jerked his head, indicating for Carl to get over and help. "Get his legs. We'll stuff him in the dungeon."

The dungeon was a six-by-six room off the garage where Jimbo kept a bench grinder and old tires.

Carl scurried over and lifted the salesman's legs.

The guy had a black splotch on his pant leg, most likely motor oil from when he hit the floor. Carl snickered at the fact that not only was the big shot dead, his suit was ruined too.

His good time was short-lived when he thought of Rafferty coming in and poking around the station. If he found the body, they would be in violation of the rules, and if Rafferty exploded, he wanted to be two towns away.

They dragged the body to the door of the dungeon, Carl grunting and cursing under his breath the whole time.

"You got no right to swear. You caused this mess and I'm gonna hafta pay for it."

"Rafferty won't find out."

"The hell he won't. That man's a fly on the wall in every building in this town. He doesn't miss a trick." Jimbo hawked and spat.

"I think you're afraid of him."

"If you were smart, you'd be afraid of him too."

"What's the worst he'd do to you?"

"Oh, I don't know. Just kill me and eat my guts out, I suppose."

Carl spoke in a soft tone, as if explaining something simple to a child. "But you're older. You've got experience on your side, Jimbo. You told me just the other day that you made your first kill before Rafferty was even thought of."

That *was* true, Jimbo thought. He did have experience versus Rafferty's toughness and youth. Then he mentally shook himself. "This is horsecrap. Get Tubby here into the dungeon before Rafferty shows up."

"I think you could take care of him, Jimbo. Honest. You could run this town if Rafferty was gone," Carl persisted.

"You're just kissin' ass because I'm mad at you."

"No, I ain't. I think you could give old numb-nuts police chief a run for his money."

The wheels began to turn in Jimbo's head. He *was* older and more experienced in hunting and killing than Rafferty. He had killed hundreds of humans and nine or ten of his own kind in one dispute or another. Maybe he *could* take Rafferty, if it came down to it. Besides, he was getting sick of taking Rafferty's crap year after year, watching him strut around town like a peacock. "Maybe you're right, Carl. Set him down and then go put the Closed sign on the door. Make sure the door's locked."

"Right." Carl dropped the salesman's legs and hurried into the office area.

Jimbo set the rest of Fatty's bulk on the floor, feeling brave right now. Why not indulge a little? Rafferty would never know. And if he did find out, he would be in for a nasty surprise because Old Jimbo was done taking his crap.

Carl came back into the garage area, his eyes wide

like a child discovering presents under the Christmas tree.

"I'm gonna feed," Jimbo said.

He closed his eyes and focused in his mind on his jaw and mouth. *Grow.* The muscles in the jaw began to pulse, first slowly and then popping like pistons in an engine. Bones ground and shifted. His jaw expanded sideways, the skin stretching like a grotesque balloon. The flesh around his mouth and on his cheeks darkened to a blackish green tint, grew leathery and tough. The teeth thickened and became elongated, tearing through gum tissue that would later heal. The metallic taste of blood filled his mouth.

"A partial change," Carl said. "That takes control!"

Squatting over the body, Jimbo pressed his mouth against the side of Fatty's neck. With a wet tearing sound, he bit the dead man's throat, spilling blood onto the white dress shirt. With his fangs, he tore away a chunk of flesh. The feast had begun.

Jill and Cora sat in the cafeteria at Lincoln Memorial. The clink of dishes and the occasional hiss from the deep fryer echoed in the background. A few surgeons dressed in gray scrubs picked at club sandwiches, their gazes blank and bleary.

"I'm positive I locked that door before I left," Jill said, and put a forkful of salad in her mouth. She was surprised that the food was actually pretty good. The salad had a mess of shredded cheese over the top and the cook hadn't skimped on grilled chicken pieces either. Cora's lunch looked good too. She had a Mount McKinley–sized mound of french fries on her plate and the remains of strawberry milk shake in a tall glass.

"You don't think he picked it, do you?" Cora said.

A page for a Dr. Salam crackled over the intercom.

"Why would he want to?"

"Maybe he's got a thing for you."

Jill sorted through her salad with the fork. "Please."

"Just watch yourself. Cops can do wrong just like anyone else. Maybe you should get some pepper spray."

"It hasn't come to that," Jill said, crunching another bite of salad. "And I hope it won't."

"After what happened to you the other night, you can't be too careful," Cora pointed out.

When they first sat down, Jill had recounted the story of her assault at the warehouse, not mentioning the strange animal.

Cora took a swig of her milk shake. "So, you heard from the Good Samaritan?"

"Not yet."

"You should call him."

"I want to, but I think it would be kind of weird. We don't even know each other."

"Most men would've kept right on driving, don't you think? Maybe there's a little something special about him."

"Well—"

"Well, nothing. Besides, you said he seemed okay. And he was good-looking too."

Jill smiled. "That he was."

"I've got a good feeling about him, Jill. The way you said he was polite and sort of sweet." Cora plucked a fry from the plate. "You should make some friends, anyway."

"You really think he sounds all right?"

"Him, yes. That cop, no. Stay away from him."

Jill shuddered at the thought of Rafferty being in her home, his eyes probing her body.

"What's the matter?"

"Just thinking about that creep of a police officer. He looked at me like he wanted . . . you know."

"To do the wild thing?"

Jill burst out laughing at Cora's description. "Yeah, only without my full cooperation."

Cora pointed at her with her french fry. "You keep me posted on that cop. I gotta go to the little girl's room."

Cora hefted herself up from the chair. Jill picked up her tray and took it to the trash receptacle. She felt the gazes of the two surgeons on her and fought the impulse to look back over her shoulder. She found it strange how people always knew when someone was watching them, almost like a sixth sense. Maybe it came from caveman days, when you had to be aware of being watched if you didn't want to end up as dinner for a saber-toothed tiger.

She didn't mind the occasional look from men. She supposed it meant she was still marketable. It had been a constant problem when she was dating Jerry, though. The two of them would go out to a bar or restaurant, Jerry would go to use the john and a guy would offer to buy her a drink. Jerry would come back and threaten to kick the guy's ass across the parking lot and make a huge scene.

But he was history and she really shouldn't dwell on him, she supposed. He was immature and hot-tempered, playing drinking games at parties and picking fights with anyone he thought had looked at him funny. Part of her was relieved when he broke it off, because she didn't want to spend her life with someone who was terminally thirteen years old, she realized now.

So maybe she *would* give Matt Crowe a call and feel him out for a friendly dinner. He seemed all right and she really didn't know too many people in town. It would be a friendly date, nothing more—but if it became more, she wouldn't mind.

Cora came back to the table, sat down and dug into her fries.

"I'm going to call him," Jill told her.

"Amen to that."

Jill punched the time clock, wished Cora good night and strolled out the ER entrance. The heat baked her skin, and she squinted against the sunlight. She unfastened the top two buttons on her blouse and fanned the material. It had to be ninety out here.

She reached the parking ramp, nodded to the attendant in the booth (she thought his name was Al, but she could never remember) and walked through the entrance to the first level. To her right was the door to the stairs and the second level where her car was parked.

She reached her car and had just inserted the key in the lock when she heard someone whistling behind her.

She jerked the key from the lock, inserted it between her index and middle fingers and made a fist so it could be used to strike an attacker. Then she whirled around, half expecting to see a hulking fiend reaching out to grab her and drag her to the shadows. Instead she saw Chief Ed Rafferty standing with his hands up as if to say, "Whoa, easy now."

He snapped his fingers. "Wow, you're quick. That's good, though, using the key like you have it. That's a sure way to disable an attacker. Go for the eyes, the throat or the crotch."

She clamped down tighter on the key. "Chief, no disrespect, but why are you here?"

"Just looking out for you, Jill. A pretty girl walking by herself to a parking ramp could be inviting trouble."

"It's the middle of the afternoon," she pointed out.

"You can't be too careful."

She looked around the ramp, hoping for someone else to walk past. "This town seems pretty quiet to me. I think I'll be okay."

The chief wrinkled his mouth to one side and said, "Hmm. I probably shouldn't tell you this, but it might help you be more safe. Keep in mind I'm not trying to scare you. A while back a nurse named Helen Devereaux was walking to the garage after her shift—she finished at three-thirty. Well, Helen strolled up to the third level of the ramp with no trouble. It was daylight, just like now, and she felt safe and secure, I'm positive. Well, when she reached the third flight of stairs there was someone waiting for her. We found her purse and a broken nail on the concrete. It was painted pink, if I remember right. That was the end of her."

Is he trying to convince me I need protection? Half of her was rattled by Rafferty following her and the other half wanted to kick him square in the family jewels and then speed away in her car. "Thank you for the warning, Chief, but I really have to get home."

"Why's that? No man to get home to, and I didn't notice any pets to feed or take care of."

"I'm tired and I want to get a shower and some rest."

"Hmmm. A shower. Good idea."

She immediately wished she hadn't mentioned it because she was sure Rafferty was visualizing her naked, soapy body in his head. The thought made her queasy.

"Pretty hot, huh, Jill?"

"Yes, it is. Now I really have to go."

Rafferty took a step toward her and leaned on the car, effectively preventing her from opening the door.

"Noticed you have a few buttons undone. Can't say I blame you."

Jill pulled the cotton material closed and held it to her chest.

"No need to be embarrassed. You're a beautiful woman. Gotta show off what you have. Am I right?"

Jill turned and slid the key into the lock. "I have to go," she repeated firmly.

Rafferty grabbed her wrist and pulled it away; the key remained in the lock.

He probably expected her to cower before him, but instead she looked him right in the face (the whole time wanting to work up a gob of spit and let it fly in his kisser) and asked him, "How did you know what time I got off, Chief? And why are you harassing me?"

He narrowed his eyes, bent down within kissing distance. "I know a lot of things in this town, Jill. I know where everybody lives and where they work. I know what time they go to bed and what time they get up. I know when they fuck their wives and even when some of them take a shit. This is my town, and I don't miss a goddamn trick. You remember that."

His placid gaze had become a look of fury; the grip on her wrist tightened and her hand turned china-white from the pressure exerted on it. He whispered, "You just remember: I see everything. Maybe if I'm lucky I'll see that body of yours naked through your window some night. You won't even know I'm there."

She pulled away from him. He stank. Like the guy in the warehouse. *Oh, Lord.*

Just when she thought it couldn't get any worse, he reached over with his free hand, seized her hair and pulled her face close to his. Twisting the hair, he turned her head to the side and slid his warm tongue into her ear.

She felt hot and dizzy, her head swollen. Tears of rage pooled in her eyes and her face felt like it was on fire. The last thing she wanted was for Rafferty to see her cry.

He let her go and backed away, grinning. "I'll be seeing you, Jill."

She immediately unlocked the car door and climbed inside, clicking the lock shut. Then she dug in her purse for a tissue. Rafferty's disgusting act had left her ear wet and slimy.

She tossed the used tissue on the passenger seat, started the car, slammed it into reverse, then screeched out of the parking ramp, half afraid that if she saw Rafferty walking she would splatter him all over the concrete with her Toyota.

But Rafferty was gone as fast as he came. After driving three blocks she settled down a little bit and eased off the gas. The first thing she would do upon arriving home was take a hot shower. The second would be to call Matt Crowe and tell him what happened. She remembered the comment he made about police corruption in Lincoln, and it turned out he was correct. But what troubled her even more was the smell that came off of Ed Rafferty's hide.

CHAPTER 8

From his prowl car, Ed Rafferty watched the nurse speed away in her Toyota and laughed out loud. That was perfect, the look of pure fear on her face and the way she had begun spurting tears. *Typical woman*, he thought.

The tongue in the ear had been a spur-of-the-moment idea, and a great one if he had to say so himself. If you beat a person down, broke them until they reached the point of tears, they usually belonged to you after that. Jill was on her way.

The air in the car felt hot in his nostrils and mouth. He rolled down the window. He picked at the peeling vinyl on the seat, thinking of his first kill, the beauty of the hunt.

When Rafferty was fifteen, his father took him to the Allegheny Mountains so he could learn to hunt. The year had been 1845, long before he came to Lincoln. They had spent two days sleeping among the pines, the air redolent with the smell of sap and needles. On the second night, they came upon a pair of hunters camped out for the night.

They had tracked the hunters for two days, his father

telling him that the anticipation of watching them would make the kill even more satisfying. They had watched them eat, sleep and even piss in the bushes. On the third night, just after sunset, Rafferty and his father changed over, careful not to shriek (even though the pain of transformation was excruciating) and warn the prey that they were coming.

After their transformation, they had moved quickly down the trail, powerful legs propelling them, the October air slicing over their bodies. The men sat by a bonfire, their knees drawn up, huddling for protection from the chilly autumn air.

His father leapt first, crashing on top of the nearest hunter and pinning him. With a slash of a talon, the man's gut was laid open and his eyes bulged in disbelief at what had just happened to him. The other one sprang to his feet and started off down the trail, but he was far too slow. In two bounds, Rafferty pounced on his back and snapped his neck.

The two of them feasted and buried the corpses, which were reduced to bones and gristle, in a small cave down the trail. Then Rafferty and his father transformed back, washed the blood off of themselves in a nearby stream and put their clothes back on. The next morning they headed home.

He had other fond memories: him and his teenage buddies burning Mrs. Hathaway's house down with her in it and then picking her off when she ran from the flames. Then there was the time he stalked a teenage girl through Dade Park, playing with her for nearly an hour before closing in for the kill. That had been back in 1956.

Jill Adams would make a nice addition to his list of memories.

* * *

Jill sat at her kitchen table and sipped Bailey's Irish Cream on the rocks, hoping to calm her nerves and warm the iciness that had seeped into her bones. Some situations called for something stronger than Coca-Cola.

That Rafferty had balls. And the son of a bitch knew there was no place for her to turn. There had to be a way to get him off her back without fearing retribution from him or one of his deputies. She needed to find an answer fast, before harassment turned into something much worse.

As she sipped her Bailey's, enjoying its cool sweetness, the phone rang. Picking it up, she almost wanted to groan. It was her mother.

"How's everything, Jill?"

"Fine, Mom."

"And the hospital?"

"Okay."

"No one's thrown up on you, or gotten blood on you? You know, with AIDS and all."

"Mom, please."

"The doctors don't have people throwing up on them."

"No one threw up on me."

God, the woman could drive Mother Teresa to murder.

"Hmm. That's okay. You probably wouldn't tell me if they did."

Jill didn't say anything, and the sound of her mother's breathing was the only noise on the line.

"Is everything okay? You sound like something's wrong."

"Nothing's wrong, Mom."

"You know you can tell me if there is."

"I'm fine."

"I don't like the sound of your voice. You sound upset. Maybe you should come home."

Jill gritted her teeth. "I'm not coming home. Mom, I really have to go. I'll call you."

She pushed the Off button on the cordless and it beeped, terminating her connection. In one way she felt like a rat for hanging up on her mother, but the woman treated her like she was four years old. "Tough titty said the kitty," she said, and laughed at the silly saying.

She polished off the Bailey's and poured herself another glass, adding more ice this time. Feeling a little brave from the Bailey's, she decided she would take the plunge and call Matt Crowe.

She picked up the scrap of paper with his number on it, went to the phone and dialed his number.

A woman answered and told her to hold on. A moment later, Matt came on the line.

"Hi, Matt, it's Jill."

"Hey, Jill. How are you?"

"Just called to see how the ankle was."

"I'll walk again someday."

"Well, I'm glad you're on the road to recovery but I'd be lying if I said that was the only reason I called."

Silence on the other end. Anticipation, maybe?

"I've been having a problem with the police."

"Rafferty or one of his deputies?"

"The head man himself. I'd like to get together with you and talk about it."

"Are you all right? He didn't hurt you, did he?"

"No, just shook me up a bit."

"Would you mind if we met at your place?" Matt said.

"That'd be fine. Why don't you come over about six? I can whip something up."

"Sounds great. See you at six."

They said good-bye and hung up.

She went to the kitchen to make sure she had spaghetti

and a jar of sauce. She was surprised that her heart rate had sped up. Feeling like a fifteen-year-old with a crush on a boy, she giggled to herself. She couldn't wait for him to get here.

Matt hung up the phone thinking he would bring her a bouquet of carnations and a nice bottle of Merlot. He hadn't been on a date in six or seven years. Hopefully it was like riding a bike.

The sun beating in the window turned the loft into a sweatbox. He felt guilty running the air conditioner all day because it meant jacking up Aunt Bernie's electric bill, but it was too hot to go without it. So he turned it to low as a compromise.

The digital clock next to the bed said four thirty and he still had a few things to take care of before he left. He had left his new weaponry on the bed; sitting down next to his arsenal, he set the shotgun across his lap, picked up a box of shells and clicked five of them home. He slid the Mossberg under the bed and a cluster of dust bunnies flew up in his face. He sneezed twice and then took the knife and slipped it under as well.

Then he loaded the Beretta and did the same with it.

Jill's revelation of the Chief's harassment made him angry, gave him even more motivation to take Rafferty down. Rafferty was a monster, a cruel beast and an all-around prick, someone he wanted dead. But Matt guessed that ten percent of Lincoln's population was Rafferty's kind, and he assumed they would turn on whoever tried to harm their beloved Chief of Police. He might be signing his own death warrant by going after Rafferty.

The best way was to hit Rafferty fast and then get the hell out of Dodge. That posed more problems, for he could never return to Lincoln again. And what if he and Jill hit it off? Started a relationship? Killing Rafferty would put an end to anything he started with her. The thought of leaving Aunt Bernie killed him, as well.

Eager to meet with Jill he decided to get a move on so he went in the house and took a shower. After he'd dressed, Aunt Bernie offered him two twenties for the two bags of groceries he'd purchased, but he refused the money. She was bound and determined not to let him pay for any food while he was here, but he needed to make some sort of contribution to the household. She scolded him, and he hurried out of the house before she tried shoving the bills in his shirt pocket.

Then he was off, more excited than he had been in years.

Rhonda Barbieri dragged her tired body out of her Audi, climbed the steps from the garage to the kitchen door, flipped on the lights and slumped into a kitchen chair. Her feet ached, her temples felt like they were caught in a vise and she could smell the sourness of her own sweat.

Rhonda, a lawyer at Goldstein and Day Attorneys, was on the verge of being made a partner, the first woman partner in the firm's eighty-year history. She had started work at seven this morning and called it quits at quarter to six. Kicking off her right shoe, she lifted an aching foot and massaged it, thinking how nice it would be to slip into a hot bath and then collapse into bed.

She kicked off her other shoe and went upstairs to the bedroom, where she slid out of her clothes and into a pink bathrobe. She looked at the king-size bed, deciding that it was nice to have the whole thing to herself this evening. Her husband, Bob, had gone to a seminar for purchasing agents in Syracuse, and would not be home until tomorrow evening.

To Rhonda's dismay, he had taken his assistant, Sheila, with him, explaining that he wanted to expose her to business settings. Rhonda knew that he wanted to expose more than just business to the little slut. Sheila Donahue. Twenty-two, red-haired, with a set of paid-for breasts. When Bob had introduced her to Sheila, the girl had been all giggles, picking lint off of Bob's suit and laughing at stale jokes even Bob didn't find funny anymore.

She'd first become suspicious last summer, when Bob told her one Saturday he was going to golf nine holes with his buddy, Ron Geiss. He had been gone six hours, and when he came home there was a faint trace of Liz Claiborne perfume on him, and that was not Rhonda's scent. She had also found a strange phone number on a piece of paper in his pocket, but she didn't want to confront him.

Yet.

Part of it was that she didn't want to admit to herself that her husband was doing the nasty with a girl half his age—that Rhonda was being dumped for a younger, firmer woman. A quick phone call to Ron Geiss would let her know if the two of them had in fact played golf, but again, that would be finding out the truth, and the truth could cut like a razor blade.

She got an image of the two of them screwing, Sheila's skirt flipped up, Bob bending her over a desk, the sweat shining on their skins. She was almost glad the son of a bitch wasn't home—now she didn't have to look at him or listen to him fart in his sleep.

She wondered if Little Miss Sheila knew about *that* charming habit.

If I wait long enough, I'll catch him, she thought. *And then I'll cut his balls off.* Maybe not literally, but she knew plenty of divorce lawyers who would love to sink their teeth into a case like this. And then he would pay dearly.

Her stomach rumbled, and she realized she hadn't had anything to eat since twelve thirty, and even then she had only scarfed down half a bagel and a cup of tea. Right about now a Stouffer's Pizza sounded good, and she decided to get one out of the freezer in the basement. First she pulled out a Diet Coke from the fridge and set it on the kitchen table.

The first thing she noticed when she opened the basement door was the smell, sour and pungent. *What in the world could cause such an awful reek?* she wondered. *Maybe a squirrel or a mouse had gotten trapped and died somewhere.*

She flipped the light switch and got nothing.

Hmm. Fuse must've blown.

After retrieving a flashlight from the junk drawer in the kitchen, she padded down the stairs in her bare feet, hoping Bob hadn't left any nails lying around. When she reached the bottom of the stairs, the odor hit her again. She couldn't place it, but it was vaguely chemical, with an undertone of raw sewage mixed in.

At the bottom of the stairs, she turned left to where the refrigerator stood against the wall. It was an old avocado-colored Amana, their first fridge. They retired it to the basement for storing frozen pizzas, pot pies, and other frozen junk food years ago.

The fuse box was to the right of the fridge, and Rhonda shone her light on the box and opened the door. The fuse in the socket for the basement and the corresponding section of the upstairs had been removed. Damnit, she'd been after Bob to get the electric updated for years. Now she had to find the fuse.

She flicked her beam to the floor and saw the fuse on the floor near the basement wall. At first she thought maybe it had simply dropped from the box, but she realized it couldn't have fallen to the floor because the door was shut and latched.

What if someone was in the house and had pulled that fuse out on purpose? And she was alone. Rhonda shivered and her hair stood on end.

Then a growl came from the shadows behind her. Spinning around, she saw to her left, opposite the stairs, only Bob's workbench and rows of screwdrivers and pliers hung on Peg Board hooks. Absurdly, she thought how he hadn't fixed anything in two months and wondered why he even bothered keeping the tools. He had even left a screwdriver on the floor. And that damned gas can he insisted on leaving down here!

There was a storage room whose wall ran perpendicular to the workbench. The door was closed. She switched the beam from the door to the window between the bench and the storage room. The glass had been smashed out.

Get to the stairs and call the cops. But don't panic, she thought.

More grunting came from behind the door. And that smell, churning her stomach.

She almost made it to the top stairs when the storage room door flew open, slamming against the wall like a gunshot. Powerful hands grasped her legs a second later, it seemed, and dragged her back down and into the darkness. Rhonda fought; a nail snapped off.

She turned her head and looked at her attacker, the face inches from hers, and smelled its fetid breath. Urine dribbled down her leg as her bladder let go.

My God, I can't die like this.

Harry Pierce flicked the light switch off, pulled the keys from his pocket and stepped outside Lincoln Firearms. He then locked the door and gave it a nudge to make sure it locked. Satisfied the door was secure, he rounded the corner of the store, passing the bow and arrow display in the front window.

He walked down Barker Avenue. Crickets chirped around him, and in a driveway across the street, a girl in a pink bathing suit jumped rope and recited a rhyme he had never heard before. He smiled. Cute little thing, she was.

He reached the parking lot at the rear. As he turned to enter the lot, a flash of hot pink caught his eye. It was stapled to the telephone pole. Usually such signs advertised garage sales or church picnics, but when he read the lettering on the sign, it chilled his blood.

He looked left, then right. The only person on the street was the jump roper. He reached up and plucked the flyer from the pole, careful not to tear it in half.

As he walked toward his truck, he folded the paper and tucked it in his pocket. This was bad. Very bad.

Matt and Jill had polished off the spaghetti. After dinner, he helped her clear the table and put the dishes in the sink. He volunteered to wash the dishes but she declined, preferring to let them soak while the two of them talked.

They retired to the living room, him in a recliner and Jill sitting across from him on the plush couch, a glass of Merlot in hand. They had talked over dinner, mostly about their pasts and her adventures in nursing. She had also been engaged, but she wasn't seeing anyone right now. That was the best news Matt heard in a long time.

She told him about the death of her father when she was young. He felt bad for her, not having a father and, from the sound of it, having a mother who didn't approve of anything her daughter did.

"I think it's great you're doing what you want to be doing," he said.

"You can't let your parents run your life. I love my mother, but if I went to med school like she wanted me to, I wouldn't be happy at all."

He had deliberately been vague about his background, mentioning that his parents were deceased, his time in the military and living in different cities out west. Luckily, she had bought the line about his parents being wiped out in a head-on collision with a semi. He felt his face start to flush when he told her the lie, and hoped she couldn't tell. Later on, when he got to know her better, maybe he'd tell her the truth about his parents.

Jill tucked her legs up under her and sat Indian-style on the couch.

"So about our encounter in the warehouse," she said.

"What about it?"

"It's obvious something strange happened. And you seem to know more than you wanted to say that night. So what was it? An animal? A howling psychotic?"

Matt wiped the sweat from his forehead with the back of his hand, not sure if it was the heat or his nerves making him perspire. "Do you believe in UFOs?"

"Don't even tell me it was an alien."

"I'm not. Maybe I should rephrase the question. Do you think that UFOs or aliens could exist?"

"It's not impossible," Jill allowed.

"How about other things? Loch Ness Monster, ghosts, psychic phenomenon?"

"No, maybe, and no."

"So you'll admit that maybe there's things in this world that are out of the ordinary?"

"I suppose so, yeah."

Matt swallowed hard. He had never told anyone in detail about the secrets in Lincoln, and it might convince Jill that he had gone off the deep end, but he had a feeling she wouldn't give up until he explained. *Here goes nothing—or maybe everything.*

"Jill, the people in this town are not all . . . people. That is, they're not what they appear to be."

"How so?"

"Underneath the skin, there's a beast. A monster, whatever you want to call it. As far as I can tell, they prey on people who are human."

"So, you're talking about vampires, werewolves, something like that?"

"Not exactly."

"And I suppose you've seen one of these things?"

He detected the skepticism in her voice and thought he must've blown it with her. Maybe she would call the Buffalo Psychiatric Center and have them cart him to the booby hatch. "I've seen them."

"When?" she demanded.

He didn't answer her for a moment, pondering whether or not he should tell the whole truth . But he had already started the unbelievable story, so why not finish it?

"Well?"

"They killed my parents. And my little brother. The Chief of Police, your friend Rafferty, was in the lead. He helped kill them all."

Her eyes widened and for a moment he thought she might throw him out on his ass.

"I suppose you don't want to hear any more."

"Matt, I don't know what to believe. You seem very nice, but this is a crazy story. On the other hand, I can't deny that something strange happened in the warehouse."

"You remember telling me that you noticed a strong smell when that guy dragged you into the warehouse?"

She said she did.

"They all smell like that. In human form you can only notice it faintly. If you're around Rafferty again, see if you detect it."

Jill stood up and Matt though she might tell him to leave.

"I'm getting myself another glass of wine. I have a feeling I'll need it if I'm going to hear the rest of your story. You want one?"

"Why not?"

She came back and handed him a glass of wine. Jill sat and resumed her cross-legged position in the middle of the couch.

"You just said your parents died in a car crash."

"I'm sorry I lied, but I didn't think telling you the bogeyman got them would be a good dinner conversation." He shrugged. "As long as I'm telling the story about Lincoln, you should know the whole truth."

She ran her finger around the rim of the wineglass. "So if I'm to believe this, Rafferty is really some creature under the skin and that's why he's harassing me."

"Basically."

"I'm sorry if it seems like I'm being snotty, but this is a little hard to swallow."

"I realize that. There is another person that knows about them too. I'm supposed to have dinner with him. I'd like you to come."

She frowned for a moment, thinking it over. "Okay."

"You're in danger. Anyone who's not one of them who lives here is in danger."

"So these things murdered your family?"

"Yes."

"Would you like to tell me about it?"

Man, this was going a lot faster than he wanted. "I've never told anyone."

"You can tell me. I'm a good listener."

"I thought you didn't believe in these things."

"I never said that. I'm skeptical, but I don't totally disbelieve."

"Okay."

He took another sip of wine.

Harry Pierce crunched a Cheez-Doodle, spilling crumbs onto his ample belly. He brushed them off, drawing a frown from Liza.

"We've been married thirty years and you still sweep the crumbs on the floor."

Harry grinned sheepishly.

They sat in recliners, an end table between them, facing the television, where Ralph Kramden was threatening Alice with a free trip to the moon. Harry had on a tank top and striped boxer shorts. It was too damn hot for anything else, pants included. He picked up his beer off the end table, took a swig and set it back down.

"Coaster, Harry."

"Yes, my love." He put it on the coaster. Man, that woman didn't miss a trick after all these years. Even with her nose buried in a copy of *Gun Digest*, she still noticed if he didn't put the beer can on the coaster or got crumbs on the rug.

But he loved that about her, the sassiness, the fire. The two of them had some incredible arguments over the years, Liza once going so far as to throw his clothes out the upstairs bedroom window and telling him never to return. He came back, they apologized and made love on the kitchen floor.

The passion had never died and even though lovemaking sessions were far and few between these days, he loved her more than ever.

He had been dancing around the idea of bringing up his meeting with Matt Crowe. Now he finally got up the nerve to mention it. "I found someone else who knows about Them."

"You told someone?" She set the magazine on her lap. "Harry, are you nuts?"

"I thought he might be one of them, so I checked him out. He came into the store and I wound up grabbing him and checking him out. He was clean. And he already knew."

Harry grabbed a handful of Cheez-Doodles and popped them in his mouth. And then he sprang the rest of the story on his dear wife. "I invited him for dinner."

"And I suppose you're cooking?"

"You know me, Liz. I could burn cornflakes."

She slid up on the edge of the recliner. "Do you trust this man? What if he's working for Rafferty?"

"I've got a good feeling about him."

"I hope you're right. Just in case, I might be packing under my apron," Liz warned.

"I love it when you talk tough," said Harry.

"I'm not kidding. Lord only knows who this man is. I wish you hadn't said anything about the beasties."

Liza always called them beasties.

"He used to live here, Liz. And besides, I sold him some weapons. I think he's planning on defending himself."

"I'm still packing. Maybe the .357."

"That's my Liza. They're planning to Harvest," he said abruptly.

She slapped her magazine down on the table and stood up.

"Are you sure, Harry? I know you suspected, but can you be sure?"

Harry set the bowl of Cheez-Doodles on the table and put his footrest down, drawing a groan from the old chair. He went to the kitchen, where his pants hung on the back of a chair.

After returning from the kitchen, he handed Liza the hot pink flyer, scratched his belly and flopped back into his recliner. "I found that on a pole outside the shop."

Liza scanned the flyer. "Their meeting's in October," she said, her brow furrowing.

"That's when it'll go down," he said.

"My God."

"I drove around after I left the shop. Those things are posted all over town, and they all say 'members only' on them. If only the nonmembers knew what the members really are."

"We have to do something, get out while we can. There's going to be damn near an army of them."

Harry shook his head. "We're not going anywhere yet. Not until I talk with Matt."

"Harold, you barely know him." Liza shook her head in exasperation.

"Just let me talk to him, okay?"

"Always playing the cowboy, aren't you?"

"You're the one talking about packing a cannon under your apron when he comes for dinner," Harry said.

Liza sat back in the recliner. "You're an old fool, Harry. But you're my old fool and I love you." She picked up the magazine. "If you want to play hero and get yourself killed, do it without me." She gave the magazine a flap and resumed reading.

The ice queen had spoken. The conversation was over, and Liza simmered in the chair. She would get over it. Liza always did.

CHAPTER 9

As daylight began to fade, coppery sunlight filled Jill Adams' living room; it wouldn't be long before the shadows started creeping in. She wouldn't admit it to anyone, but having Matt here made her feel better. With a rogue cop who had more than a passing interest in her roaming the streets, and Matt telling stories of creatures of the night, she was a little uneasy.

She chided herself for being afraid, but she couldn't help it. "Go ahead, Matt, tell me what happened." She reached over and patted his hand as if to give him reassurance that she wouldn't mock him or laugh at him, although she was still skeptical, as anyone with a full deck of cards would be.

Matt sat upright in the recliner, his drink resting on his lap, hands clasped around the glass so tight that the knuckles were white. He stared straight ahead, the sweat beading on his forehead and dribbling down into his eyes. He wiped the sweat from his brow with the back of his hand, exhaled and began the story.

* * *

That Memorial Day had begun with great expectations, with the start of summer just around the corner. Matt's mother and father planned a picnic at Emerling Park, and it was close to eighty, unusually warm for that time of year in Lincoln.

His mother made fried chicken and pasta salad, packed a bag of fresh apples and had made Matt's father go to Tops Market that morning for a loaf of crusty Italian bread. Six-packs of Pepsi and pudding cups rounded out the meal.

John and Maggie Crowe, Matt and his younger brother, Mike, had headed out in the family Bronco for Emerling Park, which was situated on the edge of a ravine ten miles out of town and was a popular spot for campers, hikers and picnickers. At the bottom of the ravine was Lincoln Creek, rippling over jagged rocks and surrounded by dense firs.

They had arrived around eleven, his mother and father unloading the Bronco and setting up on a picnic table under one of the shelters.

Mikey had tugged on Matt's arm the moment they got out of the truck, pestering him to play catch, practically putting Matt's baseball glove on his hand for him. The little turd had gotten a new mitt for his birthday in February and had been itching for the snow to melt so he could try it out. Matt gave in, and the two of them jogged over to a spot not too far from the shelter to begin their game of catch.

After about twenty minutes, Maggie Crowe announced that lunch was served, and they all dug in. Even though Matt normally loved his mother's cooking—her fried chicken especially—he told Jill the food tasted bland, like wads of wallpaper paste in his mouth. It got to the point where he actually became nauseous and couldn't finish his lunch.

He remembered it as one of the worst meals he had

ever eaten, and reflected that maybe it was a premonition that something was about to go horribly wrong.

Jill broke in, "That can't be true, Matt. I have days where nothing tastes good either."

"Everything I ate that morning tasted fine. And when my mother was cooking that chicken, it was all I could do to keep my mouth from watering over it. But once I got to the park and started eating, it tasted like crap over easy," Matt said.

After lunch, Mikey asked his dad to hit some fly balls to him with the aluminum bat he had brought, and the two of them went to the Bronco and got it out. Matt had helped his mother clear the picnic table and throw out the trash. He remembered his mother asking him if he was all right, and he responded that he would be okay, blaming it on indigestion.

The aluminum bat pinged as John Crowe began hitting pop flies to his youngest son, who was doing a better than average job of catching them. It was then that his father announced that he had a surprise; after the park they were all going to Darien Lake. Now, Matt wasn't much for amusement park rides, but his brother and father were ride maniacs. Matt planned on heading to the waterslides to scope out the girls in their bathing suits.

John Crowe got a little too enthusiastic and popped one over Mikey's head. Mikey backpedaled toward the woods, but couldn't shag the fly before it hit the ground and caromed into the woods. So Mikey and their dad went into the trees, beating the brush with sticks, but still could not find the baseball. Matt remembered that they had been in the woods for nearly ten minutes when he heard his father urging Mikey to run.

"The two of them sprinted out of the woods, Mikey first, Dad pushing him along as fast as he could. My father yelled for me and my mother to get to the truck."

"Obviously he saw something in the woods," Jill said.

"Yeah. At first my mother and me just stood there, not knowing what the hell he was talking about. My father was a sane, logical man who didn't panic easily. There wasn't much he was afraid of. But he came out of those woods yelling like a maniac and waving his arms like he was on fire."

"What was it?" Jill asked.

Matt swigged the last of his wine and asked Jill if he could have a refill. She said sure, and he got up to go to the kitchen and get it, but his legs turned to noodles and he found that he was shaking when he stood up. He collapsed back into the chair, the room spinning. The wine and telling the story had taken its toll on him physically.

"I think thats enough wine for you," Jill said. "This must be awfully hard. You don't have to continue if you don't want."

"No, I want to."

The summer night had set in outside the windows, the sunlight replaced by purple-black shadows broken by the yellow glow from the streetlights.

"You were telling me what came out of the woods."

"At first I thought it was a bear, or maybe a mountain lion. But they aren't common in this area. It took me a minute to realize that it wasn't any animal I had ever seen before."

The thing that exploded out of the woods was tall and lithe, its back hunched, with a row of spikes down the length of its spine. Its skin color was somewhere between black and green, and it had mottled yellow spots on its arms and legs. A few tufts of quill-like fur grew out of its back, along with pebble-size growths. They looked like mutant warts.

The thing was over six feet tall, Matt guessed, and it moved quickly, bounding out of the woods and pinning his father to the ground. Mikey had stopped to look back when he heard his father fall. He screamed as the thing worked on him with its claws. Matt ran to get his little brother, but Mikey took off, past the truck and toward the ravine, screaming like a fire whistle.

Over at the picnic shelter, Matt noticed that his mother was frantically trying to pack up the picnic goods and put them in the cooler. She was shaking her head and repeating, "No, no, no," unable to comprehend what had just happened.

Matt yelled at her to drop the damn food and get to the truck.

While the creature was finishing off John Crowe, two more of its kind charged out of the woods with frightening speed, one knocking his mother to the ground and scattering garbage on the concrete slab under the shelter.

Somehow Matt hit the ground in time to avoid the second creature's leap at him. It rolled in the dust and get back up for another try.

Over at the picnic shelter, a creature had Maggie Crowe pinned to the table. It slashed her across the chest, leaving the table painted with her blood. Then the thing looked up at Matt and grinned through a mouth full of razor-blade teeth, as if to mock him.

He started for the shelter, having no idea how he would stop it, since he was unarmed, his only thought to save his mom. But the other creature pounced on him, pinning him in the dirt facedown. He managed to wriggle around onto his back, only to be face-to-face with a nightmare. Saliva dripped from its jaw onto Matt's chin, a sticky fluid that smelled like rotten eggs. He gagged, his lunch churning in his stomach.

Behind him, he could hear his mother's cries for help and the beast grunting as it tore her to shreds. The beast that had him pinned raised an arm and Matt closed his eyes, hoping that one slash would result in a quick death. But he wasn't killed, and he opened his eyes and saw that the creature had cocked its head, listening.

It had heard Mikey, still running toward the ravine.

The thing leapt off of him, panther-quick, and chased after his brother.

He chased the thing, but he would have had better luck trying to stop a runaway train screeching off its tracks. Up ahead, he could see Mikey nearing the edge of the ravine, screaming, "Mom! Mommy!"

His little brother's hat had fallen off, and Matt found it and picked it up off the ground. Stuffing the hat in his pocket, he watched as his little brother ran over the side of the sixty-foot ravine, the little voice rising to a shriek, then suddenly cutting off. Matt tried to tell himself that he didn't really hear the sound of his brother hitting the rocks, a sound like a watermelon being smashed with a hammer. The creature followed.

Upon reaching the edge, Matt peered over and saw the monster shimmying down the cliff face, lowering itself with its lanky arms.

Once at the bottom, it picked up Mikey's body as easily as a construction worker might pick up his lunch box and scampered across the ravine, disappearing into the murk of the forest on the other side.

There was no saving his little brother, so he sprinted back toward the truck, his lungs burning. He glanced at the picnic area. Their bodies were gone. He reached the truck. Wasting no time and fearing they may return, he climbed into the Bronco, started it up and spun out of the clearing.

Matt cleared his throat and took a final swallow of his drink.

Jill's heart went out to him: he sat in the chair, still

staring straight ahead, but with tears streaming down his cheeks. There were puffy bags under his eyes, and he looked like he had aged ten years just by telling the story. It was an incredible tale, and Jill was convinced that his family had died in a catastrophic manner, but she wondered if maybe some part of Matt's mind had invented the creatures to cope with his loss.

After all, monsters from a B-horror flick coming out of the woods was a lot to swallow, even for someone with an open mind and a good imagination. Nevertheless, she set her drink on the coffee table, got up and went over to him.

She leaned over, put her arms around him and whispered into his ear, "It's all right."

The Barbieri basement stank of blood.

The refrigerator had a splash of blood across it, as if an artist had thrown crimson paint across a canvas.

Perpendicular to the fridge was a workbench stocked with shiny new tools. To Rafferty, they looked like they were used once, maybe twice, and pictured the owner as some prissy rich guy who bought them for show.

He found the rest of the basement unremarkable. A furnace stood on the opposite side near a storage room. It was relatively damp in the basement and the walls gave off a stale, moldy odor.

If he caught the one who did this, they would be wearing their own guts for a scarf. He didn't need this kind of attention drawn to Lincoln.

The amount of blood on the walls amazed him. It splashed in gory streaks on the block walls, the windows and the workbench. He guessed the victim struggled, maybe even got away briefly, before it finished her off.

They had received a call at the station house about ten o'clock, one of the neighborhood locals telling Clarence

that he heard some glass breaking and a woman screaming. The caller told Clarence he figured it was a domes-
tic dispute. Rafferty had had a sinking feeling in his gut
when Clarence told him the nature of the call because
the house was on Dorchester Street.

The houses in that area were all big Victorians. Hum-
mers and Volvos were in the driveways, and landscapers
did all the mowing and planting. The chances of do-
mestic dispute in Dorchester were small. That led Rafferty immediately to believe something worse had
happened.

Clarence tramped down the basement stairs. "Holy
shit, what a mess!"

Rafferty looked over at Clarence. "What'd you find
upstairs?"

"Not much. Some clothes thrown in a ball on the
bedroom floor and a can of Diet Coke on the kitchen
table. Found her driver's license in her purse. Name's
Rhonda Barbieri."

"No sign of entry up there? How about footprints,
markings on the rugs?"

"Nothing, Ed."

That confirmed what Rafferty already knew from the
broken window. The perpetrator had smashed out the
basement window, climbed in and waited for Rhonda
Barbieri to come home. When she came down into the
basement, it had attacked.

Clarence descended the stairs and entered the basement. He looked around, eyes wide. "God, this was a
bad one." He stopped at a moist pile that looked like
fleshy coiled rope. It was the woman's intestines, lying
in front of the furnace. "Tore her guts right out. That's
vicious, Chief. Even for one of us."

Rafferty secretly admired the savagery of the killing,
even though it broke the rules of the Harvest. Whoever
did this went about it the right way, caused maximum

suffering. "Page Bolster and I'll meet you in the back-yard."

"Right."

Bolster and three other officers were in charge of cleaning up messes like this one. Rafferty didn't want the county medical examiner, outside paramedics, the county sheriff or any other Outsiders messing in his business. Killings such as these had to be kept quiet. Which created a problem because the victim's relatives always came around asking questions. He'd go through the motions, assure them the Lincoln Police were on the case. Hopefully he could hold any nosy family members off until Harvest. Then it wouldn't matter.

Crossing the basement to the stairs, Rafferty slipped on the woman's blood. He threw his arms out to gain balance and silently cursed the one who killed Rhonda Barbieri.

"I feel like a goddamned idiot," Matt said, leaning forward in the chair, resting his elbows on his knees.

"There's no need. I know what it's like to lose a parent. That was hard enough, but you lost your whole family."

She kneeled on the floor, her hand resting on his leg. She could feel the warmth of his skin through the jeans. He smelled of Polo cologne and soap. She wanted to kiss him on the forehead, hug him close, tell him things would be okay. But platitudes and shallow comforts wouldn't bring his family back, would they? "What did you do when you left the park?"

"Went right to the police station. Actually, when I got to the police station, there weren't any cops there. The secretary told me they were out on a call, so I waited. About an hour later Chief Rafferty and one of his officers came waltzing in."

Jill took his hand. "Did you tell them what happened?"

Still holding her hand, he leaned back in the chair. "When I said I never told anyone this story, I really meant it. When Rafferty walked in, I was in the front reception area of the station. He asked me what he could help me with, and I knew right then that he was the murderer."

"How could you know that?"

"The smell of him. It was the same smell as the thing in the park. I've never smelled anything like that anywhere else. I wanted to turn around and run from there as fast as I could, but Rafferty took me by the arm and told his secretary to refer all his calls to Clarence, the other officer with him."

Matt knew Rafferty had recognized him from the incident at the park an hour earlier. Fear clenched his gut in an icy fist and he expected Rafferty to kill him, as well. The Chief escorted him through the office, out a back door and down three steps to the holding cell area.

They went down the hallway outside the cells to a small room. Rafferty clicked on the bulb overhead and told him to sit down in a chair.

"What's your name, son?"

"Why should I tell you?"

"I'll ask one more time. What's your name?"

"Matt Crowe."

"Well, Matt, I imagine you've seen some strange things today."

"Well, Chief, I imagine you've done some strange things today. Especially for a cop."

"Look, smart-ass. One more remark and you'll wind up like your fucking family, got it?"

Matt shifted in his chair, wanting to burst into tears, trying not to break down in front of Rafferty.

"Now just shut up and listen to me. You didn't see anything today, no bogeymen, no fairy-tale monsters, nothing. You went for a walk down one of the hiking trails, and when you came back, your family was gone, got it? Maybe they were shot, maybe aliens abducted them, but you never saw what you did."

"I'll go to the state police. You won't get away with this."

Rafferty puffed out his chest. "Oh, I think I will get away with it. Because I run this town and there's hundreds here just like me. Me and my boys will do a little investigation, but the case will remain unsolved. Or maybe I'll find someone I don't like and pin the whole thing on the poor schmuck."

"You can't control everyone." Matt hoped his voice didn't crack too badly when he said that. He was scared shitless, but he didn't want Rafferty to know that.

"No, I can't. You're right. But I can control you. I find out that you told anyone what happened at Emerling Park, I'll come after you. Put money on it. And when I do, I'll make sure you suffer. Maybe I'll tie you up and slit you open, tear your guts out while you scream. How's that sound?"

Matt didn't answer.

"Do you understand me?"

Again, Matt didn't respond and Rafferty threw the table out of the way, causing it to squeal on the floor and tip over with a thud. Rafferty grabbed a clump of Matt's hair and pulled hard. Matt's eyes watered.

"Understand now? Not a goddamn word to anyone."

In a choked voice Matt said, "Yes."

"Good." Rafferty let go and shoved Matt's head for good measure.

"Now get the hell out of here. Go out and wait for me near the front door."

Jill said softly, "That son of a bitch."

She believed that part of the story without hesitation; because of her run-in with Chief Rafferty she didn't doubt his capacity for cruelty. Anybody would have trouble believing that monsters had come out of the woods and slaughtered a family on a picnic, and so did Jill at first. But Matt had told the story with a faraway look in his eyes, and she had seen how it affected him physically. His skin had gone pale.

She remembered her great-uncle Henry, who had been in a Japanese POW camp, telling her father the story of how the Japanese soldiers had killed a man by filling his stomach full of water and kicking him until it burst. Uncle Henry had that same stare in his eyes, haunted by a horror show that played in his mind again and again. Matt was either a hell of an actor or he was certifiably insane.

"Matt, look at me."

When he did, she saw the pain in his eyes. He looked a little shell-shocked, blank and uncertain.

"I believe your story."

"Maybe you're the crazy one."

"Let me finish, smart guy. I don't think anyone could fake what you just told me, the reaction you had was too real. I believe your family was killed. One question, though. Why did you come back?"

"Revenge," he said. "I came back for revenge."

"That won't erase what happened."

"I don't care. Rafferty has to pay for what he did. And his accomplices too. I don't want what happened to my family to happen to anyone else."

"So you're planning something then?"

"You could say that."

"Killing them?"

"You'll find out at our dinner. If you still want to go with me." He removed his hand from hers and stood up. He set the wineglass on the coffee table. "Maybe you shouldn't. If things go according to plan, I'm going to have to make a quick getaway. And I don't want to hurt you. Or see you get hurt."

"I like you, Matt. But I don't like this plan of yours. You know that these things exist, and you're starting to convince me, but to everyone else it will look like you murdered cops. If that is what you're planning," Jill said.

"I'll just have to live with it."

What was it with men? She had never meet one who didn't possess a few genes that made them to do a poor imitation of every Clint Eastwood character that ever graced the silver screen. He had just opened up to her, poured his guts out, and now he was trying to act tough. "Don't go getting all stoic on me. I'd still like to go with you to that dinner. But can we talk some more about your plan?"

"How about we go out tomorrow? Is Morotto's still around? You'd like some more Italian?" Matt said.

"Maybe I can talk some sense into you."

"You can try. But I'm pretty set on this." He had a determined look on his face, like a mountain climber eyeballing Mount Everest, prepared to conquer it regardless of the cost.

"We'll see," Jill said. "I can be pretty persuasive."

"This has been eating at me for years. I think about it every day. I have nightmares about it. And I can't rest knowing that Rafferty is still alive after what he did. You say I've convinced you that these things exist, but I don't know if you're a hundred percent sure yet. You haven't really seen one. Maybe if you did, you'd know why I want him dead."

"I told you I believed you."

Matt stood up and took his glass into the kitchen, Jill following him, watching as he rinsed it out.

"Good manners. I like that," she said, kiddingly, but glad that he had put the glass in the sink. Jerry had been a number-one slob.

"Looking forward to tomorrow night," he said.

"Me too."

She wanted to stand on her tiptoes and give him a quick kiss on the lips, but she held back. Instead, she hugged him. He held on tight, then let go.

She followed him downstairs and locked the door behind him, thinking that it would be nice when that kiss became a reality.

CHAPTER 10

Donna Ricci dreaded her meeting with Chief Ed Rafferty.

Not that she was afraid of him, or anyone else for that matter, but she had heard stories about disappearances in Lincoln and investigations being covered up. She didn't think that Rafferty would attempt to harm her, but she wasn't taking any chances. She kept a Beretta Tomcat in a shoulder holster.

She pulled her Ford F150 into the parking lot at Lincoln's Police Station and parked it next to a squad car. She stepped from the car and slipped a white cotton blazer over her sleeveless blouse.

Donna was the police chief in Marshall, a town that still had a general store and boasted the State of New York's smallest post office. She had become a cop after trying a stint in the engineering program at the University of Buffalo and dropping out her sophomore year.

A friend of her dad's who had been on the Buffalo force for twenty-six years had told Donna that a police exam was coming up. "You'd be a great cop, Donna—you're whip smart and you don't take any crap from anyone. Take the exam and see how you do," he had told her.

So after talking it over with her parents, she studied for the exam and scored a ninety-eight. After passing the agility test with flying colors, she had gone on to the academy and become a Buffalo cop.

After ten years on the force, being shot once and decorated for bravery twice, she had reached the rank of sergeant. And had been passed up for lieutenant three times; each time a man got the promotion, a man who had been on the force less time than her and did not have her stellar record. So she left the big city and joined the Marshall police when she heard they needed an officer.

Within two years, she had been promoted to Deputy Chief, then appointed Chief when Hank Peterman retired. Small-town life was quiet and content. About the worst thing that ever happened was a kid busting a mailbox or breaking a window. But she liked it, because she was running the show and wouldn't be shoved aside like she was in Buffalo.

Things had been uneventful until her brother Bob had called her after returning home from a business trip and discovering yellow police tape across his door. Bob said the cops weren't telling him much, and when he tried to press them for information, the officer on the phone got nasty.

Although she suspected her brother was cheating on Rhonda (who'd kept her maiden name), Donna agreed to look into things because she had always liked Rhonda. Rhonda was a tough-minded, driven woman and, outside the courtroom, one of the nicest people you'd ever want to meet.

So she'd taken time off, the Lieutenant now acting as Chief, while she tended to Rhonda's death.

Strolling across the parking lot, she reached the front

of the station. There was a garden filled with yellow, crimson and orange blooms. A fat bumblebee buzzed from flower to flower. The flag on the metal pole in front of the station hung limp, as if it didn't have the energy to stand at attention.

She walked down a small hallway lined with chairs to a desk where an elderly woman in a dark blue police shirt sat typing.

The woman turned her head. "May I help you?"

"I have an appointment with Chief Rafferty. Donna Ricci."

"Have a seat, Ms. Ricci, and he'll be right with you. Would you like a cup of coffee?"

She said no thank you and sat down, crossing her legs. About five minutes later, a bearish man stepped around the corner and introduced himself.

"Officer Ricci? Ed Rafferty."

He offered his hand and she shook it, not liking the sweaty feel of his palm.

"Let's have a seat at my desk," Rafferty said.

Donna sat down, leaned back and stretched her legs out in front of her. She wanted to appear calm and relaxed in front of Rafferty, not giving him the intimidation edge. She had heard from some guys at the state police that he was a ballbuster, and if you were a woman he really showed no mercy.

Rafferty eased himself into his chair, leaned back and clasped his hands behind his head, elbows out. There were dark sweat stains under his arms. "So you're here about the Barbieri woman."

"Rhonda. That's right."

"What can I help you with?"

"Any suspects so far?"

"Nope. Not a one."

"Evidence?"

"Not much." Rafferty unclasped his hands and put

them on the desk. He swiveled back and forth in the chair, as if bored by the conversation.

"You have no evidence at all. That's what you're telling me?"

"None. No prints, no motive, no weapon. Nothing."

"I find that hard to believe." She leaned forward, rested her arms on the desk and looked him in the eye. Now that she was closer to him, she noticed he stank.

"Well, you can believe it. It was a messy murder, but other than a lot of the victim's blood and some entrails, we found nothing. Not even footprints."

"Look, Chief. I don't know what's going on here, but I suggest you let me in on whatever secret it is you have. I don't suppose there's a report I could read."

He picked up a pencil, twirled it around with his fingers. "It's gotta be typed up. You'd never be able to read my officer's writing. Of course, once it's typed, I could fax you a copy."

"I'll expect a copy." She pulled out a business card and handed it to him. "Will you tell me anything right now?"

"The woman is dead. That's about all I can tell you."

Rafferty set the pencil on the desk, leaned back, took a toothpick from his desk drawer and placed it between his lips. Donna liked this man less and less by the minute.

"I don't suppose you give a shit, but I know quite a few state troopers. I'm sure they'd like to hear about this case. Or maybe the county sheriff."

"You just bring in anyone you want, Donna. Anyone at all."

Arrogant bastard.

"You know, Ed. You're a piss-poor excuse for a cop. I'll find out who killed my sister-in-law," she said. "Bet on it."

He worked the toothpick from side to side, poking it around with his tongue. "Is there anything else I can help you with?"

"I'll be going."

She stood up from the chair and shoved it so it banged off the desk. Turning on one heel, she stalked out of the office, telling the receptionist on the way out that she might be better off working somewhere else.

Out by her truck, she stripped off her blazer and put it on the passenger seat. She ran her hand through her short hair and exhaled in frustration.

Rafferty was being difficult, and she didn't anticipate him cooperating any more than he had today. She doubted if he would fax her the police report (if there was one) or share any other evidence with her regarding the case. The weasel didn't even flinch when she mentioned the state police, which was a threat she could carry out. Her father had poker buddies who were state cops and she could put some heat on Rafferty if she wanted. But that wasn't her style. Hit it head-on, even if it left you bruised and bloody.

For now, she would take matters into her own hands. It was the way she always handled things.

She started the truck up and pulled out of the parking lot.

The Ford's gas gauge hovered just above "E" so she decided to pull into a service station, get gas and ask directions. After driving six blocks down Elmwood, she spotted a gas station with a sign in blue script that read JIMBO'S.

There were two gas pumps that could have been pre–Korean War, with no canopy overhead like the modern gas stations. White paint flaked off the pumps, and the paint still on the pumps was dotted with rusty blisters. The station had two overhead doors, one with the glass smashed out of six of the panels. She was beginning to think she made a poor choice in gas stations.

After parking the truck next to the pumps, she went inside to the office area, which wasn't much better than the exterior of the station. It smelled sweaty and oily, and the desk had a layer of dust on it an eighth of an inch thick. It was silent except for the ticking of a clock on the counter. She had never been in a garage where impact wrenches didn't whiz and zoom constantly.

"Hello!" she called.

There was no response for a moment and then a grizzled old man in coveralls slipped through the door from the garage. His name patch read *JIMBO* in cursive letters.

"Help you?" He said in a tobacco-frayed voice.

"Fifty dollars of regular."

"You gotta pump it yourself, you know. This ain't no full serve."

"That's fine."

"Fifty it is."

She dug in her purse and pulled out a rumpled fifty. She held it out and he snatched it from her. His eyes never left her purse.

"You're a cop, huh?"

"That's right."

He sniffled and ran his sleeve under his nose. "Saw the badge on your belt. You know Chief Rafferty?"

"I'm acquainted with him."

"What?"

"I know him a little bit."

"He don't take too kindly to strangers. That's why I asked."

"Can you tell me where the library is?"

"Across from the middle school."

Apparently Jimbo wasn't in the habit of being helpful. "Where would that be?"

"You didn't ask me how to get there."

He sniffed again, drew snot back into his throat and spat on the floor.

"They make tissues, you know."

"You want directions or you want to stand there and be a smart-ass?"

"I'll take the directions."

He told her how to get to the library, went over to the cash register and rang in her fifty dollars. The register drawer chimed open and he put the money in the till. After switching on the gas pump, he disappeared into the garage again, slamming the door behind him.

As Donna pumped gas, she thought that if the rest of the people in Lincoln were as friendly as the Chief and the gas station attendant, this would be one hell of a visit.

Telling Jill his story did nothing to alleviate the nightmares. Matt sat up, chest pumping up and down. His skin was slicked with sweat, and he stifled the scream that was building in his throat. He looked around the room. *I'm not in the park, I'm in Aunt Bernie's loft,* he thought. The clock read two fifty A.M.

He threw off the covers and swung his legs around the side of the bed.

In the dream, the creature had him pinned to the ground, all of its weight on his chest, squeezing the air out of his lungs. His limbs felt heavy, like they were made of steel, and he could not move an inch. The creature lowered its head until they were nose to nose and exhaled, forcing Matt to breathe in the foul breath. It raised its arm to swipe at him, and just as the claws reached his face, he awoke.

No, the talk with Jill had not ended the dreams. In fact, this one seemed more intense than the others. The feeling of paralysis and not being able to breathe under the thing's weight stuck with him. He slept very little the rest of the night.

At five o'clock he rose, exercising, showering and having French toast with his Aunt Bernie all before eight. She had been animated, asking him how his date went, but he had been only half listening. His mind kept drifting to Jill Adams, the way she had held his hand. It felt good, right, somehow, like it belonged there, her hand in his.

He helped his aunt clear the table and the two of them took his rental car back to Avis, Aunt Bernie following him in the truck and bringing him back to the house.

As they walked up the steps into the kitchen, Matt saw Uncle Rex sitting at the table in a flannel bathrobe and blue slippers. His hair jutted in several directions and gray stubble covered his cheeks. Matt hoped for a quick getaway before his uncle had a chance to shoot off his mouth.

"What'd you have for breakfast, Bernadette?" Rex spoke low and slow, not yet fully awake.

"French toast."

"You make him some but not your husband, is that right?"

"Rex, I'll make you breakfast. You're never up this early, though."

"Well, I am today, and I want French toast."

Matt tried to break the tension. "How have you been?"

"Just dandy now that you're here."

"How's things at the plant?" Matt said.

"Too many niggers working there."

His uncle's ignorance never failed to amaze Matt.

"You gonna make my fucking toast or not?"

"Yes, Rex."

Aunt Bernie scurried to the counter like a dog who feared abuse from a cruel master. Matt wished his aunt had the nerve to tell Rex where to put his French toast and then walk out on him, but he knew that would never happen. The bastard had intimidated her to the point where all he had to do was raise his voice and she jumped.

"Will you be okay, Aunt Bernie?"

"I'll be fine," she assured him.

"Why wouldn't she be fine, huh? You think we need you to check on us?"

"I think you need someone to teach you how to treat your wife."

Uncle Rex took a swig of coffee. A thin line of it dribbled down his chin. He wiped it with the sleeve of his robe. "Don't you mouth off to me. I'm still able to kick your skinny ass if I want."

Fat chance of that happening, Matt thought. He had knocked down his Ranger buddies in hand-to-hand training, some of them over two hundred pounds of solid muscle. Dropping a slow, middle-aged drunk with a well-placed kick would be no problem. "I've got errands to run."

He kissed Aunt Bernie on the cheek and whispered in her ear, "I'm right out back if you need me. Remember that."

She gave him a look that was equal parts gratitude and fear.

The Lincoln Mercy emergency room had exploded with activity.

There was a three-car crash on Elmwood Avenue, with two passengers dead and the remaining three brought in to the ER. One had brains leaking out of a gaping wound in his skull, and that was among the most awful things Jill had ever seen. That man had died ten minutes after being brought to the ER.

The other two victims, one a middle-aged woman and the other a teenage boy, had not fared much better. The woman had a broken neck and Jill had assisted Dr. Kessler in inserting a tracheotomy tube when her lungs began to fail. She overheard Kessler telling one of the residents that she would most likely be a quadriplegic for life. The boy's mangled left leg would need to be amputated.

What a day it had been, indeed.

Now Jill sipped her iced tea, relishing a break from her armageddon of a day. The cafeteria was silent save for the hissing of grease as the cook lowered a basket of fries into the fryer.

"Nurse Adams, how long have you been on break?"

It was supervisor Gaines; not what she needed right at the moment. Jill hadn't even noticed her approach the table.

"Ten minutes, I'm just finishing up."

"With the ER as busy as it is, we can't afford to have people taking extended breaks." Dorothy pushed her glasses onto her nose with her index finger. "Are you finished with that tea yet?"

"I am now."

Jill chugged the last of her iced tea, stood up and threw the Styrofoam cup into a trash can.

"None of the other nurses are taking breaks."

"Cora told me to come down here and take fifteen. Everything's quieted down since that car wreck came in," Jill explained.

"I could write you up if I wanted to. Unauthorized break, and maybe insubordination."

"Insubordination?" Jill couldn't believe her ears.

"That's right."

"If you're really going to write me up, then I'd say you've got nothing better to do with your time. Excuse me, I have to get back to work."

Jill brushed past her and noticed it immediately— the rank, pungent smell, the same one that she noticed on the attacker in the warehouse. The hair on her arms rose in little prickles as the odor brought back the memories of that night, stirring her adrenaline.

"You can count on that, Nurse Adams."

"Do what you have to do."

Jill hurried from the cafeteria, thinking that a smell like that on two people was more than coincidence.

Jill walked down the main hallway in the ER, past a row of gurneys and a cart filled with sheets and towels. Cora stepped from one of the exam rooms, a manila folder in her hand. She reached out and gripped Jill's arm.

"You look like you've seen a ghost. What's wrong?"

"Nothing, Cora. Just ate something that didn't agree with me."

"You putting me on?"

"Honest. I just came from the ladies' room, if you know what I mean." Jill put her hand palm down over her stomach, indicating the universal sign for intestinal distress.

"I still don't think that's it. But whatever it is, I hope you feel better."

Jill thanked her and continued down the hallway toward the nursing station. She sat down in one of the office chairs, closed her eyes, and massaged her temples.

Get through the day, she told herself. Looking at the clock on the wall, she saw there were two more hours to go on her shift. Avoiding her supervisor for that long was possible.

"Jill, possible arm fracture in one. Get his vitals, okay?" It was Cora, leaning on the counter of the nurses' station, the rubbery flesh on her arms spilling on the desktop.

Jill looked at the clock again before rising to check on the fracture.

After downing a Whopper and onion rings at the Lincoln Burger King, Donna Ricci pulled into Hill's Hardware. The building was brick, the front painted blue and the sides yellow. An assortment of lawn mowers were lined up on the sidewalk in front of the store. She walked around them, running her finger along the chrome handle of a Toro.

She opened the door and an electronic chime sounded.

An elderly man in an olive cardigan sat in a folding chair behind a counter. He leaned back in the chair, his fingers drumming on the counter to a big band tune coming from an unseen radio. He whistled tunelessly along with the music. It sounded like Benny Goodman.

Donna passed the counter and found the electrical section. She picked a sturdy-looking flashlight off the shelf and took it to the counter. She hadn't thought to bring her police flashlight with her.

"How are you tonight?" the clerk said. His green cardigan covered a madras shirt, and a pair of bifocals rested on the end of his nose. He took a tissue from the breast pocket of his sweater, wiped his nose and tucked the tissue away.

"Could be cooler out there."

He punched keys on the register and it beeped. "You don't look familiar. You live in town?"

"Why do you ask?"

"I've been running this store for thirty-eight years and I've seen just about everyone in town come in and out of here at one time or another. I know who's had kids, who's died, who's moved away. I know I've never seen you before."

"Well, you got that right. I'm from Marshall."

He took her money and counted back the change. Then he took out a brown paper bag from under the counter and slid the flashlight in.

"What brings you here, if you don't mind me asking."

Ordinarily, she did mind, and wanted to tell him to

mind his own business. But after the reception she got from Rafferty and the gas station attendant, it was nice to meet someone halfway friendly.

"Police business."

He handed her the bag with the flashlight in it. "I take it you're familiar with our esteemed chief of police."

"Unfortunately, yes."

He leaned forward over the counter toward her, so close that she could smell a mix of stale coffee and cigars on his warm breath. "Just between you and me, I personally think Ed Rafferty is a four-square revolving son of a bitch."

She liked the way this guy thought. "A twenty-four-seven son of a bitch from what I've heard."

"You have a nice stay in Lincoln—I'm sorry, I didn't catch your name."

"Donna."

"Okay then, Donna."

Tucking the bag under her arm, she headed for the door.

"And Donna. Please be careful out there. Lincoln's not too kind to strangers."

"Why did you say that?"

"Well, you didn't hear it from me, but people have a way of disappearing in this town." He took his glasses off and polished them on his sweater.

"I can handle myself."

"Don't stay any longer than you have to, Donna. Any longer than you have to, okay?"

She left the store without answering him, and the door slammed behind her. She wasn't one to scare easy or get the creeps, but she felt the hair on her arms stand at attention and a chill cascade over her body.

People have a way of disappearing in this town.

CHAPTER 11

Donna sat in the cab of her pickup. She had gone into the Lincoln Public Library, performed an Internet search and come up with one article from the *Daily Recorder* written in 1995.

Woman Visiting Neighboring Town Attacked by Animal

A Buffalo woman was attacked by a wild animal on Friday night while pumping gas at a Lincoln service station. Janice Perry, 34, stopped at Jimbo's Gas Station on Elmwood Avenue when she noticed she was low on gas. Apparently, after paying for the gas, Ms. Perry heard a strange noise from behind the station. "It was snowing hard, dark out and blowing pretty good. I heard a grunting sound from behind the station." Ms. Perry thought that it was the wind and continued pumping gas.

About five minutes later, she was attacked. "It came at me out of the snow. I could just see a shape. It walked on two legs and smelled horrible." The animal slashed Ms. Perry across the forehead, knocking her to the ground and requiring her to have twenty-two stitches.

The animal fled when another motorist pulled into the gas station. "That man who pulled into the station probably saved my life. That thing was big and mean and I think it would have killed me."

Lincoln Police reported finding no signs of an animal in the area, but have advised residents to exercise caution when traveling at night.

Donna set the printout on the passenger seat. In the library, she had done a Google search on Rhonda's name and come up with nothing. Likewise with Rafferty's. She had also picked up a late edition of the *Buffalo News* and found nothing on Lincoln or the murder. Something told her Ed Rafferty was very good at camouflage. Either that, or he repelled people so much they stayed away, reporters included.

The whole thing didn't wash. First Rafferty treated her like she had a contagious disease, and then nothing turned up in the paper.

Her cell phone rang. She picked up. It was Bob.

"Find anything out?" he asked.

"Rafferty's clamming up. I'm going over to the house, have a look."

Slurping on the other end and ice cubes clinking. "Can you do that, sis?"

"I'm sure the homeowner's association will give me a wonderful welcome."

"I mean is it legal?" Bob asked.

"You leave the fancy cop work to me," Donna said. "How you holding up?"

"You know."

"Made any arrangements yet?"

The ice chinked again. He was probably drinking J&B, she thought.

"We'll do it at Lowe's. They did a nice job with Mom's service. I guess, ah, shit."

He took the phone away from his mouth. She heard his muffled sobs.

"Sorry, sis. I was trying to say she wanted an open casket, but, uh, I guess that's not going to be possible."

Christ Jesus. He knew more than she did about Rhonda's death at this point. And she was a cop! "What'd they say?"

"Rollie Lowe told me she was in bad shape. That's all he would say." She heard his heavy breathing, and then he said, "I gotta go."

She wondered how bad it had to be in order for the casket to be closed. "I understand."

She was about to hang up when he said, "Hey, Don?"

"Yeah?"

"One other thing. Rollie told me that when they called to get the body, he had to go through the hospital and the county and they didn't have anything on Rhonda. So they dial the police station in Lincoln and they tell her their doc is examining her. That's when he found out how . . . bad she was. Is that weird?"

"Very frigging weird."

"I really got to go."

He killed the connection.

Why would the police say they were using their own doctor? The county medical examiner did the autopsies. What happened in Lincoln stayed there, was that it? At least that was the way Rafferty did it. She reached over and picked up the flashlight from the seat. After unscrewing the top, she popped in the batteries. She screwed the top back on.

Time for some digging, she thought.

He had enough roses to satisfy three dates.

Matt took a look at the heaping bouquet, the roses taking up half the bench seat in the pickup truck. He knew Jill was health conscious and chocolates wouldn't be the best idea for a fitness nut, so he opted for flowers.

A bumblebee buzzed in through the open passenger side window, humming and hovering over the flowers before landing on one. Matt shooed it with his hand and it dive-bombed him once, whizzing past his left ear before he finally backhanded it out the driver's side window.

His heart beat hard and his palms sweated like a teenager on prom night.

While stopped at the intersection four blocks from Jill's house, he did a quick check in the rearview mirror. Satisfied that his hair was in place and there was no food stuck in his teeth, he gave it the gas when the light turned green.

He revved it a little, getting the truck up to forty, knowing that most cops wouldn't stop you unless you were driving like Jeff Gordon. Anxious to get to Jill's house and liking the feel of the big V8 as it throbbed under the hood, he got it up to forty- five.

The police car's lights popped up in his rearview mirror.

"Son of a bitch," he said.

That's what I got for forgetting where I am: in Lincoln, home of the world's angriest police chief. Stupid, he thought.

Pulling the car over, he rested his arms on the steering wheel and waited. He watched in the side view as Ed

Rafferty strode toward the truck, a huge grin plastered on his face.

Rafferty popped his face into the window, his eyes obscured by the standard-issue cop sunglasses. "License, registration and proof of insurance."

Lifting his butt off the seat, Matt reached for his wallet, gave his license to Rafferty and then took the insurance card out of the glove box and did the same. He fumbled for a moment, looking for the registration and not finding it.

"Registration?" Rafferty repeated.

"It's my aunt's truck. I'm using it for the day," Matt replied.

"Your aunt's name?"

"Bernadette Lapchek."

Rafferty crossed his arms. "Never heard of her."

"She lives in town. I'm surprised you don't know the name. She's lived here as long as I can remember."

Rafferty, his head down, scanned Matt's license. "Okay. Get me the registration within twenty-four hours and we won't have a problem." Rafferty handed Matt's license and the insurance card back to him. Matt let a little sigh of relief escape. He hadn't hassled him over the missing registration, and for that Matt was grateful.

"Now, any idea how fast you were going?"

"About forty-five."

"Right," Rafferty said. "You think that's a smart idea?"

"Probably not."

Rafferty pushed his shades up with his index finger. "Well, I'm writing you a ticket."

Rafferty opened his book, took a Bic pen out of his breast pocket and began writing the ticket. After a moment, he tore it off and handed it to Matt. Matt looked over the ticket.

"So when's my court date?" Matt asked.

Rafferty started to speak and then paused. He

looked at Matt thoughtfully and those big yellow choppers appeared for a second in a grin. "You been drinking, Mr. Crowe?"

"No."

"Why don't you step out of the car?"

Matt's first instinct was to start the truck up and floor it, screeching away from the Chief. Instead he unfastened his seat belt and stepped out of the car.

Rafferty had pulled him over on Elmwood Avenue, one of the main drags in town. They were pulled over about a block from a Dairy Queen and cars passed them on a regular basis. Rafferty would not try anything out in the open with a crowd of spectators in the vicinity—or at least Matt wanted to believe that.

"Say your alphabet backward for me."

Matt did. He also walked a straight line at Rafferty's request, closed his eyes and touched his finger to his nose and touched the tip of each finger to his thumb. He expected a Breathalyzer to follow, but Rafferty didn't demand he take one.

"Well, I guess you aren't drunk, but I really don't like speeders in my town. Especially speeders that get mouthy with me. Where you from, anyway?"

He doesn't recognize or remember me, Matt realized. "The West Coast. San Francisco."

"Probably a little queerboy, aren't you?"

"No."

"They're all queer out there. I like them even less than I like speeders."

As Matt opened his mouth to say something, the butt of the nightstick stung him below the right eye. His head snapped back. He shook his head and took a few steps back. He wanted to charge Rafferty, knock him down and beat him, maybe gouge his eyes or kick him until his ribs shattered.

He touched the skin around his eye and felt the

warm, swollen flesh. He would have a shiner under that eye in the morning.

"You don't speed in this town again. Got that?"

Matt lowered his hand. He thought of the Beretta, how easy it would be right now to blow holes in Rafferty, right above the badge, spin him around with bullets.

"You got me?" Rafferty said, and lifted the nightstick as if to deliver another blow. Matt didn't flinch.

"I got you."

Matt glanced along Elmwood. A steady stream of cars whipped past. No one had stopped to gawk or offer assistance.

"Get out of here. And don't let me catch you again. Or you'll get it worse."

He turned and walked toward his patrol car, his stink enveloping him like a rotten cocoon.

It was time to shake Rafferty up a little. "Hey, Chief."

Rafferty stopped and turned around.

"This is the second time you've messed with me. There won't be a third."

A look of confusion crossed Rafferty's face, as if Matt had just spoken in Latin instead of English. "You threatening me?"

"No sir, I wouldn't threaten an officer of the law." Matt climbed in the truck and started the engine. He peeked in the rearview mirror. Rafferty leaned against the patrol car, the cop sunglasses glinting in the sun.

He half expected Rafferty to come back to the car and try and deliver another beating, but he opened the door and climbed in the police car.

As Matt pulled back on to Elmwood he said, "Think about that for a while, you son of a bitch."

Rafferty watched the punk pull away in his big Chevy.

Taking his glasses off, he rubbed the bridge of his nose with his thumb and index finger, thinking. He couldn't remember where he had seen Matthew Crowe before, but he knew it would come to him sooner or later. There had been so many Outsiders he had harassed over the years, so many times when he used a nightstick on one of them just for the fun of it. He couldn't possibly remember all of them.

He followed Matt Crowe down Elmwood and then down Wharton. He watched as the pickup pulled into Jill Adams' driveway.

Very interesting, he thought.

The cold little bitch has a boyfriend, and she was probably going to give it up for him real good. He was half tempted to follow them to wherever they were going, but he had a better idea; he would pay little Ms. Adams a visit on his own. Maybe teach her a few lessons about who her real man should be.

If Rafferty had been completely human, he would've recognized his thoughts as jealousy, but his kind only recognized hatred for others. It was raw and primitive, the emotion bubbling up inside him like rancid crude oil until it eventually hit the surface and exploded.

Pulling down the street, he decided to make another stop before heading back to the station house.

"God, Matt, he really nailed you one." Jill said, handing Matt ice cubes wrapped in a washcloth.

"Yeah, good old Chief Rafferty."

"Well, we can stay in tonight if you want," Jill said. "Maybe it's for the best, especially if Rafferty hasn't cooled down and is out patrolling. He could get you all over again. And you know how he feels about me."

"I'm not letting him ruin our date."

"What about your eye?"

"Maybe they'd give me a nice raw steak to put on it at Morotto's."

Jill laughed. "Well, as long as you're okay with this. Let me just use the bathroom and we'll go."

She went into the bathroom, peed and checked her makeup in the mirror. She only wore some pink lipstick and some eye shadow. Her mother always told her she didn't need much. *You're pretty enough, Jill, you don't need all that greasepaint on your kisser,* Mom would say.

Straightening the strap on her dress, she had to admit she *did* look pretty good. The sundress was flowered and hugged her hips, but not too tight. The hem stopped two inches above her knees, enough to show a little leg, but not enough to make her look cheap. She had caught Matt sneaking a few peeks at her tanned legs, but that was okay; she would have been disappointed if he hadn't looked.

When she came back into the living room, the ice pack was gone; Matt had set it in the sink. They went downstairs into the driveway and Matt sprang ahead of her.

"What're you doing?" she said.

"I forgot to bring these up. I was so mad when I got here, I forgot them."

He reached into the open window of the truck and wrestled out a dozen of the most gorgeous roses she had ever seen. They were wine red and she could smell them from five feet away.

He walked over to her, gave a little bow and handed her the flowers. "Flowers for the lady," he said, in a bad Cockney accent.

"Why, thank you, sir."

She kissed him on the cheek, careful not to bump the shiner that was rising below his eye.

"Your chariot, m'lady." He opened the passenger side door for her and she set the roses on the seat and climbed in.

He backed the truck up, looked both ways down the street, and pulled out.

CHAPTER 12

The sun set, streaking the sky with pinks and vermilions.

Donna Ricci knew it was time to get to her destination.

Her brother's address was 317 Dorchester. The houses were mostly big old Victorians, some with black shutters, some with pink trim, and a few with widow's walks at their peaks.

Most of the yards had towering maples that gave a ton of shade, and there was one big old oak tree that had a rope and tire tied to the branch. Maybe one of the fat cats who lived up here had it planted special.

Her brother had a room at the Radisson in downtown Buffalo so the house was still empty.

As she passed the house, she scanned the yard. The windows were dark, giving the house an odd, lonely look. It somehow reminded her of a dog waiting by the front door for a master that would never return.

She noticed an old man watering his lawn at the house next door. He was stoop-shouldered, scrawny and wore a yellowed tank top and plaid Bermuda shorts. His old-man breasts hung saggily, clinging to the fabric of his tank top. As she passed him, he followed her with his gaze, scowling and suspicious.

She didn't need the locals harassing her, or maybe getting on the phone and bringing Rafferty onto the scene. Originally, she had intended to pick the lock at the side door and slip into the house. If any of the neighbors got nosy, she would flash her tin and count on the badge intimidating them enough for them to butt out.

She had found over the years that most civilians were afraid of a badge, like a vampire backing away from a cross; it had a certain talismanic power.

After she thought about it for a moment, and especially after recalling her conversation with Rafferty, she decided to go under the cover of darkness to lessen her chances of being spotted. She would maybe slip into a basement window. Getting caught breaking and entering would serve as the death knell for her career. But she figured getting a firsthand look at the scene was the only way to find out what really happened to Rhonda. She drove to Delevan, hoping to find a restaurant.

There were a lot of shops on Delevan, and she supposed this was as close to downtown as a small town got.

There was a Rite-Aid pharmacy, a Hollywood video store, a florist and then finally Niko's Restaurant. Up ahead, more stores and shops, but Niko's was what she wanted.

She pulled the Ford over in front of the restaurant and got out.

There was an orange, lighted sign that proclaimed: NIKO'S—FINEST GREEK FOOD IN LINCOLN. Donna imagined it was also the only Greek food in Lincoln.

She entered the restaurant; inside the door was a glass counter filled with chocolates: pecan turtles, chocolate-covered pretzels, peanut clusters and goobers. There were chocolate suckers, squares of dark and white chocolates and chunks of fudge. A teenage girl with a bouncy ponytail scooped out sponge candy, placed it in a wax paper bag and handed it to a woman in a fur wrap. The sweet smell of candy filled the air.

After Donna had waited a moment, a heavyset waitress with a sunflower-colored perm materialized beside the counter.

The waitress led Donna to a table, her heavy rear end swaying as she walked. She pulled a greasy looking rag out of her back pocket and wiped the table down. Donna sat down, ordered a Pepsi, and waited for darkness.

"So how bad does it look?" Matt asked, touching the swollen area under his eye.

"Like you caught Evander Holyfield on a bad day," Jill replied, twirling her linguine.

They sat in front of the big picture window that overlooked Delevan Avenue, eating and casually watching the passersby. Presently a trio of gum-chewing teenage girls bopped past, giggling and wearing shorts that nearly exposed the bottoms of their asses.

Jill relished the food and the overall ambiance of the restaurant. Unlike most Italian restaurants, Morotto's was brightly lit and had a vase of fresh-cut flowers on each table. Watercolor paintings of the Roman Coliseum and the Leaning Tower of Pisa adorned the walls. It was a welcome change to the thick shadows and checkered tablecloths that characterized most Italian eateries.

Now on her second glass of wine, she enjoyed the pleasant rush of heat that it provided. The company wasn't bad either.

They had been discussing Matt's Aunt Bernie.

"Did you keep in touch with her at all over the years?"

"No. And I feel rotten about it. I basically withdrew from the world and focused all my energy on the Rangers. And thought a lot about my family. Still do."

"What's it like jumping out of planes?" she asked.

"Scary. Exhilarating," he said. "I'd do it again." He took a bite of veal Picatta.

"You're nuts. First jumping out of planes and then single-handedly taking on the law," she said.

"Yeah. I fought the law . . ."

"And the law won. Big-time in this case."

"He's going to kill again if someone doesn't stop him. And what about him harassing you?"

Jill looked over her shoulder and then back at Matt. "You'd better lower your voice. Remember what you said to me about people listening in?"

"Right. That was stupid of me." Matt said in a hushed tone. "Anyone could be listening. Anyone with ties to Rafferty."

Jill finished off the last of her pasta and pushed her plate aside. It had gotten dark and a swarm of sand flies buzzed around the globe lamp out front.

"So do you still believe my story?" he asked.

"I believe something traumatic happened to you. And that your family was murdered."

"But what about the part about the creatures?"

"I'm getting there. Let me tell you about something that happened to me at work."

She leaned forward and he did the same. She told him about her supervisor, Dorothy Gaines, and about the awful smell coming off her.

"That's why I don't want to go to that hospital. There's been disappearances there, Jill. And patients mysteriously dying. I'm sure they didn't tell you that when they hired you."

"It's not exactly good PR material," she allowed.

"Let me know if you run across anyone else like that. And if you do, stay away from them."

"I'll try. But one of them's my boss so it's kind of hard."

It was getting easier to believe there were strange creatures living underneath human skin running around Lincoln.

But you already knew that, right? What chased you in that warehouse?

"You're not still planning to go after Rafferty, are you?"

"I wish I could tell you I wasn't. Jill, I joined the Rangers for more than one reason. One of the main ones was so I could learn combat techniques."

"Well, I'm going to do my best to talk you out of it."

"Save your breath."

Again, a hard look of determination appeared in his eyes. It had to be awful for him, losing his whole family. When she thought about it, his desire for revenge became more understandable; the loss of her own father was incredibly painful.

"We shouldn't say any more in here."

"Matt, the only other people in here is that couple over there." Jill nodded in the direction of an elderly couple, who were hunched over plates of baked ziti.

"You let me know if he bothers you," Matt said.

"Why, so you can bash his nightstick with your face again?"

"Very funny."

"I'm sorry, that was mean. I just hate to see you get hurt again."

"Maybe I'll do a Dirty Harry on him, ask him if he feels lucky. That punk."

"I don't see you as the Clint Eastwood type."

"What type do you see me as?"

"The type I'd like to get to know a lot better."

"Why don't we take a walk when we're done?" Matt asked.

That sounded good to her.

* * *

Donna sucked down the last of her Pepsi and the waitress arrived with the check. The bill came to four-fifty. She had initially wanted only a drink, but after seeing another customer order a slice of peanut butter pie, she had to have one. She left five-fifty on the table and walked back to the truck.

She drove back to Rhonda's street and cruised by the house, scanning the street. Every third house had a streetlight with a broad rim over the lamp. The front windows were dark in the Victorian next to Rhonda's, and a look down the street showed only empty lawns and porches.

She found it strange that there was nobody sitting on any of the porches or strolling down the street. It was a nice evening, despite the temperature still reading eighty degrees at eight o'clock. She expected to see people out walking or kids on bikes, but normal summer activity seemed to have ceased.

Parking the car down at the end of the street, she checked her holster, secured the Beretta in place. She straightened the blazer to conceal the weapon, though she planned on taking the garment off as soon as she was inside. Grabbing the flashlight off the seat, she got out of the car.

She strolled down the gentle curve of the street, noticing the houses were nice, but plain. No hanging baskets dangled from porches, the gardens held only dirt and weeds, and she didn't hear so much as a radio or television from any of the homes. As she reached the house next to Rhonda's she noted its crisp white paint job and black shutters. The wraparound porch showed only white boards and railings—no furniture.

Rhonda's house, by contrast, was a pale pink with lavender shutters. As Donna turned up the driveway, she admired the arbor that marked the entrance to the front walk and the vines cascading over top of it. She walked up the asphalt drive until she reached the side door. Two strands of yellow police tape made an "X" across it. The front door would be the same.

She walked toward the backyard, flipped on the flashlight and shone it at the rear corner of the house, where a garden hose lay curled in a heap. She worked the light in an arc across the yard, which went back sixty or so feet and had a sturdy red maple at its center. Rhonda had loved that tree, had planted it herself. Nothing.

She turned back to face the rear of the house and saw the busted basement window. Shards of glass still rested in the dirt. *A way in,* she thought.

She told herself it was madness even considering entering a crime scene—and in someone else's jurisdiction, to boot! But a member of her family was dead, and who the hell was Rafferty to keep information from her? And that shit about keeping the body so his own doctor could examine it? They'd probably erect a statue to her for uncovering Rafferty's schemes.

She made her decision: a quick look around and then get out.

She killed the light and hunkered low against the back of the house, peered into the yard next door. Nobody over there. A blue SUV was parked outside a three-car garage. In the distance, a car with a rude muffler chugged down the street.

She flattened herself against the ground and slid her legs through the window. Inching backward, her legs now dangled and bumped the basement walls. The frame dug into her belly and she winced. When she was back as far as she could go, she dropped to the ground. Her shirt rose up and she scraped her belly against the concrete blocks.

"Dammit," she said.

She brushed off her shirt and popped the light back on. Let the investigation begin.

* * *

Dietrich lifted his head up from the toilet bowl and flushed.

The smell of half-digested grilled cheese wafted up from the toilet. He was sweating in places he didn't know a man could sweat. Chills racked his body as he huddled in the corner next to the toilet. If he didn't shoot up by morning, he might die, sure as shit.

He needed some smack, and in a hurry.

The last time he had needed a bag, he'd gone to toss a big house in the Dorchester area. Of course it had gone from a burglary to a murder in no time, thanks in part to his lack of self-control.

He had chosen Rhonda Barbieri's house because the lights were off and there were no cars parked in the long asphalt driveway. Once inside, he found the house to be silent as a pharaoh's tomb.

Dietrich had rummaged through the house, starting in the living room. He considered boosting the television, then decided against it because it was too heavy.

He remembered reaching the bedroom and finding silk sheets on the bed, a plasma screen television with a Bose surround sound system on the wall and a black marble Jacuzzi in the adjoining bath. These folks had bucks.

He came away with two gold chains and a ruby ring that he lifted from a jewelry box and was about to leave when he had heard the low rumble of a car engine in the driveway.

Creeping over to the window, he brushed the venetian blind aside and looked out to see the tail end of a big Audi pulling into the garage. In a matter of seconds, he decided to kill the driver.

The urge to kill washed over him. He stripped off his clothes, right in the bedroom. Kicking them under the bed, he willed himself to change into his other form. It was excruciatingly painful, so he bit his lower lip to quell a groan.

After transforming, he scampered to the basement to hide, waited in the utility room and killed the woman when she came into the basement. It had been a satisfying kill, for when she tried to escape, she had panicked like a trapped animal. She had given off heat like a radiator; he could almost see the fear rising off of her in waves.

Yes, that one had been good, especially since the woman in the warehouse had gotten away from him. As he fed, he vaguely remembered Rafferty's warning about not killing before the Harvest, but it passed through his mind like a summer breeze through the treetops.

Rafferty didn't scare him. At least, not at that moment.

Now, as he huddled in the bathroom he remembered that his clothes were probably still in the house over in Dorchester. Using the toilet for support, he got up.

Looking in the bathroom mirror, he saw a pasty-faced skeleton looking back at him. His eyes were sunken and hollow, with purplish bags under them, like the black stuff ballplayers smeared on their cheeks.

It was a risk going back to that house, back to the scene of his crime, but he needed his drugs. And when he needed a fix, the Great Wall of China could not stand in his way.

He turned on the faucet and reddish-brown water dribbled out, turning clear after a moment. After splashing cold water on his face and changing out of his sweat-soaked T-shirt, Dietrich left his apartment and caught the number three Metro bus. The house was only two miles away, but in his state, he knew he would never make it if he had to walk.

In less than half an hour, he would have his fix.

CHAPTER 13

With one hand, Donna trained the flashlight beam on the workbench standing against the basement wall. She took out her piece with the other.

There was a vise clamp screwed to the tabletop and a sheet of pegboard fixed to the wall that held an assortment of pliers, wrenches, screwdrivers, and hammers. Donna also noticed the cordless Makita drill she had bought Bob for his thirtieth birthday. It still looked brand new, never used.

She smelled gasoline and noticed a gas can and greasy rags on the floor, along with a box of Ohio Blue Tip matches. There were three taper candles on the bench, perhaps emergency lighting in case of a blackout. Donna shook her head at her brother's lack of fire safety. That was an accident waiting to happen.

Stepping away from the tool bench, she shined the beam on the floor. A cluster of brownish stains dotted the floor. She scanned the walls with the light, finding them spotted with dried blood. Rhonda's blood. What kind of monster did something like this? Rafferty had lied through his teeth. *No evidence, my ass.*

She turned her attention to the storage room. Brushing a cobweb out of her face, she opened the door; the smell forced her to jerk her head back. What the hell could cause such an odor?

An old yellow dresser stood against one wall, and some paint cans with crusty white paint on their sides were stacked in the middle of the room. Moving the beam back and forth, she looked around but came up with nothing except a mousetrap baited with peanut butter.

The smell in the room had become more tolerable and she inhaled deeply as if to ingrain the smell in her mind, trying to connect it with something. She couldn't place the odor, but sulfur kept springing to mind.

The killer had hidden here and waited for Rhonda. She didn't know how she had reached that conclusion, for there was no physical evidence to support it. She just knew the killer had been in this room.

Could it be that the killer worked in a chemical plant where they used sulfur? The nearest chemical plant was OxyChem in Niagara Falls. She made a mental note to call OxyChem.

Donna left the utility room and started up the stairs, which led directly into the kitchen. She shone the beam on the counter and illuminated a can of Diet Coke. Probably part of Rhonda's dinner or late-night snack the day she was murdered, she mused.

After probing the kitchen, the living room and the dining room, she went upstairs to the house's five bedrooms.

There was a weight bench and rack of chrome barbells in the first room and she thought of how her brother Bob had always been obsessed with his physique. The next room down the narrow hallway was Rhonda's office, complete with a huge cherrywood desk and leather office chair.

The next two rooms were filled with boxes of assorted junk; there was nothing special about them.

There was one more room left at the end of the hallway, Bob and Rhonda's bedroom. Donna pointed her beam at the door, turned the handle and entered the room.

"How's your face feeling?" Jill asked.

"Throbbing."

"You want to go back?" She touched his arm, concerned he might have a concussion, or that he might be in worse shape than he said.

"I'm enjoying the company too much to go home now."

She smiled at him. "Likewise. You sure you're all right?"

"Positive," Matt said.

They were sitting on a bench at the corner of Delevan and Thorpe. St. Mark's Catholic Church loomed behind them like a medieval fortress, its stained-glass windows darkened. Their bench was next to a streetlamp, and a cluster of moths dipped and zigzagged around the light.

Matt had taken her hand as they walked from Morotto's to the bench. She liked the feel of his hand around hers, strong and firm.

She had told him about the breakup with Jerry over dinner at Morotto's, and her mother's desire for her to study medicine at Duke or Harvard. The topic of her mother resisting Jill's nursing career also came up in their conversation.

Suddenly she found herself liking him very much. She put her finger on his cheek, turned his head toward her and kissed him lightly on the lips. "Thank you, Matt."

"For what?"

"For putting me at ease."

"You can thank me again if you want."

"Maybe later. Let's go."

They stood up and walked back to the truck, hand in hand.

They drove back toward Jill's, rolling down Delevan Street with the windows open. The air ruffled her hair and the sound of the wheels hummed on the asphalt. The air should have felt refreshing, but it served only to chill her. She rolled up the window a bit and said, "What's going on here, Matt? I mean in Lincoln. The police chief's a psycho, I almost get killed in a warehouse, the people smell weird, and according to you, there's monsters underneath everyone's skin."

"I think you just answered your own question."

"I still don't know about these things you're describing. I mean, I know something terrible happened to you and I sympathize, but monsters?"

They drove in silence for a moment until Matt spoke.

"Let's go to my aunt's. I want to show you some things. Maybe it'll sway you or maybe it won't. What do you say?"

She thought about it for a moment, a little curious, wondering what he could possibly want to show her. "Why not?"

He pulled the truck into the parking lot of Lincoln Lock and Key, did a quick U-turn and pulled back onto Delevan in the opposite direction.

Five minutes later, they pulled into his aunt's driveway. As Jill climbed out of the truck, she had to smile. She noticed the gentleman Mr. Crowe sneaking a peek at her legs.

They entered the house through the side door.

"You've got to meet my Aunt Bernie. She'll love you." They climbed three steps and entered the kitchen,

Jill noticing the wonderful smells of onion, garlic, and Parmesan cheese lingering in the air. It was a cook's kitchen, with a huge wooden spice rack on one wall, a block of expensive-looking knives on the counter and a gleaming copper pot in the sink. A stainless steel mixer and bowl sat next to the knives.

"Your aunt likes to cook, doesn't she?"

"She could give Wolfgang Puck a run for his money," Matt said.

"The kitchen smells great."

"Smells like she made her world-famous pork chops. Aunt Bernie?"

"In here!"

They entered the living room where Aunt Bernie sat in a forest-green recliner. An *All in the Family* rerun was on the tube and Arch was singing to Meathead. His aunt stood up and came over to Jill. She wrapped her arms around Jill and gave a squeeze. Jill inhaled the scents of cinnamon and brown sugar.

Aunt Bernie put her hands on Jill's shoulders and took a step back, as if to admire her. "Matthew, you're right. She *is* a beauty. Don't let go of this one!"

Jill thanked her for the compliment and they made small talk, Jill and Matt telling her about dinner. Jill also told her she was a nurse, about her apartment and how long she had been living in Lincoln.

"Would you two like some peach pie?"

They both said no thanks, that they were stuffed from dinner. Jill found herself instantly liking Bernie's warmth and friendliness, a welcome trait in any person, but especially meaningful to Jill because her own mother was such a piranha.

Matt told her that they were going out to the loft over the garage to check out some pictures.

"You two behave out there. No hanky-panky." Aunt Bernie pretended to be stern, wagging her finger at them. Her sleeve rode up, revealing a brown bruise on her upper arm.

Jill looked at Matt, checking for a reaction. A frown creased his brow, then disappeared.

"I'll be a gentleman. I promise."

Matt wished his aunt good night and he and Jill walked out to the garage and entered through the small door. They climbed a set of wooden stairs that ended at a trapdoor in the ceiling.

Matt flipped on the light switch, revealing a single bed, nightstand, a small fridge and a table with two kitchen chairs. The powder blue carpet looked plush and new. It was livable, if plain.

"Not bad. Could use a woman's touch, though," she said.

Matt rummaged under his bed and pulled out his suitcase, a big brown leather job.

"Did you notice the bruise on my aunt's arm?" he said.

"Yeah, I did."

"I'd put money on in being there courtesy of my Uncle Rex."

"He beats her?"

"I've never actually seen him do it, but I'm pretty sure he does. He smacked me around when I was living here. He's a pretty lousy drunk."

"Mean?"

"As a junkyard dog."

"Why did he hit you?"

Matt flopped the suitcase on to the bed. "I broke my curfew by fifteen minutes or so. After that I left. I'd had it with him. He liked to refer to me as dickhead or shithead or something equally flattering."

"Sounds like a real sweetheart."

"I'm keeping an eye on things. If he hurts my aunt, he'll deal with me this time."

This time Jill didn't discourage his macho talk. Any man who beat a woman deserved whatever punishment came to him. It was one thing for Matt to talk about killing the town's chief law enforcement officer, but another to defend a ninety-pound woman from an abusive husband.

Matt flipped open the suitcase and pulled out a battered Red Wing shoe box. "Let me show you these."

She had no idea what to expect, but she was willing to wager one thing: it wouldn't be dull.

Donna entered the bedroom feeling the way the archaeologists who raided the burial chambers of the Egyptian pyramids must have felt. A strange wonder at being among the possessions of the dead flowed through her.

The sheets on the bed were in a ball and a pillow lay cockeyed on the nightstand. Someone had left the dresser drawers open an inch or two. Her immediate thought was that someone had rifled through the drawers and then halfheartedly closed them when their search was complete.

Not someone. The killer had rifled through them.

She tried Bob's dresser first, opening the drawers by sticking the pen she always carried in the crack and pulling each toward her. Using the pen, she poked around, lifting up folded shirts and underwear, hoping the killer had left a clue behind. She was a little surprised that the clothes had not been ripped from the drawers and scattered all over the room.

In most burglaries, the house was ransacked.

Maybe this guy was a neat freak.

After searching the drawers in Bob's dresser (and wishing she'd remembered a pair of gloves) she crossed the room to Rhonda's.

Her foot brushed against something on the floor. Pointing the flashlight, she saw it was a pair of jeans, sticking out from underneath the king-size bed.

She hunkered down to get a closer look. Brown with white stitching on the back pockets, not Bob or Rhonda's style.

She stuck her pen in one of the belt loops and pulled the jeans from under the bed. She put her face to the floor and looked around beneath the bed. There was a yellow T-shirt under there as well.

She pulled the shirt out using the same method as she did for the jeans. Unfolding it with her pen, it became clear that the wearer was a fan of the King. There was a circular iron-on of Elvis Presley dressed in full rhinestone jumpsuit garb, crooning into a microphone, eyes closed, sweat beads visible on his forehead. The peeling, turquoise lettering above the picture read *Elvis Presley—Long Live the King of Rock 'n' Roll.*

Donna wanted to check the pockets on the jeans but was hesitant because there was no telling where the jeans could eventually wind up. Rafferty probably hadn't noticed them and wouldn't be back to investigate, but it never hurt to be careful. If she got prints or hair on the jeans, it would give away the fact that she had come to the Barbieri house.

She searched the closet and found a pair of brown leather gloves—it wasn't likely anyone would notice they were gone. She wished she'd thought of using the gloves sooner, for it would have saved her digging through the dresser drawers with the pen.

She slipped the gloves on and dug her hand into a pocket. The left front yielded two quarters and a half melted stick of Wrigley's Spearmint.

The right front pocket contained the payoff.

She pulled out a plastic baggie filled with brown powder, probably heroin. As she stuck the bag in her pocket, a bang came from downstairs. It sounded like a piece of furniture being tipped over.

What if it's Rafferty or one of his boys?

She stuffed the clothes back under the bed, as close to the way she'd found them as she could manage. She heard the thump-creak of someone climbing the stairs.

She got to her feet and quickly ducked into the walk-in closet, parallel to the bedroom door. The sliding door had been left open and she slid it shut, careful not to let it squeak or bang.

The floor squeaked as the unseen visitor came closer to the bedroom, moving down the hallway and sniffing like a bloodhound. *Why the hell was he sniffing?*

She took out her Beretta and opened the closet a crack, getting a peek at the room but also increasing her chance of being spotted. She wanted to see who she was up against if it came down to a confrontation.

The sniffer entered the room, back to the closet, a painfully thin man with white-blond hair. He immediately hit the floor and pulled the clothes from under the bed. Rifling through the pockets, his hands trembling visibly, he threw the jeans to the ground. "Fuck!"

Donna knew she was looking at the man who had killed her sister-in-law, and for a moment a very dark part of her wanted to step from the closet and empty her full magazine into the piece of crap.

Keep your cool, Donna.

She prided herself on the ability to remain calm under fire when other cops might have hurt a perp. You couldn't go around blasting bad guys like the cops in the movies. But this was different; this man had most certainly brutally murdered a woman who was like a sister to her. That trigger would be so easy to squeeze.

Stop it.

She swallowed, her throat feeling like she'd drunk a sand cocktail.

If she moved now, she could get the drop on the guy, get him on the ground and maybe get him to talk. Plus she'd be between him and the bedroom door, cutting off his escape.

Hooking her fingers around the door, she whipped it open, sprang from the closet and aimed the nine between Blondie's shoulder blades. "Hands on your head. Now."

CHAPTER 14

Matt plopped down on the bed and Jill sat next to him. Holding the shoe box in his lap, he pulled the lid off and set it between them.

The box was filled with yellowed newspaper clippings and computer printouts. Matt stuck his hand in the box and took out the article on top of the pile. He skimmed it and handed it to Jill. It was a newspaper clipping from the *San Francisco Examiner* dated October 7, 1992.

> A San Francisco woman considers herself lucky to be alive after a brush with a mysterious animal. Charlene Matthews, 31, was camping with her boyfriend when they were assaulted by what authorities believe was a bear.
>
> "We were sleeping in the tent. It was about ten at night. We heard a crashing sound in the woods and then the next thing it was ripping our tent to pieces," said Ms. Matthews.
>
> The mystery animal slashed a cut in

Ms. Matthews' leg, requiring her to have thirty-nine stitches. Ms. Matthews disagrees with local officials' contentions that a bear attacked her.

"It was no bear. It walked like a man. And it smelled rotten."

Captain Roland Lemieux of the San Francisco Police attributes Ms. Matthews' reaction to shock.

"She underwent a serious trauma, and I can see why she thinks she may have seen something out of the ordinary. But we're confident that it was in fact a wild animal. The campers left food out and that's a sure way to attract an animal."

Captain Lemieux told reporters he found a trail of beaten brush where the animal entered and left the campsite. The animal has not been found.

Apparently it was scared off when another camper heard the commotion and fired rifle shots in the air.

"Matt, this could have been anything," Jill protested.

"It wasn't a bear. I went to San Francisco and interviewed Charlene Matthews. The interview's on a tape in this box if you want to hear it."

"Sure. I'm a curious type."

"One problem. I don't have a tape player."

"Bring it to my place. We'll listen to it there."

He took a Memorex tape out of the box and set it next to him.

Matt turned on the air-conditioning to make them more comfortable and the room became pleasantly cool.

Over the next half an hour, Jill read through dozens of articles and printouts:

A Boy Scout Troop in Seattle that had spotted something in the woods that looked like a "monster."

The disappearance of the entire town of Redrock, Colorado, in 1917.

The similar disappearance of Manitou, Ontario, in 1944. The sole survivor of Manitou had been found by the Royal Canadian Mounted Police wandering in the woods nearby, bloodied and battered, muttering, "They came and got us. They got us all." When asked who "they" were, he replied, "Devils, who else?"

A detailed account of how John Snyder, a Native American who lived on the outskirts of Las Vegas, fired his shotgun at a "man-beast" that had tried beating his door down at two o'clock in the morning in 1974. Snyder, who lived alone, wounded the intruder, forcing it to flee. The Las Vegas Police found a trail of black fluid leading into the desert and tufts of wiry hair caught in the screen door. One of the officers also described, "The worst smell I've ever encountered. Like manure and ammonia mixed together."

"Did you speak with John Snyder, too?" Jill asked.

"No. He died ten years ago. Cancer of the pancreas," Matt replied. "But I did look up his daughter Sharon. She wouldn't let me in the house, but she did tell me one thing. She also said that if I told anyone she would deny it."

"Well?"

"She told me her father was haunted by what he saw that night for the rest of his life. He wouldn't go out after dark and he kept a shotgun at his side constantly. Right up until the time the cancer took him. She also told me she was in the house the night of the attack," Matt revealed.

"Did she see this thing too?"

"Yes. She would only go as far as saying she had never

seen anything like it before or since. And that her father thought it was a demon coming to take his life."

Jill sifted through the articles and printouts, reading more of the same types of accounts. A farmer in Nebraska who heard a prowler in his yard one night was nearly dragged off into a cornfield by what he described as "something from another planet." He had escaped death by fending the creature off with an ax.

The stories continued from around the country: Louisiana, Texas, Illinois, Maine, Florida. Most had been discounted as Bigfoot sightings.

Jill finished reading and handed the articles back to Matt. There was one article left in the box, which piqued Jill's curiosity. She didn't ask about it, though. Not yet.

"Matt, there's crazies all over the country. People who think they've seen Bigfoot, or UFOs or the Loch Ness Monster. Okay, maybe not the Loch Ness Monster."

He frowned. "But most people just *see* those things. These are people who were attacked. And in a lot of cases there was physical evidence left behind."

"What if they were wild animal attacks that people mistook for bizarre creatures? Bears? Mountain lions?"

"Most people know what those things look like. The things in these articles couldn't really be described by anyone."

He had that hard look in his eyes again. She had to admit that the articles did make a case, especially the cop in Nevada who described the odd smell. That she had experienced herself. Plus, the articles came from reputable newspapers and not the *National Examiner* or some other wacky tabloid that claimed Jesus had an alien twin brother.

"This town's full of them, Jill. I'm convinced. And anyone who's not one of them is probably in a lot of danger. Getting Rafferty may not be enough. There could be hundreds more of them. Just like the things that killed my family."

"So you see how crazy it is, killing the town's top lawman?"

"If there was a way to take them all out . . ."

"You can't be serious."

"They're dangerous, Jill. This *town* is dangerous. Let me show you."

Was Matt nuts or was she not being open-minded enough? "I hate to bring this up, but what about your family? Was there any account of their death in the papers?"

"Yeah. Rafferty put up a good front, even faked an investigation. Check this out."

He handed Jill the last newspaper clipping. The headline read:

Suspects Still at Large in Slaying of Family

The men responsible for the murder of three members of a Lincoln family are still at large, Police Chief Ed Rafferty told the LINCOLN GAZETTE. Police have no leads or possible suspects.

"This crime is definitely random. We have no motives for the killings. And unfortunately, the Crowe boy didn't see the killers."

According to Rafferty, Matthew Crowe, 16, was exploring the woods near Emerling Park when assailants attacked his family. When Crowe returned to the clearing where his family was having a summer picnic, they had disappeared. Police found blood and

scraps of clothing in the woods, which,
according to Chief Rafferty, indicate
the victims were killed and their bodies
dragged through the woods.

Rafferty has told the GAZETTE that
the crime was the most brutal he has ever
seen: "I've seen some bad ones, but this
was the worst. Very vicious killing."

Rafferty believes the suspects may
have been under the influence of drugs.
He has made a vow to catch the killers.
"This crime won't go unsolved. Not in
my town," the Chief said.

The victims are John Crowe, 38;
Maggie Crowe, 37; and Michael Crowe,
5. Funeral services for the victims will
be held at St. Mark's Roman Catholic
Church Saturday at 10 A.M.

Jill handed the article back to Matt.

"And they never found the killers," Jill said.

"You got it."

"Anything happen to the guy who wrote the article?"

"No. As far as I know he's still around. Name's Jack
Hanley. The *Gazette*'s out of business, though. Newspapers
don't last long in Lincoln."

"What about outside police agencies?"

"They never looked into anything, and after Rafferty
threatened me, I was too scared to tell anyone what I
saw. That, and they wouldn't have believed me."

Jill was now more confused than ever about Matt
Crowe and Lincoln. She still wanted to hear the interview with Charlene Matthews, and she suggested they
go to her place to hear it.

"Let's hit it, then," he said.

They left with the tape in hand.

BOOK TWO
The Devil
Unmasked

CHAPTER 15

Donna stepped from the closet. She kept the light on the guy. He squinted and raised his hands, as if to ward off the light. "I can't see."

He was broomstick thin, pale-skinned and had heavy dark circles under his eyes. There were purple-brown track marks up and down the insides of his forearms and he stank of ripe sweat.

"Who the hell are you?" he asked.

"I should ask you that."

He dug at the inside of his left forearm. "You a cop?"

"I'm a friend of the woman you killed."

"Don't know what you're talking about."

"Bullshit, you don't."

Loosen up, she told herself. Her neck stiffened and cords of muscle tensed in her forearms like wires pulled tight by an invisible winch. "Hands on your head. Then get down on the ground. Slowly."

He put his hands on his head but remained standing. "You've gotta be a cop. Only cops talk like that. How about dousing that light?"

"On the ground." Donna lowered the flashlight slightly. The guy stopped squinting.

"You're in here illegally, you know," he said.

He trembled, occasionally twitching at the neck and shoulders. He must've been hurting pretty bad for some smack, she decided.

"One more time. Get on the ground or I'll shoot you."

"You won't."

"Try me."

For some reason, he thought he had an edge on her, maybe because she was a woman. But she was a woman with a large gun, and bullets didn't care which sex fired them. Maybe the need for his drugs was ruling his actions right now.

Pulling the baggie from her pocket, she dangled it with one hand while holding the gun and keeping him covered with the other.

His eyes widened. "That's mine!"

"So you *were* in this house before. I found this under the bed."

He reached out his hand, palm up, as if expecting her to just hand it over. "Gimme that!"

"Answer some questions and maybe I will."

"The hell with your questions."

He charged at her and Donna spun, planting a roundhouse kick in his solar plexus. It felt like kicking a sack full of hockey sticks. The guy doubled over, lost his balance, tried to right himself by touching his hand to the floor, and teetered onto his side.

Clutching his midsection, he rolled back and forth on the ground next to the bed. "I think you broke my ribs," he groaned.

"That's quite a performance. I didn't kick you anywhere near as hard as I could have. Get up."

He pushed himself to his feet, Donna keeping the Beretta on him the whole time.

For a moment, she actually pitied him, a man so obsessed with drugs that he would charge someone with a loaded gun to get them. The fact that she had knocked the tar out of a guy who weighed a buck twenty-five didn't make her feel so hot either. She probably could've blown on his bony frame and knocked him over.

But when she thought of what he might have done to Rhonda, all thoughts of pity faded from her mind.

The room was now shrouded in plum-colored shadows. The junkie, still in the process of getting his wind back, sucked air in big gulps.

"Sit on the bed," Donna said.

"Will you give me my smack?"

You can't be serious, she thought. But having the bag of smack did give her some leverage. "Answer my questions, first."

"*Are* you a cop?"

What the hell? Maybe telling him she was a cop would give her even more leverage. "Yeah. Now what's your name?"

"Charles Dietrich."

"And you came back here for your drugs?"

"You promise I can have some?"

"I promise."

"I left them here, yeah."

"What were you doing here in the first place? When you left the drugs?"

Dietrich rocked back and forth on the edge of the bed. He hugged his midsection. "I could ask you the same question. What're you doing here?"

Losing patience with you, Charles. "I saw you breaking into the house. I chased you in here and found you looking for your drugs. And then I detained you. Anyone asks, that's my story. And I think the cops would believe me over a lousy junkie."

She expected a look of surprise or possibly resignation on his face, but he smirked instead.

"Rafferty would believe you because he's out to get me already. But then again, you're not one of us. He might not believe you."

"What does that mean?"

"Give me some of that and I'll tell you."

He nodded his head to indicate the heroin.

She thought for a moment. If she gave him the bag, he might crack and spill his guts. But he could also try and run or refuse to talk once he got what he wanted. Screw him. "What did you mean by 'one of us'?"

"We live everywhere. Lincoln's full of us." He started to stand up and she feigned another kick. He sat back down.

"Tell me what you mean by 'us,'" she demanded.

"Hunters. We feed on you."

"So you're telling me you're some sort of vampire?"

"Vampires drink blood. We consume the flesh."

The guy was putting her on, stalling so he wouldn't have to answer questions about what he was doing in the house. "Enough of this crap. Did you kill the woman who lived in this house?"

"No."

"You're lying. Do you want me to go to the local authorities? Talk to Rafferty about finding you here?"

"No!"

When she had mentioned Rafferty before, Dietrich had said that he was out to get him. And now he seemed frightened by her mentioning the police chief again. Maybe this would be her ace in the hole. "So you don't want me to go to Rafferty?"

"No. He's got it in for me. Something happened and if he finds out I . . ."

"Finds out you what?"

"Nothing."

"That's it. I'm taking you down there right now."

"Don't!"

"You killed the woman in this house. Her name was Rhonda."

"No, I didn't."

"Do you want me to bring in Rafferty?"

"He'll kill me."

"I'll take you in now. Did you kill her?"

"Fuck you! I didn't kill her."

That was it. She needed a freehand, and she wasn't dropping the gun. Donna let the flashlight fall to the floor.

She pounced on him, pinning him on the bed, one hand around his throat and the other pointing the Beretta at his forehead. She was dangerously close to the edge, her heart hammering, adrenaline racing through her body like rocket fuel. "Did you kill her?"

Instead of answering her, he inhaled deeply. The air made a snuffling, rattling sound as it passed through his nose.

"If Rafferty doesn't kill you, I might. Did you?"

"You smell good." He sniffed again. "Nice scent."

In her haste to get him to confess, she had forgotten how he had stopped on the stairs and sniffed the air like he was on the trail of something. This was getting weirder by the second.

"I killed that whore. It was fun."

His voice sounded deeper, as if it had dropped an octave.

"I'm taking you to Rafferty."

She began to slide off of him, gripping his arm and trying to pull him off of the bed, but he tugged back. She couldn't move him.

"Get off the bed. I'm done playing with you."

He gave her the same smirk he had when she'd first mentioned Rafferty.

Thrusting his arms out, he pushed against her chest, throwing her backward into the closet doors. He was stronger than he looked. She regained her balance and leveled the pistol at him.

"Smell nice. Female."

She thought her eyes were fooling her, but Charles Dietrich appeared larger. The ceiling seemed closer to the top of his head, and his red T-shirt strained at the shoulders.

He closed his eyes and bit down on his lower lip. "Ahhhhgggg . . ."

His shoulders expanded, as did his chest. She watched with horror as the arms lengthened and the muscles grew thick and ropy. Hairs, black and coarse, sprouted from his arms.

Donna's head hurt from banging it against the closet door, but her pain took a backseat to the spectacle she was witnessing now. Her mouth agape, she couldn't take her eyes off of what she was seeing. Part of her mind told her to run, to get the hell away from here, but she couldn't stop watching.

Now Deitrich looked down at his own body, then back at Donna with a look of panic on his face. The shirt had stretched to the point of tearing, and the seams gave with a *scccrrch* noise. He rolled onto his side, clutched his head. She heard the grinding and popping of bones and joints, then a squelching sound as claws split the skin of his fingertips.

She backed away, still watching.

The thing that had been Charles Dietrich rose from the bed. His clothes lay torn, strings hanging from the split material. Dietrich must've gone around six feet tall, but this thing was a good six five despite its hunched back. The raw, gassy odor of sulfur filled the room. The

Dietrich-thing opened its mouth, revealing rows of teeth designed to shred.

Snap out of it!

Instinctively, she raised the Beretta and fired, striking it in the shoulder. Black goop popped from the wound. It looked at the wound the way a person might look at a fresh mosquito bite. The creature grunted, took a step forward and slapped the weapon out of her hand, sending it skittering under the nightstand.

She knew now that this was what Rhonda Barbieri had seen during the last minutes of her life.

Matt sat on the couch in Jill's apartment, sipping ice water while she popped in the tape and hit Play.

White noise hissed from the speakers, followed by Matt's voice.

"State your name for me, please."

"Charlene Matthews."

"And the date?"

"December eighth, nineteen ninety-two."

"Ms. Matthews—"

"Call me Charlie."

"Charlie, can you tell me about your camping trip?"

"Are you sure you're not a cop?"

"I told you I wasn't."

"You better not be. I was camping with my boyfriend, Jim Sorrentino."

"Where were you camping?"

"Just north of Frisco."

"Please describe what happened."

"Me and Jim had built a campfire. We ate dinner. We had hot dogs and baked beans. The campfire died out about nine thirty."

"And after that?"

"*We poured water on it, like good campers do. Then we went in the tent and started, you know, fooling around.*"

"*You don't have to get that personal if you don't want to.*"

"*No big deal. Everybody fucks, right?*"

"*What happened after your encounter with Jim?*"

"*Actually, we were still going at it when we heard something in the woods. It was about ten o'clock. I made Jim stop and listen and he told me I was being stupid. He wanted to keep going, but I told him to shush.*"

"*What happened next?*"

"*The noises got louder. There was crashing and branches breaking, like something big was coming through the woods.*"

"*And?*"

Pause for nearly a minute. Exhaling of air.

"*Sorry, I have to collect myself. This part freaked me out.*"

"*I understand.*"

"*It closed on our tent fast. I could hear it thud across the ground. The next thing I knew it clawed through the tent and stuck its head in.*"

"*Was it a bear like it said in the paper?*"

"*No way. This thing was crazy looking.*"

"*Can you describe it?*"

"*Ugly. Mean-looking eyes. Yellow eyes. Lots of sharp teeth. And it smelled like you wouldn't believe. I think I would've puked if I wasn't so busy having the piss scared out of me.*"

"*So this creature couldn't have been any other type of animal. A mountain lion? Some sort of ape?*"

"*Definitely not.*"

"*What did it do next?*"

"*It reached for me because I was closer to it. Jim and me were screaming and the thing was grunting. It tried grabbing me by the leg, but I pulled away. It raked me with its claw and cut me. I saw the blood and Jim tells me I fainted.*"

"*What happened next?*"

"*Jim told me the next day at the hospital that another*

camper heard the screaming and came running with a shotgun. He fired at the thing and hit it. It ran off into the woods."

"Is there anything else you'd like to say?"

"I'll never go camping again. You sure you're not a cop? Or one of them reporters for the Enquirer *or one of those papers?"*

"I'm not. I promise."

"I'm sorry."

"It's okay. I can see why you'd be suspicious. Thank you for your time, Charlie."

"You're welcome. I hope this helps you."

"It will."

Jill got up and turned off the tape. She rewound it and they listened to it again. After the tape had finished, Jill sat on the couch again. "What was your impression of Charlene Matthews?" she asked.

"I think she was telling the truth. She was a little flaky, one of those New Age types."

"How's that?"

"When I interviewed her she had on hippie garb. Tie-dye shirt, lots of turquoise jewelry. She had candles and incense burning. Couple funky looking Hendrix posters on the wall, too."

"Some of those people are into UFOs and stuff," Jill said.

"I know what you're thinking. Spacey hippie-type chick, probably fresh off a bong hit thinking she saw Bigfoot. She got pretty broken up when it came time to talk about the attack. She wasn't lying."

Jill leaned forward, propping her elbows on her knees and resting her head on hands, similar to the Thinker. "Matt, I need some time to think things over."

"Put it all together, Jill."

"Let me walk you down."

He had blown it by spilling everything to her. "Let's talk some more."

"Not tonight. My head's swimming," she said.

He stood up and took his tape out of the stereo.

Jill walked him out to the truck and gave him a kiss on the cheek.

"I'll call you tomorrow," he said.

"Give me a few days."

He climbed in the truck and watched her walk up the driveway, her head down. He hoped she came around, saw things for what they were in Lincoln. Whether she believed him or not, he planned to stay.

Rafferty pulled into Jimbo's parking lot, the bumper on the cruiser scraping against the cement incline to the driveway. He squealed his brakes and stopped in front of the gas pumps. He was feeling meaner than usual, like he could break someone's nose for fun.

He had come from the Greek joint where he had downed four steak Souvlakis, an order of french fries, two milk shakes and a banana split for dessert. It tasted bland and mushy to him. What he really wanted to taste, he couldn't have. Yet. So he had temporarily satisfied his hunger with tasteless breads and meats. The waitress said she'd never seen anyone eat like that, and he had told her to hurry up and bring him the check.

When he was in the restaurant, he noticed a teenage couple three booths down from him, holding hands and drinking out of the same milk shake with two straws. They giggled, whispered and occasionally kissed across the table. It repulsed him in the way that a human might be repulsed by watching flies crawl over food.

Love, what was it? The females of his race only desired sex from the males. They kept up a good front in their human skins, pretending to be married couples or lovers. Had to keep up appearances, after all. But love? It didn't exist.

Now, he stepped out of his patrol car, his boot heels clicking on the pavement. It was a wonder Jimbo ever did any business in this place, because it was run-down, old and smelled bad, much like Jimbo.

The look of the place really made no difference to him, as long as he got free gas.

He entered the office, where Jimbo's helper Carl sat with his feet up on the desk reading a copy of *Playboy*.

"Evening, Chief."

"Where's Jimbo?"

"He never works nights."

"I know he's not here, you moron. Is he at home?"

"I dunno. Either home or out at one of the bars."

Rafferty sniffed the air. There was something underneath the smell of the grease and gasoline. He moved closer to the door that separated the office from the garage and took another whiff. He noticed Carl watching him and trying to act like he wasn't really watching him at the same time. His eyes shifted from the magazine to Rafferty every few seconds.

"Want me to pump your gas, Chief?"

"In a second."

He knew that one of them had made the change here, possibly Jimbo. The sulfurous smell lingered in the garage, and under that, the hot, metallic smell of blood. "Gotten many strangers in here, Carl? Out-of-towners?"

"No. Well, there was one guy. A salesman. But he was just passing through."

"Jimbo didn't tell me about that."

"Must've forgot."

"He's not supposed to forget. He's my eyes for whenever someone new comes through town."

Although Jimbo had always reported to Rafferty when

strangers stopped at the station, he sensed that the old coot never really liked him.

"Let me pump that gas for you, Chief."

Carl set his magazine down on the desk and rushed out to pump the gas. He was acting so skittish, Rafferty would almost put money on the fact that there had been a kill in the garage. He would stop by Jimbo's house and see if he could get the real story, for Carl was of little help.

Carl finished gassing up his car and came back into the office. "No charge, Chief."

"I know. Anything out of the ordinary happen here lately?"

"Uh, not that I can think of."

"You sure?"

"Yep. Business as usual."

Rafferty gave him a hard stare, hoping he would crack and reveal some information, but Carl stood firm.

Something had gone down in Jimbo's Garage. Maybe the old coot had lost his temper with a customer, or maybe the urge to kill had been too strong for him to resist, but someone was dead. Rafferty knew it.

Whatever happened, he would pay Jimbo a visit and find out.

He got in the cruiser and peeled out of the parking lot, leaving skid marks on the concrete.

CHAPTER 16

Donna turned and darted out the bedroom door, slamming it behind her, hoping to slow the creature down. She heard the door being opened and slammed shut behind her.

She reached the top of the stairs and ventured a peek over her shoulder. It was coming, but it moved slowly, deliberately. She could swear the thing was smiling at her.

Due to its size and musculature, Donna was sure it could be on top of her in two strides. It seemed content to play with her, letting her believe she might get away, perhaps only to pounce on her and rip her to pieces at the last minute.

She hurried down the stairs and it bounded after her. Her foot reached the third stair when it pushed her between the shoulder blades.

God, it was quick, she thought as her ankle twisted and she skidded down the steps.

She landed hard, smacking her ribs and knocking over a small table in the hallway. If she made it out of here alive, tomorrow would be an Advil day.

Shaking her head, she looked up at the stairs and her pursuer. It stood with one foot on the bottom step and one a few steps higher. Its arms hung to almost its knees and it stood in a crouch, measuring her with eyes the color of swamp water.

She got to her feet, wishing she had the Beretta on her.

It took a step down, its nails clicking on the beige tiles in the hallway.

To her left was the living room and dining room; to her right and slightly ahead was the hallway leading back to the kitchen. The front door was in the foyer, but she didn't think she could get to it and unlock it before the creature closed on her.

It took another step so that both feet were on the hall floor. She was in grabbing distance and didn't like it.

"Dietrich, if you're in there, you're dead. Understand me?"

The creature flashed its teeth. It was definitely a grin this time, probably meant to scare her by showing off its fangs. They *were* impressive; three inches long and shaped like thick needles, ideal for piercing skin.

It feinted, pretending to reach for her, as if to test her reaction.

She recoiled from it and then took off down the hallway toward the kitchen. It could have grabbed her if it wanted to, but it seemed content to let her escape again.

It likes the thrill of the hunt. The bastard.

Rounding the corner into the kitchen, she could hear its thick sniffing as it tested the air, inhaling her scent. She was lucky she hadn't killed herself fleeing in a dark house. She grabbed the doorknob and opened the basement door. Then she went through. She slammed the door but couldn't secure it, for the lock was on the other side.

Hobbling down the stairs, pain flared in her ribs and at the base of her spine. Her back was going to be a sunset of bruises.

The door at the top of the stairs banged open and she heard heavy footfalls descending the stairs.

The window was her only hope.

Rafferty climbed the cracked concrete stoop and knocked on the door. The house wasn't much of an improvement over Jimbo's service station. The numbers 1 and 9 hung on the door, the zero in between them having fallen off. The green paint was chipped and blistered, as if it were trying to remove itself from the house.

After knocking on the door, Rafferty backed down the step, and a chunk of concrete broke off, nearly sending him sprawling.

He muttered a curse and pounded on the door.

"Jimbo!"

After knocking again, he heard shuffling footsteps and then the old buzzard clearing his throat. The door opened with a soft click and Jimbo stuck his head out.

The yellow porch light illuminated his head, revealing scaly white skin on his balding scalp. The light made his skin appear waxy, like it might run off of his face.

When he saw Rafferty at the door, he opened it all the way. He still had on his grimy coveralls from the garage.

"Evening, Ed."

"Just came from the gas station."

"Carl pump your gas for you?"

"Yep. Didn't charge me either. Appreciate that, by the way."

"Any time."

Jimbo tugged at the crotch of his coveralls.

"Took a look around your place. Anything funny happen there lately?"

"Nope."

His eyes darted to the left, then to the right, and Rafferty knew he was lying.

"No kills this close to the Harvest, you know."

"Do I look like I was born yesterday?"

"Just wanted to make sure you didn't forget the rules."

"Was always a stupid rule, anyway."

"It's designed to make sure none of the Outsiders get suspicious. You know, I smelled something funny in the garage."

Jimbo spat over the porch railing. "Let's quit the dance, Ed."

"There *was* a kill, wasn't there?" Rafferty said.

"Yeah."

Rafferty felt his heart pump harder. He could feel his anger starting to rise, and if he didn't try and relax a little right now, he might splatter the old coot's nose across his face. "You killed someone?"

"No, Carl did."

"Did you feed on him?"

"Yeah."

"You stupid bastard."

Rafferty gritted his teeth. Jimbo clenched and unclenched his fists, as if he were preparing to spring. Rafferty was angry enough to slam Jimbo back into the apartment and thrash him, teach him a lesson. But he had to be careful. Jimbo was old, but he was also crafty and vicious.

"Carl needs to be punished. I need to make an example of someone."

"Why not me?"

"You might be next if you're not careful."

"Carl told me something when we were standing over the body," Jimbo said.

"And?"

Jimbo folded his arms. "He said I shouldn't put up with your crap no more. He said maybe *I* should lead the Harvest."

"You're old, Jimbo."

"I've made more kills than you ever will."

"But I killed Worthy. He was the last clan leader, so that makes me top dog. If you think you can beat me, go ahead and try. You don't have it in you."

Jimbo's eyes narrowed, bringing out the crow's feet around his eyes. He ran his tongue over his cracked lips. The old goat appeared to be sizing him up.

"I think I will, Ed."

"What?"

Jimbo's hand whipped from his side, claws revealed. Rafferty jerked his head back, lost his balance and tumbled backward. He spun and landed facedown, his nightstick jabbing him in the gut, popping the air out of his lungs.

Jimbo stood in the door grinning, his teeth the color of an old taxicab. "Forgot I could do that, huh, Ed? One of the benefits of being old. Pretty good trick, huh?"

Rafferty stood up and immediately doubled over, sucking air in big gasps, his diaphragm refusing to work. After a few seconds, he grabbed a gulp of air, thinking that if he hadn't jerked away, he would be minus most of his face.

Jimbo slammed the door, and from behind it, Rafferty heard him pounding through the house.

Donna went to the broken window. She grabbed the windowsill, pulling with all of her strength. A piece of concrete came loose and she hit the floor, landing on her back.

She heard the thing as it reached the bottom of the stairs. Its rank odor permeated the basement.

She got up and gripped the sill again. The creature took two strides and yanked her down to the floor. Her shirt ripped and she landed near the workbench. Something hard and narrow jabbed into her back and she smelled gasoline fumes.

She looked down to see the gasoline can on its side. The nozzle had poked her in the back. Cold fabric pressed against her back. It had soaked the back of her shirt.

Rising to her feet, she saw the creature ready to pounce, back on its haunches like a big cat. It leapt at her with ferocious speed and pinned her to the ground. She felt the cold concrete through her shirt.

The raw, sulfurous smell from the creature stung her eyes. Thick saliva dribbled in a runner down its chin.

The beast straddled her, then lowered its huge head and sniffed at her neck. Her lungs felt like compressed footballs. But it hadn't pinned her arms.

My arms are free. Time to do some damage, she thought.

She wanted to find something to hurt it with, but what? She turned her head left, then right, hoping for something on the floor. There! A black-handled screwdriver near Bob's bench.

She had to fight it, or she'd be seeing Dominic in the land of clouds and angels a lot sooner than she planned. She was probably doomed, but she could at least give the thing a battle before it killed her.

It reached back and dragged its claw up her thigh. She felt a burning sensation and heard the fabric pop. Then the sting of her skin being opened. She guessed it planned on cutting her to pieces, maybe seeing how many agonies she could bear before those teeth clamped down on her throat.

She stretched and got her fingertips on the screwdriver's handle. She pawed at it and it rolled toward her and she slapped her palm down on the handle.

It lowered its head and now its face was a few feet from hers. Yellowish fluid pooled in its nostrils.

She swung her arm in an arc and drove the screwdriver into its left eye, turning the eyeball into jelly. Before letting go of it, she twisted the handle, hoping that she hit the brain.

The creature reared back, clawing at the screwdriver, chattering and screeching.

She rolled to her feet, spotting the gas can as she rose. Picking up the can, she unscrewed the spout and splashed gasoline on the creature. The fluid ran down its legs and gathered at its feet.

It pulled the screwdriver from its eye, the lid closed over the ruined socket.

It snapped the screwdriver in half and flung it. Then it looked down at itself and sniffed, detecting the gasoline bath Donna had given it. It looked at her with bubbling fury in its good eye, aware of Donna's intentions.

She picked up the box of blue tip matches. Opening the box, she took one out. Its soft glow provided minimal light in the dark basement.

It swiped at her and she ducked. Its blow connected with the top of the workbench, splintering the wood and scattering tools across the floor.

She struck the match against the box, praying she wouldn't wind up lighting herself up like a road flare. Blue flame rose from the tip.

Before she could toss the match at the creature, it raked her forearm with its claw, slicing her open. God, but that hurt! The match tumbled to the floor. It hit the puddle of gasoline on the floor and a curtain of flame erupted from the concrete.

Fire raced up the creature's legs and it flung itself

against the wall, as if trying to separate the flames from its body.

Now was her chance, maybe the only one. She ran around it, getting out of the way just as the fire climbed up the workbench.

Scrambling up the stairs, hoping she wouldn't pass out, she hurried through the kitchen.

She heard the thuds coming up the basement stairs and smelled the thing's skin cooking, a mixture of spoiled meat and sewer gas that made her stomach lurch.

She reached the front door in the foyer, flipped the dead bolt and pulled it open. Goddamned police tape. She clawed through the tape and it fell to the floor like giant limp noodles. A siren screamed from down the block. Good, here comes the cavalry. God knew she needed it right now, even if it happened to be Rafferty.

She turned the screen door knob and flung it open.

The flaming horror caught up to her and drove its fist into her lower back. It felt like a two-by-four to the kidneys.

She flew forward, palms scraping the wood on the front porch. Fresh pain traveled up her wounded arm.

It busted through the screen door and the door flew to the right and hung on a remaining hinge like a marionette on a string.

This would be the end. She was sure of it.

The blood leaked from her arm, making her head feel muddy. She looked up and the treetops spun.

Her ears split again as the cop cars pulled up. She could tell by the sounds of the sirens they were prowl cars.

A blast from a big gun. A .357?

Darkness.

* * *

Jill stood in front of the mirror, brushing the snarls out of her hair.

The air felt thick enough to slide down your throat and choke you. She had the window open, but it provided no breeze to cool the room. Occasionally a car whizzed past or a group of kids strolled by, hooting and hollering, but no breeze came.

The lamp on the nightstand provided a murky cone of light. She made a mental note to get a bigger, brighter lamp. The lack of light and the oppressive heat made the room seem smaller, confining. Almost claustrophobic.

Maybe she would invest in an air conditioner if she got some money saved.

When she finished brushing her hair, she set the brush down and picked up a tube of rose lotion from Bath and Body Works. It was her favorite scent, and she rubbed it on her hands, arms and legs, enjoying its coolness.

She had wiped the mascara from her face that had run in rivulets down her cheeks. After asking Matt to leave, she broke into a crying fit, and the force of her sobs scared her. She hardly knew Matt, and yet she liked him a lot.

Her sobbing had come when she thought of the lousy luck she had with men in the past four or five years.

The guys she had dated had mostly been after one thing. Their eyes would glaze over when she tried talking about history, current events or books. They would steal glances at her breasts or her legs, paying little attention, waiting only for their turn to talk. A guy she had dated twice tried slipping his hand up her skirt on their second date. They were in the middle of a General Cinema movie theater at the time.

When she got up and stormed out, he had followed her, ham-handedly trying to apologize for his advances.

She slapped his face and told him to perform a certain sex act on himself.

There had been other dates, other guys, and then Jerry. By the time they had broken up, she began to believe all the good men were taken. And then there was the incident in the warehouse and Matt had come dashing in to save her.

Maybe she wanted to believe that it had been fate, or a sign this was the man she would be with. It wouldn't hurt if she got to know him better.

But then the stories started, stories about monsters and hidden beasts living in Lincoln, all seeming to crazy to believe if not for the small kernel of truth that stuck in her mind. She had seen something in that warehouse, despite all her attempts to deny it.

The memories of the smell on Dorothy Gaines and Rafferty's creepy behavior floated into her head and she told herself to shut up.

The inner voice, possibly the voice of reason, the voice that for most people spoke the truth, kept butting into her thoughts. *They're real, Jill. Matt's right.*

Why couldn't she get Matt Crowe out of her head if she wanted him gone?

A bead of sweat dribbled down her forehead. That was it. Too hot for clothes. She stripped, ripped the blankets off the bed, flopped down and turned off the light.

She would call Matt tomorrow and tell him they should go their separate ways. She would thank him for helping her, and that would be it.

If she plunged herself into her work, she would forget about him and another man would come along. One that didn't believe in bogeymen.

CHAPTER 17

Carla Reese dragged the pack of Wrigley's gum across the scanner plate and the register beeped. "That be all?"

"How much for you?"

The customer, a teenage kid, maybe seventeen, leaned across the counter. Carla had never seen him before, even though he appeared to be around the same age as her. His shoulder-length hair was parted in the middle, brown and fluffy, as if he had spent a lot of time blow-drying it. He had on a faded denim jacket and bleached jeans.

The jacket had patches with the names of heavy metal groups sewn on them. She could make out a few of them: Metallica, Slayer, and Judas Priest. He was a throwback to the eighties, a headbanger. A species believed to be extinct.

"Excuse me?" she said.

"How much for you, sweetie? Are you for sale?"

"That'll be twenty-seven cents."

"For the gum?"

"Right."

He dug in his pocket, pulled out a crumpled dollar bill, and threw it on the counter. She picked it up and unrolled it, not liking the sweaty feel of the paper.

"What time you get off?"

"None of your business."

She punched the amount into the register and the drawer popped open, bumping her in the groin. She frowned. That drawer always opened a little fast and normally she stood to the side so it wouldn't catch her in the crotch. But the jerk had distracted her.

"If you don't tell me, I can wait outside for a while. I got all night."

"I'm off at midnight."

That was a lie. In ten minutes it would be ten o'clock, and her shift at Wilson Farms would be over. They were open twenty-four hours and she expected her replacement, Liz Chaney, any minute.

"I'll come back at midnight. To see you."

She left his change on the counter, not wanting to touch his hand. He pressed the change against the counter with his palm and dragged it. The scraping noise made her hair stand on end.

"Me and my friends'll be waiting," he said.

He stuffed the change in his front pocket and bounced out of the store.

What an asshole.

She was used to being hit on by guys, but never by somebody that forward. What did it mean when he said him and his friends would be waiting for her?

Last year she nearly made the cover of *Seventeen*, and her mother was talking with some big-time talent agent in New York named Barry Barker. Carla was custom-built for modeling. Five-eleven, weighed one hundred fifteen; and according to the photographer at *Seventeen*, she had better cheekbones than Kate Moss. Thus she became the target of horny teenage boys.

She thought about calling Ronnie at Home Depot to come pick her up, but he wasn't off work for another hour, and she had her own car at the store. Besides, the kid who came in the store was probably long gone by now. Maybe he was just trying to rattle her, or maybe one of his buddies had dared him to come in and hit on her. It would be better if Ronnie didn't find out some-one was hitting on her, for there would be a fight if he did.

She wondered if all that weightlifting he did for foot-ball made him aggressive.

The clock read five minutes to ten.

Liz Chaney walked through the door, her brown apron draped over one arm.

"Hey Liz," Carla said.

"Hey."

"Did you see anyone out there?"

"Outside the store?"

"Yeah."

"No, why?"

"Some jerk was in here hitting on me. He said he'd be waiting for me when I got off work."

"Must be nice to get that kind of attention."

Liz wore Coke-bottle glasses with flaming pink frames. She also had a face full of throbbing acne. Carla didn't know much about her outside of work, but she didn't think Liz went on many dates.

"It was no big thrill. He was a real loser."

"I have to take what I can get."

Carla smiled awkwardly.

Liz walked down the cereal aisle and disappeared through the silver double doors at the back of the store. She came out a moment later, hands behind her back, tying her apron string.

Carla punched in her cashier number, signing off

the register. When Liz got to the counter, she would punch in her own number and take over.

Removing her apron, Carla brushed past Liz on her way to the back room.

"Have fun on your date."

"He's probably not even out there." She hoped.

She went through the double doors near the coolers, unlocked her locker and took out her purse. Stuffing the apron in the locker, she closed it and clicked the padlock in place.

She paused at the door, scanning the parking lot for any sign of her admirers. Her Firebird and Liz's Taurus were the only cars in the lot. An elderly man in a madras shirt talked on the pay phone at the edge of the parking lot.

The coast looked clear, but her heart rate sped up just the same. She hurried to her car.

Carla's keys slipped from her hand and jingled on the pavement. Her palms were slick with sweat.

She bent down, picked them up, and unlocked the car door.

"Hey sweetheart."

She turned around and saw the guy from the store standing ten feet from her. There were two other people with him, the friends he mentioned in the store, she guessed.

The guy to the left of him had a ponytail, though the sides of his head were shaved. He had a narrow, ferrety face and held a black boom box in his right hand. The other one was a girl, maybe fifteen. She had on a black crop top that showed off a pale, round belly. The crop top was complemented by a denim miniskirt that appeared to be groaning from stress being placed on it.

Carla eyed all three of them. "Piss off."

She flung open the car door, hoping to climb in quickly

and speed away. Her nail chipped and broke on the door handle.

The leader of the group grabbed her by her left arm.

She gasped and tried to pull away, but his nails dug in tight.

"Look down."

Six inches of chrome flicked open. He had his back to the store window so the knife would be out of sight.

She glanced over to the phone booth, hoping the elderly man was still there, but he was gone.

Frantic, she looked to the store window, but Liz was out of sight.

"Your friend ain't there. And if you scream, I'll stick you. Try me if you think I won't."

The other two closed in on her.

"Get in the car. You're taking us for a ride. Cooperate with me and you'll be okay."

She wanted to believe that, but she couldn't. She was positive her body would be found in a ditch or an abandoned warehouse.

She jerked her arm, trying to free herself. He poked her in the thigh with the tip of the knife, and a dot of blood stained her khakis.

"Get in. Now," he said through clenched teeth, and she noticed they seemed odd. Canine. Fang-like. God, he stank too!

She crouched into the car, the knifepoint in her ribs.

"Get in with her."

The girl and the guy with the shaved head went around to the passenger side. The one with the knife told Carla to unlock the door and she did. The other two climbed into the backseat.

"Take it, Rick. Keep it on her."

He handed the blade to the guy with the shaved head, who held it to her throat as she got into the car.

The leader climbed into the passenger seat.

Carla burst into tears. If only she had called Ronnie!

Matt turned on the radio; Billy Corgan and the Smashing Pumpkins were singing about the world being a vampire. Even at this time of night, Matt switched on the air-conditioning. The dashboard lights glowed luminescent green, providing the only illumination in the truck's cab.

He couldn't understand why Jill was hesitant to believe his story. After all, they had been chased by one of Them in the warehouse. And she had been the one who wanted to meet and talk about it, so that made it all the more puzzling.

Granted, it sounded crazy. Monsters living under human skin and hunting people for food. Had he not witnessed them firsthand, he wouldn't have believed the story either.

He pulled the truck into his aunt's garage and got out. Tucking his speeding ticket in his back pocket, he climbed to the loft, and once inside, turned on the light.

His suitcase lay on the floor, open. A green T-shirt hung over the side.

It reminded him of all the places he had been in the last ten years. And how he had run from the problems with his uncle and kept on running. He initially ran away because he didn't want to deal with Uncle Rex anymore, but once he was on the road, he began to search for the creatures. Each time he heard about a strange murder or disappearance, he would travel to that city or town to investigate.

That type of lifestyle wasn't conducive to building a relationship with a woman. There had been some here and there; Monica in San Francisco was one of the better ones.

They had been together three months when he left. He had jotted a note on a piece of legal paper and left it on her kitchen table. It was cowardly, and he knew it.

He told her about his nightmares, but instead of the monsters, he lied and told her it was escaped convicts that murdered his family. He had walked out on her after seeing a news report about a Boy Scout troop in Seattle that spotted a strange creature in the woods.

After that, he spent most nights in hotel rooms, eating take-out Mexican or burgers, watching pay-per-view until falling into fitful sleep. And playing back that day in Emerling Park in his mind. Over and over and over.

For the first few months after they died, he fully expected them to pull up in the Bronco and take him home. He had even caught himself glancing out Aunt Bernie's picture window, watching. He gave up on that idea after a while, as he did on the idea of settling in one town and being at peace.

But why should he give up on Jill? He'd been running too long, pushing people away, putting up that proverbial brick wall around himself and not letting anybody in. And if you did that for too long, you could go nuts, become one of those guys who climbs a clock tower with a high-powered rifle.

There had to be a way to convince her.

First he would call Harry, the gun store owner, and see if dinner was still on. He took the folded piece of paper with Harry's number written on it off the nightstand.

He dialed the number and a woman answered.

"Is Harry there?"

"Who're you?"

"Matt Crowe. I met him at his store the other day."

A pause.

"Hang on."

He listened as she set the phone down and yelled for Harry.

"Hello, Matt."

"Hope I didn't disturb you. Your wife sounded upset."

"That's just her usual pleasant demeanor shining through."

"Dinner still on?"

"Yep. You still bringing a guest?"

"Maybe."

Matt heard a musical tone ring in the background. "Hang on a second, Matt, it's my cell."

Matt heard Harry mumbling in the background but couldn't make out the words. A moment later, he came back on the line.

"That was Donny Frank, buddy of mine," Harry said. "They found a body."

Matt felt the hairs on his neck prickle. His first thought was that the secret residents of Lincoln had struck.

"Where?"

"Griffith Park."

"Are you thinking what I'm thinking?"

"Exactly. I'll pick you up. Where you live?"

Matt paused for a moment, wondering if he could trust Harry, if he should just go off riding with him. Why not? He was a big boy, capable of handling himself if Harry gave him trouble.

Matt gave him directions.

He hung up and went down to the truck. It occurred to him that he might want the shotgun in case there were any of them still around. But there was nowhere to conceal it. Plus there would be a ton of cops around, and a loaded twelve-gauge might not get him invited to the policemen's ball.

"Hell with it," he said.

Harry pulled up five minutes later in a cream-colored Lincoln Town Car. He was surprised at the vehicle, taking Harry for a truck guy all the way.

Matt climbed in the car. "Nice wheels," he said.

"I wanted a truck. One of those Ford Expeditions. The big sumbitches. But the wife outvoted me."

From hearing his wife's voice on the phone, Matt had a feeling Harry got outvoted a lot.

Rafferty pulled his Magnum and ducked through the door, fully expecting Jimbo to be waiting for him. But Jimbo was gone.

The television set threw off a bluish-white glow, the only light in the room. A metal oscillating fan whirred, scattering papers. Rafferty swept his gun back and forth across the room. Jimbo could be crouched in a corner in the dark, ready to pounce on him.

Satisfied that the room was clear, Rafferty stripped off his clothes and tossed them on the floor.

He would be vulnerable while changing into his true form, but if he wanted to kill Jimbo, it was his best chance. He could do more damage with claws and teeth than with any gun.

Rafferty willed the change to come, his human skin replaced by a rough, leathery hide. He grew seven inches, bringing his height to seven feet. His muscles expanded and bulged, bringing his weight to over three hundred pounds.

It took minutes for him to become a beast. When the change was complete, he made a fist and punched a hole in the living room wall. Plaster dust puffed and chips spattered on the rug.

He howled, a low guttural sound starting in his chest

and rising to a shriek. A neighborhood dog answered him.

Rafferty didn't care who heard him. He wanted Jimbo to be shaking right about now.

The hunt began with the scent. He tilted his head back and sniffed. He smelled spoiled meat, sweat, oil, hops and barley from the beer bottle on the floor.

He ducked his head and entered the dining room. In this form, his night vision was poor. He flipped on the light switch in the dining room and a cockroach danced across the dining room table. He sniffed again, able to smell the bug, and if the bug had taken a crap, he could've smelled that too.

Jimbo was above him. The scent came through the ceiling.

Rafferty found the stairs and climbed them. At the end of a narrow hallway was an open door.

Blackness beckoned him from beyond the door. Jimbo had surely left it open as an invite for him to climb the attic stairs.

He stuck his head into the open doorway. Dark in here. He flipped the switch, but no light came. Had his enemy unscrewed the bulb?

He sniffed. The scent of the hunted grew stronger and along with it the smells of dust, old leather and mothballs.

The first attic step groaned as he put his weight on it.

Movement came from above.

He retreated as a heavy object slammed into the stairs from above, splintering wood. He picked it up, palming it in one hand. A bowling ball his adversary had dropped from over the railing.

It wasn't enough to even scratch him, and Jimbo knew that. He was just messing with Rafferty, trying to rattle him.

I'll rattle you.

He took the stairs in three strides, attempting to reach the top before Jimbo could hurl another object at him.

There couldn't be many places left for him to hide, even among the junk. Stacks of boxes littered the attic, along with a rusted red bicycle, a copper floor lamp and an old army cot.

Rafferty proceeded to the far end of the attic, creeping down the narrow aisle between the boxes and past the chimney. The scent grew stronger.

The boxes to his right came crashing down and he deflected them with his arm.

Jimbo in his true form leapt at Rafferty, claws outstretched and ready to kill.

He backed Rafferty up, pushing against his chest and bashing him into the wall. He jabbed at Rafferty's throat, but Rafferty got his arm in the way and smacked the clawed hand away.

Jimbo tried to bite next, opening his jaws and cocking his head at an angle, trying to get under Rafferty's chin and bite the soft flesh at the throat. Rafferty slammed his forehead into Jimbo's face before the old bastard could bite him, and it snapped Jimbo's head back.

Rafferty clubbed him across the face with his forearm; Jimbo staggered, but did not fall. Jimbo rushed him again, leaping at Rafferty, but Rafferty let himself fall backward, and Jimbo sailed over him and slammed into the chimney.

Wobbly and looking drunk, Jimbo tried to stand, but Rafferty, having the killer instinct of a big cat, pounced, pinning him to the ground.

Jimbo raised his arm to protect himself, but Rafferty slapped it away.

He bit into Jimbo's throat and ripped out a hunk of

flesh. Then he bit again, hard, right through to the spine, snapping it and killing his adversary.

It was good to be king.

Harry pulled the Town Car into a small lot that divided the park in half. The lot also served the community center, a small brick building located near the picnic shelters. Matt saw an ambulance and a police cruiser parked on the grass near a picnic shelter. Sirens flashed and strobed across the shelter roof.

A group of teenage boys, some of them with skateboards tucked under their arms, had gathered near the shelter. *Didn't these kids have a curfew?*

Harry pulled into a space and put the Town Car in park. He shut off the engine, reached across Matt and opened the glove compartment.

"Excuse me. This don't mean we're dating."

He took out a little .22 and a clip. He jammed the clip home, untucked his shirt and sucked in his belly. Tucking the gun into his pants, he opened the car door.

"That gun goes off, you won't be having *any* dates," Matt commented.

"No one likes a wiseass, you know."

They walked toward the picnic shelter, Harry strolling casually, Matt with his hands in his pockets.

"You think that twenty-two'll be any good against one of Them?"

Harry looked thoughtful for a moment.

"Probably not. But it makes me feel better."

CHAPTER 18

A thud. The ambulance door shutting?

Donna saw faces through a haze. It was like looking up at someone from the bottom of a pool. They shimmered.

She felt weak, her head throbbing, and she vaguely remembered her head slamming against the porch deck. Her arms and legs trembled, her stomach swirled and her back felt as if someone had taken a sledgehammer to it.

The siren howled and the ambulance began to move. The faces became blurred and faded out.

She was on an elevator. The floor light indicators flashed ten, eleven, twelve. It stopped on twelve and a pretty blonde in hospital scrubs stepped into the elevator.

"Thirteen, please," the woman said, smiling at Donna.

The elevator stopped at thirteen and the woman in the scrubs stepped off the elevator. She looked over her shoulder at Donna.

"You're going to be surprised. He's doing so well."

She knew the hospital was Buffalo General, for she recognized the sandy carpet in the elevator. That, and the button for the ninth floor was missing. She had always taken this elevator when . . .

When she came to see Dominic.

The elevator stopped at the fourteenth floor (she couldn't recall pressing any buttons). She got off and made a right, then a left. Dominic's room had been 1420. The hallway seemed longer than it used to, as if it would take hours to reach the end. The halls were empty save for a laundry cart and a lonely IV stand.

She entered Dominic's room to find the bed made, the sheets crisp and white. There was a note on the pillow, written on yellow steno paper and folded horizontally.

It read "Sweet Thang" on the front. Dominic had called her that whenever he knew she was mad and he was in trouble. It usually managed to get a smile out of her, even when she was so mad she could have strangled him.

She unfolded the note.

Look behind you.

She turned around and stood face-to-face with Dominic Ricci.

"My God. You look great, Dom."

"Thanks."

He looked healthy, his skin a glowing olive color, his hair shiny. The strong jaw was there, the deep brown eyes, the smile that had slain her the first time he had flashed it. Nothing like the Dominic who had weighed eighty pounds when he died. Before cancer claimed him, Dominic's skin had been waxy and stretched over the bones. His cheekbones flared out, like they might pop through the skin. He had been too weak to have his hair washed, and the lush head of hair he once had became stringy and greasy.

But here was the old Dominic, untouched by disease.

"Hey, sweet thang."

"Where are we?"

"I'm dead. Where are you?"

"But your face, your appearance. The cancer's gone, right?"

"It's never gone, sweet thang. Ask anyone who's had it. It stays with you, even when they tell you it's gone. In your mind, sweet thang."

Dominic only called her "sweet thang" when she was mad or when he was trying to jolly her out of a bad mood. His use of it started to bother her, because this wasn't like the old Dominic.

"Am I dead too?"

"No. Not yet. Do you burn?"

"Do I burn?"

When she had first seen him, she wanted to throw her arms around him and squeeze, cover his face with kisses. Now she wanted to be away from him. He was acting weird, not like the man she knew.

"It's coming back, sweet thang."

"Stop calling me that."

"The rot's coming back."

The skin near the corner of his eye became brown and bumpy. The patch of brown started spreading, becoming darker and turning black. It made its way down his cheekbone in a tributary until it reached the corner of his mouth. It was like watching time-lapse photography. The side of his face looked like a rotten banana in a matter of seconds.

He took a step toward Donna. She backed up.

Dominic brought his hand to his face and poked a hole in the rotting skin with his index finger. He hooked the flesh and pulled, his cheek ripping.

Donna backed up farther, stumbling onto the hospital bed.

His eye was visible in the socket. His cheekbone gleamed and maggots squirmed from the open ruin that was his face.

Donna heard herself yelp, an involuntary sound.

Dominic came closer.

"Get the hell away from me!"

The floor near her feet exploded open, sending pieces of tile ricocheting off the walls. She looked down to see flames burst *out of the hole. They licked at her pants, raced up her leg. Her legs and lower back were on fire.*

A clawed hand reached out of the hole, gripping her flaming pant leg. It dragged her down. She reached for the sheets on the bed, trying to keep herself from being pulled into the pit. The flames scorched her as it took her down into the fiery hole.

The thing that had been her dead husband put his hand over her face and pushed her down into the hole. His hand felt like a rubber glove filled with ice cubes. She felt herself draining, slipping away. She closed her eyes, the glow of the flames visible through her eyelids.

She opened her eyes again. The overhead light hurt, and she squinted.

The paramedic popped his head back into view, fuzzy at first and then clearer. His head was shaved bald, and a Fu Manchu mustache covered his upper lip and grew down the sides of his mouth like some crazy shrubbery.

"Hang in there. We're almost at the hospital."

The siren cut out and the ambulance slowed. As the paramedic opened the rear door, the world spun and she passed out into oblivion once again.

Matt and Harry brushed past the teenagers. The cops had wrapped police tape around the shelter's support beams. A sheet-covered corpse lay on the picnic table. Whoever covered it had done a sloppy job, because a hand with lavender-painted nails hung limply over the side of the table.

A police officer, a lanky guy with a comb-over, shouted at the crowd to disperse. Nobody moved.

"Wonder where the medical examiner is?" Matt said.

"Maybe he's on his way."

Matt noticed with distaste that blood had seeped

through the cracks of the picnic table and pooled on the concrete pad.

"Looks like quite a bit of blood," he said.

"Sheet's soaked with it," Harry agreed.

The ambulance crew stood in front of their rig, gurney at the ready. One of them had a big duffel bag with a white cross on the side of it draped over his shoulder.

Medical supplies, no doubt, although they wouldn't need them. The victim was long dead.

The two paramedics looked confused. They both kept looking around, perhaps waiting for the medical examiner to arrive on the scene. The whole thing looked awfully loose and sloppy. No other officers on the scene, no medical examiner, nobody being questioned as to what they saw.

Somebody called the police, and yet it didn't look like a report was being taken.

"I heard the cop tell the ambulance crew it looked like there were bite marks on the body," someone said from behind Matt.

Matt turned around to see where the voice came from. Its owner was a pudgy kid, maybe seventeen. His belly hung over the waist of his cargo shorts.

"What did you say?"

"About what?"

"Bite marks."

"Oh. The girl told the officer and the officer told the medics that it looked like there were bite marks on the body."

"What girl?"

"The girl who found the body."

"Where is she?"

"Over there. By the police car," he said, pointing to the cruiser.

"Thanks. Harry . . ."

"Here comes the cavalry."

Another police cruiser pulled up onto the grass, its siren blaring.

"The kid behind us told me there were bite marks on the body," Matt said.

"Did he see them?"

"No. The girl who found the body told the cop that."

"Where's the girl?"

Matt stood on his tiptoes to look over the crowd. He saw a blond girl of about fourteen leaning against the car. She wiped tears from her face with her shirt.

He wanted to find out what she'd seen. The cops would be busy with the crowd and the crime scene, so Matt had an idea.

"Let's go talk to her," he said.

"And the cops?"

"They're preoccupied. She'll give us the best information."

The red-haired cop who'd pulled up in the cruiser hitched his belt and approached the ambulance crew. After a word with them, the crew got in the ambulance, backed it up and drove away. That was weird. How were they planning on getting the body to the morgue?

The red-haired cop approached the balding cop at the shelter.

"Now's our chance." Matt tugged at Harry's sleeve and they walked over to the girl.

Matt and Harry approached the girl. She leaned against the rear of the police car, arms folded across her chest. Mascara ran down her cheeks, and even in the dark Matt could make out the redness in her eyes. Her bottom lip quivered.

Matt wished he had a tissue to offer the kid.

She had on a pink T-shirt cut so that her navel showed. A pair of in-line skates lay on the ground at her feet. She had a thousand-yard stare going, her big blue eyes looking right through Matt and Harry.

He felt like a shit heel for what he was about to do, but he had to know about the wounds on the body. "Can we talk to you?"

Matt waited a few seconds and asked her again.

She snapped out of it, her head twitching like a person coming out of a bad dream.

"Who're you?"

"Detectives Rand and Wilks. Lincoln Police."

"Oh," she said.

Matt wanted to breathe a sigh of relief. If the girl hadn't been in a state of shock, she might not have bought the fact that they were detectives. She might see that neither one of them had a badge clipped to their belts.

"What's your name?" Matt asked.

"Sally Perski."

"Where were you headed when you found the body?"

"Home. I was going home from my friend Laura's house."

"Did you see or hear anyone? Was there a struggle?"

"Yeah. Three of them. Lights started coming on in the houses and they ran. Then there were sirens."

"Did you get a good look at anyone?" Harry said.

"They were big, I remember that. And . . . That was it, just big."

Matt sensed she wanted to say something else. "And what? You were going to say something else, Sally."

"You'll think I'm weird."

"Try me."

She looked back and forth from Matt to Harry, maybe trying to gauge if she could trust them.

"They looked like animals. Only they walked on two legs."

She sniffled and wiped her nose with the back of her hand.

"Where did they go?" Matt asked.

She pointed to the six-foot chain-link fence that separated the houses from the park. "They jumped the fence and ran through that yard." Sally craned her neck to look past Matt. "Where's you guys' car? I didn't see you pull up."

Harry broke in quickly. "We're plainclothes, honey. Our car's unmarked."

She might be coming out of the shock, Matt thought, ready to notice that their impression of detectives was not exactly Dennis Franz quality. They might only get in a few more questions before she realized they weren't cops. Speaking of which, Matt glanced over to the real ones at the shelter.

The balding one was taking names on a notepad, and the red-haired one was busy peering under the sheet. He stepped right in the pool of blood on the concrete. Matt didn't know much about crime scene investigation, but he did know that the cardinal rule was don't touch anything. The redhead was butchering the scene.

Harry said, prompting the girl, "So these people ran. Then what happened?"

"I went to see if I could help the person under the shelter. The one they attacked. And . . ."

Sally's lip quivered and she put her hand over her mouth, as if to hide her shame from Matt and Harry. Fresh tears welled in her eyes. Matt admired the hell out of the kid. A woman was being assaulted, and the attackers were still in the vicinity, but instead of running, she'd tried to help. In a day where so many people had a "don't get involved" mentality, the girl tried to help, and that took guts. Matt wanted to give her a hug and tell her she would be all right, even though she probably wouldn't. The corpse would appear in her nightmares for years to come.

"I know this is hard, honey. But we need your help if we're going to catch these people," Harry said. He put a big hand on her shoulder, a decidedly fatherly gesture.

She wiped the tears from her cheeks and took a deep breath. "Her body was all bit up. And her throat was sliced. There was a lot of blood."

"You're sure there were bites?" Matt said.

"Yeah. It looked like chunks were missing. Poor Carla."

"Carla? You know her?"

"Carla Reese. She went to Millard Fillmore."

The balding cop approached. His red-haired counterpart was shooing the crowd away.

Matt wondered if any of them would have helped Carla Reese as she was being torn to pieces. Maybe or maybe not. But they were plenty glad to stop and try to get a peek at her mutilated corpse. God, people were morbid.

"Thanks, honey. You take care," Harry said.

"The officers will take you home. Let's go, Detective," Matt said.

They hurried back to the Town Car, Matt wondering if there would be more attacks. And how would Lincoln's finest handle this case?

He also worried about the girl. When Rafferty questioned him about what he saw the day his family was killed, he put the fear of the devil in Matt. Would he try and scare Sally Perski too?

"I wanna check on that girl tomorrow, Harry. I don't trust that son of a bitch Rafferty."

"You think she'll be all right for tonight?"

"He won't risk another murder. I have a feeling they'll try and cover this one up. Like another murder I know about."

"Get her address and stop by the house tomorrow."

As they walked away, Matt saw the girl duck her head and get into the back of the cop car. He was pretty sure he heard the cop say, "What detectives?"

Matt and Harry parked next to the Lincoln Community Center, a one-story brick building that was formerly an elementary school. Grubby bushes surrounded the building, stopping just below the first-floor windows. To one side of the building was a wooden playground set with bridges and tunnels and slides. They had a good view of the crime scene. Matt guessed a hundred feet from the shelter. Hopefully not close enough to draw attention.

The car windows were down; a mosquito whined and landed on Matt's arm, tickling him with spindly legs. He smacked it, leaving smeared blood on his arm. "Damn bugs."

Harry looked at him and laughed. "You would've lasted about five minutes in Vietnam. Mosquitoes the size of hummingbirds over there."

"You were in 'Nam?"

"Got a Purple Heart too. Took shrapnel in the ass for Uncle Sam. Show it to you some time."

"No offense, but I have no desire to see your bare ass."

"I meant the Purple Heart, wise guy."

The red-haired cop remained at the shelter. The crowd of onlookers had departed, and now the cop paced back and forth, agitated.

"What do you suppose he's waiting for?" Matt whispered.

"Your guess is as good as mine."

They got their answer when a white van pulled into the parking area, swung around, and backed up to the picnic shelter.

Two men got out, one from the driver's side and one from the passenger side. The back doors flew open and another pair of men jumped out. They had on coveralls, either blue or black, with no markings. Matt found that strange, because if they were police or worked in some other official capacity, they would've had some kind of identification on their clothes.

The men who had been in the back of the van took out an old army-type stretcher, the kind used for taking wounded off the battlefield, and set it on the tabletop next to the body. Then one of them got the corpse's feet, while the other grabbed the shoulders. They flopped her on the stretcher; one arm poked out from underneath the sheet. The man at the body's feet stuck it back under the sheet.

The sheet glowed phosphorescent against the night and the darkened blood that soaked it. Luminescent.

Matt was not a religious man, but the sheet reminded him of an angel's robe. He hoped an angel had escorted the girl's soul to a better world, for she had met an awful fate in this one.

They lifted the stretcher with the body and slid it into the back of the van. The cop yelled at them to hurry up.

Once the body was in the van, one of the men took out a plastic bucket and ran to a waterspout near the picnic shelter. He filled the bucket and brought it back to the shelter. The other men brought two mops out from the van and they went to work mopping the concrete pad.

"They're trying to erase any sign of the murder. But why?" Matt said.

"To keep their fellow creatures hidden," Harry replied.

"We have to tell that girl's family what happened. The cops'll feed them a line of bullshit about what happened. I wish we could get this on videotape."

Matt heard the rumble of a big engine coming. A diesel.

A turquoise dump truck pulled into the parking area. He could make out LINCOLN D.P.W. painted on the door. Its backup alarm beeped as it neared the picnic shelter.

For a cover-up, they were making an awful lot of noise. Matt was surprised that none of the lights in the houses near the park came on, or that no one peered out the windows. Perhaps the people in the houses were also demons, fully aware of the events in the park. They would have no need to look, for it was a familiar scene taking place in front of them.

But what about the people who weren't creatures underneath? They probably knew better than to watch, aware that the men in the coveralls and the cops were not the good guys. They probably feared retaliation if they were caught spying.

The men set the bucket and mops back in the van and then all four of them picked up the picnic table, two to a side. They leaned it against the tailgate of the dump truck and tipped it into the bed with a hollow crash.

The cop took one last look at the concrete pad and then gave a thumbs up. The men in coveralls got into the van, and the cop jogged to his police cruiser.

The dump truck pulled out first, followed by the cop car and the van.

They had cleaned the site as if it were picnic trash instead of a human being they were dumping. Matt felt his stomach knot. "You believe this?"

"This town, anything's possible," Harry said.

* * *

Rafferty stepped out of the patrol car and slid his baton into his belt. Clarence stood at the picnic shelter, rubbing his hands together, as if trying to warm them. As Rafferty approached, he shifted his weight from foot to foot.

Clarence had radioed Rafferty on his way back from Jimbo's and told him there was a murder in the park. Rafferty told Clarence to meet him there pronto.

Now, Clarence waited for him like a ten-year-old boy who's broken a window and sees his father coming up the driveway. Rafferty stopped three feet from him.

"The boys took the body away?" Rafferty said.

"Yep."

"Witnesses?"

"There was a group of kids. I got their names."

"Others?"

"The ambulance crew."

"Our guys."

Clarence nodded. "Charles called them. He was the first one on the scene."

"Why didn't Linda call you?"

"Don't know."

Rafferty punched the wooden support post that held up the shelter's roof. All calls came right to Linda at the station, for Lincoln had no central dispatcher. She was supposed to call Rafferty, and if he wasn't around, Clarence. At least it didn't get out over the scanner.

The ones who murdered the girl must've gotten spooked or been stupid. Besides taking a victim before the Harvest, they violated the essential rules: make the kill in a remote location and consume the body fully. The murderers had left behind evidence, and Rafferty didn't want strangers poking their noses into his business. Evidence led to questions by Outsiders. Every murder like this meant having to go through a cover-up.

Each of them made on average one or two kills per year. Most went to neighboring towns and cities to make the kills, so as not to draw attention to Lincoln.

Rafferty knew what was happening; it was too close to the Harvest. The need to hunt and kill was welling up inside his fellow creatures like a geyser ready to gush. He was losing control of his followers.

"There was a little girl who found the body."

"Where is she?"

"I dropped her at the station house."

Rafferty hunkered down and examined the concrete pad that served as the shelter's floor. He took out his flashlight and shined it on the floor. The clean team had done a good job mopping up blood, for there was no visible evidence of a kill.

"Any idea who did it?"

"No. There were three of them according to the girl."

"Where'd they go?"

"Over that fence." Clarence pointed to the fence that separated the houses from the park.

"Something else. The girl said some detectives questioned her."

"Son of a bitch. What detectives?"

"I don't know. And the press was here too."

He felt like slamming Clarence up against one of the posts and knocking some sense into his skull. Where the hell would detectives come from? Lincoln didn't have a detective bureau, it was too small. The nearest city that did was Buffalo, and the Buffalo cops wouldn't have known about the murder.

Shit was getting worse by the moment.

"Things are going downhill. Jimbo killed someone at

the station. And I got into it with him tonight. He challenged me, tried to kill me."

"What happened?"

"I tore out the old bastard's throat."

Clarence's mouth opened in an O of surprise. "Jesus, Ed."

"Never mind that. Did they take the body?"

"They did. Got rid of the picnic table too."

"The crowd that was here, were they Outsiders?"

"There were a few."

"Give me the names. I want to talk to all of them."

Clarence pulled a sheet off of his notepad with a list of names written on it in blue ink.

"Things are getting out of control," he repeated. "It'll be hard to keep this up."

"There's more," the redhead warned.

"Now what?"

"Some woman cop got into it with one of ours in a house on Dorchester. The house burned down."

It was that little bitch Donna Ricci who had tried to grill him on the Barbieri murder. He knew it. "What happened to it?"

"Burned to death. One of the other boys put a few holes in it too."

"The body?"

"In the garage at the station house."

"Let's go see it. Where's the woman cop?"

"Lincoln Mercy."

"We'll see her too."

CHAPTER 19

Rafferty entered the squad room with Clarence behind him. He went to his desk and set his nightstick on the desk. "Where is the girl?"

"In the room," Clarence said.

Clarence leaned against his desk, arms folded across his chest, watching Rafferty, maybe expecting an explosion.

"What about the other item?"

"In the garage."

"Anybody see it?"

"Don't think so."

Rafferty turned to him; the fluorescent lighting beating on Clarence's face made him look pale and drawn, like a suspect under interrogator's lights. He hoped that's how Clarence felt, because he had fucked this one up but good.

Too many people got an eyeful of that girl's body in the park. He didn't know who he was angrier with—Clarence or the murderers. "You're sure no one saw it?"

He scratched his chin and tucked his arm back into the crossed position. "No one saw it."

"What about the other officer?"

"I sent him home from the park."

Rafferty half laughed and half snorted. "At least you did something right tonight."

Clarence looked down at his boots.

"I'm gonna talk to the girl, then I'm gonna look at that body."

Thumbs in his belt loops, he hitched up his pants and went through the door to the cell block. He opened the door to the interrogation room.

A blond girl of about fifteen sat on the chair, her knees drawn up to her chest, arms wrapped around her legs. She had bony knees and her collarbone jutted out underneath the skin. Someone should start feeding the kid.

He would start off playing the good guy.

"You cold, honey?"

"Yes."

"Clarence!"

Clarence poked his head in the doorway.

"Get this young lady a jacket."

"Right," Clarence said, and disappeared.

He returned with one of the winter coats from the storeroom. It was three-quarter length, midnight blue, with a fuzzy blue collar and lapel.

Rafferty took it from him and draped it over the girl's shoulders.

She wrapped it around herself and held it closed at the throat.

"So you saw something in the park? Something unpleasant."

"Yeah."

"Would you like some hot chocolate?"

"No."

Rafferty pulled out a chair and sat down, hands folded in front of him on the table, trying to appear the epitome of concentration. "Where were you going?"

"I already told this to the detectives. Do I have to tell it again?"

"What detectives?"

"The ones at the park."

"We don't have detectives here. The town's not big enough."

"If you say so."

"Do you remember their names?"

"Rand and Willis. No, Wilks! That's it."

She set her feet on the floor and sat up straight, nestling into the coat.

"Why don't you tell me what happened anyway."

She told him she was walking home from her friend Laura's house, where they had spent the past few hours in-line skating.

When she got near the shelter, she saw three large men crouched over a woman, who was lying on top of a picnic table. She was struggling, and Sally said the woman screamed.

"It sounded like an animal getting killed," she told Rafferty.

Lights had come on in the houses bordering the park, and the three men hopped the fence, ran through a yard and were gone, she told him.

"Then what happened?"

"I ran to see if I could help her, and . . ."

"And what?"

Tears rolled from her red-rimmed eyes. She wiped them on the sleeve of the jacket.

He was getting impatient. "Tell me!"

She recoiled from the force of his voice.

"It was Carla Reese, all bit up."

"Two questions. How did you know who she was, and how could you tell they were bite marks?

"She went to my school, Fillmore. And there were chunks taken out of her. Can I go now?"

"Not yet. Tell me more about these detectives."

She slipped the jacket off her shoulders and sat forward on the edge of the chair. She nudged the jacket and it slipped off the chair, rumpling on the floor. It was as if she didn't want it coming in contact with her skin any longer.

"One was a fat guy. He had on a flannel shirt."

"How old?"

"About fifty."

"And the other one?"

"Young. Dark brown hair. He was cute."

"I don't care about cute. How old?"

"About twenty-five."

His blood began to hum like motor oil through a V-8. Thrusting the chair away from the table, he stood up. The girl winced.

He turned his back to her and put his hands on his hips, the vein over his right eye pulsing and twitching, close to blowing his cool. If he didn't control himself, someone might be dead soon. The whole situation made his stomach churn and go sour.

First he had phony detectives poking around asking questions, and absolutely no idea who they were. Or worse, maybe they really *were* from Buffalo Homicide and had gotten word about the killing.

It was only a matter of time before people from the state or county came nosing around. He couldn't keep covering things up much longer.

He took a deep breath.

Facing the girl, he said, "Don't talk to anyone about what you saw. No reporters, no other police, no one except me. There's things about the murder only the killer would know, and we need to keep that private. Understand me?"

"Yeah."

"You'd fucking better."

His explanation about only the killer knowing certain details was bullshit, but she didn't know that. If it kept her quiet, then it was okay with him.

"Get up. I'll drop you off at home."

Rafferty returned to the station house afterward. Before Sally got out of the car, he told her again not to mention what she saw to anyone. Normally, he would've threatened violence, but there was enough trouble stirred up right now without some girl telling her parents the cops hassled her.

He walked into the station. The front of his shirt was moist with sweat, and he peeled fabric away from his chest.

Clarence sat at the deputy's desk hunched over, entranced in a game of solitaire.

He didn't look up as Rafferty approached the desk.

"Anyone else here?" Rafferty said.

"Nope."

"Good."

He grabbed Clarence by the hair, just above the crown of his scalp, yanked his head up and then smashed his face into the desktop. Cards flipped and scattered onto the floor.

Rafferty let go.

Covering his face with his hands, Clarence rolled away from the desk in the chair. He took his hands away from his face; rivulets of blood trickled from his nose and lower lip, which would be fatter than Dom De-Louise in no time.

"Jesus, Ed."

It came out "Jeethus, Ed."

"Don't act fucking surprised. You knew you had that coming."

"Could've at least given me a warning."

"What fun would that be?" Rafferty said.

Clarence pulled a white hanky from his back pocket and dabbed at the blood running from his nose.

"We're getting in deep, Clarence."

"Deeper than deep," Clarence agreed.

"I got dead people showing up all over my town. Killed by our own kind. Other things I can go after like a regular crime, but when one of us kills, it gets hard."

Clarence leaned back, his head over his knees, pinching his nostrils together with the handkerchief.

Rafferty almost never had to discipline Clarence, but he knew better than what he did tonight, and he had to be reminded that mistakes were costly. "I can't have you making mistakes like this. Got it?"

"You're right."

"I'll need your help."

"You got it. You know that."

Rafferty rubbed his chin. "Let's go look at the body."

They walked out into the garage. Next to a patrol car on the oil-spotted floor was a blanket with a clawed foot sticking out from underneath.

Rafferty went to the blanket, squatted down and pulled it back.

Someone had killed one of his kind, something that had never happened while he was chief.

The skin was charred black and blistered. Shit. This made it tough to ID. Once one of Rafferty's kind switched into their true form, it was impossible to identify the human it had once been. If they died while in that form, they stayed that way, unlike those werewolves in the movies, which turned back into humans after being killed by a silver bullet.

"Any idea who it was?"

"None."

"Did anyone see it?"

"I covered it with a blanket I had in the squad car. I don't think the medics saw it."

"Who took it here?"

"The van."

"And who took the woman to the hospital?"

"The paramedics."

Rafferty draped the blanket back over the thing's face.

"Have it taken to Krasner's. You took the Reese girl's body there, right?"

"Uh-huh."

Elliot Krasner owned Krasner's Funeral Home and Crematorium, and he was one of Rafferty's kind. Sometimes when Rafferty needed to dispose of a body, he had it brought to Krasner's and cremated. Looking at the corpse, he hoped it would fit in the oven, for he'd never had to burn one of his own kind before.

Rafferty stood back up and motioned for Clarence to follow him.

Once inside the squad room, he sat at his desk, opened the middle drawer, and took out a pad and Number 2 pencil. He flipped the first page over the top of the pad and touched the tip of the pencil to his tongue.

"Bring a chair over."

Clarence wheeled his own chair to the front of Rafferty's desk. His nosebleed had stopped, but he continued to blot blood from his lower lip.

"I'm moving the Harvest up."

"Can you do that?"

"No choice. It won't wait until October. Someone's gonna come in with all the commotion here and find us out. It has to be sooner."

He wrote at the top of the page:

TO BE ELIMINATED

"We got some planning to do."

* * *

Jill fanned the neckline of her blouse, trying in vain to cool herself off. The temperature had spiked to eighty-three degrees and it was only quarter to seven in the morning. She felt sticky already.

She entered the break room to find Cora putting her Masterlock on her locker.

Jill knelt down and opened her own locker.

"You hear about the one they brought in last night?" Cora kept her ear to the ground, and she was always the first to have the hospital gossip.

"I just got here," Jill said. "What happened?" She put away her purse, clicked her lock in place and stood up, holding her bag lunch.

Cora grabbed a Styrofoam cup and poured herself some java from the Mr. Coffee. "They brought in some woman. Sheriff's deputy. No, wait, Chief of Police. Marshall, I think. Minor burns on her back, laceration on her arm."

Cora pulled out a chair from the break room table. She sat down, Jill wondering with shame if the chair would hold under her weight.

"They pulled her out of a burning house."

"What was she doing in the house?"

"Chasing a suspect."

"That's a little strange. Not that unusual, though."

"Hold your horses. I'm getting there."

Cora took a loud sip off of her coffee. "She came in raving about some sort of monster that attacked her. Over and over again. Wanted to know if the cops killed it."

Jill dropped her lunch. A container of yogurt and an apple spilled out, rolled onto the floor. Cora's statement left her feeling numb.

"You gonna catch your lunch, honey?"

A monster. The lady had to be delirious.

Jill bent down and gathered her lunch off the floor.

"You all right?"

"What room's she in? They admitted her, right?" Jill asked.

"Yeah. Don't know what room."

Jill put the yogurt and the apple back in the bag and stuck it in the refrigerator. Cora tilted her cup back and shook it, as not to miss a drop of coffee. She got up, crushed the cup and tossed it in the trash can.

"Who told you the story?" Jill said.

"Renee Tutweiler. She was leaving when I came in."

Matt Crowe might be telling the truth after all, Jill thought. She would have to hear the woman's story herself to be certain.

Cora left the break room.

Jill realized she still held the handle of the open refrigerator door. Feeling foolish, she let go and the door closed.

Lunchtime. She would see the patient at lunchtime.

Jill stepped onto the elevator holding copies of *People* and *The National Enquirer*. She had stopped at the gift shop and bought them, hoping to use them as a peace offering.

Being stuck in the hospital could be about as exciting as watching grass grow. She hoped Donna Ricci would like them. Besides, if she showed up empty-handed to visit a sick person, she would feel guilty.

She pressed the button for the fifth floor. Maggie Clark at the admissions desk had given her Donna Ricci's room number, five hundred two. The doors closed and the elevator shot up, her stomach lurching at the rapid ascent.

The elevator stopped and she stepped out. She swung by the nurses' station and got an idea of Donna's condition: arm laceration, minor burns on back, some bumps and bruises. Donna would be released in a day or two.

She thanked Donna's nurse. Then she went to the end of the hallway and found Donna's room, number five hundred two.

Jill entered and found the woman laying on her side, facing the door. She had spiky blond hair. A bandage covered her right forearm. Her arms were thin but corded with muscle.

She looked up at Jill as she entered the room.

Donna Ricci had a pouty mouth and brown eyes that radiated toughness without saying a word. Cora had said she was a cop; that toughness must've served her well on the force.

"Let me guess, more needles."

"Not this time. Donna, right?"

"Yeah. Who are you?"

"Jill Adams. I'm an ER nurse."

"What're you doing up here?"

"I want to ask you some questions."

She pointed to the magazines tucked under Jill's arm. "What are those?"

This was going to be tough. "Thought they might help you pass the time." Jill set the magazines on the hospital tray next to the bed.

Donna propped her head up on her hand. "Did the hospital send you up here?"

"No," Jill said. "I want to know something for myself and you can help me."

The room had one other bed, which was empty. Jill shut the door and pulled up a chair next to Donna's bed. Donna looked at her as if she had just discovered a new species of insect.

"What did you see in that house?" Jill asked.

"None of your damn business."

"Please, I need to know."

"Don't know what you're talking about."

Donna winced as she spoke.

"Do you need more painkiller?"

"I'm fine."

"Will you tell me what you saw?"

"Don't waste my time. All I saw was a scumbag junkie. I chased him through the house."

"The ER nurses told me you were raving about a monster."

"I was delirious."

"How did the fire start?"

"Look, I don't know what you're talking about. And you're getting on my nerves. I want to get some rest, so why don't you leave?"

"Okay," Jill said. "Hope you feel better." She paused at the door. "It smelled like rotten eggs, didn't it?"

Donna's brow creased, a slight frown. Perhaps she was trying to ignore Jill's comment. Not show any chinks in the armor.

"All right, then. I'll go."

Jill turned the door handle.

"Wait."

Jill returned to the chair and sat down.

"Tell me what *you* know. Maybe I saw something in that house and maybe I didn't. I want to hear your story first," Donna demanded.

Letting out a sigh of relief, Jill told Donna about the encounter in the warehouse, meeting Matt, her encounters with Rafferty, and the story of Matt's family. As she spoke, she began to think that the stories sounded less absurd. The more she talked, the more she convinced herself that the nightmares were real.

When she finished, Donna scowled at her. Maybe she was wondering whether or not to believe Jill's stories. After a moment, she took a cup off of her hospital tray and sipped out of it.

"What you're telling me would be pretty hard to make up," Donna said.

"I've had trouble dealing with the whole thing, but I'm becoming a believer. The worst part is I may have alienated someone because of it. Will you tell me what happened in the house?"

"You're sure you're not a reporter or something?"

To ease her suspicions, Jill unclipped her hospital ID badge from her blouse and handed it to Donna, who took a good, hard look at it before handing it back.

"All right. This is what happened."

She told Jill about her meeting with Rafferty, Rhonda Barbieri's murder and the incident in Rhonda's house where Dietrich changed from a man to a monster. She finished by telling Jill how she tried to off the creature by setting it on fire and nearly wound up a human barbecue herself.

"It took guts to fight it off like that. I probably would've had a heart attack," Jill said.

"I'm not so sure about that. From the way you said you clubbed that guy with the pry bar in the warehouse, I'd say you got some piss and vinegar in you."

"Thanks. What'll you do when you get out of here?"

"Well, my days as police chief are probably numbered. I entered a crime scene out of my jurisdiction and burned it to the ground to boot. I don't think the town council will be all too pleased," Donna replied.

"What about your sister-in-law?"

"I'm going to have a talk with Rafferty. Tell him about the junkie."

"He's one of them, you know," Jill said.

"Doesn't matter. Someone I care about is dead, and he's the one in charge. I want to see what kind of half-ass explanation he offers me about the investigation."

"That guy I mentioned, Matt, wants to kill him."

"Not a bad idea. Not a smart idea, but not a bad one."

That led Jill to wondering what she should do about

staying in Lincoln. The town was full of murderous creatures, the Chief of Police one of them. If she went back home, her mother would think she'd won. Jill would be little Jilly who couldn't handle being a nurse. Her mother would all but hang an *I told you so* banner across the front of the house.

Going home was out of the question.

It would take months to find another apartment and another job, and who knew what could happen by then? What if Rafferty didn't just harass her and go away the next time? What if he changed into a beast like the junkie had and chased after her?

Then there was the issue of Matt. She liked him and wondered where a relationship with him might take her.

She knew now that he wasn't a flake, and Donna's story confirmed that for her. But would she be risking her life staying here? It seemed like it. She didn't think she could go out in public anymore without wondering who the creatures were and who the people were.

"You look like you're in deep thought."

"Just debating whether or not to pack it up and leave town."

"Whatever you do, stay away from Rafferty. It sounds like he has more than a casual interest in you."

"You're going to see him," Jill pointed out.

"He tries anything with me, I'll blow his nuts off," Donna said grimly.

Jill laughed. Somehow, she didn't doubt Donna would hesitate to blow said testicles off of the Chief of Police.

"You own a gun, Jill?"

"I hate guns."

"It might be a good idea to start unhating them. There're classes that can teach you how to shoot. I can give you some numbers if you want."

"I'll pass for now."

"Think about it."

"You know, I'm supposed to have dinner with Matt and a guy he met who knows a lot about the townspeople here too. Maybe you should come."

"I'll think about it. Give me your phone number."

Jill took a notepad and pen off of the nightstand and wrote the information down.

"Can I ask you something?" Donna said.

"Sure."

"One of these things chased you, even had you around the neck. How come you needed my story to convince you they were real?"

"I guess I was fooling myself into thinking something like this couldn't exist. I wanted things to go so smoothly for me that I pushed the idea of something so horrible away. I needed more proof, and your story gave me that extra push I needed."

"Fair enough."

Jill looked at her watch: ten minutes to one. Time to get back downstairs. She stood up and pushed the chair against the wall. "Can I get you anything before I go?"

"A free pass out of this place."

"Don't hold your breath."

Jill got her to smile. She wished Donna well and left the room. After work, she would call Matt Crowe and invite him over. She hoped that she could explain why she didn't swallow his story at first and apologize to him.

If he still wanted to see her. She wouldn't blame him for not coming over after the way she'd given him the cold shoulder last night.

She almost wanted to call him right now, but she only had five more minutes to get downstairs and get back to work. It felt like she would burst until she could call him.

The rest of the day was sure to drag.

CHAPTER 20

Matt's heart did a steady jitterbug in his chest. Pulling out of the driveway in the truck, he'd almost hit a black Nissan coming down the street. His head felt fuzzy and unfocused. All he could think about was his destination.

Jill had called him just after four and told him she wanted him to come over. She wouldn't say why, just that she had something important to tell him.

Then she hung up.

He pulled the truck into her driveway and parked. He had the air blasting in the truck, and when he stepped out, the heat leapt on him and hung on for dear life. He took a few steps up the walkway before he saw her.

"Over here," she said.

He climbed the wooden steps, stumbling on a loose plank. Jill sat on a glider, swinging back and forth, legs crossed, one arm draped lazily over the side.

"Have a seat," she said.

"To what do I owe this hospitality?"

"To the fact that I acted like an idiot."

"I wouldn't go that far."

"Can I tempt you with a drink? A peace offering?"

A pitcher of lemonade and two glasses sat on a table in front of the glider.

"Ah, bribery. Very persuasive."

He sat down next to her and immediately he noticed her fresh, clean scent. Roses and soap, maybe the yellow bar of Dial.

Jill poured a glass of lemonade for Matt and one for herself. He took a sip. It was a little tart for his taste, but still pretty damn good on a hot day.

She turned around to face him and sat Indian-style.

"You'll get splinters with bare feet on this porch."

"I don't care. I've been dying to sit on this glider since I moved in."

"So why did you call me here?"

"To apologize."

"For?"

"Well, for one, kicking you out last night. And two, for not believing your story. You poured your guts out to me and I treated you like you were a flake."

"Apology accepted on the first count. But why do you believe me all of a sudden?"

"Because of a patient that came into the hospital."

She told him about her conversation with Donna Ricci.

"This woman actually saw one of them?"

"Saw it and tried to kill it."

"Did she say what happened to it?"

"No. It was on fire, and then she passed out."

He needed to talk to this mystery woman. Maybe he could gain an ally, or at least some insights into how the creature reacted to the fire. That could be a way to take them down. "Things are getting worse. They're showing themselves more."

"How's that?"

He told her about the body in the park, and how the

young girl who discovered it said there were bite marks on it.

"I wish I never moved here. Except for one reason."

He gave her a puzzled look.

"You, silly."

"Aw, shucks, ma'am."

"Are you still mad?"

"No. I don't blame you for thinking I was weird."

"I really am sorry, Matt. Even though I know one of those things chased us through that warehouse, I just couldn't admit to myself that it existed."

"You don't have to be sorry. I must've sounded like a lunatic."

"Well, at first," Jill said. "I believed something traumatic happened to you, but I wasn't convinced it was an attack by these things. And after my last relationship, I was afraid of someone unstable."

"I thought I dropped the ball with you. I was kicking myself for telling you the story."

"I'm glad you felt comfortable enough with me to tell it."

She gripped his forearm and gave it a small squeeze.

"So you think we can be an item?" he said.

"My sources say yes."

He leaned over and kissed her on the mouth. As he finished the kiss and pulled away, she caressed his cheek.

"What do you say to dinner. Pizza maybe?" Matt asked.

"Bring it on."

They sat in silence, sipped lemonade and held hands.

After three pieces of pizza and two glasses of lemonade, Matt's stomach was stretched to the limit. The Pizza Hut box and the empty pitcher sat on Jill's coffee table.

They sat next to each other on the couch. Their legs

touched, and he placed his hand on her bare thigh. The skin was warm and smooth. She didn't seem to mind his hand.

"That beat cooking," she said.

"I'll clean this up."

He picked up the pizza box, pitcher, glasses and empty paper plates and took them to the kitchen. When he returned, she was fiddling with the stereo.

"Any preferences?" she said.

"How about ninety-seven?"

"Format?"

"Classic rock."

"Good enough."

She pressed a button and Ronnie Van Zandt's voice came out of the speakers, singing about an aged blues singer.

"Did that cop—what was her name?" Matt said.

"Donna."

"Did she describe it to you?"

"No. She mentioned the smell, though."

"She saw the man change?"

"Right in front of her."

Matt had never seen one change, but he suspected it was an awesome, if repulsive, sight. "I'm anxious to meet with Harry."

"I told Donna about the meeting at Harry's. I hope you don't mind."

"The more the merrier."

"Do you still want to kill Rafferty?"

"Yes. But I'm not going to. Yet."

"What do you mean?"

"Killing him won't solve the problems in Lincoln. There's probably hundreds of Them living here. They'll keep taking victims. Besides, if I kill Rafferty, I'll never get out of here alive."

"So what are you thinking?"

I don't know. Nukes? "I'm hoping for a way to get a lot of Them at once."

"Then what?"

"Skip town. Hopefully with you."

"It'll look like you murdered innocent people."

"That's the thing. I need a way to get Them to change into their true form. Then do it."

She paused for a moment. Matt thought for a moment that he might be pushing her away again with talk of murdering hundreds of residents of Lincoln. "Think of it, Jill. We're in danger just by being here. There's already been killings. Donna's sister-in-law, the girl in the park. I can't let this go on. Not after what happened to my family."

"I guess you wouldn't be hurting actual people."

"Exactly. And Rafferty's targeted you, the scumbag."

He saw goose bumps raise the hairs on her forearms. "I'm sorry. I didn't mean to frighten you."

She crossed her arms. "It's not your fault. Just when I think of his tongue in my ear, like a snake. Yuck."

"If you don't want to get involved, I'll understand. But I like you. A lot."

Jesus, that sounded like it came from the mouth of a virgin on prom night, he thought.

"Really? You must have had some girlfriends along the line."

"There were a few here and there."

"Well, I can't go home. And it'll take me time to move. If I'm going to be here, I might as well help. Besides, I don't want to miss out on you either. Just no guns for me. My dad and all."

It was frightening that someone could walk into a store to buy milk or bread, and get killed for no reason. You could walk out of your house and be shot, stabbed, robbed or raped. And Jill's father had been one of the unfortunate ones to experience this.

"I won't bring it up again. You don't have to get within ten feet of a gun if you don't want to. I know how hard it is to lose family."

"The worst part about the whole thing was that when I got the news, my mother pushed me away. I went to her expecting hugs and kisses. She told me we both needed to be alone and sent me to my room. I cried all night. Alone."

"That's pretty damn lousy."

Matt gave her credit for pursuing her own life and forging ahead, away from her mother. From what Jill had told him, the woman sounded like a domineering control freak. "Your mom sounds like a cold person."

"Like a Fridgedair. Every year for my birthday, you know what I got? A card."

"Money in the card?"

"Nope. No presents and no parties. Mother always said that was a sure way to spoil a child."

"That's lousy too. No, that's beyond lousy, that's shitty."

Matt couldn't have imagined going without birthday parties as a child. If Christmas was the Holy Grail of childhood, then birthday parties were a close second, perhaps the Ark of the Covenant.

"What was your family like?" she said.

"Well, my brother was a typical pain in the ass little brother. Scratched my records, pulled the wheels off my trucks, ripped my baseball cards. But I wouldn't have traded him for anything. My mom and dad couldn't do enough for us. They took us everywhere. Darien Lake in the summer, the circus, which I never liked but Mikey loved. The beach, picnics, movies. My dad worked a lot of hours, but he always had time for us when he was home, no matter how tired he was. I miss all three of them."

"They sound great. But we're survivors, right?"

"I guess we are."

She smiled at him. She had her hair drawn back in a ponytail, and strands hung down over her forehead, down the side of her face. He reached over and brushed it away. He didn't think he'd ever seen a woman look prettier than she did now.

She moved closer to him, reaching for him and running her hand over his cheek, through his hair and to the back of his head. Tiny jolts of electricity pricked his neck and crackled down his spine.

She drew him close and kissed him, her tongue slipping past his lips. He kissed her back hard.

Drawing back, she offered him a wry smile. "That wasn't too forward, was it?"

"I'm not complaining."

She kissed him again, this time pushing him back so that she was on top of him. His heart sped up and he ran his hands up her back to her hair and untied her ponytail.

Her hair spilled down in tight curls.

She straddled him. Then she pulled off her shirt. He slid his hands up her belly, over her rib cage, cupped her breasts over the bra. She moaned and leaned forward.

Jill whispered in his ear, "This couch could use a good workout."

After making love on the couch, and again on the floor, they went to the bedroom and fell asleep on top of the covers. Now, Jill lay with her head on Matt's chest. He smelled pleasantly of perspiration, and the hairs from his chest tickled her cheek.

The clock-radio alarm whined like a hungry baby and Jill flicked it off. Taking Matt's arm by the wrist, she gently lifted it and slipped out of his embrace. Then she kissed him on the chest, just above the nipple. He stirred.

"Morning," he mumbled, half asleep.

"Morning. I've got to get ready for work."

She tossed the covers aside, got out of bed and stretched, feeling Matt's gaze on her naked body. With Jerry, she was always self-conscious about her nudity, preferring to throw on a robe, but Matt watching her didn't bother her at all.

The room was still in shadows, as the sun hadn't risen yet. She took her silk robe off the hook on the bedroom door. As she slipped it on, she remembered that it had been a Valentine's present from Jerry. It was the only gift of his that she kept. The stuffed animals, earrings, cards and letters were all taking up space in a landfill right about now.

But the robe was comfortable, so why not keep it? She loved the feel of the cool silk against her skin.

A breeze blew in the open window, rattling the shade and sneaking under her robe, tickling her butt. The breeze could be a good sign, for it might mean an end to the brutal heat that had plagued Lincoln and the entire northeast all August.

She turned and looked at Matt before leaving the room. He was on his side snoring softly, his right arm bent, hand tucked under his head. The outline of his bicep was clearly visible. She smiled as she remembered how she kissed *all* of his muscles last night.

It would be nice to wake up next to someone like him every morning. She realized that was the giddiness that came with a new boyfriend and good sex. But she felt good and wished she had time for a run. She could go two extra miles today.

She went into the bathroom, showered and blow-dried her hair.

After the shower, she returned to the bedroom to

put on her makeup. Matt was doing push-ups, the muscles in his back and arms flexing and pumping.

"Too bad I'm already showered. You look like you're working up a sweat," she said. "I could help you with that."

"You're too much woman for me. I don't know if I could handle you again."

She nudged him in the ribs with her bare foot, knocking him off balance, causing him to fall on his side.

"I'll show you too much woman."

"Brutal. You're a beast. How about I make some coffee?"

"Sounds good. It's in the third cupboard on the right on the bottom."

He got up, put his clothes on and headed for the kitchen.

After putting her uniform on, she joined Matt in the kitchen.

Two green mugs of steaming coffee sat on the table.

"So did you enjoy last night?" he said.

"God, yes. Couldn't you tell?"

"It's been a while, that's all."

"You were great."

"I aim to please."

"What've you got planned for today?" Jill said.

"I've got to make a couple visits."

"To who?"

"The Reese family. I have to tell them what happened to their daughter. The cops probably gave them a line of crap."

He took a sip off his coffee. Jill went to the cupboard and took out a box of Grape Nuts and a bowl and spoon. Taking a half-gallon carton of milk from the fridge, she brought everything to the table and sat down. Then she poured the milk and cereal in the bowl and stuck the spoon it.

"Where else are you going?" she asked.

"The girl who found the body. I want to make sure she's all right. That Rafferty didn't harm her."

"Be careful," she said, and took a bite of cereal.

"You too. I don't want him harassing you again."

The company of a boa constrictor was preferable to the company of Lincoln's police chief. If she never saw him again, it would be too soon.

"Pick you up at six?" he said.

"Yeah. I've got to get going in a few."

She looked at the clock hanging over the fridge: it read six twenty-five. The two of them sat in pleasant silence while she finished eating. When she had crunched the last of her cereal, she rinsed the bowl and spoon and left it in the sink.

Slurping the last of his coffee, Matt got up and put the cup in the sink. He went to the door. She moved in close to him and kissed him. Then she wrapped her arms around his neck and hugged. He returned the hug, slipping his hands around her lower back and squeezing. She closed her eyes.

"See you tonight," he said.

"Can't wait."

After leaving Jill's, Matt went back to his Aunt Bernie's.

He showered, shaved and changed into clean clothes. He also took the Beretta and the hunting knife with him. On his way to the truck, which he had parked in the driveway, he heard the window screen click as his Uncle lifted it.

Rex Lapchek stuck his unshaven face out the window and said, "You put gas in that?"

"Of course, *sir*."

"You'd better. Better not scratch it either, numb nuts."

He gave his uncle a big grin. "Wouldn't dream of it, dear uncle."

"Better keep that grin off your face too."

Or you'll wipe it off, right?

His uncle drew his head back inside and slammed the screen shut.

Matt hopped in the truck and slid the knife and gun under the passenger seat. Jill probably wouldn't even get in the truck if she knew what he had hidden under the seat. But he felt slightly better with the weapons in the truck. Slightly.

With the murder last night, and with the creatures' heightened activity, traveling unarmed would be a health hazard. He wanted to bring the Mossberg with him, but that was a little harder to conceal, and if he ran into Rafferty again, he didn't want to wind up in the slammer. A handgun and knife fit nicely under the seat. A shotgun didn't.

He arrived at the Reese home ten minutes after leaving his aunt's house. He'd looked up the address in the phone book; it was an easy one to find—they were the only Reeses in Lincoln.

The house was a gray English Tudor covered partially in ivy. Had to be at least five thousand square feet. A triple-paned bay window looked out over the front lawn, which was lush and emerald-like. He didn't think an artist could paint a more vivid green with a palette full of colors at his disposal.

The Reeses must've spent a lot of time on that lawn—with the heat, everyone else's on the block was sick yellow and brown. It was like comparing a young man's lush head of hair to a wizened geezer's thinning locks. The hedge that separated the property from the neighbor's was clipped square, and a short wall of decorative stone snaked along the front of the house.

As he walked up the driveway, he looked up at the chimney. It was slate gray with a letter "R" set inside the brick in a lighter shade of gray. A custom-built job, probably in the family for generations.

He rang the doorbell at the side door. While he waited, he looked around at the black Humvee parked in the driveway. It looked as dark and imposing as a killer whale.

The woman who answered the door was nearly his height. She was thin as a sapling. He noticed her hands, the long, slender fingers gripping the door handle.

She opened the door wider. "May I help you?" she said in a slight British accent.

The woman wore a white silk blouse and black silk pants. Her hair, polished ebony, flowed to one side and draped over her right shoulder. She seemed to glow, a contrast of light and shade.

"Is Mrs. Reese home?"

"I'm Lila Reese."

"Carla's sister?"

"Her mother. What do you want?"

"My name's Matt Crowe. I have some information about your daughter. She's missing, isn't she?"

"She's probably with Ronnie."

"Ronnie?"

"Her boyfriend. Not that it's any of your business."

"Did you call the police?"

"No."

"I don't know how to tell you this, but Carla's body was found in the park last night. I saw the police take it away."

"That's nonsense. She's with Ronnie."

"Can you prove that?" Matt said.

"I don't have to prove anything, especially to a stranger."

"Where was your daughter last night?"

"Working."

"She never came home, right?"

"Her boyfriend has a place, Mr. Crowe."

It was a damn shame that a college girl didn't come home and the mother just assumed she was staying with her boyfriend. She hadn't even checked up on the girl from the sound of it.

"Mrs. Reese. Do me a favor. Call her boyfriend. Please?"

She eyed him the way the lion must have eyed the mouse, deciding the fate of the prey. "Why should I believe you?"

"You don't have to. For your daughter's sake, please call."

She waited a moment, rolled her eyes and sighed in exasperation. "Wait here."

She returned with a white cordless phone in her hand. She dialed a phone number and put it up to her ear.

Matt listened.

"Hello, Betty?

"Fine, how are you?

"Did Ronnie go out with Carla last night?

"No?

"She's not at your house?

"Can you ask him if he knows where she is? She didn't come home last night.

"He hasn't talked to her? Okay, thank you Betty. Good-bye."

She pressed the Off button, a blank look on her face.

"She didn't go to Ronnie's. She didn't go. Where could she be?" she asked Matt, as if he would say, oh, she's in the trunk of my car, I'll unlock it and get her for you right now. He knew where Carla was, but he had a feeling this woman wouldn't hear it even if he told her again.

The blank look disappeared and her face changed, a clear blue sky turning into a black tempest. "How do I know you didn't do something with her? Maybe you abducted her."

"Number one, I'm not a murderer or a kidnapper. Number two, if I was, I wouldn't show up at the victim's house."

"I suppose not."

"Look, Mrs. Reese. My family was murdered here. I know what the police are like. If you call them, they'll lie to you. They'll tell you they never found a body."

"That's preposterous."

"If you don't want to talk to me, I'll leave."

"Wait here."

She disappeared, shutting the inside door behind her. It was ivory colored with a frosted oval window. The door opened again, and it was apparent she still didn't believe he was completely harmless.

She held a .45 at her side.

"Now you can come in, Mr. Crowe."

She led him through the kitchen and dining room, then through a pair of white French doors.

Brilliant sunlight poured through the bay window at the front of the room. Likewise through a skylight in the ceiling. A creamy Persian rug with an inky pattern partially covered the honey-colored hardwood floor. With the sunlight and the abundance of white furniture, it looked like the waiting room to get into heaven.

"Sit down, please."

The couch swallowed him whole. Getting up in a hurry would be a definite impossibility. He propped his elbow on a pillow, only to have it slide off the shiny material. Satin.

Lila Reese sat on the matching love seat directly

across from him and crossed her legs. She set the .45 on the cushion next to her, but kept her hand on top of it.

"My father was a Mossad agent. This gun belonged to him. And he taught me how to use it. Just in case your intentions are not as you say."

"Whatever makes you more comfortable."

"Now what's this nonsense about my daughter?"

Matt told her the story of how the body was found, what the witness saw, and the body being carted away in an unmarked white van.

"How can you be sure it was Carla?"

"The girl who found her told us it was Carla. She graduated from Millard Fillmore, right? The girl recognized Carla from school."

Lila Reese looked to the mantel, where an eight by ten photo in a black frame was propped up. The girl in the picture was a younger, prettier photocopy of Lila Reese.

Because the picture was in black-and-white, he couldn't tell the eye color, but if he were a betting man, he would bet the farm that they were fiery blue, like her mother's. Even in black-and-white they were extraordinary.

She remained silent, staring at the photograph.

Matt felt awkward, like being in an elevator full of strangers. "I know how hard it must be to hear this. I lost my family here too. The killers were never found."

"Not my Carla," she said. "It's impossible."

She looked through him, like she was watching something through the bay window, a passerby on the street. He wondered if her mind had snapped, or if she was starting to shut herself off from reality, retreating into the part of the mind that didn't have to face reality, the part responsible for daydreams and denial.

"It was some other girl. The girl who found the body must be mistaken."

"It was her."

"Then why haven't the police contacted me?"

"The police in this town are crooked, Mrs. Reese. Don't trust them."

"You're obviously some sort of paranoid, delusional man."

"This town is dangerous. Have you lived here long?"

"Eight months. We have several homes around the country."

"I suggest you use one of them and get out of town."

If her gaze were any colder, ice crystals would've formed on her lashes. "I'm sure Carla will be home in time for supper."

She stood up, and with her right hand, smoothed the front of her pant legs. The .45 hung in her left, the barrel pointed at the floor. He had no problem imagining this woman bringing the gun level and pulling the trigger. Especially if she thought he was a maniac.

"Leave, Mr. Crowe. I'll be talking to the police, and if you're lucky, I won't mention this discussion."

Matt pushed himself out of the quicksand couch, lost his balance and flopped back into the cushions. The second time he tried, he planted his fists into the cushions and used them to leverage himself up.

He paused at the French doors and turned toward her. "She's gone. I'm sorry."

"Get out. Now."

He left before he wound up with a bullet in the back.

The phone conversation with her brother had left her saddened and angry. Donna wiped the tears from her face with the back of her hand, then dried it on her hospital gown. The cup of water she had thrown across the room lay on its side against the baseboard.

She couldn't have been more stunned if Jesus Christ walked into her hospital room and sat down to watch

Wheel of Fortune. She knew Bobby was cheating on Rhonda, but for him to view her death and the burning of their home as a liberating experience made her wish she could choke him through the phone line.

Ed Rafferty walked into the room, thumbs in his belt loops. He paused for a moment, legs spread, feet planted shoulder-width apart, like a gunslinger entering a saloon. The day wasn't getting any better.

Who was he trying to impress? she wondered.

He stepped forward, hit the water on the floor, and slid. His hand shot out and he gripped the door handle, regaining his balance. Donna stifled a laugh.

"Good afternoon. Officer Ricci, right?"

"You forget my name already?"

The man looked like he'd been beaten with the ugly stick. He had a crooked nose and squinty eyes, and his mouth was a thin slash.

"Mind if I shut this door? I have some police business to discuss with you."

"Go ahead."

He shut the door, careful to step around the water on the floor this time.

"I'm glad you came to see me, Chief Rafferty."

"Oh?"

"I was actually planning on paying you a visit when I got out of here."

"Then it looks like we're on the same page."

He came back over to the side of her bed and stuck his hands in his pockets, all except for the thumbs, which poked out like sausages. She was still lying on her side, looking up at him; she felt vulnerable. She pushed herself up so that she was sitting against the partially reclined bed.

She tried not to wince from the pain.

"You were in the Barbieri house when it burned."

"That's right."

"What the hell were you doing in there?"

"Finding you a murderer."

"Is that so. Who?"

"Name was Charles Dietrich. Thin, blond, a junkie. He killed my sister-in-law."

"This isn't your jurisdiction, Officer Ricci."

"That's *Chief* Ricci. I extended you the courtesy."

"Still isn't your jurisdiction. Even if it was, you had no business being in that house."

"Maybe I didn't. But I found the killer."

"How do you know he was the killer?"

"He admitted it to me. I believe his words were 'I killed that whore.' "

"What happened to this Dietrich?"

"I chased him through the house. I blacked out. I don't know what happened to him."

"My men on the scene didn't find a body. They didn't see anyone leave the house either."

"I'm not making this up. Did they find my gun? I had it on him and he slapped it out of my hand."

"No gun."

"Don't you care that someone was killed in your town?"

He smirked, then turned away from the bed, looking at the floor. He started pacing back and forth across the room.

"I'll investigate this on my own, Officer Ricci. If you're smart, you'll keep your nose out of my business."

"You don't seem to be doing much investigating. No leads, no clues. And I just named the killer."

He continued to pace. "What else did you see in that house?"

"What?"

"You saw something else in that house."

"You're full of shit."

He was on her in one stride, gripping her bandaged

arm and squeezing. She gasped, unable to draw a breath for a moment.

"I know what you saw in there. And you know what you saw."

"You're crazy."

"You can deny it if you want. If you go telling anyone else what you saw or what happened, I'll come looking for you."

He squeezed harder, her bones feeling as if they might turn to powder if he squeezed any more. Donna yelped. Gritting her teeth she said, "I'm not hard to find."

He clenched his teeth. He was almost nose-to-nose with her, still gripping her arm. The smell of him was too much. The same smell that was on Dietrich after he turned into the creature.

It became clear that Jill Adams was right; Rafferty was one of them.

"Stay the hell out of my town. And not one word to anyone about any of this, bitch."

A vein pulsed over Rafferty's eye, and his face flushed.

"Let go of my arm."

"Promise me you'll stay out of this."

"Can't do that."

He squeezed even harder. She thought she felt some stitches rip. *He's really going to break my arm,* she thought.

Drawing her head away from him, she slammed it forward, mashing his lower lip. There was a crunching noise and she felt a stab of pain in her forehead, but it was better than the pain in her arm. He let go of her and reared back, his hand covering his mouth.

"You little—"

The door opened and Donna's nurse, Brenda, walked in. She looked at Rafferty, then at Donna, unsure of what was happening inside the room.

"Is everything all right?"

"Fine," Donna said.

"I was just going," Rafferty said.

He put his hand to his lip, got some blood on his fingertips and then looked at them as if to confirm the fact that he was bleeding.

"What happened in here?" Brenda said.

"I slipped on some water. You ought to clean it up," Rafferty said, and walked out the door.

"I'll get one of the aides to clean it up."

Donna's left arm was bleeding, a bright red splotch seeping through the bandage from Rafferty ripping her stitches.

"We better take care of this as long as you're here," Donna said.

"How'd you do that?"

"Bumped it on the bedrail."

"Just like the police officer slipped on the water. I don't believe either one of you."

"Believe what you want, as long as you sew me the hell back up."

CHAPTER 21

When he thought his hands would stop trembling, Matt let go of the steering wheel.

He was parked outside of 109 Chestnut Street, home of Sally Perski.

He wiped his damp palms on the front of his jeans, and then the sweat from his brow. The air-conditioning in the truck was going full tilt the whole way over here, but he still dripped perspiration.

The Reese woman was in severe denial, and if he had pressed her, he may have wound up with an extra orifice in his body. He wondered if she believed him and was pushing the truth away, or if she completely refused to accept the notion that her daughter was dead.

Despite the fact that he had nearly pissed himself when she leveled the gun at him, he couldn't help feeling sorry for her. Rafferty and his band of goons would lie to her, tell her there were no leads in the case, that her daughter had simply disappeared. The witnesses would be intimidated, threatened or removed, and the story would die out, one more person who simply vanished from Lincoln's streets without a trace.

He got out of the truck and walked up the weedy, cracked walkway to the front porch, which sagged as if an invisible giant were using it for a footrest.

He climbed the steps and stood in front of a wooden screen door. The screen inside the frame was rusted red and had a tear in it. He looked around the porch and saw a wicker couch, now missing its cushions.

After ringing the doorbell, he waited for a moment.

A toddler with a mess of curly blond hair scampered to the door and looked up at Matt. His baby gut hung over his diaper.

"Hiya!" he said, and darted out of sight.

"Brendan, don't answer the door!"

Sally Perski appeared behind the door. "You're that guy from the park."

"Can I talk to you?"

"You're not a detective."

"How'd you know?"

She crossed her arms and put her weight on one leg, hip thrust out as if to say "here's how I know." "The police told me there's no detectives in Lincoln."

"I'm sorry I lied to you, but we needed to know what you saw."

"Why?"

"To find out what killed that girl."

"It wasn't a person, was it?"

"No."

"What, then?"

"I'll tell you if you want to talk to me."

She measured him with her gaze. "You're not some kind of pervert or weirdo, are you?"

"I let my membership to the perverts and weirdos society expire last month."

She looked behind her, and looked back at Matt. "Okay, come in."

He entered the living room, half expecting to find

the inside as run-down as the exterior. The beige rug had vacuum tracks on it, and the room smelled of peach-scented air freshener.

The furniture was the same sandy brown as the rug, and a massive oak entertainment center covered one wall, a thirty-five-inch television encased inside. The entertainment center was flanked by a cherry grandfather clock, which gonged twelve times.

"Have a seat."

Brendan darted into the room, a toy fire truck clasped in his arms. He came up to Matt, held up the truck for inspection and chirped, "Cuck! Firecuck!"

"Brendan, sit down," Sally instructed.

He wobbled to the center of the room and plopped onto his rear end in a manner only a two-year-old could without having a sore tailbone for a week.

"I'm keeping an eye on him. My mother's at work."

"Only brother?"

"One's enough."

"Be glad you have him."

"I guess I am."

"Good."

She went into the adjacent dining room where a red Eureka vacuum stood, its cord unraveled like a snake. She picked it up and began winding it around the prongs on the vacuum designed to hold the cord.

"What happened after you left the park?"

"One of the cops took me to the police station. I waited in a little room for a while. I don't know how long because I didn't have my watch on."

Rafferty's tactics hadn't changed, as Matt remembered that small, dank room and the fear he had felt the day Rafferty threatened to kill him if he talked about the murders. "Do you know which cop you talked to?"

"The one who drove me there had red hair. The one I talked to at the station was big and ugly."

"Do you know his name for sure?"

"I forget his name but he told me he was the chief."

"Did he threaten you?"

"Not at first. He was nice at first."

She finished winding up the cord and rolled the vacuum into the kitchen. When she came back in, she had a can of Pledge and a dirty white T-shirt, presumably a dust rag.

"I'm going to clean while we talk. My mom'll be pissed if the house isn't clean."

She aimed the can at the end table and pressed the button. Polish hissed out. Using the rag, she rubbed it into the wood surface.

"What did he tell you?"

"He was pissed when I told him about the detectives. He told me there weren't any detectives in Lincoln."

"How about threats?"

"He just told me not to talk to anyone. But he looked all crazy and messed up. Like he was about to lose his temper."

She finished dusting the end table and moved to the entertainment center, wiping down the television screen.

"Did he say anything else?"

"Not really. Like I said, he started off nice and then got nasty. I was sort of scared."

Brendan looked up at his big sister, momentarily interested in her cleaning activity, and then went back to rolling his fire truck back and forth on the rug.

She stopped dusting and looked at Matt.

"What did I see in the park?"

"This is gonna sound nutty, but you saw, well, creatures."

"I don't think you're nutty. I told the police chief they were men. But I know they weren't men. No men look like that."

"There's a lot of Them in town, Sally. They live under people's skin."

"Is that why so many people smell?"

"Exactly."

The girl noticed the smell of them, which he speculated was something not everyone could detect. If everyone in town could detect the strange odor of the beasts, they would know something was not right with a good portion of Lincoln's townspeople.

Maybe certain people were born with the ability to detect the scent, and the same people might not have that much trouble believing that the creatures existed.

"What are they?"

"I don't know for sure. But they're very dangerous. You make sure not to walk through that park by yourself. Don't go anywhere by yourself."

"You don't have to remind me."

"And watch out for Chief Rafferty. He's one of Them."

"I noticed he smelled funny too."

"I'm gonna go now, so you can finish your housework."

"You can hang around if you want to."

"Thanks anyway, but I don't think your mom would be too crazy about finding a strange man in the living room," he said. "Be careful, Sally."

Matt got up and Brendan said, "Bye-bye!" and waved his hand enthusiastically. Matt reached down and ruffled his hair.

He was at the door when she asked him, "How do you know about these things?"

"I had a bad experience with them when I was about your age. I also sat in that little room at the police station and had the police chief threaten me."

"No shit?"

"No shit. Talk to your mom about getting out of Lincoln."

He opened the screen door and stepped into the heat.

* * *

Rafferty jammed his finger into the elevator's L button and pressed hard, turning the skin under his fingernail white.

The doors slid closed.

His visit with Donna Ricci had been infuriating; no one told him what to do in his own town or talked back to him, especially another cop. This was his turf.

He'd lost his temper again, first with Clarence then with Ricci, nearly snapping her arm in half. If he didn't get control of himself, he didn't know what would happen.

People will die, that's what will happen, Ed. Just as sure as shit, people will die.

The only positive thing that came out of the meeting with Ricci was he could now pin the murder of the Barbieri woman on Charles Dietrich. And since Dietrich had burned in the fire, he didn't have to worry about anything going to trial. As an added bonus, he doubted anyone would miss Dietrich. Missing junkies didn't show up on the side of milk cartons.

He wanted Donna Ricci out of his town, and if there wasn't so much shit hitting the fan right now, he would've made sure she disappeared. He would have to gamble for now that she wouldn't talk about what she saw in the Barbieri house. He didn't think even a dumb bitch like her would ruin her career by spouting off about monsters chasing her through a burning house.

The elevator slowed and stopped. The L button lit up, the doors opened, and Rafferty stepped around an elderly woman in a wheelchair. She had a cast on her right leg, and Rafferty bumped her as he passed.

"Ow! You clumsy asshole!"

He decided he would play polite; he didn't need anymore incidents at the moment. "Excuse me, ma'am. Are you okay?"

"Watch yourself."

Maybe when you got that old you didn't care what you said to anyone, cops included.

He walked past the security desk and the guard, a man with the name James on his tag, nodded to him. A boy of about twelve hopped past him on crutches, his mother walking beside him, haranguing him for going skateboarding.

Walking past the emergency room entrance, he spied her out of the corner of his eye.

Jill Adams, hair done up in a ponytail, wearing a green top and white pants. She hadn't seen him, so he slipped behind one of the columns in the lobby. She was hunched over a laundry cart, sorting through a pile of hospital gowns.

She hadn't been on his mind this morning, but seeing her had jarred his memory a little; he wanted to pay her another visit and scare the hell out of her.

Jill Adams had some fire to her, and he liked that. It would be a challenge to take her when the Harvest came. She would put up a fight, and that got him a little excited. Intimidation was his favorite tactic, but once in a while it was nice to get one that fought a little and then crush them like a cockroach.

She took one of the gowns off the cart and then turned and walked down the long emergency room hallway.

"See you soon," he said.

Jill climbed the porch steps and looked at her watch. It was ten to four and Matt was coming at five o'clock to pick her up. That would leave her plenty of time to shower and change, as well as have a tall glass of something cold.

She had no air-conditioning in the car, and she knew when she got in the house, she would have to literally peel her clothes off.

Pulling her keys from her purse, she unlocked the door and went upstairs. She set the keys and her purse on the kitchen counter, then took the pitcher of lemonade out of the refrigerator.

She took out a glass and poured herself a tall one.

Something was odd in the kitchen but she couldn't figure out what it was. There was something out of place, not the way she had left it this morning.

"What the hell is bothering me?"

Unable to place what was wrong, she took her lemonade and went into the living room. The light on the answering machine flashed and she pressed the Play button.

"Hi, Jill, it's your mom. You do remember your mother, don't you? I'm the one you haven't called in over a week. Call me back if you haven't forgotten my number."

"Jesus Christ, Mom. Nothing like a little guilt," Jill muttered.

After setting down her lemonade, she flipped on the stereo and Molly Hatchet blared from the speakers. She forgot they'd left it on Ninety-Seven Rock last night. Buffalo's only classic rock station, as they claimed. She wasn't a big classic rock fan—her tastes leaned more toward John Coltraine—but it would suffice.

She went into the bedroom and changed into a tank top, jean shorts and sneakers. Realizing she forgot her lemonade, she walked back to the living room.

"I'm losing it."

The lemonade was not on the coffee table where she had left it.

"What the hell?"

Maybe she left it in the kitchen. No, that wasn't right, because she had brought it into the living room, but she'd check the kitchen anyway.

She got halfway through the dining room and gasped.

"Pretty damn good lemonade."

Ed Rafferty leaned on the wall in the archway between the dining room and the kitchen. He took a rude sip off of the lemonade and sucked an ice cube into his mouth, crunching away.

How could she not know he was in the apartment? The stereo was how. He must have sneaked into the living room while she was changing in the bedroom, his footsteps masked by the music.

"What are you doing here?"

"Just came for a visit. You should clean out that attic. It's a mess."

She suddenly realized what had been out of place in the kitchen: the chair pushed away from the table. She always pushed the chair back in, and she knew for sure that she pushed it back in this morning. It occurred to her that he must've pulled the kitchen chair out and sat in it. Waiting.

Rafferty chugged the glass of lemonade and belched.

"Sweet. I could taste your lips on the glass."

"What do you want from me?"

"Just concerned about you is all."

"So concerned that you picked my lock?"

"You shouldn't leave your door open."

"I didn't."

She was getting hot, her blood rising and making her skin flush pink. This was the second time he'd invaded her home, solely for the purpose of surprising her. The thought of him sneaking around the apartment made her skin feel like beetles were dancing on it.

He dropped the glass on the dining room rug and it tipped over, the liquid dribbling onto the carpet.

"Get out," she said. "You have no legal right to be here."

He started toward her.

She backed up into the living room, bumping her calf on the coffee table.

"You're an outsider, Jill, and I have to keep tabs on all the outsiders in my town. It just so happens that you're also a particularly lovely one."

Her eyes darted back and forth, looking for a weapon to fend him off with. Her best shot would be the brass candlestick on the mantle, but she wasn't sure she could bring herself to actually hit someone with it. It could cave in somebody's skull if swung with enough force.

And if Rafferty changed forms, she wouldn't have a chance.

"Tell me about your experience in the warehouse."

"I don't know—"

"Don't lie to me, you dumb cunt."

"Don't call me that, you son of a bitch," she said through clenched teeth.

"C'mon. A junkie named Dietrich chased you through the furniture warehouse. You couldn't miss him. Pale, whitish hair, lips like a woman."

He was only five feet from her, a sour odor coming off of him like heat from a radiator.

"No need to worry about him anymore. He's dead. But I would like to question you, Jill. I worry about you. A pretty girl all by herself. There's some nasty people around this town."

"I'm finding that out."

He stepped closer again. She backed up against the couch.

He slumped in the lounge chair next to the couch and set his feet on the coffee table, blocking the path between the chair and the table, trying to trap her.

She saw an opportunity to run.

She planted her foot on the coffee table and pushed off, bounding over it and running through the dining room to the kitchen. Rafferty's footfalls pounded on the floor behind her.

Her scalp caught fire as he yanked her hair from behind, jerking her backward, her sneakers squealing on the kitchen floor. Rafferty whipped her around and shoved her back against the stove, rapping her lower back on the door handle.

"Where do you think you're going?"

"Anywhere away from you."

"I knew the first time I saw you I had to have you."

He leaned in toward her, his rank smell overpowering. He reached for her arm.

Her left hand struck like a cobra, jabbing hard into Rafferty's right eye. He growled and slapped his hand over his wounded eye.

Seeing an opening, she bolted out the door and down the back stairs, Rafferty following, clunking on the stairs.

She reached the side door, yanked it open, and hit the screen door handle with her palm.

"Open, dammit!"

The wind whooshed from her lungs as Rafferty's shoulder plowed into the small of her back. The screen door flew open, the two of them hitting the concrete, Jill rolling away, heaving for air.

He must've jumped off the landing to get at her, she thought dazedly. Judging from the force of the blow, and from Rafferty's sheer size, she was lucky that her spine hadn't snapped.

He was coming at her again, teeth bared, growling low in his throat like a wolf.

She was still on the ground sucking air when Rafferty clenched his hands around her right ankle and began dragging her. The skin on her right elbow shredded on the concrete.

He moved backward, dragging her like a woodcutter might drag a freshly cut pine tree through the snow.

If she let him get her in the house, there was no telling what horrible things he might do to her.

His back at the screen door, he took one hand off her ankle and pulled it open. It slipped from his hand and slammed shut, Rafferty yelling "Fuck!"

This was her chance.

She slipped her free foot between his legs and drove the point of her sneaker into his crotch.

Grunting, his grip on her ankle loosened, and she twisted her leg free. She crawled away, scurrying like a mouse from an owl.

The full weight of him slammed into her again, banging her chin into the concrete and making the ground start to spin.

"I should've done this in the first place."

She heard metal jingle and clank behind her.

Handcuffs.

He jerked her left arm behind her back and slapped the cold metal on her wrist. Then he did the same with the right.

Gripping her upper arm, he hoisted Jill to her feet with little effort. Chin throbbing, vibrating like a tuning fork, she knew she was in trouble.

Would he try to rape her? The thought of him forcing himself between her legs made her stomach churn.

He turned her around, still gripping her upper arm.

"No one gets away from me."

She saw his eye was swollen and pink, looking like raw hamburger.

"Let's go."

She was aware of a sticky wetness dribbling from her chin and running down her throat. The fall on the concrete had cut her open. Absurdly, she hoped none would get on her tank top, because blood was a bitch to get out. Surely the least of her problems right now, but it sprang to the forefront of her mind.

He gave her a shove and they started up the driveway when Matt pulled in.

CHAPTER 22

Donna pointed to her truck and the cab driver pulled up next to it. The driver turned around and through a tangled beard said, "There ya be."

She paid him with a rumpled twenty she'd found in her pocket. Then she climbed out of the cab. The cab pulled away, its muffler rumbling.

The hospital had released her with instructions on how to care for her wounds. She didn't relish coming back here, but she needed to get her truck. Donna stepped on to the sidewalk. Looking around, she saw no sign of any police cars. She walked down the block and stopped at Rhonda's house.

I can't believe this.

Rhonda was dead, the house was burned, and Bob was acting like he didn't have a care in the world. It was amazing how the status quo could get so fucked up in such a short amount of time.

How did it come to this?

The house was a total loss, the paint around the windows scorched black where the smoke and flames had jumped out. The acrid tang of smoke and charred wood hung in the air, like the world's biggest bonfire. The right side of the roof was caved in, beams and joists burned black and sagging, leaving an open wound in the house. More likely than not, the town building inspector would deem the house unsafe and an emergency demolition would be performed.

Looking at the house, her throat tightened and she willed herself not to cry again. But she felt like she had let Rhonda down by not bringing her killer to justice.

The excursion into the house had left the murder suspect dead and the house ruined. Not to mention that she had witnessed a monstrosity take shape and chase her through the house. To top it off, her days as police chief were probably numbered once the full story of the incident got to the Marshall Town Supervisor.

She had to pull it together, somehow find a positive in this whole mess. If ever she needed redemption, it was now.

Calling Jill Adams would be a start.

Matt flung the car door open, making the hinges whine. He sprawled over, stuck his hand under the passenger seat and poked around until he gripped cold steel. He pulled the Beretta out and slipped out of the car.

Today was the day Ed Rafferty might die. Upon seeing Matt pull up, Rafferty had shoved a dazed-looking Jill up the driveway and into the side door of the house. If Rafferty hurt her, he would put one bullet hole in his body for every mark on Jill.

Keeping the gun pointed at the ground, he moved in a crouch to the side door. He tried the doorknob and found it locked. Matt kicked the door and it rattled. He lowered his shoulder and slammed into it. Still, it didn't give. He didn't want to resort to blasting the lock, but he had no choice. In a few minutes, neighbors would all be coming out of houses and gawking anyway.

Leveling the gun, he fired twice. The bullets splintered the wood and gave a ping as they shredded the lock. He kicked the door and it flew open.

Opening the screen door, he padded up the stairs to the landing between floors. Again he listened but heard only an appliance humming in Jill's apartment.

A refrigerator?

If he's hurt her . . .

He moved to the landing outside the kitchen door. To his dismay, that door was locked and he had to blast it as well. His ears rang from the gunshots.

He nudged the door open with his foot, both hands on the nine, in a shooter's stance, ready to fire.

He slipped into the kitchen, where one of the chairs lay on its side. Positive the kitchen was clear, he advanced to the dining room, where a glass lay on its side, a pool of water sinking into the rug.

Matt moved through the arch that separated the living and dining rooms, expecting Rafferty to pop out at him any moment. Rafferty had taken his family from him, and now he faced the possibility that the police chief had taken Jill. This gave him more reason to waste Rafferty, but the rate at which today's events had accelerated made him feel dizzy. He also felt vibrant, alive.

The living room was empty save for the furniture.

Sweat dripped down his back, plastering his shirt to the skin.

There was only the bedrooms and bathroom left.

He advanced to the windowless hallway.

Jill's bedroom was the first room on the left; its door was closed.

Matt braced his back against the wall and faced the door.

Coiling his leg, he kicked the door right below the knob. The door flew open and hit the wall.

Matt pointed the nine straight ahead, ready to fire. Instead of finding Rafferty behind the door, he found Jill.

She lay on the bed, one arm over her head, tied to the bedpost with a scarf. Her top was slit down the middle and sticky blood covered her abdomen. A brown leather belt covered her mouth, serving as a gag.

"Jesus, no."

She covered her wounded belly with her free hand, the blood staining her fingers.

Matt sat on the bed, setting the Beretta next to Jill's right arm, the one covering her wound. She shook her head furiously, motioning to the doorway.

"Let me see the wound."

He moved her hand to look at it. They were just scratches. Thank Christ.

Matt untied her hand and the gag, and kissed her on the cheek.

"I'm gonna get you out of here."

"Matt, he went and hid when he heard the gunshots. He's still here."

From behind him, Rafferty said, "Damn right I am."

Matt didn't have to turn around to know that Ed Rafferty had him covered with a gun.

"You should've checked the porch, loverboy."

The son of a bitch was hiding on the upstairs porch. How could he be so careless as not to check the porch?

"How do you like my artwork? You can't see it but it says 'bitch.' I couldn't finish the rest of my carving because you showed up."

Matt turned around to look at Rafferty. He held a big chrome revolver on Matt. "I'm gonna fucking kill you."

"I think not."

"Here's a souvenir for you. The artist's tool, if you will."

He tossed something onto the floor next to the bed. It was a steak knife, fresh with Jill's blood.

"Hands on your head."

Matt put his hands on his head and clasped his fingers. "Do you know who I am?"

"You're the little prick I stopped for speeding the other day."

"Close but no cigar."

"There's something else I should know?"

"Emerling Park. Family of four. You killed my parents and my little brother."

Rafferty raised an index finger, wiggled it back and forth. "I knew I knew you from somewhere else. Well, maybe I'll pick off the last family member today. Who knows?"

"You're gonna die, Chief Rafferty."

"If you say so," Rafferty said. "Get on your knees."

Matt looked down at Jill. She had inched her hand over to the Beretta, and now she gripped it.

Rafferty hadn't seen her grip the gun, for Matt was blocking his line of sight.

She mouthed, "How do I fire it?" to him.

"Point and pull," he mouthed back.

Rafferty said, "Enough of the sweet nothings. Get on the floor."

"Are you sure you want to do it?" Matt said to her.

"I'm sure," she said.

Matt nodded toward the floor, hoping that she would get the message that he was going to hit the deck. He hoped Rafferty would follow him with the gun and not have it pointed at Jill. She was putting herself in harm's way, and given the fact that she hated guns, he loved her for what she was about to do. It took incredible guts.

He nodded to her.

"On the ground now!"

Matt dove right, toward the foot of the bed. Rafferty tracked him with the revolver.

Jill raised the gun and fired, the gun bucking upward, causing the bullet to go high. Luckily Rafferty was a big target. The bullet caught him in the side of the face and spun him around, forcing him out the door and slamming him into the hallway wall.

Rafferty worked his way to his feet, ready to bring the big revolver up. Matt pushed himself up, ready to do damage.

Jill couldn't believe she had fired a gun at somebody.

Her wrist ached from the recoil of the weapon, and ringing buzzed in her ears. If they got out of this alive, she hoped her hearing would eventually come back to her.

Her stomach felt raw and sticky, thanks to Rafferty's artwork. He had thrown her over his shoulder and carried her up the stairs with tremendous speed. On the way into the apartment, he took a steak knife from one of the drawers, took her to her bedroom and tied her to the bed with the belt from her silk robe. To top it off, he took another belt off the dresser and gagged her. Then, working with quick strokes, he carved up her abdomen.

She hadn't given him the satisfaction of crying out while he was cutting her.

He told her he would wait for Matt to come upstairs, enter the room, and then sneak up behind him. If Matt were lucky, he would only frame him for Jill's assault. If he was unlucky, Rafferty would kill Matt, rape Jill and then get rid of both their bodies.

Now, Rafferty rose to his feet. A flap of ragged skin hung from his cheek where the bullet had grazed him.

The exposed bone gleamed; black fluid leaked down the side of his ruined face. She obviously hadn't scored a direct hit, because his brains would've been all over the wall. Although, who knew how much damage the thing under Rafferty's skin could sustain? Maybe it was immortal.

He started to raise the gun when Matt charged him. Matt drove his shoulder into Rafferty's gut and knocked him off balance. The revolver discharged, thundering a blast through the window and spraying glass across the floor.

Jill flattened herself against the bed, angry with herself for not pulling the trigger again before Rafferty got up. She felt numb, disconnected. It was like being in a slow-motion movie.

Matt wrapped his arms around Rafferty, tried to throw him to the side. Rafferty brought the revolver butt down on Matt's shoulder. Matt grunted but hung on to the Chief.

Matt hooked his leg behind Rafferty's and shoved, toppling him into the clothes hamper in the corner, hitting his head against the wall. Rafferty lifted the revolver again, but Matt slapped his wrist away, causing Rafferty's shot to blast a hole in the plaster.

Matt gripped his wrist, but Rafferty was too strong. He broke away and swung the gun at Matt, clipping him in the side of the face and knocking him aside.

Jill saw Rafferty swing around again, aiming the gun at her. The barrel looked as big as a subway tunnel.

"Die, bitch."

She rolled off the bed and onto the floor as he fired, the bullet taking out the plaster in chunks, spraying dust and chips on her head.

Rafferty got up, and Matt caught him in the throat with a punch. The blow sent Rafferty back against the wall, holding his throat, but still gripping the gun. Matt charged him, but Rafferty had the presence of mind to get his boot up, catching Matt in the gut and sending him to the ground.

Rafferty choked and gurgled in the corner. Jill hated herself for thinking this, but she hoped his windpipe was busted and he would choke to death.

He took his hands away from his throat and grinned. He aimed at Jill. Matt got his hand up and knocked Rafferty's hand aside before he could fire. Rafferty kicked him again.

Flat against the ground, Jill looked underneath the bed and saw Matt on the other side, his face still contorted in pain from Rafferty's kick.

"Matt!"

She slid the gun under the bed and it hit him in the chest. He looked surprised, as if the gun had dropped from the sky, and she yelled, "Shoot him!"

Matt picked up the gun, rolled on his back and fired. She closed her eyes and prayed for Rafferty to die.

CHAPTER 23

The bullets exploded out Rafferty's back, taking chunks of flesh and spraying the ebony blood on Jill's walls.

He gurgled once and collapsed against the bed, a big man in a small space, his arm folded at an odd angle over his head. The revolver fell to the floor next to the bed.

Matt had done what he came to Lincoln to do: kill the man who had taken his family from him. It all happened so quickly, he didn't have time to tell Rafferty exactly what he thought of him, or express the rage that had built up in him over the years like steam in a radiator. But the bastard was dead, and that was what mattered.

Matt said, "You can get up. He's dead."

Jill peeked over the mattress and then stood up. Her shirt was torn, exposing her stomach. Blood stained her skin, soaked her shorts.

"Are you sure he's dead?" she said.

"He looks dead enough."

"What about the thing underneath the skin? Do you think it dies with him?"

"Good point. Maybe I should finish him off."

"How?"

"Cut his head off."

"Omigod, Matt, no."

"Any better suggestions?"

"I suggest we get out of here. You and I know about the monster underneath, but other people may not. It looks like we just killed the Chief of Police."

"How long to get a few things together and patch yourself up?"

"Fifteen minutes."

"Make it five," Matt said. "I'll get the first-aid stuff."

Jill rifled through her dresser, pulling out underwear, shirts, shorts and jeans, and kept her head as far down as possible, trying not to look at Rafferty's corpse.

Matt checked the medicine cabinet in the bathroom and found a tube of Neosporin and some Band-Aids. He yelled to Jill, asking if she had any big gauze pads, and she answered no.

He dug through the linen closet in the hall and found a blue washcloth and matching towel. He ran the water in the bathroom, letting it get steamy hot, then soaped up his hands and scrubbed them vigorously. After wetting the washcloth, he returned to the bedroom with it, the towel and the Neosporin.

He glanced at Rafferty, half expecting him to jump up and leap at them. But his corpse remained in place, arm cocked over his head.

"You got any crop tops? You don't want anything rubbing against that."

"I'll throw my scrubs on. They're nice and loose."

"Now it's my turn to take care of you."

He touched the washcloth to her abdomen and she

winced. He mopped the blood off of her belly and then cleaned up her legs. Once the blood was wiped away, he could see the marks Rafferty had made, crude strokes that luckily were only superficial cuts. If Jill were fortunate, they would heal without leaving any scars.

"How'm I doing, nurse?"

"It'll do under the circumstances."

He unscrewed the cap from the Neosporin and squeezed a dab onto his index finger. Gently, he applied it to the cuts, her abdomen tightening with pain. When he was done, he put the cap back on the Neosporin and stuck the tube in his pocket.

"We'll stop and get some gauze pads for that."

She stripped off the shorts and her panties, surprising Matt.

"Don't look so surprised. We've got no time for modesty. Besides, you've seen it before."

She took a set of gray scrubs from the closet and put them on. After tying her hair back in a ponytail, she slipped on socks, and grabbed her spare clothes off the bed.

"Let's get going. He's giving me the creeps."

The phone rang, jolting them both.

"Forget it," she said.

It rang four times before the answering machine came on. Jill's voice came on the recording, sounding fuzzy. The beep went off.

"Jill, you there? It's Donna from the hospital. If you're there, pick up."

Jill took two leaping steps to pick up the phone before Donna hung up.

Matt overheard Jill telling her that they were in bad trouble, and that Rafferty was dead. He wanted to tell her to keep it quiet, not tell this Donna what had happened, for Matt hadn't met her and didn't know if he could trust her. But Jill had let it out of the bag, and they had to trust Donna not to turn them in to the cops.

Matt took out the phone book from underneath Jill's desk and looked up the number for Lincoln Firearms. He didn't have Harry's number with him, and he couldn't remember it off the top of his head. Hopefully Harry would be in the shop.

Jill said she would call Donna back and then hung up the phone.

"Ready?" she said.

"One more call and then we go."

Hands shaking, he punched in Harry's number and the phone rang. Eight rings, nine rings.

"Lincoln Firearms. Yello."

"Harry, it's Matt."

"Looking forward to our dinner. Still bringing that date?"

"Listen to me. We killed Rafferty. He was waiting for Jill in her apartment. He's dead."

"Jesus Christ!"

"We're getting out of town. We'll hole up at a hotel."

"No, don't do that. I've got a cabin up in Pottsville. Take Four Hundred to the end and turn right on Sixteen. Make the first right you see and take that road up into the hills. Cabin's at the top. There's a spare key inside the mailbox."

"Thanks, Harry. You sure you want to do this?"

"The shit's gonna hit the fan here anyway, Matt. I'll be up in the morning with a care package for you."

"And you can tell me what you know."

"Get going. I'll see you in the A.M."

The line clicked on the other end and Matt hung up the receiver.

"Where are we headed?" Jill asked.

"Pottsville. Harry's got a cabin off of Route Sixteen

we can stay in. He's gonna bring us some goodies tomorrow."

"Guns?"

"Hopefully. We might need them."

"We'd better go."

They linked hands, Jill carrying a blue duffel bag with her clothes in it.

Jill locked the door behind them and they went.

The tingling started in his fingers. His arm was bent over his head as if he were doing a crazy aerobics stretch; he wiggled his little finger.

His limbs were paralyzed and his chest burned like hell, but he was alive, and even better, he had heard every damn thing the two of them said. Rafferty had taken worse punishment than this and lived to tell the tale. Once he was hunting a gang member named Johnny Fernandez, and Johnny surprised him by flicking open a switchblade and stabbing him in the throat. The wound would have killed an ordinary man. Rafferty had torn Fernandez's arms off before he killed him.

He wiggled all his fingers, then rolled his hand in a circular motion at the wrist, the paralysis slowly fading. Within ten minutes he had sensation back in his entire body, although his tattered face and wounded chest hurt like hell.

His skin itched as it mended itself together, the slugs that had entered his body falling out like gumballs from a machine. Reaching up to his face, he held the tattered flap of skin to the cheekbone and it fused with the flesh.

Crowe had mentioned cutting his head off. That was one way to kill Rafferty's kind. The other was fire.

The ability to self-heal from even the most devastating wounds made Rafferty's kind superior to humans. If a regular man had taken those bullets, he would be lying on a morgue slab right now. His kind cut down by bullets rose to fight again in a matter of hours. Both the human skin that disguised him and the beast underneath were healing by the minute.

He stood up and looked in the mirror over the dresser. The skin on his face was flawless again, no sign of a scar or any trauma. The only signs of being shot were the black bloodstains on his face and the bulletholes in his uniform.

After picking up his revolver and holstering it, he left the apartment and walked around the block to where he had parked his cruiser. An elderly woman in a wool coat pulled a shopping basket as if it weighed as much as a Volkswagen. She looked at his tattered uniform and said, "Are you okay?"

"Mind your own business," he said. She looked as if he had reached out and grabbed her tit. Scurrying away, she muttered to herself.

He plunked himself into the driver's seat of the cruiser and called Clarence from his cell phone.

"Yeah, Chief."

"Keep your eyes peeled for a red Chevy pickup. Fifteen hundred model." He went on to describe Matt and Jill.

"What'd they do?"

"Put a couple new holes in me where I didn't have holes before."

"They shot you?"

"You catch on quick."

"Well, where are they? Let's go get them."

"I don't know at the moment, numb nuts. But I think they're heading to a cabin in Pottsville."

"You want me to set up a roadblock?"

"No. They left a few hours ago. We'll let them get up there and then take them. We're gonna do some hunting."

"Before the Harvest?"

"Fuck that rule. Meet me at my house in an hour. We have a lot of people to take care of. But first call up to Pottsville and find out who owns cabins up there. It's a small town, so someone should know."

He hung up the phone.

The drive to Pottsville took forty minutes, most of it down Route 400. Pines and spruce lined the road, creating dense woods where sunlight dabbled through in places, but never really penetrated. Not somewhere you'd want to be lost, Jill thought.

They took the last exit on 400, Route 16 South, and made the first right down a dirt road cut out of the pines. Matt urged the truck up a hill, the road winding left and then back to the right until the cabin was in sight.

The cabin sat five hundred feet off the road, in among the pines and cloaked in shadows. They pulled up the stone driveway and parked the truck at the side of the cabin.

It was constructed of brownish-black wood, with red shingles on the roof. The chimney sagged to the right, and the bricks looked ready to topple. There was a four-foot wood cutout stuck into the lawn, painted like Uncle Sam and holding a small American flag.

They approached the front door and Matt reached into the mailbox that hung on the front of the house. After fumbling around for a moment, he pulled out a brass key and stuck it in the lock. He jiggled it left, then right, before the lock clicked and the door opened.

The cabin smelled of wood smoke but it seemed to have the things they would need to stay here for a while. A double bed faced the door, and next to the bed was a stand with a clock radio on it. The place had a stove, a card table and chairs and, to Jill's relief, a phone.

"Looks homey enough. It's got a wood stove in case we get cold," Jill said.

"Don't think we have to worry about that yet. I'm going to run outside, so why don't you bandage yourself up?" Matt suggested.

They had stopped at a Rite-Aid and picked up gauze, tape and more Neosporin.

Matt headed for the front door.

Jill said, "Do you think they'll come after us?"

"I think it's a pretty safe bet."

"Harry's bringing guns, right?"

"Right."

"Good," she said. "I never thought I'd hear myself say that."

She crossed her arms and rubbed them for warmth. The thought of things coming out of the woods to hunt them gave her the shivers.

Picking the Rite-Aid bag off the table, she went into the bathroom to put gauze over her wounds.

The bathroom was done in bubble-gum-pink tiles, and the toilet had a furry hot pink cover over its seat. It smelled a little damp, but the place was free of mildew, and the sink gleamed.

The door banged as Matt went outside. She liked the way he had insisted on taking care of her at the apartment—sweet, but not overbearing. He had applied the ointment to her stomach with such a light touch, careful not to hurt her in any way.

She was used to caring for others, putting in an IV or bandaging a wound, so it was nice to have someone take care of her, even in a small way.

As she took the gauze and tape out of the bag, she hoped this Harry was good on his word to deliver weapons to them.

Although she disliked guns, a firearm had saved their lives today, and it was a good bet that wasn't the last time they would need one.

But could she bring herself to fire one again? That she didn't know.

Matt walked around the back of the cabin. He had the hunting knife in the sheath on his belt and the gun tucked into the rear of his pants.

A cord of firewood rested against the back of the cabin, and there was a picnic table and a rainbow-colored lawn chair in the backyard. The yard sloped away from the cabin, a dirt trail leading down into the pines and the forest beyond.

They were on a hill, and that was a plus, because it was a good defensive position. The only ways to get at the cabin were the main road and that dirt trail. Matt hoped the creatures couldn't attack from the trail. The possibility of a front *and* rear attack presented even greater problems.

Still, it made him nervous because he had seen Them in action, the way they tore out of the woods that day at the park. If they came at the cabin in any type of numbers, he and Jill wouldn't last long.

He had a bad feeling in his gut, a gnawing, that the Chief of Police might have survived the bullets. Who knew how much damage one of them could take and still keep going? Despite his concern, he snickered to himself, visualizing Rafferty as an evil Energizer Bunny with pink ears.

Regardless of whether Rafferty was dead or alive, the Lincoln Police would be looking for the suspects, combing the area. Hopefully no one saw them leave the scene, and if Rafferty really was dead, he couldn't describe his killers.

Even though they were nearly forty miles from Lincoln, it didn't seem far enough.

He took another glance into the woods, where columns of sunlight broke through the trees. Not much light and plenty of darkness to conceal an attacker.

He hoped Harry was bringing them some heavy-duty weaponry.

Matt walked back around and went in the front door. Jill came out of the bathroom. A small Band-Aid covered the cut on her chin. She had also plastered gauze over the wound on her arm.

"You look like you just fought a war."

"You don't look so hot yourself." Jill said.

"I know. Seriously, how are you?"

"It stings, but I'll live. How about you? Rafferty clipped you good a couple of times."

"Oh yeah."

He was so high on adrenaline that he hadn't felt much pain, but now that Jill mentioned it, he had a dull throb in his stomach where Rafferty kicked him. His left cheekbone also felt tender, and upon touching it, he knew he was going to have one hell of a shiner from getting clocked with the revolver. He already had a purple bruise under the other eye from the assault with the nightstick.

"Damn. I was just starting to feel better from the damage you did to me in the warehouse."

She offered him a thin smile. "What are we going to do? We're fugitives. And God knows how many of those things are looking for us right now."

"I figure we stay here at least until morning. See what Harry brings us, then decide from there."

She moved in close to him and looked him in the eyes. "Whatever happens, I'm glad I found you."

She wrapped her arms around his neck, careful not to press her belly against him. He could feel her heat, smell her scent. He hugged back, banishing sexual thoughts from his mind for now, trying to focus on what lay ahead of them.

"Ditto for me," he said.

He would not lose her to Rafferty like he did his family.

Metal banging in the yard. Garbage cans being turned over?

Sally Perski set her Harry Potter book on the bed, got up and peered out the window. Nothing out there, save the darkness.

It was probably a neighborhood cat rummaging for scraps.

"Sally, turn that fan down," her mother called.

"But it's hotter than hell!"

"Watch your mouth, young lady. Turn it down."

The window fan, old and yellowed, thrummed and rattled on the highest setting. Sally clicked the knob to Low and lay back on the bed with her book. She and her mom were alone tonight; Brendan was spending the night with her Aunt Katherine in Buffalo.

She would spoil him rotten for the evening, giving him one chocolate chip cookie after another and renting all the Barney videos that Blockbuster had to offer. She wished someone would spoil her like that.

Something thumped on the outside wall of the bedroom.

Again she put the book down and rolled off of the bed. She couldn't look out that window because the fan was in the way. Something hit the wall again.

"What the hell?"

She had just begun to curse this past year, liking the sounds of the words but not brave enough to use anything other than "hell" or "damn" around her mother.

Drawing the miniblinds aside, she looked out the window that overlooked the yard.

Something like black velvet streaked toward the house. "Mom!"

Glass shattered and the wood in the window frame gave with a hollow crack. The fan banged against the ground.

A creature from a nightmare stuck its head in the ruined side window. Sally moved away from the rear window, just in time, as a clawed hand burst through the glass.

The creatures Matt Crowe described had come for her.

The one at the side window crammed its lanky frame into the bedroom, ducking its head to avoid hitting the ceiling. Its amber eyes focused on her and it grinned, showing nasty teeth.

They smelled so bad she thought the SpaghettiOs she had for dinner would come back up.

She managed to take a step toward the door before it wrapped its arm around her waist and yanked her off her feet.

All she could think was that she was glad Brendan wasn't here.

Across town, Lila Reese held a stinking bag of garbage at arm's length. At their home in the Hamptons, they had a cleaning woman to handle menial chores like this, but not here. She would have to suffer through it.

She opened the garbage can lid and dropped the bag in. After replacing the lid, she rubbed her hands together, as if to get the filth off of them.

Arthur Reese was out of town, negotiating the sale of one of his hotel chains to some Texas millionaire. She could care less who or what as long as the money kept rolling in. Arthur was on the verge of becoming a billionaire, and damned if she wouldn't try and spend every last cent of his money.

On top of it all, Carla still hadn't come home. Her calls to the Lincoln police had gotten her nowhere. The officers told Lila she should give it some time. *Give it some time!* She had called Arthur, who put in a call to a private investigator.

She told Carla a thousand times a day to be careful, that she was a pretty girl, and there were a lot of creeps out there who would love to get their hands on her. In her heart, she always knew something like this would happen. Carla was just too pretty, and the world was full of weirdos.

She walked back to the side door and opened it.

Something smelled rotten in the hallway. Then she caught sight of it and felt a knot of fear in her stomach.

There was something big and black and hulking waiting for her. It growled like an animal. Twin yellow globes glared at her from the darkened hallway.

It moved forward and leapt down the stairs. It grabbed her arm and pulled. There was no initial pain, only a sharp tug and a popping noise, and she thought it dislocated.

When she looked at her shoulder, the spurt of blood and torn fabric told her different.

The last thing she saw was the thing coming closer, her severed arm in its claws.

CHAPTER 24

Nothing like a good stroke to kill the time.

Carl pulled his coveralls up and zipped the front closed. Even when he worked at night he still wore them— even if there were no cars, it made him feel more mechanic-like. He stuffed the August issue of *Playboy* magazine in his rear pocket and sauntered back into the office.

He sat in the squeaky chair and propped his feet on the desk, something Jimbo couldn't stand him doing, but Jimbo was nowhere to be found. Carl and the other mechanic, Don Gerritt, had kept the place open without Jimbo.

Carl felt like a liberated slave. He could put his feet on the desk or sneak off to the john whenever he wanted. He had even managed to skim a hundred and forty dollars from the register in Jimbo's absence.

Hell, no one had come looking for that salesman he had killed. The body had been consumed, and his Lexus was at the bottom of Lake Erie. By the time they found the car, the Harvest would come, and they would be on the move, looking for other towns to occupy.

"Fuck you, Jimbo. Carl's running the show now."

A crash came from the garage. It sounded like one of the toolboxes had been tipped over and everything had spilled out onto the concrete.

Carl shot up from the chair and grabbed the metal Swingline stapler off the desk, it being the only weapon available.

Facing the door, he tried scaring them off.

"Whoever's in there, I got a loaded Magnum!"

He stepped back toward the glass door leading to the pumps.

The door to the garage bay squeaked open like a coffin lid in a Dracula movie.

"I mean it! I'll fucking blow your head off!"

Something flew through the door and rapped him right on the kneecap. Pain flared, and he instinctively hopped on one foot. He looked down and saw the impact wrench lying on the floor.

A chrome revolver appeared in the doorway, its owner guarded by the shadows in the garage.

"Turn the lights off and put up the Closed sign, now."

Carl didn't want to argue with a loaded gun, so he flipped the lights off and turned the sign around.

"Now sit down."

He hopped on his good foot to the chair and sat down, his knee a mess of throbs and aches.

Ed Rafferty stepped from the shadows, stark naked, his skin white as an eggshell.

Rafferty naked? If he was naked, that meant he must've been on a hunt.

"What do you want, Chief?"

Even as he asked the question, Carl knew it was a foolish one, because in his heart he knew Ed Rafferty hadn't come here to wish him happy birthday. He meant to hurt Carl.

"Seen Jimbo around?" Rafferty said.

"Not for days. I been runnin' the station myself."

"Good for you. Have any more salesmen drop in?"

Oh, shit. "Salesmen?"

"Don't play dumb, Carl. Jimbo told me about the salesman you offed. I hope it was a good one."

"I didn't mean to, Chief. But he was causing trouble. You're not gonna kill me, are you?"

Rafferty reached over and clapped him on the arm. "Relax, Carl, I'm not going to kill you. Hey, you got a smoke?"

"Uh, yeah, sure."

He'd never seen Rafferty smoke before. Maybe he only did it once in a while.

He pawed at his shirt before feeling the battered pack of Winstons tucked in the breast pocket. After removing the pack, he plucked a cigarette out with his thumb and index finger and gave it to Rafferty. Then he picked up his Bic from the desk and lit it for the chief.

Rafferty inhaled, the butt glowing in the dark office like an ember. He blew smoke over his head, and it circled him in a gauzy haze.

"That was a big mistake, Carl. Killing like that. You know the rules."

"Yeah. I know."

"I'll forget about it this time because you're young and stupid."

Carl didn't respond, instead transfixed by Rafferty's total lack of shame or embarrassment at standing nude in a gas station.

"Before I go, I'd like a favor."

Carl swallowed hard. Was Rafferty going to ask him for something weird, like a blow job? He'd rather take a bullet in the guts than do that.

"What?"

"One of those little gas cans to keep in my patrol car. In case I ever run out of gas."

"Oh yeah. Sure!"

Carl pursed his lips and blew out a breath of relief. He pushed himself up with his good leg and limped past Rafferty into the service bays. He remembered leaving a half full gallon can near the compressor.

He returned to the office and handed it to Rafferty.

"Even got some gas in it for you."

He hoped that would satisfy the chief. Carl wanted him out of here.

"I'm not going to kill you, Carl. But you will have an accident. A horrible one."

Rafferty set his weapon on the floor and unscrewed the cap and spout from the gas can. In one quick motion, like a quarterback flipping a shovel pass, he doused Carl's face in gasoline.

It felt like liquid fire in his eyes and he screamed, rubbing his eyes and only succeeding in irritating them more.

Rafferty has a lit cigarette. A hot pinprick kissed his cheek and then there was nothing but searing orange light.

He fell to the ground screaming, beating at the flames.

Rafferty left Carl's flaming body and hurried out the front door.

He looked back, seeing the flames spread across a throw rug and to the magazine rack, whose contents would provide more fuel for the fire. If he were lucky, maybe the flames would get to the gas tanks buried under the pumps, and the place would go up like the Fourth of July.

Jimbo's place was gone. The old coot dead. That served him right for ever messing with Rafferty.

He accelerated around the back of the station, the night air rushing over his body, making him tingle. He hopped a fence and cut diagonally through a yard with a small pool and swing set, jumped another fence, and bolted down a driveway.

He was being especially ballsy, running naked through yards back to his patrol car, but tonight he felt invincible.

He had survived bullet wounds that would've buried a man, and now he felt unstoppable. So what if someone saw him running through yards? As far as he was concerned, no one could touch him. All that worrying about being found out by Outsiders and sneaking around was useless. His kind was the superior race, and they didn't need to worry about humans anymore.

After taking the Perski girl, her mother and the Reese bitch, he had changed back into human form and elected to leave his clothes off when he took care of Carl. He wanted to see the look on the little punk's face when he showed up naked. It was priceless.

Now, he knifed across a front lawn, feeling the same exhilaration a big cat must feel when on a hunt.

His patrol car was in sight, and he leapt over the hood, landing squarely. He got into the car and closed his eyes, relishing the night's work.

A murder witness was out of the way, the murder victim's mother was taken care of, and he had removed Carl, something he'd been wanting to do for a long time. His officers and other volunteers were taking care of the humans in the park who had stopped to stare at Carla Reese's body. They would disappear, and their homes would be burned to the ground.

If anyone wanted to know what happened, they could come and see him. He didn't care. The Harvest was soon, and the Outsiders who lived in town would be slaughtered, so let them come and see him.

He felt like he was in control again. The only thing left was for Clarence to find that cabin where Jill and Matt were staying. Then his remaining problems would end.

* * *

Donna had waited for Jill's return call. Her phone rang at six in the morning, the day after Jill had said they'd killed Rafferty. Jill had given Donna directions to the cabin and now she cruised down the expressway, both sides lined with trees. Hopefully the cabin wasn't much farther. She hated driving in the boonies.

She was a city girl, born and bred, and being out in the country like this was the equivalent of landing on Jupiter. Marshall was about as far from the city as she wanted to get, being twenty miles away from Buffalo. It was a small village, with a population just over ten thousand, most of them wealthy.

Now she was on her way into the heart of the country, suspended from work and dealing with movie monsters living in a town not thirty miles from her home. She felt she had to join the fight against them (if there was going to be one) and take action to avenge Rhonda's death.

Her Colt Anaconda rested on the seat next to her, the backup weapon to her automatic, lost in the fire. It was a .44 Magnum, and after seeing that thing chasing her through the house, she had her doubts about even a .44 being able to do much damage to one of them.

She got off the 400 at Route 16 and nearly passed the dirt road; she had to screech the brakes and crank the wheel to make the turn.

She parked behind a red Chevy pickup, holstered the Colt and approached the front door. The grass had a filmy frost on it, and the cabin was draped in shadows. She was surprised to find herself shivering on the last day of August.

She knocked on the door and took a step back.

A boyishly handsome guy opened the door, pointing a piece at her. He also had a large hunting knife in a sheath on his belt.

"That an automatic in your hand or you just glad to see me?" she said. "I'm Donna Ricci."

He laughed and the ice was broken. He lowered the weapon and invited her inside.

"Sorry for the greeting, but we can't be too careful."

"No problem."

Jill sat on the bed, pulling on socks.

"Donna, this is Matt Crowe," she said.

She shook his hand.

Matt said, "Jill tells me you saw one of them."

"I did more than saw it. The son of a bitch chased me."

"What did it look like?"

"Tall. Yellowish eyes. Claws. Smelled like someone took a dump in a bucket of spoiled eggs."

"That's about right. You're lucky you got away."

"You're familiar with Them?"

"All too."

Jill stood up off the bed and slipped into sneakers. "They killed Matt's family."

"Rafferty was with them," Matt said.

"I'm sorry to hear that. They got my sister-in-law too. That's why I was in her house."

"Who was it?"

"Some low-life junkie named Charles Dietrich. He must've been waiting for Rhonda when she got home," Donna said.

Donna took off the light cotton jacket she was wearing, set it on the card table and then sat down. "I questioned Rafferty on what happened, but he gave me the runaround. So I tried checking things out for myself and wound up burning down my brother's house."

Jill joined her at the table.

"What does your brother think about all this?" Matt asked.

"I actually think he's glad to be rid of her. He told me that this was a new beginning for him."

Donna still felt a surge of acid in her stomach at the

thought of the fight she had with Bob. "But that's Bob for you. Diddling his assistant on the side."

"That's awful," Jill said.

Donna pointed to Matt's weapon. "So what kind of firepower you have? Those things are pretty damn strong."

Matt held up the gun. It was an automatic, maybe a Beretta. "This is it, so far. But Harry's supposed to be bringing us more."

"Can he get his hands on any artillery? How about an M-1 tank?"

"Maybe some nukes," Jill chimed in.

"Or how about a nuclear sub? We could blow the bastards back to the Stone Age."

Matt threw up his hands. "You two are out of control."

From outside came the sound of a car engine.

"That's gotta be Harry. No more comments from the peanut gallery, okay?" Matt said.

"We promise," Donna said.

"Scouts' honor," Jill said.

Donna liked the two of them already.

Matt opened the front door and watched the big Lincoln roll up the driveway, smooth and quiet. He expected Harry to stop, but instead he swerved the car to the right, drove around the two pickup trucks, ran over a big root and then pulled around the back of the cabin.

Turning toward the dirt trail, he gunned the engine, pulled down the trail and then backed up, nearly turning the picnic table into splinters. The guy needed a reverse alarm on his vehicle.

He got out of the Lincoln, brushing yellow crumbs off of his flannel shirt.

"Nice piece of driving," Matt said.

"Good morning to you too."

Donna and Jill came out to see what was going on. Matt introduced them both to Harry and they all shook hands and exchanged hellos

"Shit, I almost forgot," Harry said.

Matt was puzzled.

The big man opened the driver's side door and reached over the seat, producing a brown shopping bag. "Here we go. Gotta have breakfast."

He thrust the bag at Matt, who opened it. Fresh blueberry muffins and a gallon of orange juice.

Donna took the bag from Matt. "I'll take these in and get some plates."

"No sampling until we come in," Matt said.

"Then you'd better hurry," Donna said.

She disappeared around the front of the cabin.

Harry popped open the trunk, nodded toward Jill. "So this is the date you were going to bring for dinner? You've got excellent taste, Matt."

"A one-man army *and* a flirt," Jill said.

"Only the best for Matt Crowe. No non-pedigrees," Matt said.

Jill whacked him on the arm.

"Here," Harry said, and gave him a burlap sack. It had a round object in it that felt as heavy as a bowling ball.

"Jill, how about taking these in, please?"

Harry took out two Winchester Model 1300 Defender shotguns and handed them to Jill, who took them by the pumps, barrels pointing up. He then took out a wooden crate and Matt immediately smelled gasoline. There were a dozen dusty glass bottles stuffed with rags and filled with gasoline.

Molotov cocktails.

"You drove up here with those in your trunk? What if you had an accident?"

"If I didn't die in Vietnam, I ain't gonna die in no car

wreck," Harry scoffed. Then he hauled out the real goodies: an M-60 machine gun and an M-79 grenade launcher. He set those on the ground and told Matt to take the grenade launcher in the house and the M-60 upstairs.

"Upstairs?" Matt said.

"You didn't notice it?"

"Can't say I did."

"I'll show you later."

Matt took the grenade launcher inside and returned for the M-60, while Harry pulled out two wooden crates, presumably full of ammunition. He also revealed two M-16 rifles with grenade launchers under the barrel.

"You got Jimmy Hoffa in there too?"

"You'd be surprised what's been in this trunk."

They hauled the M-60 and the crates inside and set them on the floor next to the table. Donna had washed a stack of plates and was drying the last one with a paper towel when they came in. She had also taken out four blue plastic cups and set them on the table.

"That's some serious firepower," Donna said.

"Yep," Harry replied.

"Harry, Donna's chief of police in Marshall," Jill said.

"Well isn't that just wonderful, a police officer. Do you have any ATF agents you want to introduce me to?"

"Relax," Donna said. "I won't tell if you won't."

"Deal."

They all sat down at the table and dug into the blueberry muffins and juice. They were slightly warm, sweet-tart and delicious.

Through a mouthful of blueberries, Harry said, "Let me tell you what I know. You're in for a lollapalooza."

The muffins were all but crumbs.

Harry leaned back in his chair, content, his hands folded on his belly. Matt took the plates and cups to the sink while the others settled in. Jill felt a mild tingle of excitement race through her at the thought of Harry's story. She had always been a little too curious for her own good, one time when she was little unscrewing a cover plate for an outlet to see the wires inside and slipping the screwdriver into the slot by mistake. She got one hell of a jolt for her troubles and a sore arm for two days.

Matt joined them at the table.

Harry stood up, brought the burlap sack to the table and set it down. "Exhibit A," he said.

He shuffled the cloth off of the object. The top of it was grayish white, smooth and domed. More of the sack came off to reveal two huge eye sockets, a nasal cavity and wickedly sharp teeth that jutted from a bear trap–like jaw. The skull was three times the size of a human cranium.

"Where the hell did you get that?" Matt said.

"My father. He killed one of these things," Harry said, with some amount of pride.

Jill reached out, eager to see just how sharp the teeth were. She tapped her finger against one of the teeth and was rewarded with a pinprick of blood.

"My God, those are sharp," she said, and sucked blood off her fingertip.

"These things have existed for hundreds of years. Maybe thousands," Harry said. "My father kept a diary about them. Knew a lot."

"How did your father know so much about them?" Donna said.

Harry straightened himself up and leaned forward, elbows on the table. "Dad had an encounter with one when he was about nineteen. He was hunting up in these woods. This cabin was his. Anyway, he's on a trail tracking a buck when the woods go dead silent. He hears branches crunching off the trail and the next thing he knows it was exploding out of the woods at him."

"What'd he do?" Matt said.

"Fired the shotgun right in its face. It ran off into the woods, shrieking, and Dad ran back to the cabin, got in his truck and took off. He rarely came back up here after that."

"Then what?" Jill said.

"He became somewhat of an expert on them. Interviewed a lot of old-timers who'd seen them. All over the county."

"How did he come upon the skull?" Donna said.

"I grew up on a farm in Holland, about forty miles from Lincoln. One night Dad hears our horses making a terrible racket, like they want to bust out of the barn. He took me and his Winchester out to see what was the matter. Well, we get in the barn and isn't there one of the bastards with one of our horses pinned to the ground. Old Buddy. Buddy's got a bite out of his neck the size of a melon."

Harry ran his hand over the top of the skull, as if petting a dog. Jill thought he was trying to calm his nerves.

"It charged us, and Dad fired, but it kept coming. So he tells me to run and tosses a kerosene lantern at the thing. It went up like a Roman candle, screeching and screaming. He put a few more shots from the Winchester in it too. If I live to be a hundred I'll never forget that night. I can still smell it burning."

"What else do you know?" Matt said.

"From what Dad learned about them from his interviews, they live inside people. He was never sure if they take over a host body, like a parasite, or if they have a natural disguise that they use. Meaning a human body. And there's this too."

He took a hot pink piece of paper from his pocket, unfolded it and placed it on the table. Jill snatched it up.

HARVEST SOCIETY TO MEET
St. Mark's School Gymnasium
September 3
Time: 7 p.m.
MEMBERS ONLY

She passed it to Matt, who then passed it on to Donna.

"What the hell does this mean?" Donna said.

"They're preparing to Harvest."

"Harvest what?" Jill said.

"People."

Jill's blood temperature felt like it dropped twenty degrees.

"They hunt sporadically. They can't draw attention to themselves, so their kills have to be selective. They sustain themselves for most of the time with huge amounts of food. But they're hunters by nature, or so my dad thought. About every hundred years the sons of bitches all show their true forms and go on a mass hunt. They'll try for as many as they can get in Lincoln, then they'll move on and start in another town."

"Sweet Jesus. I have articles about entire towns disappearing off the map." Matt said.

Donna said, "And this meeting. What's it for? To plan the attack?"

"Not sure. All I know is I've been planning to stop it for a long time," Harry said.

"How?" Donna said.

"I've got a small arsenal built up under my gun shop. Lots of explosives. C-4, satchel charges, hell boxes, blasting caps, the works. I figure we can blow them to pieces."

"Sneak into the meeting place?" Matt said.

"You got it. I figure explosives are the only way. Maybe bring in some gasoline too. For some extra insurance."

"Don't people try and join this society? Or wonder what goes on there?"

"Anyone can talk to Rafferty about joining, but they're always turned down for one reason or another. People think it's some kind of exclusive club, but they really have no idea what it is. They just want to be a part of it."

If they only knew, Jill thought.

"How long have they controlled Lincoln?" Donna said.

"For as long as anyone could remember. If you corner some of the old-timers, they might tell you what they know."

They would be taking a huge risk in trying to stop the Harvest, but if they didn't act, hundreds of people in Lincoln would die, not to mention anyone else who got in the way. It was quite possible that they could all be killed trying to stop the Harvest. The thought of trying to stop them made her guts feel weak, but she had never been one to stand by and let others suffer. She decided to speak up. "I say we do it. Come up with a plan and try to stop them."

Matt smiled at her—a proud smile? She knew he wouldn't leave the town without a fight.

"Or we could cut our losses and skip town," Donna said.

"And just let this happen?" Jill said.

"You're right," Donna said. "I owe Rhonda something."

"Then we do it?" Harry said.

Matt stood up. "Let's hit the bastards," he said. "Hard."

Rafferty told Clarence he'd given him this assignment because he couldn't trust anyone else to undertake such an important mission. In Clarence's book, it was another way of saying that you had been elected for shit work.

Keeping low to the ground, he pushed his way uphill, branches catching him on the cheek and arms, leaving little white scratches. Not enough to hurt, just enough to be annoying.

Sweat trickled from his scalp and matted his hair to his forehead. It was only ten o'clock in the morning and already hotter than the devil's sauna.

Rafferty had given him the task of snooping around Pottsville and finding the owners of cabins in the area.

He had stopped at the 7-Eleven on Route 16. The kid behind the counter wore a black T-shirt with the name KORN emblazoned on the front of it. The punk had blue hair and rings in his eyebrow, nostril and lower lip.

Clarence wondered how the little freak had ever gotten hired.

The kid had responded "I don't know" to most of his questions before becoming agitated and telling Clarence to take a walk. Clarence was dressed in jeans and a plain blue tee, out of his uniform. The kid failed to notice the shield clipped to his belt, as well as the automatic holstered at his side. Or maybe he just didn't care.

Clarence was about to turn and go when an old man in a John Deere hat with saggy, wrinkled skin spoke up. "Hear you're looking for owners to cabins. There's two in town here. One's owned by George Grey. Fella named Pierce owns the other one. Out of towner."

After getting directions to both cabins, he left, flashing the punk behind the counter a dirty look.

He had called Linda at the station and asked her to look up the names in the phone book, and sure enough, Harry Pierce lived right in Lincoln. Linda also told him that her sister knew Liza, Harry's wife, and that they owned the gun shop in town.

That could be important, because they could be armed to the teeth up there.

Now, he continued climbing until he was a hundred yards from the cabin, then he flattened himself out against the earth and took out a small pair of binoculars.

A squirrel bounced across his path, making him flinch. "Fucker," he said.

He lifted the binoculars to his eyes and scanned from left to right. There were two pickup trucks parked next to the cabin, a Ford and the Chevy Rafferty had described to him. No one in sight yet, though.

After watching on and off for five minutes, someone stepped from the front door, a tough-looking broad with short blond hair. She had a shotgun cocked under one arm, pointing at the ground, and she seemed comfortable with it.

He wondered what other weapons they had in the cabin.

An older fat guy came out to join her, and he had a funny-looking gun in his hand. Clarence wasn't sure, but he thought it might be a grenade launcher.

Rafferty would appreciate this reconnaissance. He'd better.

The squirrel darted in front of him again, and he was half tempted to put a round in its hide.

Damn, he hated the woods.

He watched the blond woman again, and this time she seemed to be looking at him, as if she had spotted him.

He made himself one with the forest floor, pressing tight against the dirt.

BOOK THREE
Harvest

CHAPTER 25

Donna had agreed to keep watch out front while Harry and Matt set up some of the defenses.

They had all agreed to try and stop the Harvest, and all four would stay at the cabin tonight, even if it meant fending off an attack.

She focused her attention back on the pine trees. It was amazing how little light filtered through them, making them seem like the woods of Hansel and Gretel and all the other fairy tales meant to scare children. The deep, dark woods where witches and big bad wolves waited to snap up little kids.

There was a shape on the ground a hundred yards away, but Donna couldn't tell if it was a log, an animal carcass or a person. Would they be so bold to send someone up here? Knowing Rafferty's arrogance she answered her own question; she was surprised Rafferty didn't come and knock on the door himself.

She stuck her head inside the cabin and motioned for Harry to come out. He was in the midst of prying the top off of a crate with a crowbar, his face getting redder by the second.

He pushed himself up off of one knee and instinctively grabbed the grenade launcher off the table. Maybe he sensed something was wrong too.

"What's up?"

"Take a look down there, about a hundred yards."

She pointed to the general area and Harry squinted.

"What am I looking for?"

"Maybe a log, maybe a visitor."

He moved his head forward and used his hand to shield his eyes from the sun. "Too dark to tell for sure. Unless we go down there."

"What if it's a trap?"

"That's what I'm thinking. It's probably nothing, but if we go down there, we could be ambushed. Keep watch. We're gonna have to hustle to get this stuff ready."

Harry trotted back into the cabin.

Donna hunkered down like a catcher, the shotgun resting across her knees.

They wouldn't attack this early, this time of day, would they?

They had seen him. He knew it.

Now the blond lady was squatting down, and he could feel her gaze on him. Why hadn't he been more careful?

He took another look through the field glasses, confident the woods were dark enough not to reflect light off the lenses. Her head turned back toward the cabin, as if someone was calling her, and then she stood up and went through the door.

This was his chance. He could go back down the hill, get in the unmarked and take off, or he could cut farther up the hill and flank the cabin, getting a better look at everything. He really didn't have enough information to bring back to Rafferty, just that they had a shotgun and a grenade launcher. They could have a how-itzer set up behind the cabin for all he knew, and when the attack came, he and the others could be devastated.

No, he needed to bring more information back to Rafferty.

He got to his feet, brushed the dirt off of his jeans and started up the hill and to the left of the cabin.

Matt wiped his forehead with the front of his shirt. He was up in the cabin's crawl space, which was accessed by sliding away a wood panel in the ceiling and lower-ing a ladder. He hadn't even noticed it when he and Jill had arrived at the cabin.

He was hunched over, the roof joists six inches from his head. It was full of spider- and cobwebs, and he had squashed a pile of mouse droppings upon stepping into the crawl space.

The M-60 was a bitch to get up into the crawl space, and Matt hoisted it up with one arm while gripping the ladder rungs with the other. Jill had passed him up the ammunition, which made him think of "Praise the Lord and pass the ammunition." He had snickered to himself and when Jill asked what was so funny, he said, "Noth-ing."

After pounding on the small window, he managed to open it, and set the stand for the machine gun on the sill. It provided a good field of fire, and put the entire front area of the cabin within the gun's range. Because it was so cramped, he would lie on his stomach the length of the crawl space to fire the weapon.

He hoped that the gun would pack enough punch to kill those things.

From downstairs, Harry said, "Matt, come down for a second."

He backed himself up and climbed down the ladder.

Matt brushed himself off and a tiny dust cloud appeared around him, like Pigpen in the *Peanuts* comic strips.

"There might be a scout out in the woods. What do you think about taking a walk down?" Harry asked

"It might be an ambush. Or it might be nothing," Matt said.

"My thoughts exactly," Harry said. "Whoever they are, they won't learn much. Except I do have one more thing to show you, but that's out back."

Harry jerked his thumb toward the back wall of the cabin.

"I say we keep a constant watch," Jill said.

"Yeah," Donna agreed.

Matt nodded in agreement with them.

"We'll take shifts. I'll keep the first watch. Someone can relieve me in an hour," Donna said.

Jill agreed to take the second watch, Matt the third, and Harry the fourth.

Harry slapped his forehead. "Son of a bitch! I almost forgot!"

They all looked at him as if he were an escaped lunatic. At first Matt thought it would be really bad news, like Harry forgot the magazines for the M-16s or worse, forgot the grenades for the launchers, which would be one of their most effective weapons.

"The fires. There were at least a dozen houses set on fire last night. In Lincoln. There were fatalities. I heard it on the scanner."

"Addresses?" Matt said.

"All over the place. Jimbo's gas station went up too."

"I'd bet a dime to a dollar that Rafferty and his crew were responsible," Jill said.

"If there were only some way to find out," Matt said.

If he had to guess, he would say that Sally Perski and Lila Reese were two of the victims whose houses went up in flames. Rafferty wouldn't want family members or witnesses snooping around and leaking his secrets out, so he most likely had killed them.

"Without being in town, it's pretty impossible," Harry said.

The young girl, Sally, had seemed like a nice kid, and although Matt hadn't particularly cared for Lila Reese, he felt sorrow for her too. Two more innocent people murdered by that son of a bitch. "I was just thinking that Sally Perski and Lila Reese are probably two of the victims."

"More cover-ups," Donna said, shaking her head.

Matt said, "As sad as it is, we can't let it distract us. They could come for us at any time. Jill and I are putting you two in harm's way. Are you sure you want to stick around?"

"I've got nothing to lose at this point. If I can deal out some payback, then so be it," Donna said.

"And I've been preparing for the Harvest for years. I was gonna tangle with them sooner or later," Harry added.

"Besides, we couldn't leave the two of you to the wolves, could we?" Donna said.

There weren't many people who would stick beside you when the proverbial shit hit the fan, and the fact that Matt had found three of them made him believe that there were still decent people in the world. They were around, but you just had to look a little harder to find them.

Jill gave Donna a hug, who accepted it awkwardly, and then kissed Harry on his cheek. His face immediately turned the color of a Valentine's Day heart.

Harry said, "Enough with the mushy stuff. We've got preparations to make. Jill and Matt, follow me. Donna, keep your eyes peeled. And take one of the M-16s. It has better range than that shotgun."

Harry seemed to be hitting his stride, and Matt could imagine him twenty-five years younger and a hundred pounds lighter, a lean, tight leader of men, barking orders and doing his best to fight a lost cause. He was in his element.

"You're forgetting something," Donna said. "I don't know how to fire one of these. Especially the grenade launcher."

"Oh yeah. Jill, you watch this too."

Harry took the gun from Donna and gave an impromptu lesson on putting in a clip and firing the M-16, and loading and firing the grenade launcher. It took fifteen minutes.

"Got all that? It ain't that hard."

Donna and Jill nodded in assent. Harry took one of the M-16s and handed it to Jill.

"What's this for?"

"Target practice. Let's go."

They followed him out the back door of the cabin and Donna went out the front to stand watch.

The sun hit them in the face as they entered the backyard.

The gun in Jill's arms was bigger than she imagined; the ones on television and in the movies seemed like toys compared to the one she was actually holding. She had to admit she felt safer carrying it around and, although she would never tell anyone, it made her feel powerful.

Matt carried one of the Defender shotguns, and Harry the grenade launcher. They followed him to the trail behind the cabin, a ragtag little squad hoping to hold out against a powerful enemy. She began to understand how Davy Crockett and his crew at the Alamo must have felt.

They made their way down the path, Harry in front, Jill in the middle, and Matt bringing up the rear. Harry scanned left and right, watching the woods for any signs of movement.

They came to a small clearing, a shaft of sunlight sneaking through the pines, the morning mist burning in the sunbeam.

Harry stepped ahead of them, into the middle of the clearing, and began stomping his foot on the ground. He breathed in sighing gasps, running out of wind.

At last his foot struck metal, and a hollow clang reverberated through the forest.

He bent down and clawed at the dirt, grabbing handfuls and tossing them aside.

"Aha! You two come here."

Jill glanced at Matt, who looked as puzzled as she felt.

They joined Harry, Matt kneeling and Jill bent over at the waist.

He had scraped away the dirt to reveal what looked at first like more dirt, but then Harry pinched a piece of brown cloth between his fingers and lifted it slightly. She realized it was camouflage for something underground.

Pulling a corner of the cloth away, he revealed a flat piece of brown metal.

He knocked on it; it sounded like a steel drum.

"Escape route. And shelter. There's two doors under here, like storm cellar doors."

"And under the doors?" Jill said.

"A concrete bomb shelter, and a tunnel leading to the cabin. There's a trapdoor under the throw rug."

"You're full of surprises, Harry," Jill said.

"Thank you," Harry said.

"Were you expecting a nuclear holocaust anytime soon?" Matt said.

"No, big mouth. But my dad did. He had it built right after the Cuban missile crisis. I improved on it after September 11. I wanted to have a place to retreat to if I needed. If they come and get in close to the cabin, this is a way out. It's only a hundred feet from the cabin, so it might not give us much time, but it's better than nothing. C'mon, I'll take you down."

He grunted and pushed himself to his feet.

They started out of the clearing and headed back toward the cabin.

The fat guy, a girl and a younger guy were looking at something on the ground, but what?

Clarence had parked himself behind a tree trunk, ducking out with the binoculars and snatching quick looks at the trio in the woods. There were at least four of them, counting the blond woman he'd seen before, and they looked like they were well armed. That shouldn't matter, because Rafferty was planning on twelve of them coming up here to attack the cabin. Twelve of his race versus four humans was no contest, heavy armament or not. Still, it helped to have all the intelligence you could gather on your enemy for the battle ahead.

After the fat guy did some talking and pointing, they started back toward the cabin. What was under there? Mines? A booby trap? A pit for them to fall in?

He would wait and find out.

Before returning to the cabin, Harry had Jill practice shooting with the M-16, picking off beer bottles he'd arranged on a log. Matt had seen a lot worse shooting from raw Ranger recruits, and he thought that Jill would do okay. She hit three out of five bottles with her first try, and then went back and knocked off the other two.

"We could've used you as a sharpshooter in 'Nam," Harry said.

"That's pretty good shooting for your first time," Matt said.

"Yeah, except now my shoulder aches. What about the grenade launcher?"

"We'll only use that on the real enemy."

"Aw. I was kind of having fun."

Matt was surprised to see that she felt comfortable with the gun at all. Most people who'd never fired or held a gun treated it like a rattler that was about to bite them. Even though Jill was comfortable, Matt noticed she always kept the barrel pointed at the ground when carrying it. There was a saying that as long as you realized there was no such thing as an unloaded gun, you'd never have an accident. He was glad to see her treating it with respect.

"You look pretty comfortable with that," Matt said. "I'm surprised."

"Now why'd you say that? Is it because she's a woman?" Harry said.

"No. I've been opposed to guns all my life," Jill replied. "My father was killed by one in a robbery. But in this case I almost feel safer with it. In a weird way it's comforting."

She looked down at her feet, and Matt wondered if she wasn't feeling a little ashamed, like she had betrayed herself by changing her stance on guns. He didn't want her to feel that way, because this wasn't an everyday situation. Creatures out of a horror movie were most likely coming for them, and if they couldn't fend them off, they were all going to die in unpleasant ways. The guns were a necessity.

He sidled up to her and slipped his arm around her shoulders, giving her a squeeze.

She kissed him on the cheek.

"Let me show you the tunnel," Harry said.

Donna stood watch at the front of the cabin, the M-16 resting in the crook of her arm, the barrel hanging and pointing at the ground.

"Anything new?" Matt said.

"Nada."

She stood like an eagle looking to snare a rabbit, her eyes focused, watching every shadow in the forest. He was glad to have her on their side.

Inside the cabin, Harry pulled the oval, rainbow-colored throw rug to the side, balling it up at the foot of the bed. Underneath was a four-by-four wooden trap-door with an iron handle.

Harry slipped his fingers under the ring, lifted it and pulled the trapdoor open.

The smell of damp earth rose from the hole.

Harry started down a small ladder.

Matt peered over the edge of the hole to see Harry shining the light on his face, the way kids did when telling ghost stories. He almost expected Harry to yell, "Boo!"

"Call Donna in here too."

"She should stay on guard," Matt said.

"Follow me, then," Harry said.

They followed Harry down the ladder into the cool, moist earth. The chamber at the bottom of the ladder allowed them to stand at full height, but they had to duck under the concrete that jutted out from the tunnel's ceiling.

The three of them hunched over, following Harry down the concrete tunnel. As they progressed, Harry's heavy breathing echoed in the tunnel.

They came to a set of double steel doors painted olive green.

"Stand back. I haven't opened her in a while."

Tucking the flashlight under his chin, he gripped the handle and pulled as hard as he could. Even in the dim light, Matt could see a vein bulging in Harry's temple. He hoped Harry didn't put too much pressure on the old plumbing and blow a gasket. That would be all they needed.

"Harry, how about I give you a hand?" Matt asked.

"No way. Almost got it."

He grunted and groaned the way a power lifter doing a clean and jerk might.

"Harry, let me . . ."

The doors gave with a loud scrape, and Harry nearly tumbled backward before regaining his balance.

Harry disappeared into the doorway, his short, squat frame and their surroundings making Matt think of Bilbo Baggins padding around Bag End.

There was a click and bluish fluorescent lighting came on inside the shelter.

The three of them stepped through the opening and into Harry's very own Little Big Horn, where he most likely planned to make his last stand against something.

The concrete walls in the shelter were painted a blinding yellow, made even more dazzling by the fluorescent lights reflecting off of them. When Matt commented to Harry on the color of the room, he responded by saying, "Studies show that bright colors improve mood. If I'm gonna be stuck down here with a bunch of guns and ammo, I sure as shit don't wanna start feeling depressed."

There was a bunk bed against one wall made up with brown surplus army blankets. The wall opposite the bunk was stacked with supplies including gallon jugs of water; canned vegetable and tomato soups, pineapple chunks and Dinty Moore beef stew; and brown plastic packages that Matt recognized as Meals Ready to Eat.

There was also a boxy white first-aid kit with a green cross on it, stacks of batteries, flashlights, Blue Tip matches and a black boom box.

Harry patted the wall. "Yep, she's built pretty solid. I figure two people could survive down here for about two years before the food ran out."

"What about using the john?" Matt asked.

"Over here."

He motioned with his hand and they followed him into a smaller chamber that Matt hadn't noticed, for he'd been too occupied looking at the supplies.

Six concrete steps led up to the steel doors that Harry had shown them from the outside. To one side of the steps was a toilet that had a retractable flowered curtain on a track, much like privacy sheets in a hospital room.

"I've got septic tanks down underneath here. You wouldn't believe what that cost me, but it was worth it."

"Why didn't you have them install running water and a sink then?" Jill said.

"Don't trust that outside water to drink. If there's a biological or nuclear war, the drinking water's gonna be shit."

Matt couldn't imagine living down here for two years, or even two hours. He felt as if the walls were going to push in toward him, getting closer and closer until they pinned him, crushing his bones and choking off his breath. Jill didn't seem to mind the place, but he could feel himself start to sweat.

Once when he was four, he was playing underneath the rickety old porch outside his house's back door. It was propped up on concrete blocks that passed as supports, like crutches holding up a three-hundred-pound man. He had tempted fate on a winter afternoon, digging a tunnel through the snow and burrowing under the porch.

When he was halfway under the porch, the tunnel collapsed around him, the snow pinning him facedown against the ground. Wet, slushy snow filled his mouth and nose, and his limbs were pinned. He remembered feeling paralyzed.

Immediately he began to scream until it got too hard because the weight of the snow was constricting his chest. His guardian angel was working overtime that day, because their neighbor, Mr. Fitzsimmons, happened to be taking his golden retriever, Shotzie, out to do his business. He heard Matt's faint screams and dug him out.

The bomb shelter felt the same way. He hoped they wouldn't have to come through here at all; it could very well be a tomb.

Harry worked himself into the corner near the steps and felt around for something. He pulled an L-shaped bar from two rungs on the wall.

There was a four-by-four-inch cutout in the concrete where a hex-shaped green metal socket stuck out. Harry stuck the L-shaped end of the bar in there and Matt realized that it was a crank to open the doors.

"Just crank her and the doors will start to open."

Harry turned the crank for a moment to demonstrate, and the doors didn't seem to budge at all.

"It takes a while to get them open, but it works," he said.

The doors began to open, making a sound like someone punching a cookie sheet. Sunlight speared through the cracks.

Matt started back down the tunnel, unable to stay in the chamber any longer.

CHAPTER 26

Twigs snapped; Clarence swung around the tree to take another look with the field glasses.

At first he thought his eyes were fooling him. The earth rose as if something big and buried were trying to force itself out of the ground. The dirt fell away from the rising object, and its brown skin fell away to reveal flat, gray metal.

They were doors to a cellar!

He took a good look at the doors, then looked back to the cabin and guessed the distance to be about sixty yards.

This would be useful information to give to Rafferty. Hell, he might even promote Clarence for this.

He didn't want to chance being spotted, so he hurried down the hill, ducking low to avoid detection.

Matt returned to the table after calling his aunt and telling her he and Jill decided to go on an impromptu camping trip and wouldn't be around for a few days. He ended the conversation by telling her that he loved her, and to keep her doors locked and stay inside if she heard any strange noises. She said she didn't know what he was talking about, but not to worry because she was going to visit her friend Ethel in Pittsburgh for a week. He breathed a sigh of relief when she told him that. It was a huge load off his mind knowing his aunt would be safe.

Harry sat with his fingers locked behind his head, leaning back, his gut swollen with a Big Mac and fries. Matt had run into town and picked them up a meal at the local McDonald's. Donna looked ahead, eyes focused somewhere faraway.

Harry said, "Feels like I'm back in 'Nam. I mean the getting ready for a fight part."

"What's it like? Being in a war?" Donna said.

"A lot of boredom and waiting broken up by fear and extreme violence."

Matt nodded in agreement. Desert Storm had been no Vietnam, but it was no tea party either. "Where were you stationed?"

"Khe Sahn."

"Wow," Matt said.

"Those gooks shelled the shit out of us. They had their big guns up in the Co Rock Mountains in Laos. Our artillery couldn't touch 'em. My ears ring pretty much all the time now. From all the blasts."

Donna focused in on the conversation and said, "That must've been a little taste of hell."

"You bet. Like I said before, if I didn't die over there, I'm not gonna die here. Let me tell you something. Me and two of my buddies were huddled up behind some sandbags. Well, don't old Charlie start raining shells down on us. They come whistling in and I don't know how I knew, but I knew we were gonna take a direct hit."

His eyes glazed over, and Matt was worried that he might have a flashback.

"I got up and told the guys to run. I hauled it out of there and sure enough the shell hit just as I ate dirt. I got some shrapnel in my keister. They found my buddies' body parts twenty yards away. I got to go home not too long after that," he said. "We left some good guys over there."

"I'm sorry to hear that, Harry," Matt said, realizing how lame and inadequate it might sound.

"Don't be. You probably weren't even born when that happened."

Harry picked up one of the paper McDonald's bags and crumpled it in his hands. "It's a hell of a thing to lose people that quick."

"You ain't kidding. Not a day goes by I don't think about my Dominic," said Donna.

"Dominic?" Harry said.

"My husband. Lost him to a brain tumor."

Matt and Harry expressed their sympathies.

For the first time Matt realized that all four of them had lost people close to them. Maybe that was the common bond that brought them together, making them stick the whole thing out and not run away.

Donna said, "I miss him. And I feel like I owe him for letting him die. Maybe I can redeem myself."

"It wasn't your fault. How can anyone stop a brain tumor?" Matt said.

"I still feel like I let him down. My sister-in-law too. I couldn't prove who killed her."

Harry said, "I know what you mean. Sometimes I feel like if I could've moved faster and warned those guys, they would be alive. But you can't torture yourself over it."

"I know I shouldn't."

They sat in silence for a moment until Harry said, "Well aren't we a bunch of jolly assholes."

Matt broke into laughter, at first snorting through

his nose, trying to contain it and then starting to laugh so hard his belly hurt. Soon Donna and Harry joined him, Donna with tears streaming down her face, Harry's face pink and glowing with sweat. Maybe it was the combination of the words "jolly assholes" that had struck him so funny, or maybe they just needed a good laugh to break the tension and somber mood. Whatever it was, it had broken him up. "I'm gonna check on our perimeter guard," he said, wiping tears from his cheeks.

Matt got up and went outside, muttering "Jolly assholes, that's too much."

The shadows grew longer.

The sun began its descent beneath the horizon, turning the sky shades of pink and lavender.

Matt stood in front of the cabin, an M-16 slung over his shoulder, waiting for Jill to round the cabin. It was her turn for guard duty, with Matt's coming next, but he wondered if after dark they shouldn't put two people on and have two sleeping inside the cabin. They had agreed to walk a perimeter around the cabin and scan the woods for any signs of trouble. If they suspected an attack was coming, they would fire a flare gun over the area where they had heard noise, lighting it up so they could see what was coming.

The spotlights mounted under the eaves flipped on, illuminating the yard in cones of mustard-yellow light.

Jill approached from the left, her head turned, looking to the woods for any signs of movement, listening for branches cracking or footsteps.

An M-16 hung on her shoulder, and her fingers drummed a steady beat on the strap. She also wore a beat-up army backpack that held six extra magazines, a flare gun and extra grenades. Matt joked with her before she went on duty that she'd better not trip or she'd be a one-woman Fourth of July spectacle. She had responded with half a peace sign.

She approached him and stopped.

"Anything yet?" he said.

"Nothing. A couple of snaps and cracks, but it turned out to be 'coons."

"You okay with the weapons? All set on what to do with them?"

"Yes, Sarge."

"Just checking."

The crickets began to play their song, chirping in the woods.

He moved closer to her. "We're gonna get through this. And we're going to stop them."

A branch snapped, and a brown rabbit darted out of the bush, stopped to observe them and scampered under a fallen log.

"Can I distract you from your guard duty for a kiss?" he said.

"Certainly."

He kissed her long and warm on the mouth, as if it were their last.

"Back to duty, soldier," Jill said. "I don't know if I can concentrate after that." She peered into the woods. "I can't see very far into the woods. We might not know they're out there until they're on top of us."

She was right. With light fading, you could see a couple hundred yards into the woods, and when darkness fell, that would be reduced even more. The creatures could cover ground quickly, and fifty or so yards wouldn't leave much time. They needed to think of something, and quick.

"Keep your eyes peeled," he said.

"Where are you going?"

"Last-minute plans."

He rushed into the cabin. He tore through the door

so fast that he caught his foot on the step, stumbling in and grabbing the table, stopping himself from going ass over tin cup.

Harry and Donna stood at the sink, Harry putting the bags and wrappers in the garbage can, Donna rinsing dishes. They looked at him, both suppressing laughter at his less than graceful entrance.

"I've got a few ideas, but we're going to have to hustle to get them done."

"What've you got?" Harry said.

"We might not have enough warning before we see them coming. They can move damn fast," Matt said.

Harry scratched at his scalp, as if trying to stimulate his brain by massaging it through the skull. "That's a good point. They could be almost all the way up the hill before we know it."

"Well, they have to come from the road—at least start from there, right?" Donna said.

"Yeah. There's really no other way. The other side of the woods, the side behind the cabin, ends at Old Mill Road, fifteen miles away in Newsome."

"What if we put a sentry down by the road? With one of the flare guns," Donna said.

"Who's crazy enough to do that?" Harry said.

Donna said, "You're looking at her."

"If they come, you'd be caught out there," Matt said.

"I agree," said Harry, still holding a McDonald's bag in one hand.

"Not really. You're both forgetting we have three vehicles. I can take my truck to the bottom of the hill. Put someone on guard duty up here. When I see them, I'll fire a flare and haul ass in the truck."

Matt looked at Harry, whose face was screwed into a look of concentration. Matt was developing a tremendous amount of respect for Donna; there was steel at her core, as if her will had been forged in a furnace.

"Let me go with you," Harry said.

"Don't patronize me. Just give me some weapons and let me get down there."

Harry exhaled out his nose. "All right. But the first sign of trouble, get your ass back up here."

"Yeah, the first sign," Matt added. He didn't want to say too much more to Donna, because number one, he didn't need to (she could handle herself), and number two, he suspected she might sock him one if she thought he was being a patronizing jerk.

"An escape route. A better escape route!" Harry said.

"Where?" Matt said.

"The logging road that cuts through the woods and eventually ends on Sixteen. Not many people know about it. Goes for about five miles. What do you say we park one of the vehicles out back near the bomb shelter? If we need to run, we can drive down the trail until we hit the logging road."

That was actually a pretty good idea, giving them a retreat option. Matt liked it a hell of a lot better than the idea of being holed up in a bunker not much bigger than a walk-in closet.

"We'll use my truck for the escape vehicle. It'll handle the hills better than a car. Plus it's got an extended cab, so we all can fit," Matt said.

"Then let's get moving. Before our company arrives," Donna said.

Donna's visibility ended five feet from the front of the truck. Fog rolled into the woods. It swirled in loops and rose and fell like a sheet in the wind, taking on a life of its own. The temperature had dropped by twenty degrees. Maybe the cold was a precursor of the attack.

You're being ridiculous, she thought.

The fog ruined her line of sight, so her ears were her only means of detection.

Driving the truck down the hill had been no problem, for the fog had set in after she had parked. For the first hour or so, it was clear and visibility was good, but then, almost as a bad omen, the fog had come.

She had backed the Ford into a small clearing and angled it toward the cabin to allow for a fast escape. Her arsenal included a Defender shotgun, four Molotov cocktails, her Colt and the flare gun. She had the Colt in a holster, the Defender across her lap, and the cocktails and flare gun resting next to her on the seat. A lighter stuffed into her shirt pocket completed her armaments.

The gasoline smell was giving her a headache, so she cracked the window. The open window made hearing them easier, although for some reason she felt safer with the window closed. That was ludicrous, really, because she had seen one of those things in action, and she knew it could tear through glass like paper. Still, she felt more secure, as many people did in their cars. That's why ninety-year-old ladies felt safe flipping the bird to two-hundred-pound truckers. The automobile provided false security, like a womb.

Another hour passed with no noises other than cars whizzing past on Route 16. The only thing she had seen were headlights flashing by.

Looking at her watch, she saw it was ten twenty-eight.

The fog had stopped swirling and settled in like a white blanket over the woods.

Her tongue felt like a piece of sandpaper, and when she pressed her lips together, they almost stuck from dryness. She licked her lips to moisten them.

Another half an hour passed before she heard them.

Dull thuds came up the hill, quick, scampering movements. Feet were hitting the ground fast.

What if it's just an animal? A deer?

The smell wafting into the truck told her otherwise.

She readied the flare gun, and then paused. She rolled down the window. With her other hand she grabbed the shotgun and pointed it out the window. Her stitches itched.

A big branch snapped like a whip cracking, and leaves rustled as they moved closer. The noises were getting closer to her truck, and she knew that they hadn't moved past her yet, because she would've heard the noises get farther away.

Instead they got closer. They must've smelled her, she realized.

She pointed the flare gun out and up.

A shape charged the truck. It slammed into the driver's side door. She dropped the flare gun. *Shit.* The creature poked its head in the window.

She raised the Defender and pulled the trigger, the cacophonous blast stinging her ears, the buckshot tearing off half its face. She pumped the gun. Still it came. It ripped the door open.

She kicked at it but the creature grabbed her by the legs and pulled her from the truck. Her back slammed against the ground. It stood directly over her and lowered itself. Donna swung the shotgun up and stuck the barrel in its guts. She pulled the trigger and blasted it backward. Then she rolled twice, trying to dodge in case it attacked again.

She got to her feet and saw it had gotten between her and the truck. It stood. Even in the darkness she saw murder in its yellow eyes. Black, viscous fluid dripped down its legs. Its grayish guts hung from its abdomen.

It hissed at her, and out of the corner of her eye, she saw two more of them, bigger than the first one, step into the clearing.

She racked the pump on the Defender and grunted

"motherfuckers" under her breath, trying to be brave and screw up her courage.

The wounded one grunted, and two *more* of his buddies materialized out of the fog like wraiths. Now the wounded one was in front of her, two were off to her left and another two on the other side of the pickup.

If she waited for them, she'd be dead; she had to make a move.

Letting out a war cry, she charged the wounded one, shotgun raised. It actually took a step back. She aimed high and pulled the trigger, fire blazing from the barrel. The shot tore off the left half of its skull.

It gripped its head, letting out a wail as it fell aside that made Donna's teeth hurt.

She threw herself in the truck, slamming the door behind her. She started the Ford up and frantically engaged the electric locks.

The other ones slammed into the truck, one leaping onto the hood, two more into the bed, while the one she wounded pressed its ugly mug against her window. Drool flecked from its lips, and it bared its teeth and clacked them together, as if trying to intimidate her.

Sensing that the wounded one was the most immediate threat, she decided to do something about it.

She reached for the Colt, but before she could draw it from the holster, the rear window smashed in and a clawed hand gripped her wrist. Her wounded arm sang out in pain, and she bit on her lower lip, drawing blood.

The wounded one at the driver's side window smashed its head through the glass and brought its face inches from Donna's.

She might be joining Dominic at the pearly gates sooner than she thought.

* * *

Matt didn't like the fog creeping in on them like this; he kept imagining that someone was watching him and he couldn't see them back.

Rounding the front edge of the cabin, he shivered, amazed at the drop in temperature from the sweltering heat that had been engulfing western New York. He had on a short-sleeved polo shirt. *Deal with it, Crowe,* he told himself.

It was nearly eleven o'clock when he heard gunshots from down the hill.

The flare hadn't gone off yet, but that didn't mean anything, for they might have attacked Donna before she could get off the warning.

He ran inside and shook Jill awake, who lay in the bed, hands together and pressed underneath her head. She awoke, fuzzy and mumbling. "They're here," he said.

Harry was in a sleeping bag on the floor, snoring softly. Matt shook him. "Hurry! Hurry!"

Harry jerked awake. He unzipped the bag and climbed out. "What? What is it?"

"They're here. I heard gunshots."

Awake now, Jill sprang out of bed.

Matt gave Jill his M-16, and Harry took the other one and a Defender shotgun. Tucking his own nine millimeter into his belt, Matt slid the panel in the ceiling aside and pulled the ladder down. He patted his side to assure himself the knife was still there too. Harry had insisted Matt take the M-79 grenade launcher, and encouraged him to rain hell on them.

Harry kicked the throw rug aside and pulled on the rung that led to the tunnel and the bomb shelter.

Matt started up the ladder.

"Keep sharp," Harry said.

Jill took a position by the right front window, Harry by the left, holding onto the M-16, with the shotgun and a supply of Molotov cocktails lined up. He had given some to Jill, telling her to throw them hard at the ground to make the bottle break.

Matt got up into the crawl space, and he heard Harry say, "Wish I had a flamethrower."

He kicked up dust in the attic, and the musty stuff got into his nostrils and made him sneeze violently. He sprawled out onto his belly and readied the gun, prepared to fire and make a sweep across the front yard if he saw anything. He had only fired an M-60 one other time, in the Rangers, and he hoped he would remember how to use the weapon properly.

He cleared dust from his throat and spat.

And waited.

CHAPTER 27

Jill drummed her fingers against the handle of the M-16, waiting for something to come out of the woods at them.

Harry was hunkered down, but every few minutes, he got up and peeked out the side window, looking out on the driveway.

They had opened their windows to allow themselves to toss out the Molotov cocktails, and milky fog crept into the cabin.

"Could've done without the fog," Jill commented.

"Looks like it cleared up a little," Harry said.

Very little, but at least she could see out into the front yard of the cabin, maybe fifty or sixty feet.

"Harry, what do you say we barricade the door?"

"That won't stop them."

"I know. But it might buy us some time if we need to get out through the tunnel."

The glow from the spotlight allowed her to see Harry frown in thought. "You're right. If we have to hightail it out of here, it might slow them down."

He stood up and went to the bed. Grabbing the mattress, he dragged it and flipped it up against the door. He then pushed the kitchen table over to the bed and flipped it up onto the mattress. Then he grabbed the kitchen chairs and tossed them on top. Jill supposed it was better than nothing, but it seemed incredibly inadequate.

"Five more minutes and I'm going after Donna," Harry said.

"That's noble, Harry, but it's thicker than milk out there. You'll never find your way down the hill."

"I'm not gonna leave her down there."

"But we need you here."

"We'll see."

Men are so stubborn at times, she thought.

The one behind her pulled her arm backward, pressing the forearm against the seat, straining her muscles and tendons. She thought it might tear her arm off if she couldn't get loose soon.

Pain bit through her shoulder and she jerked her head around to see the wounded creature sinking its teeth into her, right around the collarbone.

She screamed in pain and anger, expecting her arm to be ripped from the socket.

She looked at the one in the back. Her barrel was lined up with its face.

Stupid bastard.

She squeezed the trigger, and its head snapped back, but more importantly, it let go of her wrist.

The recoil from the Colt and her weakened wrist caused the weapon to clatter onto the floor of the cab. The thing to her left had its teeth locked into her, and she felt herself being lifted off the seat.

She hooked her arm around the steering wheel, realizing it might snap, but not willing to give up. It was the only thing keeping her inside the truck.

It pulled, and she felt her collarbone snap. The pain was enormous. Her stomach felt as if she'd swallowed ants, and her head spun like she just got off the Tilt a Whirl at Six Flags.

Still have the shotgun.

The stock was pointed at her, the barrel pointed at the gas pedal. She had one chance to free herself before she was dragged from the pickup and killed.

It meant unhooking her arm from the steering wheel and giving the beast leverage for a second, but she had no choice.

She let go.

For a moment, her rear end left the seat, and the heels of her shoes dragged on the floor mat. But she managed to grip the stock of the shotgun, pull it toward her and point it at the roof of the cab.

Her attacker doubled its efforts, thrashing her around like a puppy with an old sock, banging her forward into the steering wheel then back into the seat, over and over.

Again her head swirled, and for a second, everything went black, the light disappearing like a fade-out in a movie.

When she came to, her torso was halfway out the window. She brought the shotgun perpendicular to her body, barrel pointing back over her head. She moved her head to one side and squeezed the trigger, hoping she wouldn't take the side of her face off.

The blast shut off sound in her right ear.

The teeth came loose from her shoulder, and then she felt the blood skimming down her chest and arm. For the moment she was free, but she could hear the bastards on the truck bed, bouncing it up and down like a demented child with a pogo stick.

She wriggled back in through the open window.

One of them reached a greedy claw inside the cab and grabbed blindly for her, and for a moment she just sat and watched it, wondering if it were real, feeling detached and fuzzy. It was like being on cold medicine, the feeling that your head was floating three feet above your body, everything moving in slow motion.

Monsters are here, the bogeyman's here, they're going to get me, get me, take me away.

The claw swiped at her hard enough to make air whoosh and tore into the seat cushion, exposing snowy stuffing.

She brought her good arm (or better one, for they were both hurting) up and gave herself a stinging slap across the cheek.

Snap out of it!

She took a quick peek to her left to see the monstrosity that had bit her flailing away on the ground, its head a charred mess from the shotgun blast. She must've hit it dead center with the shotgun, for after a few seconds more of flopping around, it lay still.

Hey, I got one.

She fired the ignition and stomped on the gas pedal, the truck lurching out of the clearing. A quick look in the mirror revealed three of them in her truck bed, the one that took the shot from the Colt laying prone, and the other two coming toward the cab.

She stepped on it, and the truck responded, growling up the hill like an angry bear.

The searching claw came through again, this time swiping her on the arm just above the elbow, taking a cut of flesh an inch deep. She yelped.

She had to get rid of her passengers, because she was

giving them a free ride right to the cabin, and that wouldn't do. She fought the truck, which seemed to sway left and right, a symptom of her wooziness and blood loss.

Hit the brakes, like they do in the movies. They'll go flying!

She gripped the wheel, white-knuckle tense, and stomped on the brake pedal, the tires kicking up dirt. Donna lurched forward and rapped her head on the steering wheel.

The passengers in back slammed into the back of the cab, squealing in anger, but remained in the truck bed, shooting her plan to pieces.

She considered just turning into the woods, taking them with her and buying her new friends a little more time.

A claw shot at her, but missed, tearing off the rearview mirror instead.

Dazed, shaking her head, she put the truck in reverse. Sticking her head out the window, she looked behind her, the rearview mirror being only a memory. One of the creatures lay still, its arm hanging over the side of the truck.

Was it dead too?

The other two glared at her, hissing.

She gave it gas, driving backward down the hill. She sensed that she was over to one side too far, but couldn't be sure due to the fog and the cloudiness in her head.

Again she hammered the brakes, and this time her passengers lost their balance, windmilling their arms, which would have been comical if they weren't so hideous.

They flopped over the tailgate, and Donna heard a thump as the truck backed over them and lurched to her right, the rear end out of control.

The next thing she knew, up was down and down was

up, and it was like being in a steel garbage can while someone beat it with a baseball bat.

In the midst of being jostled around the cab, she realized that she had come too close to the side of the road, where the ground sloped off, and the tires on that side had gone down the embankment, causing the truck to flip.

It rolled three more times before coming to a halt and pinning her between the passenger seat and the dashboard.

The passenger side window had busted, and now her cheek was pressed against the dirt on the forest floor, with tiny pebbles digging into the skin.

Her body hurt everywhere, and she could feel the blood running down her arms and covering the tops of her hands. Her stomach lurched; she vomited down the front of her shirt.

Grunts and growls came from outside the truck, her attackers coming to deliver the coup de grâce. But hey, she'd done all right, and had taken one, maybe two of them along for the ride, she thought.

One of them stuck its face in the windshield, now cracked in a spiderweb pattern, and she could swear the thing was smiling at her. It punched out the glass and diamond-like fragments exploded into the cab.

Her eyes half closed, she looked at the creature. Its face was all jutting angles. The nostrils were large and porous, the mouth and jaw wide and filled with grayish teeth honed to a point. It had bat-like ears, flattened against the sides of its skull. Spittle dripped from its jaws, giving the mud-colored skin around the mouth a shine, even in the darkness.

God didn't make you, did He?

The blackness came again, but this time it became lighter and lighter, first charcoal, then light gray, then transparent, then white. There was dazzling light, so bright it hurt to look at it, might take your sight away if you did.

She saw a white castle keep, its stones whitewashed, reflecting the light, set upon clouds. A drawbridge lowered, and a figure approached.

Dominic approached her, his skin flawless olive, hair blow-dried into a perfect wave. He had on a white Nehru jacket and matching pants, and white beads hung from his neck.

"Waiting for you, sweet thang."

He reached his hand out to her, and for some strange reason, as he unfolded his hand, she saw that his fingernails were painted white.

Was she seeing heaven, or was her brain so overloaded with endorphins that she was hallucinating? Dominic would never have anything to do with religion, so the fact that she was seeing him in some type of quasi-heaven made no sense.

He smiled and his teeth dazzled, reflecting beams of light back at her. Her eyes ached from looking at him.

With his smooth skin and slick pompadour, he reminded her of an old crooner from the forties who made the bobby-soxers swoon, like a young Sinatra.

"C'mon, Donna. It's time. Even though you let me down, you can still come to the castle. Let go."

He reached out and touched her arms with his fingertips, and warmth spread through her like whiskey on a cold day. She felt all her limbs start to relax, as if they were turning to liquid. *I'm dying. But it feels so nice and warm.*

"I'll forgive you, Donna. You knew I had the brain tumor, but you didn't tell me. But that's no problem, sweet thang."

"I couldn't have known," she said to hallucination Dominic.

"Oh, but I think you did. Just like you knew that Rhonda would die."

"But I didn't."

Was she at war with her own conscience? Or was she really dying and was her dead husband giving her grief about his death?

"It wasn't so bad, Donna. The tumor only hurt most of the time. Morphine doesn't last forever, you know."

"Stop it!"

There was a *whumpf!* The entire truck shook.

She opened her eyes to see the creature face-to-face with her, but now it turned its ugly head outside the truck and left her alone. There was another *Whoosh!* The ground shook again.

Light flashed, like being in a storm cloud when lightning popped. She closed her eyes again, and for a moment all she could see was the reflection of the trees imprinted on her eyelids like a negative.

There was a shriek, and she smelled something like rotten meat burning.

Her arms felt like they were made from lead, and her head filled with helium, ready to float from her body.

"Holy shit, she's in a bad way."

"You got that right," she whispered to the voice.

Then she passed out as something hauled her from the truck.

If there was one thing the Rangers drilled into Matt's head, it was that you didn't leave a man behind. Ever.

While Donna was on the hill and trying to shake off her unwanted passengers, he had heard the sound of metal being rended, the big crash that came from down the hill. Donna was in major trouble, maybe already dead, and if they didn't get to her soon, her death was a certainty.

Matt scooted down the ladder and yelled to Harry, "I'm going after her."

"Not if I get there first," Harry said.

Like Matt, Harry had been a military man and in all likelihood had the same credo drilled into his head, to never leave a comrade behind. Military or not, Matt wouldn't have let someone die down there alone on the hillside. The training the Rangers gave him had only strengthened a belief that already existed.

"You both can't go," Jill said.

"Someone should stay here. No sense of us all getting killed down there," Harry said.

"Why don't Jill and I go? She can drive while I fire."

Harry got a wounded look on his face.

"Harry, we need you up here. You know these weapons better than anyone, and I don't want to lose you down there."

"Yeah, I guess I do know them better than anyone," Harry said.

"Let's go then."

They rounded up an M-16, some grenades for its launcher, and Matt's nine millimeter, which felt woefully inadequate against the enemy they were facing.

Matt and Jill stepped into the fog, now deteriorating into yellowish wisps, allowing them to see patches of trees through the murk.

They climbed into Harry's Lincoln, Jill behind the wheel, Matt leaning out the passenger window, ready to fire the M-16 at the first sign of movement in the woods.

Jill maneuvered the Lincoln down the hill, the high beams glaring off of the remaining fog.

Matt heard movement in the woods to his left, but the intruders remained unseen, and there was no way to get a clear shot. He'd be wasting ammunition.

He hoped Harry was ready for them, and he wondered if they made a mistake by leaving someone alone up there.

Jill drove fifty more feet, and the road began to curve, getting steeper.

Matt saw the Ford tipped on its side and caught a whiff of gasoline; the gas tank must've ruptured.

Then he saw them, lurching, big limbs carrying them toward the truck, no doubt ready to tear Donna apart. They were about a hundred fifty feet away. He knew he could fire the grenade launcher from about a hundred feet, minimum.

"Stop the car."

The brakes squealed as she stopped, and one of the monsters looked up and furrowed its brow, scowling at Matt.

He aimed the rifle, intent on ripping it to shreds with a grenade. Realizing that he might catch the gasoline on fire, he decided to take a chance and fire anyway. They would get to Donna before he could pick any of them off with the rifle.

"I'm going to fire. Then I'll go get her. Can you turn the car around on this road?"

"Yeah."

"Do a three-pointer and be ready to roll. Here."

He handed her the nine millimeter, hoping that they would stay away from the Lincoln. "Keep the car running. Hopefully I'll be back." They exchanged a quick smack on the lips and Matt stepped from the car.

He propped his elbows on the roof of the car and aimed the launcher.

He pulled the trigger and the grenade tore into the middle of them, spitting up dirt and sending two of them flying, as if they had jumped off a trampoline.

"Go!" he said to Jill, advancing across the road toward the truck.

She pulled the car away.

He had two more grenades, and he quickly opened the breach and reloaded with one of them.

One of them charged, an arm hanging at a crazy angle, the bones broken. It came at him with frightening speed, and even in the darkness, he could see the sinewy muscles in its legs pump.

Matt opened up with the rifle, hitting it in the chest, the beast still charging him. He had some idea of how a matador must feel.

He aimed for the head and skimmed one off the side of its skull, but still it came, leaping as it came within ten feet of him.

Purely on reflex he raised the gun and emptied most of the magazine into its gut. It landed on him, spilling him backward, his back scraping the ground.

Both of them were on the ground, and it prepared for another lunge. Matt released the empty clip from the rifle, slapped home another one and pumped the trigger as fast as his finger would allow. The bullets hit the thing in the head, snapping it back and spraying fresh blood on the ground.

Jill was turning the Lincoln around, swinging the lumbering vehicle back up toward the cabin.

It spasmed once more, then flopped onto its back in a final death agony.

Matt was on his feet and rolling again, ducking and firing into the mist, expecting one of them to charge at him any moment. He could hear them moving up the hill, branches crackling underfoot, tree limbs snapping as they were pushed aside. Harry had better be ready.

He reached the overturned truck and peered in the missing windshield. Donna lay inside, her limbs twisted and cramped against the dashboard. Her skin was the color of skim milk, and she looked ahead with a blank stare.

"Dominic?" she moaned.

"Not Dominic. Chirst, she's in a bad way."

The acrid smell of smoke and scorched wood drifted to him, as the forest lit up around the truck. His grenade launcher had started a fire, and the flames threw themselves against the fog like a movie against a screen, creating a glowing curtain.

He swept the rifle back and forth, watching for them.

In order to get Donna out of the truck, he would have to put the gun down, which he didn't want to do. But even in the dark he saw her shirt was soaked with blood; if he didn't get her out soon, she would die.

Propping the M-16 against the roof of the truck, he squeezed his torso into the cab and got Donna in a front bear hug. She whimpered.

"I'm sorry. This is going to hurt, me moving you like this. But I have to."

"Okay."

He counted three and pushed off the seat with his legs, pulling Donna out and on top of him. He rolled her over on her back, and for a second her eyes rolled white into her head, and he figured she was a goner.

It was only when she whispered, "Thanks for coming back for me, Dom," that he knew she was still alive.

The smoke rolled around them, making his eyes water and his throat burn. He could see shapes moving in around them, shadows visible because of the flames.

He readied the gun and two of them charged out of the gloom.

Two short bursts cut them down at the knees, but they got up and raced at him again. It was way too close to fire the grenade launcher at them.

They were twenty yards away and he fired again, this time barely slowing them down.

He fired again, knocking one down, but the other,

seemingly indestructible, kept coming and leapt at him, pinning him back against the truck.

Instinctively, his hand shot up to its throat, holding the head back, and more importantly, the jaws.

It pinned his left arm to the ground, and with his right he held the clacking jaws at bay.

Its warm, fetid breath blew in his face. The teeth were inches away, and if they connected, he could kiss what little good looks God had given him good-bye. He glanced at Donna, who lay motionless on the ground, moaning.

The creature's weight compressed his rib cage, and a stitch burned in his side. It had to weigh a good two hundred and fifty pounds. His grip on its throat started to slip, and if he lost it, he was a dead man. It would probably go right for his throat.

The face pushed closer to his.

He had one chance.

He let the grip around its throat go and jabbed his finger into its eye, jamming the knuckle halfway into the socket.

The thing screeched and Matt wriggled away, but it still held firm to his wrist.

He was at arm's length, the thing's arm outstretched, pulling him as if the two were in a tug-of-war. He yanked, trying to pull away from it, but he was losing.

His feet slipped through the dirt, and he dug in with his heels, but it continued to reel him toward it.

More of them materialized at the edge of the woods, making noises that sounded almost like purring, perhaps anticipating the kill and the feeding.

He was going to die like his family did, at the hands of these abominations.

Another stepped up behind the creature that had him in the tug-of-war. This one stood well over six feet, maybe closer to seven. It ducked underneath a branch and angled itself between two trees so that its shoulders and back would fit.

He knew it was Rafferty.

They would be on him in a moment if he didn't break free.

The knife. Use your knife.

With his free hand, he pulled the hunting knife from the sheath and it glittered in the firelight. He stepped forward toward the creature and swung the knife, burying it to the hilt in its throat. Its eyes widened and it gurgled before Matt pulled the knife out. When it let go of his arm he pulled away and scrambled over to Donna. The creature thrashed, swinging its arms and then falling to its knees, hands over its throat. The rest of them seemed transfixed by its death throes, as if they were astonished that someone had slain one of their own with only a knife. Matt took this as his opportunity to make a break.

With no choice, he slung Donna over his shoulder in a fireman's carry. She groaned, and he felt the dampness seeping into his shirt and knew she was losing a lot of blood.

He reached for the M-16, pushing up off the ground with Donna on his shoulder, as if performing a barbell squat.

The creatures snapped out of their momentary daze.

Slipping around the front of the pickup, one of them charged, hitting the hood and scrabbling up the overturned truck, its claws screeching on the metal. It stood on the truck near the wheel well, perched and ready to strike. Every muscle in its body flexed.

Before it could pounce, Matt raised the gun, firing one-handed, the gun jerking wildly. One of the shots winged the beast and spun it enough so that it lost its balance before it leapt. It hit the ground short of him and growled.

He started back toward the road, his shoulder and arm burning from Donna's weight, his lungs starting to ache. Part of it was from exertion, part of it from the fact that his heart was pumping at a thousand miles an hour from adrenaline. Collapsing now meant a very unpleasant death.

He summoned the voice of his drill sergeant, Hollis Daniels, inside his head.

You gonna quit on me now, boy-ya! I don't want no pussies in my platoon. You quit now and you ain't nothing!

Sergeant Daniels was quite the motivator, a six-five, two-hundred-fifty-pound black man from the Louisiana bayou. If he told you to shit Tiffany cuff links and then polish them, you did it. Calling up his drill sergeant's voice gave him the extra juice to keep moving.

More of them were crashing through the woods, stomping over branches.

He made his legs move, but didn't think it would be fast enough; they were coming like a hot wind on his neck.

One of them grabbed his shirt, scratching his back. The fabric ripped and he broke away, but not before hitting a root and losing his balance. He landed face-first in the dirt, Donna landing on top of him like a sack of concrete. Grainy dirt covered his lips, and he spat it out.

The gun bounced away, end over end, and landed five feet from him.

He rolled Donna off of him, and she lay on the ground like a rag doll, helpless.

He looked up and they stood over him like redwoods, amber eyes reflecting the burning forest like molten drops of lead.

The big one, the one he knew was Rafferty, pushed the other two away.

It bent over and took a handful of his shirt.

He took a swing and connected with its jaw. It felt like smacking heated marble; if he lived, he knew his knuckles would be swollen in the morning.

It spat in his face, a viscous yellow fluid that ran down his cheek. It smelled like raw sewage, and he gagged, forcing his gorge down.

The Rafferty-thing licked its lips, its tongue black and pebbled.

He prayed it would be over quickly, but he knew that was futile.

CHAPTER 28

Hissing noises came from within the fog.

Harry was vaguely aware of their positions, for although the fog had thinned, it still provided cover for anything in the woods.

He stood ready at the window, peering into the yard, the spotlights shining down on the dark, hard-packed earth.

Crouched at the window, his back muscles bunched up, feeling like someone was wringing them out. Cold sweat covered his palms and his heart beat like a hummingbird's wings. He squeezed the M-16's handle as if to assure himself it was still there, hoping that his sweaty palms wouldn't let the weapon slip and fail him at the moment of truth.

He didn't like this scenario for obvious reasons, but there were other reasons too; it reminded him of Khe San. If he squinted hard enough, the pine trees turned to jungle. He remembered the B-52s coming during the day, flying too high for Charlie to hear them, the enemy unaware the big bombers were there until the deadly payloads rained on their heads. The enemy was different now—there weren't twenty thousand NVA waiting to storm the cabin—but that didn't comfort him.

The brush rustled and cracked, and Harry expected one of them to come plowing out of the woods at any second.

One of them tore out of the fog, a gray blur until it reached the spotlights. He felt the predatory eyes boring into him, oblivious to everything around it except its prey.

He fired several bursts, and the bullets struck, making it dance a jig, limbs flailing but still coming with locomotive power.

It fell and slammed into the cabin wall just below the window. Harry popped out the clip, reached beside him and grabbed another one.

It rose and lunged through the window, and Harry reared back, avoiding a bite aimed at his throat. It came around quick with its arm, battering the rifle from his hands.

The creature swiped again, not content with just knocking the gun away, but trying to remove his face instead. Harry ducked again, and the fish-hook claws whizzed past his right ear.

He reached out and grabbed the shotgun propped against the wall, at the same time stumbling backward, away from the creature.

Harry got his balance, steadied himself, then pumped the shotgun and fired. The buckshot hit the thing below the jaw, and it clutched its throat, wheezing through the wound as it sucked air, sounding like a drain unclogging. Blood poured from the wound, but it kept coming, throwing its leg over the windowsill and ducking into the cabin.

Harry pumped and fired again, vaguely aware of another noise under the din of the shotgun. His volley hit the beast in the face, tearing skin from the bone and sending it to the floor clutching its head.

Harry racked the gun, and it spat out an empty shell. Lowering the barrel, he pointed it an inch from the ruined face and pulled the trigger. It gave one last spasmodic kick and then was still.

In the midst of the chaos he felt a sick dread, wondering if he should have left Liza all alone. When she asked where he was going, he told her there were a few things that needed doing at the cabin before the fall and deer season. Loose floorboards, insulation that needed repair, setting mousetraps, things like that.

She had given him a look of suspicion, staring him down, waiting for him to crack like a dam that can't hold any more water. On the rare occasion when he tried to slip a fib past her, he usually broke under the look and spilled the real story to her.

But this time he'd held against the raging river that was his wife.

Besides, if he had told her the truth she would have wanted to come along. Liza always wanted to be in on the action. She was too curious for her own good, and once she got a taste of something that piqued her interest, she dove into it headlong. If Liza found a subject she liked, she read every book on it, becoming an expert in no time.

She had seen a beastie one time, and he knew her curiosity overrode her fear of them. Most people who saw them and lived never wanted to see one again. She would want to be right by his side holding one of the shotguns. He imagined her safe at home, curled up on the couch in her green bathrobe with a cup of Earl Gray and some Pepperidge Farm Milano cookies. It made him feel better.

He turned his attention back to the stinking hulk on the cabin floor.

He cocked his ear and despite the ringing in his head he heard something behind the cabin. It started off as a pounding noise, a steady *thump thump thump*, then turned into the high squeal of metal on metal. They had gotten around to the back of the cabin, and at first he thought they were taking apart Matt's truck.

The noise continued and he realized what it was; they'd found the door to the shelter and the tunnel and were breaking it open. After a moment, he realized why only one of them had attacked the cabin head-on: so the others could sneak in through the tunnel. While the first one kept him busy, the others were coming up the tunnel.

So they *had* been watched yesterday.

Stepping around the dead creature, he picked up a Molotov cocktail and fished a Bic lighter out of his pocket. After setting the shotgun down, he tilted the bottle at an angle, flicked the Bic and touched the flame to the rag. It gave off oily smoke, making Harry cough.

He yanked the trapdoor open and again cocked his ear, straining to hear them. Scratching, like chalk on cement; they were in the tunnel and they were coming.

Harry threw the Molotov cocktail hard, the glass breaking on the tunnel floor with a *chink!* The fire crackled, sending heat washing up out of the hole. He lit three more cocktails and fired them into the hole.

"Sorry, Dad," he said, looking upward. His father had built this cabin with nothing but simple hand tools and sweat. With one toss of a bottle, Harry was about to destroy the whole thing.

He stooped down, picked up the Defender, dug some shells out of his pocket and reloaded, clicking them home.

Then he backed up, keeping the shotgun aimed at the trapdoor. The ones in the tunnel squealed like pigs in a slaughterhouse. Fire was probably the only damn thing that scared them.

He picked up the M-16 from near the window, deciding that he could get off more shots with it and not have to reload as frequently as the shotgun.

The flames raced up the wooden ladder to the tunnel and caught the floorboards of the cabin, creating a ring of fire around the trap door.

The screeching in the tunnel got louder, and he bet it wouldn't be long before one of them took a run at the flames in order to get up into the cabin. The way he saw it there were now two options; either stay in the burning cabin or go outside with them running around. Neither option gave him a warm fuzzy feeling inside.

The flames began to spread, lashing angry orange and yellow heat at him. They had spread six feet from the trapdoor, and now thick smoke began to fill the cabin.

The noises in the tunnel stopped for a moment (or was it he couldn't hear them over the flames?). Then a guttural growl arose from the tunnel, and something big slammed into the floor, just beside the trapdoor.

A clawed hand, gnarled and flaming, shot out of the hole, its nails reaching for purchase. It got its grip and the other hand followed, the monstrosity pulling itself out of the hole like a man doing a chin-up.

The skin on one side of its face was scorched away, revealing raw pink tissue. It glared and him and screeched.

It wriggled itself out and came for him, scrambling low across the floor, a ripple of flames lighting up its back. It was too quick, and before he could raise the gun to fire, it knocked him down, racking his shoulder hard on the ground. He rolled onto his belly, intent on getting to his feet, but it squashed him to the floor.

Hot pain, like a heated nail, dug into his back and he screamed, doubting his friends would hear him.

Matt stared into the eyes of a devil, one that held his fate in its hands. The spreading flames cast an orange glow, bathing the demons in queer light, making it feel as if he had gone directly to hell.

The Rafferty-thing held him up, his feet a good six inches off the ground. The other beasts stood watching. Matt glanced sideways and saw some of them licking their lips in anticipation.

Looking the thing in the eyes, he said, "I know who you are. I should've cut your fucking head off when I had the chance."

Its eyes narrowed in fury.

"Go ahead. Get it over with. Finish what you started in the park with my family."

The grip on his shirt tightened. It raised its free hand, the claws hooked and ready to kill. Matt winced, preparing for the final blow.

Twin beams slashed through the remaining fog, the hum of a V-8 filling the clearing. The Lincoln swerved left, catching one of the beasts, sending it up the windshield and over the roof of the car. Upon impact, the grill crumpled like tinfoil.

Jill swerved right and Rafferty tried to leap out of the way, but the fender grazed him and knocked him to the ground. Matt fell to the ground, free of Rafferty's grip.

Jill threw the door open and fired the nine millimeter, catching one of them in the throat and sending the others scattering.

Matt got to his feet, opened the rear passenger door, and dragged Donna's limp body into the backseat. She flopped inside and her head lolled at an angle. Then he scooped up the M-16, Jill ducking inside and closing the door as one of the monsters plowed into the side of the Lincoln.

Rafferty rose to his feet, stood in front of the Lincoln, raised his arms and half-howled, half-screeched. Then he made two fists and slammed them on the Lincoln's hood, dimpling the metal.

"Get us the hell out of here!" Matt yelled.

If Harry weren't still back at the cabin, he would've told her to tear ass down the hill and take off down Route 16, but they couldn't leave Harry behind.

Jill put it in reverse and floored it, the suspension bouncing like a pogo stick as it hit the incline at the side of the road. One of the beasts leapt onto the trunk and Matt shot it off, blowing out the rear windshield and spattering glass on himself and Donna. The shards stung his hands.

He brushed the glass off her face; her cheek felt like cold modeling clay. Her skin was ashen, and there were dark circles under her yes. She was dying, and if not for the slight rising and falling of her chest, he would have thought her already dead.

Jill cranked the wheel, backing up out of the woods and onto the road, facing the cabin. White steam puffed from the front of the now crumpled hood, and Matt knew the radiator had taken a fatal blow.

Please, Lord, let this car get us to the top of the hill.

Jill pushed hard on the accelerator and the Lincoln chugged on.

Another creature burst out of the woods, and Matt fired at it, sending it to the ground momentarily. It got to its feet, dragging a wounded leg behind it as it climbed the hill.

He had to come up with a way to get Harry from the cabin, get to the pickup truck, and get them all down the hill without getting ripped to pieces. It might come down to sacrificing himself, or at the very least putting

himself in harm's way, but it was something he was willing to do. He wasn't thrilled about the idea, but he
would do it if necessary.

They reached the edge of Harry's driveway, and when
he saw the cabin, Matt actually twitched in surprise.

Flames lashed out from the window and thick smoke
rose in mini-cyclones, creating a black curtain around
the cabin. The glow from the fire had to be visible from
the road, and someone would be calling the fire department before too long. Those firefighters would be
in for one hell of a shock when and if they got here.

They were within fifty feet of Matt's pickup truck.

"It's not gonna go much farther," Jill said.

"Keep pushing. We're almost to the truck."

As if the car had read Jill's mind, it gave a dying
cough, a bang and then it stopped in its tracks. Puffs of
steam rose from the grill. Matt was surprised the Lincoln made it up the hill at all. That said something for
American-made cars.

"I'll get you and Donna to the truck."

A look of panic crossed her face. "What about you?"

"I'm going into the cabin for Harry."

"I'm not leaving without you," she said.

He slapped a fresh clip into the rifle. "Fine. We might
actually be safe for a little bit if we stick near the cabin.
The fire will keep them off of us for a few minutes."

He bent across the seat and kissed her quick.

The thinning fog gave the effect of looking through
a dirty glass with milk residue on the sides. Through the
blown-out rear window of the Lincoln, Matt saw them
standing in a semicircle at the top of the ridge, spaced
about ten feet apart. The biggest one of them, the one
he knew was Rafferty, stood in the center. Matt hoped
that it was the fire keeping them at bay, that they
weren't just biding their time and waiting to attack,
knowing they had the cabin hemmed in.

Matt counted twelve of them. Not good odds. "We're getting out. I'll go first and cover you. Can you drag her to the truck? Harry didn't put it as far back as he said."

"Yeah. They're afraid of the fire, aren't they?"

"I think so," he said.

Matt backed out of the rear driver's side door and aimed the M-16 over the Lincoln's roof. Jill slipped out the front passenger door, the nine millimeter still in her hand.

She ducked around Matt and hooked her arms under Donna's armpits. Then she grunted and dragged her from the car as gently as possible.

"She's got a few minutes. Her shirt's soaked. She's lost a lot of blood and she's way beyond shock," Jill said.

Donna's shirt was blotted red and damp. Jill was right; she would be dead very soon and there was nothing any of them could do to save her life.

Jill rested Donna's head in her lap and then did something that Matt thought crystallized Jill's essence. She kissed Donna's forehead lightly and brushed a strand of hair away. When she looked up at him, there were tears in her eyes.

Donna's body jerked, her eyes fluttered; she lifted her head and said in a gurgle, "I got two of them." Then her head lolled to one side and she stared up at the sky permanently. Jill closed her eyelids.

I'm sorry, Donna. Why the hell did they let her go down that hill by herself?

Matt clenched his fists hard, the nails digging into his palms. They would have to leave her body.

He focused his attention back on the beasts, who began to creep toward the cabin, all of them low to the ground. If they all charged at once, Jill and Matt wouldn't have a chance against them.

"Let's go," she said.

Matt opened fire with the grenade launcher, aiming

into the left side of the circle where they had clustered together. The ground shook and dirt exploded into the air. Two of them were torn in half, and the other one dragged itself along the ground, its legs two scorched stumps. He fired the M-16 at it, catching it in the side of the head, and it stopped moving. He retreated to the pickup truck.

Jill reached the truck. "Go get Harry. I'll wait for you."

"Yeah, but *they* won't. Start driving!"

"Not without you and Harry. I've got a gun to protect myself."

Matt shook his head in exasperation, and then loaded the last grenade into the M-16's launcher. Jill started up the truck and swung it around to the side of the cabin.

"Since you're so goddamn stubborn, take this and use the grenade on them. Just point and fire. Give me that."

He took the nine millimeter from her and handed her the M-16.

He thought it near impossible that he could pull Harry out of the burning cabin and make it to the truck before they closed in for good. He hoped Jill would put herself ahead of Matt and take off in the truck so at least one of them would live to tell about this little adventure.

He took off, running to the far window, the one with less smoke coming from it.

He climbed over the sill, sucked in smoke and immediately starting hacking. He dropped to the floor on his hands and knees knowing that it was smoke that did most people in and not the actual flames. He had minutes to find Harry, maybe less.

Crawling forward, he yelled, "Harry!" The only hope was for Harry to be alive and able to answer Matt, because smoke made seeing impossible.

Something creaked in the roof, and there was a sound like a tree crashing after a lumberjack chopped it. He looked up and saw the flames advancing across the ceiling. The roof was on the verge of collapsing.

The flames roared and crackled around him, making it difficult to hear, but he could make out another sound; thudding followed by a screech of pain. It was directly ahead of him.

He scurried like a roach toward the noises and purely by instinct threw his hand up in front of him as a fireball rocketed at him, knocking him on his side. The flaming thing landed five feet from him. It was one of the beasts, its arm and chest in flames, beating at itself wildly to extinguish them.

Before it could move again, he fired six shots into it, and it fell back into the smoke, howling.

"Did you get the fucker?" Harry's weak voice.

"Harry! Make some noise!"

"Here!"

Matt crawled ahead and stuck his hand out, reaching until he made contact with lumpy flannel. He moved forward until they bumped heads, Harry on one knee, trying to get up.

"Can you walk?"

He nodded and hacked like a twenty-year smoker. They started out of the cabin.

CHAPTER 29

They were getting ready to charge.

The remaining nine monstrosities spread themselves out, twenty feet between each of them, until the two on the end were parallel with the cabin. They were trying to outflank the cabin, the flames no longer a deterrent to them.

She stood at the open truck door with the M-16 ready to go in case they rushed her.

Two of them on the left started forward, and she fired the grenade launcher, rocking the earth and reducing the monsters to flaming body parts. That was the last grenade, so she tossed the weapon on the seat and climbed in the truck, feeling better in the cab than standing outside with them.

She started up the Chevy and put it in reverse. Three of them darted toward her.

One leapt and got a chest full of the tailgate as the 1500 slammed into it, slapping it to the ground and running it over. The truck thumped as the wheel crushed the beast.

One down. Hopefully.

She braked hard, put it in Drive and sped forward, over the lawn and toward the cabin. A quick check in the side mirror showed two of them in pursuit.

She pulled up to the cabin. No sign of Matt or Harry. They were almost out of time.

"Put a hole in my back," Harry said.

Matt had one arm around Harry, gripping his belt to hold him up while he held the gun in the other. Sticky wetness pressed against his forearm where it came in contact with Harry's back. Harry sucked in air hard with each step, then coughed it right back out as his lungs took in a breath of smoke.

"Almost to the window, Harry."

"Thank Christ," he whispered.

Outside he had heard the grenade launcher plowing into the earth and wondered how Jill was faring. He hoped she was at least able to take out a few of them with the grenade launcher, but they were probably spread out and would be hard to get in a group.

They shuffle-dragged themselves across the cabin. They had been in the cabin only minutes and it already felt as if someone had rubbed salt in Matt's eyes and blowtorched his lungs. If they didn't get out of here pronto one or both of them would pass out.

They staggered to the window, Harry retching. It was like dragging ten sacks of concrete. He started to slide and Matt yanked him upright and shoved him toward the window.

Harry bumped the sill then threw his leg over it, losing his balance and falling out of the cabin. At least he was out of the smoke.

Popping sounds came from the roof, and it took Matt a second to realize it was the ammo from the M-60 going off from the heat. It would be a cruel twist if he survived the attack and bought it from one of his own stray bullets. Good old fate could be a real hoot sometimes.

Matt straddled the sill, ready to exit when he was yanked backward like a fish being plucked from the water on rod and reel. A steel grip crushed his chest and he kicked furiously to free himself, but the grip only strengthened. It lunged forward, still holding on to him, and after a moment he passed out, the air in his lungs stolen by constriction and smoke.

Harry flopped out of the cabin's window.

He staggered to his feet. Dazed and soot-stained, he wandered in a small circle.

Jill reached over and opened the passenger door, yelling, "Harry, get your ass in here!"

He looked at her, befuddled, eyes narrowing before recognizing her. Then he climbed up into the cab, slipping and then gaining his balance before landing on the seat. His red flannel was spotted with soot and smoke.

"Where's Matt?"

"He was right behind me. Saved my big fat butt in there," Harry said.

"We have to get him out."

The yard turned as black as a coal mine as the fire shorted out the electrical system in the cabin, killing the spotlights.

Jill gripped the gun, ready to leap out of the truck and storm into the cabin, when she saw one of them leap from the window. It took her a moment to realize what she was seeing.

It had Matt in its clutches, carrying him across the yard where it was met by the largest of the creatures. The big one tore Matt from the smaller one's arms and threw him over its shoulder.

It made a clicking noise in its throat and growled, whipping its head around in the direction of the truck, obviously giving a command. Then it pointed at the truck, turned and ran down the hill.

Jill flipped on the truck's headlights and the twin beams speared the darkness. Then she backed the truck up so it was facing the road. She surveyed the situation.

She counted five of them, standing in the darkness and looking like grotesque shapes cut from black construction paper. Their eyes shone like lanterns.

To hell with them. I'm going after Matt.

"Hang on, Harry."

"My back," Harry groaned.

She cranked the wheel hard and gave it gas, pulling the truck toward the driveway, the steering column whining. Behind them lumber crashed and crackled as the cabin's roof gave in.

She accelerated, and the attackers moved together in a cluster, trying to block the road. The truck gained speed, humming. Jill was intent on splattering them all over the road, thinking that this was what a bowling ball must feel like.

She rammed them, sending two off to the side, limbs broken and twisted. One of them managed to cling to the side of the truck, hanging on to the mirror. The other two had leapt out of the way, and she was glad, for if she had hit one head-on, the truck might have suffered the same fate as Harry's Lincoln.

Jill felt reckless and frenzied, her thoughts whipping past like Indy cars at top speed.

It clutched at the truck, snarled at her and bared its teeth like an angry Doberman.

"The hell with you," she said.

She sped up, and there was a towering pine tree

coming up fast on the driver's side. She eased the truck over until they were almost off the road.

Even in a daze, Harry looked concerned. "What the hell are you doing?"

"Watch."

The truck sideswiped the tree with a bang-screech, flinging the creature and mirror off the truck with a *thock!*

The truck swerved left, wanting to continue off the road, and Jill cut it back to the right, nearly tipping the Chevy over.

Harry said, "Where's Donna?"

"Lost her. Neither one of us wanted to leave her body behind for them, but we had no choice. She killed two of the bastards, you know."

"We shouldn't have let her go down that hill. God, I feel sick."

"I know, Harry. But I have a feeling she would've gone whether you wanted her to or not. She had something left to prove to herself."

"Still."

"I know."

"Keep an eye out for Matt. That big one took him down the hill."

"Any weapons left?"

It hadn't crossed her mind what they would do if they actually did catch up to Matt's captor, for all she cared about was getting him back. Would they yell at it? Kick it in the shins? Taunt it until it cried and gave up?

She scanned the woods on both sides but saw nothing. There weren't even any tracks on the road visible in the headlights.

Was he really dead and gone, or would the beast keep him alive for a while? She refused to accept the possibility of Matt's death, instead hoping that they would keep him alive, at least until Jill and Harry could attempt a rescue.

Harry groaned again.

She looked at him and saw blood smeared on the seat near his lower back. In her haste to escape down the hill, she hadn't noticed Harry's wound.

"Where are you hurt?"

"It poked a hole in my lower back. Hurts like hell."

Looking in the rearview mirror, making sure nothing was following them, she put her blinker on and pulled over on the shoulder of Route 16.

"Let me see."

Harry turned his back to her and she lifted up his shirt. He had a round red puncture wound the size of a quarter three inches above the waist. It didn't look too deep, but she had to get him to a hospital anyway. If it went too deep, it might have got his kidney and then he would be in serious trouble.

"You're going to the hospital. Can you hang on until we get to South Buffalo Mercy?"

"Yeah."

She pulled the truck off the shoulder, taking one more look in the mirror. The woods glowed orange, as if a giant sun were setting in the center of the forest. Sirens whooped and fire trucks blatted their horns in the distance. She hoped for the firemen's sake that all of the attackers were dead. If not, they were in for one hell of a surprise.

They drove the rest of the way in silence, arriving at South Buffalo Mercy in half an hour, Harry shifting his weight back and forth the whole time, trying to keep the pressure off his back.

She pulled up to the main doors where a statue of the Virgin Mary stood, arms splayed, palms up, as if inviting all to come. The inscription on the statue's base read *Mercy For All.* Two women in bland hospital scrubs sat smoking on a bench.

Harry stumbled out of the truck and the women in scrubs gave him a funny look. But they continued smoking. Both of them looked fresh out of nursing school, much like Jill.

She leaned across the seat so they could hear her.

"How's about giving my friend a hand into the ER?"

"We're on a break," the pudgy one said.

"Well, end it right now. This man needs help."

The pudgy one rolled her eyes, flicked her cigarette to the ground and got up as if it were the biggest chore in the world. She took Harry by the arm and led him through the automatic doors.

Jill parked the truck in the neighboring parking ramp and walked back to the main entrance. She entered the lobby; a white sign with a blue arrow said EMERGENCY ROOM.

She walked down a corridor and into the waiting room, where a sallow girl of about sixteen rocked a wailing infant back and forth. The only other people in the waiting room were an elderly man and woman, the man holding an ice pack to his head while the woman thumbed through a *National Geographic.*

The nurse sitting at the desk in triage stood up and asked Jill if she needed help. She was tall and bony, with curly red hair packed tight by barrettes.

"They just brought my friend in. Harry Pierce."

"You two were in a fire?"

Jill wondered for a second how she knew that then remembered Harry looking like he just came out of a coal mine.

"Yeah. There was a small barn fire. He's also got a puncture wound on his back. Pitchfork fell and got him."

"We're treating him right now. Why don't you have a seat and we'll let you know when you can see him."

"Thanks."

Just then a dark-skinned doctor with a heavy mustache poked his head through the set of double doors.

"Are you Jill?"

Jill came out *Jeel*.

"Yes."

"How did your friend injure himself? The wound on his back? He says he does not remember."

"It was a pitchfork. He got hurt in his barn."

"Okay. Thank you. He will need a tetanus shot then." The doctor disappeared through the doors.

She sighed in relief and then took a seat in the waiting room. Her head throbbed, her body ached and all she could think about was Matt.

She buried her face in her hands and cried softly, the tears coming against her will. If anybody noticed, they didn't say anything to her, and she really didn't give a shit if they did.

The hospital treated Harry for smoke inhalation, cleaned and dressed his wound, and released him five hours later.

While Harry was being treated, two auto accident victims and a stabbing were brought in to the ER. She knew the scene well; doctors and nurses in a frenzy, wheeling gurneys around, hooking up IVs and cutting away clothes. Harry was all but forgotten, and no one second-guessed the story about a barn fire.

When they walked out the main entrance, daylight had broken.

Both Harry and Jill agreed they needed rest, and despite being only ten miles from Lincoln, they agreed to stay in the city. Even though it was closer than they wanted to be to Rafferty and Lincoln, they could disappear in the city, affording them some security.

They wound up checking into a Best Western. Harry used his Visa to pay for two single rooms against Jill's objections; she was trying to save him money by getting one room.

They took the elevator to the fifth floor and found their rooms, Jill in 515 and Harry in 517.

"I need some sleep," Harry said.

"You said it."

"Why don't we sleep until around one and then get up and figure out what the hell we're gonna do?" Harry said.

She wanted nothing more than to take a hot shower and collapse on the bed. "Sounds good."

"Hey Jill?"

"Hey Harry."

"Thanks for sticking around up there. You could've taken the truck and bolted, but you didn't. For all you knew I was dead in that cabin."

"I wouldn't leave a friend behind," she said.

"You would've made a good Marine."

She gave him a tired salute and he grinned. Jill took out her key card and unlocked her room. Harry unlocked his and slipped behind the door.

The room had a lush burgundy rug, with bedspreads done in hunter green and white. An ice bucket with a stack of wrapped plastic cups sat on the dresser.

She entered the room and faced the bed, admiring a pen and ink sketch of Buffalo's Central Railroad Terminal depicting a steam locomotive pulling away from the monster train station, a fifteen-story tower in the background that served as New York Central's offices.

She peered at herself in the dresser mirror. Like Harry, her face was smeared with smoke, only lighter gray, for she hadn't actually been inside the burning cabin. A spiral of hair stuck straight up and she smelled like a combination of campfire and stale sweat.

And me without my deodorant.

She forced a laugh, which quickly snowballed into a sob, wet tears dribbling down her cheeks.

Donna was dead, Matt was in all likelihood dead and they still had to contend with Rafferty and the others. Rafferty had probably killed Matt. Jill thought it was naïve to think that a devil like Rafferty would show any mercy, especially to someone who had done him harm.

She sniffed, wiping away tears with her right hand and feeling about as attractive as a bag lady. She looked in the mirror; her tears had made tracks down her cheeks, cutting through the dirt and smoke.

"Jill, you look like some sort of crazy raccoon," she said, and broke into laughter.

She needed a shower, both to cleanse the dirt from her body and refresh her.

After stripping off her clothes, she took a hot shower, scrubbing her skin pink and clean. When she was done, she towel-dried her hair, wrapped another towel around her body and curled up on the bed.

She fell asleep instantly.

Jill heard hollow rapping on the door, and rose from the bed, still fuzzy and half asleep. She was almost to the door when she looked back and saw her towel in a pile on the floor.

"Who is it?"

"Harry. I've got food!"

"Hang on."

She put her clothes on, still damp with sweat and smelling of smoke. She looked at the alarm clock on the nightstand; it read one twenty. Harry was early.

Once she was dressed, she went to the door and

peered through the fisheye lens, knowing it was silly but not taking any chances after the nightmare that was last night.

It was Harry, pacing back and forth, a brown grocery bag cradled in one arm. She slid the chain over, turned the lock and pulled the door open.

Harry said, "There you are. I was getting worried."

"I was fine."

"You took a while to answer."

"I was also naked."

"Oh shit, I mean, I'm sorry, I mean—"

"Don't worry about it, Harry. What you got there?"

"Oh, this." He came in and set the bag on the dresser, then began to unpack it, whistling the theme to *The Andy Griffith Show*. He pulled out two Styrofoam containers, two take-out bowls with plastic lids and two twenty-ounce Pepsis.

"You like turkey?" He said.

"I'm here with you, aren't I?"

"Smart-ass," he said, grinning.

They feasted on roasted turkey sandwiches, served on crusty French bread and dripping with spicy mustard. Jill only ate half of hers, for Harry had also bought a mound of curly-q fries and a bowl of minestrone soup with each sandwich.

Harry cleaned out his containers to the last crumb. When he opened his mouth to speak, a belch rumbled out, and he slapped his hand over his mouth. Jill laughed. Harry rolled his eyes as if to say, *What did I do?*

"I called Liza."

"How's she doing?" Jill said.

Harry licked mustard off his fingers. "She saw through my story. I told her I was going to the cabin to make some repairs before hunting season came along. I wound up telling her everything that happened. Can't get nothing past that woman."

"You shouldn't be lying to your wife, anyway."

"Oh, I don't. Not often, anyway."

She had been bottling up a thought and finally said to Harry, "We have to go after Matt."

"I've been thinking about that too."

"Then you think he's alive then?"

"Yeah. And let me tell you why." He cleared his throat. "Rafferty's a real son of a bitch, agreed?"

Jill nodded. *No argument there.*

"Matt almost killed him. Probably the only person who's come close."

"How do you know he's alive? Rafferty, I mean."

"He organized that attack. They wouldn't have come after us like that without his okay. He's their leader, and he rules with an iron fist. I'm positive he's alive."

Jill threw the garbage from lunch in the trash can and went to the mirror. She ran her fingers through her hair, pulling here and there, trying to bring it to some type of order. It looked like a mess of coiled springs, the curls taking on a life of their own.

She turned to Harry. "He's got him locked up somewhere. I don't know how I know that, but I do."

"I think you're right. He'll try to make an example out of Matt."

"We have to get him out."

"I agree, but I don't think they'll give us a warm welcome. How do you propose we get him out?"

"Can you get more weapons?"

"Liza can bring them."

"Then get her on the phone."

Hard concrete pressed against his cheek. Matt lifted his head. He opened his eyes to a harsh, white light.

What the hell happened?

It came to him slowly, like remembering a vivid

nightmare upon awaking. He had gone into the burning cabin after Harry and swallowed more smoke than most firemen do in a career.

He sat up and looked around. He was in a jail cell. The accommodations weren't exactly five star: a look at the bed revealed a thin, yellowed mattress, and from the smell of it, the toilet had backed up long ago and never been fixed.

He stood up and moved to the bed, rubbing his temples, trying to ease the splitter of a headache that ran down the center of his head. He coughed, spat some blackish phlegm on to the floor.

After a moment on the bed, he approached the bars and scanned the cell block. He wanted to get an idea of the layout. It was rectangular in shape. At the right end was the door to the interrogation room where he'd been taken after his families' death. In the center of the block another door, and still another at the far right end. That one probably led into the station.

He sat down on the bed.

A door creaked open and the click of shoes echoed on the concrete floor. Rafferty appeared in front of the cell. He folded his arms and looked down on Matt with a self-righteous grin.

"How do you like the place?" Rafferty asked.

"It isn't the Hilton."

"I see you've got the cell with the air freshener. I like to leave the toilet like that to discourage people from returning."

The sight of him standing there acting like the king of the world made Matt want to gag. "I should've finished you off when I had the chance."

"When I was lying there I heard you and your bitch of a girlfriend talking. You mentioned cutting off my head. That would've done it, but you were in too much of a hurry."

A cockroach scuttled across the floor, bumped into Matt's foot and darted away in the opposite direction.

"I have to give you and your friends credit. You killed nine of us. I don't think that's ever been done before."

"I'll kill more of you before I'm done."

"Tough talk. Like I said, I give you credit, but you'll still have to die. The girl and the fat one too. We got the blonde, though, didn't we?"

Until now, Matt had kept his head down for most of the conversation to avoid Rafferty's smug expression, but now he raised his head and looked into Rafferty's eyes. "She was worth a hundred of you."

"When will you accept the fact we're superior to you? I survived wounds that would've killed a man."

"Just how did you find us?"

"The local yokels know everyone up there. All it took was one of my officers asking some questions at the local minimart. Plus, like I said, I heard you two talking about your escape at the apartment."

Matt stood up, deciding that he didn't want Rafferty having the upper hand, standing over him and looking down. He stopped two feet short of the bars and looked up at Rafferty, who was a good six-five to Matt's six feet.

If Rafferty were a man, Matt could've taken him, despite the size advantage. He had a paunch, and his pants were too tight, clinging to his thighs. Had there not been a demon under that skin, Rafferty would be nothing more than a slow, flabby middle-aged man.

"Why did you pick my family?"

"We needed to feed. You know, I liked killing your father. He screamed like a woman."

"Just like that? You kill for the hell of it?"

"No. I told you we're superior to you. It's not just for the hell of it. It's a need to hunt, to kill, to eat."

"So basically it's hunger."

"More than hunger. It's a drive. Did you ever want

sex so bad you were about to explode? I mean, say you hadn't done it in six months and your woman starts teasing you?"

"So you're reduced to base urges? I don't see how that makes you superior to us. We can control urges."

"I could kill you with one bite to the throat. Or maybe the back of the neck, snap your spine."

"In that case big cats would be superior to men. I'm sure a tiger could do the same thing to me."

Rafferty frowned. "Enough of this! I've got plans for you and the other two. I'll dare them to come help you, and they will. Your kind is always rushing to help each other. It's pathetic if you ask me."

"That's what makes *us* superior, asshole."

"You won't be talking so tough when you find out what I've got in store for you." He pulled his nightstick from his belt and raked it across the bars. "Sleep tight, sweetheart," he said, and strolled down the hallway.

The bastard was planning something to draw Harry and Jill in and Matt had to warn them before they walked into an ambush. He couldn't let them die, especially after what happened to Donna. Dying ten times would be preferable to letting any harm come to Jill.

Maybe she and Harry took off, headed farther south, or maybe they crossed the Peace Bridge into Ontario, Matt thought. At least they would be safe, and that gave him some comfort.

But he knew different. Harry and Jill were made of good stuff (as his father was fond of saying about people he admired). They would come for him, and that troubled him.

What was Rafferty planning?

CHAPTER 30

"That man's gonna be the death of me."

Liza finished packing the weapons into the trunk of her sister's Honda Accord, including two shotguns, an M-16 rifle, and some C-4 with the necessary blasting caps and radio detonator. There was also Harry's blue steel forty-four and enough ammunition to arm a third world nation. If her sister knew what was being stowed in her car, she would get her tit in the wringer about it right quick. Liza told her she was taking the car to do some grocery shopping.

She had the Accord parked in their garage, connected to the gun shop by a breezeway. The wind chirped through a hole in the concrete near the garage door and climbed up Liza's leg, chilling her. Harry was fond of calling the breezes snow snakes because they crawled up your leg in winter and nipped you on the ass.

She closed the trunk and hugged herself, shivering. Her circulation was poor to begin with, and she never went anywhere without a cardigan, even in the summer.

I was never cold like this when I was a girl. Getting old is really hell, she thought.

It didn't help that the temperature had gone from the nineties and sweltering to the chilly fifties in the space of two days. The dampness made it feel like someone was twisting corkscrews through her kneecaps.

Getting old *was* hell.

She slammed the trunk and hobbled over to the door.

Harry's favorite red-and-green flannel shirt, a pair of socks and Wrangler jeans rested on the passenger seat. She patted around her rib cage, feeling the blunt hardness of a thirty-eight comforting her like an old friend.

Old Harry had really gotten himself in deep now, and when she met him, she never bargained for what *she* was getting into.

He started ranting about the hidden monsters shortly after they were married, and she seriously thought about a divorce. He made her promise to be careful when she went out and gave her a thirty-eight revolver to carry. That wasn't a problem because her father taught her how to shoot back on their farm in Indiana when she was a girl.

After about six months of warnings to watch out for "Them," one day she packed her suitcases and waited for him to come home from the gun shop. She showed him the packed bags and told him she would be on the next Greyhound back to Indiana if he didn't stop. That was the end of it. Harry didn't mention another word about "Them."

She quietly wondered about his sanity until she saw one herself.

That same summer she threatened to leave him (was it '63 or '64? It was before he went to Vietnam), she was walking to the drugstore to pick up cough syrup for Harry. He had developed a summer cold and was hacking like he had TB.

She had to travel the alley between a hardware store

and the Laundromat on her way to Glosser's, and she remembered the icy chill that danced over her back. She saw a flicker, amber lights in the darkness, like a jack-o-lantern.

The smell nearly flattened her. It was like sulfur and under it the stench of feces, blood and entrails. There had been a meat-packing plant five miles from their farm. It smelled now like it had then when there was a hog slaughter, and she remembered sitting on the porch with Zelda, perfume-soaked handkerchiefs over their noses.

She stood frozen by fear and morbid curiosity, wondering exactly what had happened in that alley.

The chain-link fence at the back of the alley jingled, the moonlight catching the beast as it reached the top. It had a corpse slung over its shoulder, the skin bleached out from blood loss. It looked right at her and damned if it didn't smile before leaping the fence and disappearing into the night with its quarry.

She ran all the way home.

She had arrived at the house huffing and puffing, with Harry wondering where his cough syrup had gone. She told him Glosser's had closed early and he gave her a quizzical look and dismissed the issue for the moment.

The next morning she told him what she had seen, and apologized for not believing him. He had smiled, patted her hand and said, "That's okay, I don't blame you." He could've gloated and said, "I told you so," but he didn't, and she loved him for that.

She had a feeling Harry was up to something involving the beasties, and he confirmed her suspicions this morning, calling to tell her the story of the siege at the cabin. She'd known his tale about him doing repairs at the cabin was bull chips, because Harry never did any work up there until a week before shotgun season. He was never good at slipping things past her.

Harry told her one of his friends was missing, and the other had died during the fight. The cabin was a total loss, and they needed weapons to go after Rafferty and stop the Harvest.

There were no second thoughts about bringing them the guns; it was automatic.

She clicked the garage door remote and the door creaked on its tracks. The plan was for her to meet Harry at the old Buffalo Tool and Die Works two blocks from the hotel. After delivering the weapons she was to return to the gun shop.

Harry had wanted her to stay at the hotel, but she responded, "Then who's gonna run the shop?" Harry knew it was better not to argue with her when she got like that.

She pulled out of the driveway and turned left, heading for the entrance to the 190 South.

The shivers returned again.

Rafferty watched the old woman pull out of the driveway, confident she did not see him following. His vehicle of choice was a beige '83 Buick, impounded from a drunk driver who never returned to pick it up.

He knew she would lead him to Crowe's friends if he trailed her. Instinct at work again.

She was a nice little bargaining chip, as well. Taking her would not be a problem.

He stayed five car lengths back, able to take his time for traffic was light and he didn't have to worry about some jackass cutting in front of him and ruining his line of sight.

He trailed her to the ramp for the 190 South, the expressway that ran through the heart of downtown Buffalo.

Content with himself, he smiled, leaned back and drove, a man at ease.

Liza pulled the Honda into the lot of the old Die Works. It must have been the shipping and receiving dock, for there were four rusted roll-up doors, one of them spray-painted with the words GOODYEAR CREW. Liza had heard about them on the news, a gang that had terrorized most of the eastside, dealing drugs and shaking down neighbors for protection money.

She was flanked on both sides by sawtooth-style buildings, and the six-story main manufacturing complex towered in front of her. The lot only had access on one side, where she had entered through a busted chain-link gate. Because there were walls on three sides, the area could only be viewed from behind; that made it perfect for keeping prying eyes out.

She pulled up farther into the wasteland.

Empty syringes and glass vials littered the ground. The whole lot had become a microcosm of the inner city. Decay, garbage and a dreary hopelessness had settled over the old plant. Manufacturing jobs that once paid sixteen or eighteen dollars an hour were long gone, much like the days when you could walk these streets without worrying about taking a bullet.

There were old tires stacked in a heap, a washing machine with bullet holes in the side, an orange recliner with a spring popping out, and even a child's doll with a bleached-out pink dress. It was a sad, broken-down area.

She engaged the electric locks, and after waiting a very long five minutes, a Chevy pickup pulled in, Harry driving and a sweet young thing in his passenger seat that had to be Jill.

They killed the engine and got out, Liza doing the same, stepping over broken glass and crack vials. She and Harry met halfway and she smoothed her hand across his cheek.

"How are you, you old fool?" she said.

"Still alive and kickin'."

He kissed her on the lips.

"No time for that. Your goodies are in the trunk," Liza said.

He introduced her to Jill and they shook hands.

"Not getting fresh with the old boy, are you?"

"He *is* awfully handsome."

"Will you two cut it out?" Harry said, a blush creeping into his cheeks. He opened the Honda's trunk and pulled out a green duffel bag. Then he dragged it over to the pickup and hoisted it into the bed.

He stopped long enough to peer across the lot, toward the opening at the chain-link fence, where Liza had entered the property.

She noticed him staring at something.

"What are you looking at?"

"Was that beige car there when you pulled in?"

When she turned around, the driver swerved out of his spot and sped away, the tires squealing.

"My guess is you were followed. That looked like an unmarked cop car."

"You shouldn't go home. Stay with us," Jill said.

"Nonsense, missy. I've got a store to run, and I'm not letting anyone stop me from running it, cop or no cop."

Harry said, "Stay with us."

"Hogwash. I can handle myself," Liza said.

"But—"

She lowered her voice and glared at him. "Harold."

"Dammit, Liza."

"Dammit yourself. Now listen to me, both of you."

She approached Harry and placed her hands on his

cheeks, tilting his head so he looked down at her. "You two worry about yourselves. If you don't stop them, a lot of people are going to die. They don't want me, anyhow. I fully expect both of you to come out of this alive, got it?"

"Sheesh," Harry said.

"I don't want you to do this, Harry, but someone has to. It won't be any worse than worrying if you were lying dead in some Vietnam rice paddy. Just get out alive."

"Promise me on Harvest night you'll either leave or lock yourself in the bunker."

"Another bunker?" Jill said.

"Under the gun shop. Built like a brick shithouse. No way would they get in there."

"I promise," she said.

She pressed herself against him and he hugged her. The body had softened and expanded with age, but she still relished the strength in Harry's arms, the way he embraced her. That was something that would never burn out or grow old.

He let her go, and she squeezed Jill hard. She looked surprised, as if she hadn't expected a tough old broad to give her a hug.

She climbed back into the Honda and lowered the window.

"Careful going home. This ain't exactly Beverly Hills," Harry said.

"Don't worry. I'm packing."

She tooted the horn and pulled out of the lot, immediately looking for a beige car.

She had been foolish, allowing herself to be followed to the meeting, and by a cop, no less.

On the ride back to the gun shop, she checked the rearview mirror every few seconds, scanning the road for the beige car. The only vehicle behind her the whole way home was a titanic white Cadillac.

Still, her stomach quivered.

A fine mist tapped on the windshield, and the wipers beat it away. The cold had seeped into her bones, gnawing on them like a pit bull with a T-bone in its jaws. She had the heater going full tilt, but she still shivered.

It was as if the cold was buried deep in the bones, and no amount of external heat could penetrate to warm her.

Once again, the thought of her own carelessness, of being followed, entered her mind, an unwanted guest that wouldn't leave. She prided herself on the fact that she was always quick to spot a bullshit artist or a con man, and her lapse in watchfulness made her wonder if she was losing something with age.

No one put one over on Liza Pierce.

Then why did you let that car trail you?

It didn't matter now, for the damage was done.

She pulled into the garage fifteen minutes later, and while in the breezeway, she made sure to lock the door to the garage. She did the same in the house, checking all the locks and closing all the miniblinds.

She patted her breast to assure herself the thirty-eight was still there.

Still feeling chilled, she turned the thermostat up to seventy, the furnace coughing out a dry, dusty smell indicative of the first lighting.

She still felt frozen, so she boiled some water and made herself a cup of Earl Grey. Lord, it was chilly! And not even September yet.

It was when she sat in her recliner that the cold became the least of her problems.

She heard footsteps on the kitchen floor.

She stood up and whirled around to see Ed Rafferty standing three feet behind her chair.

He moved fast, grabbing her wrist before she could take a step to get away.

"How the hell did you get in here?"

"I beat you back here. You really should lock your doors."

He dragged her across the living room and out of the apartment.

Matt heard a woman's voice, thin and reedy, echoing down the hallway of the cell block.

Now what was Rafferty up to?

He gripped a wiry, elderly woman above the elbow. Her hair was tied up in a bun, streaked gray-black. The struggle with Rafferty had wrinkled her cardigan and ankle-length skirt.

"You're breaking my arm," she said.

"You'll be lucky if that's all I break," Rafferty said.

He produced a key from his belt and unlocked the cell door next to Matt's, shoving the woman inside. She lost her balance and sprawled onto the concrete floor.

"You sure they're aren't any Boy Scouts or cripples you want to rough up while you're at it?" Matt asked.

"Shut your hole."

Rafferty slammed the door and the clanging noise bounced around the hallway.

The woman pulled herself to her feet and dusted off her sweater, as if dirty clothing were the only thing that concerned her right now. He looked away from her, trying to spare her some dignity, and her heard her mutter "Asshole cop" under her breath.

Good for you, lady.

Rafferty glared at him and stalked off down the hallway.

"You wouldn't know my Harry, would you?" she asked.

"Gun shop Harry?"

"Yes."

"I do. Know him, I mean."

"You must be Matt."

"How'd you know?"

She looked over her shoulder and stepped closer to the bars that separated the cells, lowering her voice to a whisper.

"I don't know how good their hearing is, but it can't hurt to whisper. Harry and Jill are alive. They're holed up at the Best Western in Buffalo."

Thank the Lord. Jill was alive.

"Are they okay?"

"A little battered and bruised, but otherwise fine. I brought them some provisions."

"Rafferty wants them. They can't come into town. If he gets all three of us it's really over."

"Well they've got enough firepower to level this place and put a serious hurt on those bastards, pardon my French."

"God, the Harvest. I've got to get out of here."

She peered over her shoulder like a child sneaking cookies from the jar. "This might help you."

She plucked her sweater away from her chest, then slipped the other hand in and pulled out a snub nose revolver. He should have been surprised at an old woman producing a revolver from under her sweater, but somehow he was not. She seemed to be full of piss and vinegar.

"How did you manage to get that in here?"

"That stupid oaf probably figured I was just a harmless old lady."

She handed him the revolver and he slid it under his mattress, smoothing it over as not to leave a bulge.

"Why did they bring you in?"

"Rafferty followed me, the weasel. And I was silly enough to let myself be followed. Lord, it's cold in here!"

"He wants to get them too. They'll be walking into a trap," Matt said.

"Not much we can do sitting in here. But if we could use that gun . . ."

"Let me think about how."

Footsteps clicked down the hall, and Liza backed away from Matt's cell and sat on the bed.

Rafferty appeared, took out his keys and opened the doors to Liza's cell. She turned her head away, refusing to look at him. He had a lumpy paper bag tucked under one arm like a football.

"Let's go."

He dragged her to her feet and took her down the hallway to the room at the end of the corridor. It was the same room where Rafferty had taken Matt as a teenager and threatened to kill him if he squealed about the murder of his family.

"You'd better not hurt her, you son of a bitch."

"Wouldn't dream of it," Rafferty said.

He pushed her into the room and closed the door. Maybe he was just going to talk to her.

Matt doubted it. He had to get out of here.

Fifteen minutes later, a red-haired cop came to Matt's cell and instructed him to turn around. The cop opened the cell door. Then Matt felt his arm jerked behind him. The cop slapped on a cuff.

Matt considered the gun under the mattress, about making a move for it, but he didn't know what had happened to Liza. He couldn't abandon her in this hole.

The cop pulled Matt's other arm back and completed the job. He was led out of the cell block and into a garage, where a beige car was parked.

The cop told him to sit down and gave him a shove to help him to the ground. Matt landed hard, jarring his tailbone on the concrete.

"Stay there," the cop said.

"Like I have a choice."

Five minutes later, Rafferty stepped through the door

with a small cardboard box tucked under his arm. It was sealed with clear packing tape.

"Take this to your friends at the Best Western."

So he *had* gotten information from Liza in that little room.

"Be back here in an hour. If you're not, I'll kill the old bitch. I'm not fucking around on this one, so don't get cute on me."

The red-haired cop stepped behind him, bent over, and unlocked the cuffs. Matt rubbed at his chafed wrists.

Rafferty handed him the box. It was light, not even a pound.

"What the hell is this?"

"A message. Don't open it until you get there. The keys are in the car. Open the door, Clarence."

The other cop pressed a red button on the wall and the garage door rolled open.

Matt got in the car, started it up and backed out of the police garage.

He screeched into the hotel parking lot, catching a sour look from the doorman. The guy was dressed in a bright red uniform that reminded Matt vaguely of the witches' soldiers in *The Wizard of Oz.*

He parked the car, entered the lobby and stopped at the front desk. The clerk, a bronze-skinned woman, flashed him a smile and told him which room Harry was staying in.

Matt took the elevator to the fifth floor and stepped off, nearly crashing into the cleaning woman and her cart of mops and disinfectants. He stopped at 517 and knocked on the door.

Harry opened the door.

"Matt!"

Harry's eyes bulged like moons and Matt thought

the big man just might grab him in a bear hug. Thankfully he only shook Matt's hand heartily.

Matt stepped into the room, brushing against Harry's belly as he entered the room.

"What's that?" Harry asked, jabbing his finger at the box.

"Rafferty sent it with me. We've got to hurry up—I've only got forty minutes before I have to be back, or he'll . . ."

"He'll what?"

"He's got Liza. I'm sorry, Harry."

"That son of a bitch. How is she?"

"Holding her own. She snuck in a revolver. That's some woman you got there."

"That's my girl," he said.

"Where's Jill?"

"I'll summon her."

Harry banged on the connecting door. Jill asked who it was and then opened it when Harry said, "Us!"

"Look who I found."

Her eyes got bigger than Harry's had, and she threw herself at Matt, pressing her face into his chest. He hugged her close with his free arm and kissed the top of her head.

"I'm so glad you're alive," she said.

"I wasn't sure I'd see you again," he told her.

She stepped back, smiling, her eyes tearing.

"Now don't go getting sentimental on me. I've got to leave in about twenty minutes."

"What's with the box?"

"Let's find out."

He led the way into Jill's room and opened the desk drawer, digging until he came up with a pen with BEST WESTERN on its side.

Before opening the box, he held it up to his ear. He had set it on the seat in the car on the way here, and it didn't sound like it was ticking, but you could never be sure. Better to be safe than to get blown to bits.

Satisfied it wasn't a bomb, he used the pen point to split the tape, then pulled the flaps open.

There were wads of balled-up newspaper inside, and Matt pulled them out and tossed them on the floor. Underneath the paper was a small white box and a sealed envelope.

"Anyone want to do the honors?" he said.

"Let's see the box," Harry said, picking it up.

Matt tore open the envelope, while Harry opened the small box.

Harry took the lid off, sucked in air in a heaving gasp and backpedaled, sitting on the bed hard. The box landed on the table, remaining upright.

Harry's face had gone dead pale.

"What is it?" Jill said.

Harry clamped his hand over his mouth.

"Look in the box," he said.

Matt picked up the box and Jill peered over his shoulder.

It took him a second to realize what he was looking at, that what he was seeing was real, and not some grisly Halloween prop.

It was a severed finger, slightly crooked, sitting on a bed of wadded cotton. The skin was liver-spotted; and a gold wedding band rested below the knuckle.

Matt wanted to fling the package across the room, but he stopped himself. It was Liza's finger, and to do that would be disrespectful, like walking on a grave. Instead he set it gently on the dresser and closed the lid.

Behind him, he heard Jill whisper, "Oh, my God. Matt, is she . . . ?"

"She has to be alive. Rafferty said if I didn't come back in an hour he would kill her. He needs her for leverage."

"Read the note," Jill said.

Matt removed the paper from the envelope and un-folded it.

Nice touch, don't you think? Took me a while to get her to hold still, but once I started cutting, she lost some fight. The three of you turn yourselves in to me in one week. The place of surrender is St. Mark's Catholic School, twelve midnight. I'll expect Harry and Jill to show up. If they don't, I'll chop up Crowe and the old woman piece by piece and send them to you. If you surrender, I'll let the old woman go.

> *Sincerely,*
> *Ed Rafferty, Chief of Police*

"We have to stop him and free you and Liza," Jill said.

"I can work on getting the two of us out. Harry's wife brought a gun into the jail," Matt said.

"We'll show up there, but we're not gonna come in quietly," Harry said.

"You've got guns?"

"Liza brought them," Jill replied.

"Can we put together a quick plan?"

"Why don't we just take these weapons and blow them to hell, get Liza out now?" Harry said.

"That won't stop the Harvest. And if Rafferty senses something's up he might kill her before we could bust her out," Jill said.

"I suppose you're right. I don't like it, but I suppose you're right. Now what's your plan, Matt?"

"This is what we should do."

Ten minutes planning to stop an army of devils. If they were going to succeed, they would need an angel on their collective shoulders. Better yet, a whole legion of them.

CHAPTER 31

Matt pulled into the parking lot to find Clarence standing with his arms crossed outside the garage doors. He reminded Matt of a cigar store Indian, big and ugly.

Matt hit the brakes in front of the garage door, and the cop waved him out of the car.

"Slowly!" he said.

Once he was out, the cop instructed him to turn around, put his hands on the hood and spread his legs. He patted Matt down, giving him a little jab in the crotch when he reached Matt's inner thighs.

"How'd that feel?"

"Piss off."

He escorted Matt into the cell block, where Liza lay on her cot, motionless. At first he though she was dead and Rafferty had left her body there as a surprise for him. Her arm was draped across her forehead, as if she had a bad headache and was resting on her couch at home.

A piece of gauze was taped over the spot where her ring finger used to be. It was brown with dried blood.

Her chest rose and fell, the only sign she was still alive.

Clarence, the red-haired cop, unlocked Matt's cell door and pushed him in. Did these guys think that you got in the cell quicker if they shoved you? It seemed to be the norm around here. Maybe they could start an Olympic event: the inmate shove and toss.

The first thing he did after Clarence was gone was slide his hand under the mattress and feel for the revolver. He had a tense moment when he couldn't find it, but then he felt it. He had expected to turn and see Rafferty on the other side of the bars, dangling the gun, mocking him with it. But the cell hadn't been searched, and their get-out-of-jail card was still tucked safely away.

Matt said, "How are you holding up?"

"Ugh."

"That bad? Did the bleeding stop?"

"Yeah. The dear Chief of Police cauterized it for me with a propane torch," she said. "But not before he jammed it in that toilet in your cell. I think I'm getting an infection."

"Painkillers?"

"None. I think it might be infected," she repeated.

She must be in incredible pain, pain beyond his comprehension.

He lowered his voice and said, "We've gotta get out of here. You bringing that gun in was a small miracle."

"Thank heavens for them," she said.

"We've got a plan. Just try and hold on."

"I'll do my best," she croaked.

The door from the squad room opened and somebody approached the cells.

It was Rafferty; he leaned against Matt's cell door and held onto the bars.

"They agreed to surrender. But you have to promise not to hurt Liza anymore."

"What did the fat one say when he saw his old lady's finger?"

"That he wanted to tear your guts out."

"How quaint. They really agreed to turn themselves in?"

"Yeah."

"We'll see about that."

Matt jerked his head in Liza's direction. "And we'll see if you let her go."

"If everyone cooperates, I see no problems."

"Uh-huh."

Rafferty let go of the bars and walked away. Matt trusted him about as much as he would an angry rattlesnake.

Harry sat in a chair facing the hotel room door, his head bobbing, fighting the tight grip of sleep that wanted to pull him under. One of the shotguns was draped across his lap.

Jill rested on one of the twin beds, fingers twined behind her head on the pillow. She had a wonderful view of the ceiling tiles, and she'd resorted to counting the tiny dots in the panels to try and make herself sleepy. It hadn't worked. The alarm clock read 2:15 A.M.

She felt like she had downed a pot of coffee; every few minutes she twitched or rolled over, and her skin felt itchy. The pillow had lost its coolness and felt as if it were stuffed with knotted-up sweat socks.

Resigned to the fact that she wasn't going to get much sleep, she kicked the covers off and swung her legs over the side of the bed.

They had moved from the Best Western to the Adam's Mark. Since Rafferty knew where they were staying, the switch would keep him off balance.

She stood up and looked out at the city lights, most notably City Hall's top floors. They were kept lit at night, making her think of a king with a giant red electric crown.

She tiptoed over to Harry and shook him gently. His head jerked back and a snort erupted from his mouth. Jill had managed to talk him into staying in the same room for the sole reason that there was safety in numbers.

They'd had a long day, going shopping at the Main Place Mall, Jill buying sweatshirts and jeans, Harry flannel shirts. They also stocked up on toiletries: soap, toothpaste, toothbrushes and deodorant. The whole time they had constantly peered back over their shoulders, trying to look at everyone and no one at the same time.

Rafferty was miles away, but that didn't make her feel any safer.

They had agreed to take turns standing guard, and Harry's shift was over. He had dozed off, but she cut him some slack because she knew he must be incredibly worried about his wife.

Harry had been pretty quiet since getting Rafferty's package, choosing to slip the ring off the severed finger and throw the remains in the Dumpster behind the Best Western. She could almost see the stress carving fresh wrinkles into his face.

"Hey," he said, coming out of his doze.

"Go to bed and get some real sleep, Harry."

"Every time I close my eyes I have nightmares."

"You should get some rest anyway."

"I'll try."

He rose slowly from the chair, handed Jill the gun and lumbered across the room, looking like a woolly mammoth slogging through a tar pit.

Jill took his place in the chair, trying not to think about the size of the task ahead of them. *What if we can't get Liza and Matt out? Can we destroy a small army of nightmare creatures and get out alive?*

Their lives were not the only ones at stake, for entire families would be slaughtered. Never in a million years had she bargained for this when she took the job at Lincoln Mercy Hospital.

She had the same numb feeling that she'd had when she found out her father had been killed. Was this really happening?

Unfortunately, yes.

For the hell of it, she picked up the phone off the nightstand and dialed her number, punching in the code for her answering machine when it picked up. While the tape rewound, she looked over at Harry. He jerked his head back and forth on the pillow and murmured in his sleep.

The first voice on the machine was her mother's, whining that Jill wouldn't call her back. Then her mother again, this time in tears.

The third message was from Dorothy Gaines, telling her not to bother coming into work, that she found a real nurse to do the job. If only that new nurse knew what she was getting into.

Her mother again, threatening to call the police, then a beep and no more messages. She hung up the phone and set it back on the nightstand.

Too bad, Mom. She couldn't possibly explain what was happening to her mother; she would tell Jill to seek help from a psychologist and say something like the job was getting to her.

She returned to the chair, propped the shotgun against the wall and waited for the night to pass.

In the week leading up to the Harvest, Jill and Harry had hit the Mobil Station downtown, filling five-gallon cans with gasoline. Harry had stopped at Home Depot, picking up rags and a pair of tin snips. The two of them had also stopped at Tops Markets and purchased a case of Mason jars.

Harry rented a van from Avis so they could drive around with the supplies in the back and not draw attention to their cargo. The van also allowed them to work in relative privacy.

After they rented the van, they stopped and bought four Zippo lighters. Harry said they were the most reliable things ever made.

They had caught a news report about the fire at the cabin. It seemed the state police had cordoned off thirty acres of land around the site of the fire. Channel 2 reported a host of government vehicles, some of them military, driving in and out. A Humvee remained parked at the entrance to the cabin road. Not the civilian kind, either. This one had camouflage paint and a machine gun on the roof. Upon seeing the report, Jill reflected that maybe Rafferty and his followers would finally be exposed.

Harry had called St. Mark's School to see if any events were scheduled for September 3, and they caught a break because the Fall Fair and Craft Show was scheduled for the day before the Harvest Meeting. That gave them the opportunity to sneak in their supplies without breaking into the joint.

Harry had the weapons resting on the bed, looking black, shiny and deadly. He had checked them again and again, cleaning, inspecting barrels and chambers, making sure they were ready to fire.

"I'd feel better if I could test a few rounds."

"I don't think hotel management would appreciate bullet holes in the walls," Jill said.

"I'm worried about the van," he said.

They had parked the van in a parking garage across the street.

"Most people will probably ignore it. And a six-dollar-an-hour security guard isn't going to give it a second glance."

"Pretty sad," Harry grunted.

"Where will we park in proximity to the school?"

"I figure on the same street."

"I don't think so."

"Why not?"

She twirled her hair around her finger, thinking.

"Too suspicious. One of us is going to have to bring the van around the back and unload the supplies. If we do it on the street, someone might see us and call the cops."

"You're right. One of us will wait in the school. There's a side door near the cafeteria and gym that we can use. We'll pull the truck up there and unload. I think we'll be safe because there's nothing else on that side of the building. It's a red door," he added.

"What about a security system?"

"None. At least there wasn't when I worked there."

"You worked there?"

"After I got back from the war things were slow at the shop. So I took a part-time maintenance job at the school. Besides, the school will be open when we go in, with the craft fair going on and all."

The supplies were ready to go. They had cut holes in the lids of the Mason jars with tin snips to allow a rag to be stuffed in. The two of them took turns in the van, fifteen minutes at a time, creating Molotov cocktails.

When they were done, they had two dozen Molotovs, two full gas cans, two shotguns, the M-16 and Harry's forty-four magnum. Harry also had his fireworks ready to go; the plastic explosive, cord, blasting caps and the radio transmitters for detonation went into the bag. Would they be able to get out of the building before the Fourth of July show started? Jill wondered.

Jill thought about how she'd gone from hating guns,

blaming them for the death of her father, to thinking of them as the reason she was alive right now. She had established an uneasy truce with them, not entirely comfortable, but able to fire one if needed.

Everything still felt dreamy, as if they were getting ready to go on a deer-hunting trip rather than fight monsters. If it was possible, she felt tired, battered, confused and jumpy at the same time.

Picking up on this, Harry said, "You'd better get some rest. Tomorrow's the start of it."

She took Harry's advice and stretched out on the bed.

Matt's back throbbed from sleeping on the lump in his mattress, but it was the only way to keep the gun concealed. If it meant getting out of here, then a sore back was a small price to pay.

The week had been uneventful, most of it spent running a film in his mind, rewinding it and playing it again. When he would make his move, how he would get Liza out, and how to hook up with Jill and Harry once they were out of here. Things might go as smooth as a Hollywood action flick in his mind, but real life was never like that. Guns jammed, ammunition misfired and no one ever got knocked out with one punch.

He had to prepare himself for any eventuality, because if he didn't plan for the unexpected, they would be dead in a hurry.

Tension seeped into his head, a dull pounding sensation. He massaged his temples, hoping for relief and getting none.

Liza's condition had grown steadily worse; she had become delirious, babbling about going back to the farm from time to time and moaning loudly. Matt feared she had gone septic from the infected wound. If they didn't get her out of here soon, she would end up dead.

He had appealed to Rafferty to bring a doctor in and look at Liza, and he had gotten the middle finger for his trouble. That man was a real sweetheart, all right.

"Liza, how are you?"

"Okay," she said, her voice barely above a whisper.

"Is there anything I can do for you?"

"Cut my arm off."

"Can't help you there. Just hang on as long as you can, okay?"

"Yup."

He felt like pounding the bars with his fists until they bled. If he paced any more, he would wear a hole in the concrete floor. Anything was preferable to sitting here, especially while he knew Liza was suffering so badly.

He wanted Rafferty to come for him so he could use the revolver and get the show on the road. The timing needed to be perfect, and he wasn't sure if he should wait until they came right up to the cell or blast them as they came down the hall.

He decided to wait for them to come close, then have them open Liza's cell door first. If they took Liza out first, he could shoot one of them and have her grab the keys for him.

"Liza."

"Uh?"

"Can you get up?"

"Do I have to?"

"Yes."

She looked like a pile of rags, lying on her side with her knees curled into her body.

She rolled over slowly until she was on her back.

Matt tapped a steady beat on the floor with his foot, worried that Rafferty would come waltzing in while they were talking. This part of the plan was crucial, and he didn't want Rafferty to hear any part of it.

Besides, the less Rafferty suspected, the better. Let him think he had a couple of lambs, ready to be led to slaughter.

After more groaning, Liza stood up and leaned against the bars. Heat radiated from her skin and sweat dripped down her face. She had to be running a pretty high fever.

"When they take us out, I'm assuming to the school, do whatever you can to get them to let you out first."

"I don't follow."

"I'm gonna use the gun then. I need you to get the jailer's keys. If they come to get me first, they'll put cuffs on me and then the gun will be useless," he explained. "Besides, I'll need someone to let me out of my cell."

"What if they put cuffs on me?"

"They won't."

He hoped.

"Okay. We'll do it."

"Just make sure you get out of the way. I'll need a clean shot."

"Mmm-hmm."

"Go back and lie down. Get some rest."

She shuffled across the floor and collapsed on the bed, her arm hanging limp over the side, hand touching the floor.

Liza had to recover for both of their sakes.

The night of the Fall Craft Show, Jill checked them out at the registration desk while Harry walked to the parking garage to retrieve the van. He had volunteered to go out in the rotten weather, sparing her from getting soaked. The temperature barely hit fifty and silvery rain fell sideways, pelting the windows like small pebbles.

Jill finished settling up their bill and waited in the lobby near the revolving doors. Harry finally pulled up in the van and Jill scurried through the rain and hopped in. They had left the pickup truck in the garage and would come back for it if this whole thing worked out.

She wiped droplets of rain off of her face, thankful that she only had to run a few feet to the van. Harry had taken it worse, his hair slicked wet by the rain and his clothes made darker by the dampness. He shivered like a wet dog.

"Ready for this?"

"About as ready as I'll ever be."

"Weather's not so hot, huh?"

"I'm sorry you got soaked."

"All in a day's work."

They pulled away. The van smelled of gasoline fumes, so despite the steady rain, Jill cracked the window. A fat raindrop landed on her cheek.

"Do you think Liza's okay?"

She wanted to tell him yes, put his mind at ease, but that wouldn't be fair to Harry, because she didn't know if it was the truth. Liza was in the custody of a maniac who'd already amputated her finger just for kicks, and there was no way of telling what he would do next. Telling Harry everything was peachy keen would do nothing but give him false hope. "I honestly don't know."

He let out a sigh.

"Not what you wanted to hear, huh?"

"No, you're just being honest. We have to remember who and what we're dealing with here."

Harry swung the van onto the expressway, headed for Lincoln. The rain came harder, creating a crystalline waterfall on the windshield. Harry turned up the wipers.

Twenty-five minutes later, they were pulling up to their destination.

Jill's belly cramped. She checked the side mirror every few seconds; at any moment she expected a police cruiser's lights to flash behind them and put an end to their plans.

"Try and relax," Harry said, picking up on her mood.

"Fat chance."

The school was on their left, a three-story structure made of sand-colored brick. A pine tree stood on the front lawn and towered twenty feet over the school's roof. A silver cross hung over the main doors, and under it, in block letters, SAINT MARK'S SCHOOL.

Harry turned left into the driveway between the school and the church rectory, then into the lot behind the school and parked next to a Ford Expedition.

They got out of the van, Harry opening the rear doors and pulling out the green duffel bag with the weapons and ammunition in it. Jill took the two cardboard boxes they had filled with the Molotov cocktails and draped a sheet from the hotel over them. They still had the gas cans to bring in, but they would have to make another trip for those.

They hurried to the school's side door, and Harry gave a pull on it. At first it didn't open and Jill feared it was locked, but it gave with a rusty screech and they stepped inside.

Ahead and to the right was a stairway leading downward, across the hall to the left were stairs to the second floor.

"Those go downstairs to the cafeteria," Harry said, pointing.

A murmur and the sweet smells of brownies and pies rose from the stairway. The ladies' auxiliary or the PTA had most likely set up tables to sell their wares, Jill figured.

"Looks like the cafeteria's out as a hiding place," she said.

"Yeah. Wait over there while I get the gas cans."

Harry set the duffel bag on the stairs going up and Jill followed him, setting the boxes with the Molotov cocktails down on the landing. She climbed up three steps to stay out of sight, hoping that if someone entered the door, they would walk past without noticing her.

"Be right back," Harry said.

The cramp in her stomach knotted again.

Harry went outside and as the door swung she could hear the rain piddling on the blacktop.

She stood on the steps, chewing on her thumbnail, a nervous habit she hadn't done since she was nine years old. Jittery, she sat down, stood up, then sat on the steps again. *Come on, Harry, did you go to Texas for that stuff?*

"Can I help you?"

Jill looked down the steps to see a woman with an egg-shaped figure, all butt and thighs, staring up at her. It looked like an airbag had deployed in her screaming pink pants. The combination of the slacks and the flowered top with pinks and purples in the petals made Jill think of an Easter egg.

"I'm sorry?"

"Can I help you?" Easter Egg Lady repeated, her fleshy jowls jiggling.

"Just waiting for someone," Jill replied.

"Are you a crafter?"

"Yes, in fact we make the best doilies in all of western New York."

"Oh, how lovely." The woman clasped her hands together. "You know you don't have long to set up. Can I help you down to the gym?" She started up the steps, arms outstretched, ready to grab the duffel bag and haul it off to the gymnasium.

"No!"

Easter Egg Lady stepped back as if she'd walked into a bug zapper. "Well, I was just trying to help."

More interested in seeing what I had in the bag than helping, I'm sure.

"I'm sorry. My partner will be back any second. He's kind of touchy about anyone else handling the merchandise."

She could not let this woman, see Harry come in with the gas cans. Her radar might be up already, and Jill didn't want to make her any more suspicious.

Hopefully she didn't smell the gasoline from the cocktails, either.

Easter Egg Lady peered around Jill at the box; then, apparently satisfied, said, "All right. Just hurry to the gym. Time is short." She spun on her heel, her butt jiggling as she did so, leaving in a huff.

She wasn't gone down the cafeteria stairs two seconds when Harry opened the door and peeked in.

"All clear?" he asked.

Jill looked around the corner, and not seeing anyone, gave him a thumbs-up sign.

Harry swung the door the rest of the way, leaned against it to keep it propped open, and lifted one of the cans over the threshold. He did the same with the other, and then let the door close behind him.

"Let's get out of sight," Jill said.

"Up the stairs. We'll cut across the upper floors and find a classroom. What's today, Saturday?"

"Yeah."

"Mind's a little fuzzy. No school tomorrow means we can hide out in here."

Jill slung the bag over her shoulder, then crouched and lifted the boxes of Molotov cocktails. She started up the stairs and Harry followed, a five-gallon can in each hand.

They reached the second floor and Harry protested for a break, but Jill urged him to keep moving until they were farther away from the activity two levels down. "If I can handle this, so can you, soldier," she said. The muscles in her arms felt like they were on fire and her shoulder ached from where the strap dug in, but she didn't want to slow down until they were out of sight.

They went down the main hallway, flanked by classroom doors eight feet high, painted chocolate brown with a silver number screwed into the center of each door.

"This is the old wing of the school," Harry said, huffing and puffing.

The walls were painted a light color (she couldn't tell if they were mint blue or the equally attractive mint green), and the paint cracked in little tributaries. A pink Barbie lunchbox sat against the wall, looking lonely and no doubt missed by some elementary school girl.

Jill's arms felt like putty, so she stopped and set the boxes down. Harry came to a halt behind her, nearly plowing into her before setting the gas cans down.

"If we can find an unlocked classroom it would be ideal," Harry said.

They spent ten minutes going up and down the wing, jiggling doorknobs and hoping a careless teacher had left one open, but they were all locked.

"Shit!" said Harry.

"Don't say that in front of Him," Jill said.

"What are you talking about?"

She pointed to the end of the hallway, opposite of where they entered the wing. A full-size crucifix hung on the wall, Christ's pale, flaking body dripping blood from dozens of wounds. The Christ looked toward heaven, his face a mask of crushing sorrow, the eyes seeming to plead for mercy, looking all too realistic.

"That'd make me behave if I had to walk by it every day," Harry said.

"It's a little creepy, with the blood and all."

"I guess we're stuck here until the show's over," Harry said.

"You think anyone will come up here?"

"Not likely. I was really hoping for an unlocked room, though."

"This'll have to do. What's around that corner?" Jill said, pointing to the junction where the crucifix hung.

"Doors to more stairs. One of them will take us back down to the gymnasium."

They shoved the supplies against the wall, near a door with 201 on its face, and under that a hand-lettered sign stating, MRS. RANDALL—8TH GRADE.

The cramp hit her belly again, and she told it to get lost, but it hung on, keeping her in knots. She sat on the floor, drawing her knees into her stomach, hoping for relief from her stomach pains. Harry sat next to her.

For now it was quiet, with just her, Harry and the Savior of the World in the hallway.

She hoped for no other company that evening.

CHAPTER 32

It remained silent, save for the occasional murmur echoing down the hallway, or shrieking children running up and down the stairs.

Harry squinted at his watch.

"Time?" she asked.

"Ten thirty. The craft show was over at nine. I haven't heard anyone for about forty-five minutes."

"Let's get set up, then."

She literally couldn't sit still a minute longer. Maybe if she got moving, got a sense of purpose, it would take her mind off of her nerves.

They picked up the equipment and hauled it toward the end of the hallway near the crucifix. They turned right at the cross and reached a beige door with a small window cut into it.

Harry set the cans down and a flutter wiggled through Jill's stomach. She wondered what would happen if the door was locked.

Harry opened it.

They started down the stairs, reaching the first landing outside an office marked PRINCIPAL. There was a boys' lavatory across from the office, directly ahead was a bright yellow door.

"That the balcony?" Jill asked.

"Yep."

The balcony looked over the gymnasium on both the north and south walls, and was key to their plans: it was a good position from which to fire down on an enemy.

Jill said a small prayer that the door would be open, for if they couldn't get to the balcony later, their plan would stall in first gear.

Again, Harry opened the door. He let it swing shut and it boomed in the empty school, sounding like the door to a tomb being sealed shut.

They continued down the stairs to the next landing. There was a set of red double doors with a silver panic bar, and above the doors a glowing exit sign.

"Where do those go?"

"To the foyer. And the main entrance," Harry said.

They took the last five steps down into a small hallway flanked by two beige doors. A third door lay straight ahead; it was the door to the gymnasium.

Harry set his can down at the bottom of the stairs and shook his arms vigorously to work out the muscle burn. Jill set the boxes and bag down as well.

"This is the only door into the gym. No, wait, I take that back. This is the only door that ninety-nine percent of the people who come to the school know about. There's another service door behind the stage. It connects to the cafeteria." He pointed to the door at the left. "This one's the locker room."

"What's behind door number three?"

Before he could answer she gripped the handle and yanked. The door swung open and a mop handle flew out and rapped her on the forehead. Jill shoved it back in among the assortment of push brooms, buckets and bottles of green and blue cleaning solutions. The closet smelled wet and dirty.

"Guess it's a janitor's closet," she said, rubbing the spot where the broom had conked her.

"We'll put the gas cans in here until it's time to set things off."

"That's awfully close to the gym."

Harry picked upon her vibe that being close to the gym also meant being close to Them, increasing the chances of being found out and torn to pieces.

"There's nowhere else to store them. We can't just leave them sitting here. Too suspicious."

He was right and she knew it. She didn't like it, but he was right.

She pushed aside a yellow bucket on casters and stuck some of the mops in the back corner of the closet in order to make room for the gas cans.

"Okay."

Harry sighed and squatted like an Olympic power lifter, then lifted the cans and moved them into the closet. Jill slammed the door shut.

"Now the moment of truth," Jill said.

She yanked on the doorknob and the gym door opened.

Harry picked up the duffel bag and Jill took the box containing the Molotovs.

The gym was lit with a queer, yellow and murky light, thrown off by dim lamps on the walls. It was the color of poison gas.

Their shoes chirped on the floor as they walked. The balconies ran along two walls, twenty feet in the air, painted bright yellow. Harry informed her that the school colors were yellow and blue, hence the canary-colored balconies.

"Let's get up on the stage," Harry said.

The stage had a dusty green curtain drawn across it, with steps flanking either side. They climbed the steps up onto the stage and it rewarded them with an enormous creak.

Jill didn't like it in here, for it wasn't supposed to be this quiet. She imagined children running across the gym, kicking red rubber balls, playing jump rope, tag or basketball. Their sneakers would squeal like a hot rod's tires as they ran across the floor, full of energy that adults envied.

Their footsteps echoed through the gym, giving it a sepulchral feel and making Jill wish she were just about any place else right at the moment. They ascended the stage steps, and Harry went to the curtain, felt around for the seam and slipped through.

Although she knew he was directly on the other side, an irrational corner of her mind told her he had been swallowed up, never to return.

That feeling dissolved when he stuck his head through the seam.

"You coming?" Harry asked.

She snapped herself out of it and set her supplies down next to the duffel bag, then ducked through the opening in the curtain. Harry was down on one knee, sliding his hand back and forth over the floor.

"What are you doing?"

"Looking for a trapdoor ring. Here it is."

Reaching into his back pocket, he pulled out a Swiss Army knife and opened the blade with a soft *click*. Using the blade, he pried at the floor until a rectangular piece of wood popped up and rattled on the stage.

"Your trapdoor?"

"You got it."

He stood up and pulled the trapdoor open, then started down a flight of steps that led underneath the stage.

"Wait here. I'll find the light."

The darkness under the stage engulfed him as he descended into the hole. A moment later white light cascaded out of the opening and Harry said, "Come on down."

Jill climbed down a set of rickety wooden steps into a basement that smelled dry and dusty, like old newspapers. A naked bulb hung on a wire at the bottom of the stairs, and a string for switching it on dangled from the fixture.

Plastic Santas, reindeer, a kneeling Mary and Joseph and a glittery star with the word NOEL scrawled across it were among the props in the storage area. There was also a wooden cradle filled with straw, and timbers used for constructing the manger scene.

The room also held stacked metal folding chairs and a backdrop painted to look like the yellow brick road as it approached the Emerald City.

"One time when I was working here I came down after school hours and found Mrs. Kelleher and Mr. Abernathy, the seventh grade teachers, naked from the waist down and going at it like rabbits." Harry chuckled. "Abernathy offered me a thousand bucks to keep my mouth shut."

"Did you take it?"

"Nah. I just told him if I ever caught him again I would go right to the principal."

"I guess they were really into their work."

"I'll say. I'll go get that bag and start setting up down here. You mind taking the cocktails up to the balcony? We should've left them there. Wasn't thinking."

"Not a problem," she said.

She walked up the stairs, grabbed the boxes and headed to the balcony. Once on the balcony, she set the boxes down and stretched, trying to take some of the ache out of her muscles.

She wanted to get the Molotovs out of sight, so she hunkered down and pushed them across the floor, the cardboard boxes swishing as she shoved. There were old green file cabinets against the wall, and she found a space wide enough between them to slide the box in.

There was a yellowed tarp draped over a table, and she took that and used it to cover the box, making it less conspicuous. The only thing that would give them away was the slight odor of gasoline coming off of the jars. She hoped no one sniffed them out and removed the cocktails before the time came to use them.

Looking out on the gym floor, she tried to imagine it crowded with the creatures, their grotesque forms squirming and writhing as they transformed from men to beasts. She felt disheartened at the task ahead, going up against an army of predators.

Then there was Matt and Liza to worry about, whether or not they could escape from Rafferty, and whether or not the four of them could all get out of the school alive.

They had planned hastily, and much of their plan depended on luck. Maybe whatever malevolent force had created the creatures had an equally powerful enemy on the side of good and light that would come to their aid. Would it be God, or some other deity that gave them a push?

Or maybe there was no evil force behind the creatures; perhaps they had crawled out of the ooze and had been stalking the earth since prehistoric times. She liked to think that someone was watching over them, that if there were a God, He would not let this go down. They were on the side of good, right? That should count for something.

Sure Jill, and so are Luke Skywalker and the Lone Ranger, and they always beat the bad guys in the end, she thought. Those were convenient endings cooked up by scriptwriters, but in the real world sometimes even the good guys got their heads handed to them.

Still, she had to hope.

She left the balcony, taking one last peek to make sure the cocktails were out of sight, and joined Harry underneath the stage.

He was on his knees at the front wall, the one facing the gym, molding grayish explosives to the blocks.

"C-4?"

"Yeah. How'd you know?"

"Robert Ludlum novels."

Harry dropped a piece of it and it rolled between his legs.

Jill gasped. "Be careful!"

"Relax. This stuff is highly stable. It won't do anything without a detonator to set it off."

He bent over and picked up the C-4, then molded more explosives behind a steam pipe that ran along the bottom of the wall. He took a white cylindrical object with an antenna jutting from the top from the bag. When he was done, cords ran from the explosives to the cylinder.

"Is that the detonator?"

"Sort of. Actually it's a receiver."

He took out a similar white cylinder with an antenna and a metal switch on top of it. The transmitter to set off the blast.

"If you need to blast, flip this switch. This goes with us."

Harry tucked the receiver and wires behind a stack of cardboard boxes. Someone would have to be looking very hard in order to find it. "Let's just hope no one decides to investigate," he said.

"I put the cocktails up on the balcony."

"Good. Now all we have to do is wait."

That would be the hardest part.

* * *

Something shook Jill from the comfort of sleep.

Tilting her head up off the floor, she listened hard, but despite her straining could hear nothing. She chalked it up to nerves and the fact that she was over-tired. Might as well get back to sleep.

She rested her head on her hands, which itched from the wool blankets they had laid on the floor. The blankets had been covering three plastic wise men from the Christmas display. They'd decided it was better than sleeping on concrete.

She closed her eyes.

Sleep had almost gripped her when she heard a noise, the type that makes small children cover their heads with blankets in the middle of the night.

It was a long creak, then a slam. A door.

"Harry. Harry!" she hissed, reaching over and shaking him.

"What?" He smacked his lips, half-awake.

"Someone's here."

"In the room?"

"No, the gym. Listen."

A thud, metal banging.

"Sounds like its coming from the balcony," he said.

He sprang to his feet faster than Jill thought possible and grabbed the shotgun.

The door slammed again, booming in the empty gym.

"They must've left the balcony," Jill said.

Harry bent over, unzipped the duffel bag and took out the M-16, which he handed to Jill.

"This might be easier for you. It has a little less kick than the shotgun. Just point and pull the trigger. Easy, though, 'cause it's automatic."

She took the M-16 from him.

"Listen," she said.

Thumps came from the left of them, near the stairs. Whoever it was decided they were going to check out the stage.

The footfalls advanced until they were right above them, the floorboards groaning. A wet, sniffing sound came from above, like a bloodhound on the trail of a convict in those old prison movies, only much louder.

"It's trying to get our scent," Harry said.

"Your heart pumping as hard as mine?" she whispered.

"Is your heart going a thousand beats per minute?"

"Yeah," she said.

"Then I'm right with you."

More sniffing, then thuds, moving quickly from left to right, then from front to back, punctuated by grunts and growls.

"It can smell us but it can't find us. Be completely still," Jill said.

"I hope it can't break through the stage."

"The one that chased me and Matt busted through a brick wall."

"Well, there's a comforting thought."

"Comfort's got nothing to do with this situation," Jill said.

The thumping slowed and then stopped at the front of the stage. The beast let out a roar that made her teeth vibrate. She propped the gun against her leg and slapped her hands over her ears to muffle the din.

It sounded pissed off and frustrated that it couldn't find its quarry.

There were two strides across the stage, then a thud as it hit the floor and took off. The next sound was the door shutting, and then the gym was silent again.

"Do you think Rafferty knows we're here?" Jill asked.

"I don't know. Maybe he sent that one here to keep an eye on things."

"Do you think it was him?"

"I doubt it. Don't ask me why but I don't think it was."

She paused for a moment and then said something that shocked even herself.

"I think we should go find it and kill it."

"What?"

"Look, we have to leave the stage before tomorrow night. What if Rafferty left that thing in here as a guard dog? We'll have to go upstairs eventually, and we'll have to face it. And I'd rather us hunt it than it hunt us."

Harry scratched the back of his neck, and his brow furrowed.

"I hate to say this, but you're right. We're gonna have to eliminate that thing. I just hope there's only one of them in here."

She would rather take a hot poker in the rear end than go looking for one of the creatures and she knew Harry felt the same way. But they had to make sure it was dead and not somewhere waiting to ambush them.

"Fire is our best chance. We'll go to the balcony and grab a Molotov cocktail."

"Let's just hope we don't burn the joint down in the process," Jill said.

With a sigh of resignation, Harry took the Zippo from the bag and then dug around and pulled out a box of shotgun shells. He filled his shirt pockets until they bulged like misshapen breasts. He also gave Jill a spare clip for the M-16.

"Keep sharp. That damn thing could be hiding anywhere," Harry said.

They started up the steps, Jill feeling as if she were about to go hunting a tiger armed with only a slingshot.

Somewhere in a dank corner of the cell water dripped a steady beat. Liza's breathing became a series of moans and groans as her health grew worse. Rafferty better come for them soon, or Matt's little plan wouldn't work. He needed Liza to be alert enough to get out of the line of fire, scoop up the keys and unlock Matt's cell. Maybe he was asking for too much, but it was all they had to go on.

He sat on the edge of the cot tapping his feet, feeling the lump that was the revolver jabbing him in the rear end. In his mind he ran the scene over and over again: whipping out the gun like an old-time western gun-slinger, praying that he was quicker on the draw than Black Bart. If he missed, they were dead. He had no doubt that they would be killed right here, and the hell with taking them to the school as hostages.

"How goes it?"

He looked up and Rafferty was there, propped against the cell door as if he were sidling up to the bar to order a tall cold one.

"You really want me to tell you?"

"Not really. I could give a shit."

"What do you want? If you want me to deliver another package you can put it where the sun don't shine."

"No, nothing like that. Although that was quite effective, I'll bet. I'd give my left nut to see the look on the fat guy's face when he opened that box and saw his old lady's ring finger."

"I'm glad you find it so amusing."

"Oh, I do. Even more amusing than the plot I think your friends are hatching."

Matt did his best to look puzzled and didn't think it worked.

"Come on. You don't honestly think I thought they would go quietly. Not after the fight you all put up at the cabin."

"You're nuts."

"Am I? Well, maybe. But just in case I sent a watch-dog over to the school, to make sure no one crashes the party early."

If there were only some way to warn Jill and Harry. But his ass was stuck in this cell, and the chances of Rafferty letting him use a phone were next to nothing. They would have to fend for themselves until he found a way out of here.

Harry went first, nudging the trapdoor open with the barrel of the shotgun, looking like a Neanderthal emerging from a cave.

He held the trapdoor and then pushed it all the way open, holding onto it with his free hand and setting it gently on the stage floor so it wouldn't slam. On her way up the steps, Jill brushed against the opening and kicked up a cloud of dust. The need to sneeze was immediate, and she stifled it by shutting her eyes tight and bunching her nose.

They crossed the stage, the boards creaking, each groan sounding like a wrecking ball slamming into a brick building. In reality Jill knew the noises were nowhere near that loud, but who knew how sharp the beast's hearing was?

They made it across the gym floor to the door, Jill watching the balconies, half expecting the creature to come swooping down from above like a hawk. Its scent hung in the air, chemical and putrid all at once.

They climbed to the balcony, and twice Harry thought he heard something. They stopped to listen, but it turned out to be Harry's ears trying to put one over on his brain.

Once they were on the balcony, Jill threw aside the tarp that covered the Molotov cocktails and removed one of the firebombs. Then she closed the box and replaced the cloth.

"We'll try cutting through the lobby over to the other wing," Harry said.

"It could be anywhere out there."

"There are a lot of places to hide in here," Harry agreed.

The sensible part of her mind, the part that told her not to pet strange dogs or play on train tracks, screamed at her to turn around and leave the building immediately. She did her best to stifle those thoughts and instead focus on the fact they were heavily armed and a match for their enemy. It wasn't working very well.

"Maybe it's gone," she said.

"And maybe I'll grow angel wings and fly off the balcony," Harry said.

"Aren't the doors to the lobby locked?" she asked.

"Yeah, they probably are."

"That means it has to be on this half of the building," she said.

"Not necessarily. If it came in on the top floor—not through the front doors—it could circumvent the lobby by traveling on the second floor and going to the other side. You really don't even have to go through the lobby to get to the other wing."

"But how much do you want to bet it's on this side, waiting?"

"I'd bet more than a dollar on it."

They resigned themselves to keep going, Jill feeling like a mountain climber who simply can't continue up Everest. Her joints ached, and her eyes felt heavy and grainy from lack of sleep. But they had to keep moving toward the top of the proverbial mountain, where something was waiting to tear them to pieces.

The lobby doors were locked, so they decided to check the second floor.

They went back into the hallway, past the principal's office and up the stairs until they were at the full-size crucifix. Jesus was still staring with His weepy, glassy eyes, looking toward heaven. They could use a hand from Him right about now, even if the statue wasn't the real deal. Maybe they could lure the beast to the statue and it would collapse on the bastard and crush it.

Harry growing those angel wings seemed more likely.

"Do you smell it?" Harry said in a whisper.

She hadn't noticed an odor when they entered the old wing, but she took a good sniff and detected it, a wild animal smell, thick and sour. There was no doubt that it was in the hallway with them.

They moved straight ahead to the other side of the T-junction, where there was one classroom and another beige door leading to the stairs. Jill peered through the small window in the door and saw only blackness.

They turned around and made a right down the long hallway, the smell of the creature getting heavier as they went.

Jill whispered, "We know it's not in the classrooms because the doors are all locked. I doubt they can pick locks either."

They moved, both of them in a semi-crouch, scanning up and down, side to side, watching for any flicker of movement that might indicate their enemy's presence.

As they reached the stairway to the third floor, the scent grew thicker.

One set of stairs, black with yellow grip tape on them, led up, and another led back to the first floor.

"Up or down?" Jill said.

Harry looked back down the hallway, then up the stairs. Jill thought he was stalling, indecisive.

"Up."

"Any particular reason?"

"Nope."

"What's up there?"

"No more than a landing with two rooms. One's the music room and one's an old classroom that hasn't been touched since the fifties. And the door to the roof."

The more Jill thought about it, the less she liked the idea of heading upstairs; it could become a trap if their pursuer sneaked up behind them. She didn't think St. Mark's School was lax enough to leave the roof door open, so that eliminated another possible escape route.

"I say we go downstairs. If it comes up behind us, we'll be trapped up there," she said.

"Jesus, you're right. I can't believe I didn't think of that."

They turned to go down the stairs when Harry put his hand on her shoulder as if to stop her from moving any further.

"Wait. Hear that?"

Jill cocked her head to one side. She heard footsteps coming from the third floor. The footsteps stopped. Harry raised the shotgun, ready to fire.

"It's waiting on the landing," Harry whispered.

"Wish it wasn't so damned dark."

"C'mon. What are you doing?"

As if on cue, something bounded down the stairs and charged toward them. Harry fired, the shot hitting the beast in the arm, but it kept coming.

It plowed into Harry, knocking him back, the two of them rolling over and over each other, Harry pushing its head back to keep the jaws away from his face. It was a small one, just over five feet, but no less ferocious than its bigger brethren. It hissed and spat at them.

They stopped rolling, the creature on top, and Harry pushed it up like a man doing a bench press until there was a foot of space between the two of them. Then he balled up his knees, planted his feet on its legs and pushed off, thrusting the beast away from him. It rolled into the wall and got up, the quizzical look that had crossed its face turning into insane rage.

Jill stood stunned, the whole thing unfolding too quickly. A little voice inside her told her to get moving.

Harry picked up the shotgun, but the creature charged again and he couldn't turn the gun around, so he swung by the barrel, cracking his foe in the head. The blow sent the beast staggering like a drunk, and it nearly plowed into Jill.

She sidestepped quickly, moving to her right as the assailant sailed past her. She snapped herself out of her fog and raised the gun, but by then the attacker had regained its bearings and lunged for her, pushing her onto her butt.

The Molotov she was holding hit the ground, and she expected to hear glass break, but there was only a hollow *ping!* The jar was still intact.

It got on all fours and scrabbled toward her; she crab-walked backward, the beast advancing on her too quickly. The muscles in its legs flexed, ready to pounce, when Harry brought the shotgun down on it like an executioner swinging an ax. He connected at the base of the skull.

Jill tried pushing it off of her, but even stunned it was too heavy to move.

"Harry!"

Harry dropped the shotgun, took two steps back, lowered his shoulder and charged like a linebacker drawing a bead on a running back. He slammed into the creature, knocking it off of her.

Jill got on her hands and knees. She hurried over to the Molotov cocktail and gripped it, prepared to throw it before realizing it wasn't lit.

Harry got to his feet and saw what she meant to do. "Jill!"

The Zippo came flying at her quick, and she caught

it one-handed and flicked it open, the flame licking her hand. She held the flame to the rag jutting from the jar's lid and it lit.

Harry backed up and Jill threw the jar to the ground, smashing it at the creature's feet. The flames raced up its legs as it flailed and spun around, beating at the fire. Harry and Jill retreated down the hallway, a good twenty feet from the flaming beast. Jill snatched up the M-16, and as the demon advanced toward them, still aflame, she fired, exploding its head with two bursts from the rifle.

It fell to the ground, dead.

Harry grabbed a fire extinguisher from a glass cabinet in the wall, pulled the pin, and sprayed powdery white foam on the burning corpse. The fire was out in seconds, and Harry looked up at the ceiling.

"Lucky we didn't set off the sprinklers," he said.

A half-charred, stinking body caked with white powder lay on the floor. Tendrils of smoke floated up, and it smelled like someone had cooked a spoiled steak.

"God, that stinks," she said, trying not to gag.

Even in the dim hallway light, she could see that Harry's skin had turned three shades lighter.

"Man, that's nasty," Harry said, holding the extinguisher in one hand and clapping the other over his mouth and nose to block out the smell.

"We've got to get rid of it," Jill said.

"And how do you propose we do that?"

"You said there's some rooms on the third floor?"

"They'll be locked."

"They're worth trying," she said.

She took off down the hallway, jogged up the stairs and found three doors on a small landing. There was a piano in front of the door directly across from her and another steel gray door marked ROOF—UNAUTHORIZED ACCESS PROHIBITED. She tried the doors on the left and right and found them locked. Likewise for the door to the roof.

She gave the piano a shove just for the hell of it and found that it was on casters.

They could move the piano and hide the corpse behind it. It wasn't the best plan, but given the options, there really were no options. Hopefully Rafferty and his crew would stay off of the third floor.

She went back downstairs and told Harry her idea.

"All right," he said.

Harry rolled the beast over with a shove of his foot so it was on its back. He got it in a bear hug around the chest and lifted the torso up.

"Man, this thing stinks," he muttered.

Jill took the legs, which were charred black and flaking. The skin felt like warm, dead leaves.

They lugged it to the stairs, and after fifteen minutes of grunting and struggling, they had the body stuffed behind the piano. If you stood in front of the piano, you couldn't see it, but that wouldn't matter because it smelled bad enough to singe nose hair.

If anyone came up here they would find it.

"I hope they stay off the third floor," Jill said.

"I don't see any reason for them to come up here."

Wearily, they worked their way back downstairs, leaving foam on the floors, with nothing to clean it up. One more calling card they needed Rafferty to overlook.

CHAPTER 33

The night before the Harvest, Matt dreamt.

In his dream, the red-haired cop came and opened Liza's cell door, then dragged her out by her hair. Matt reached under the mattress and took out the revolver, but the cylinder swung open and the shells dropped to the floor.

When he bent over to pick up the bullets, he found them covered in a thick, mucusy gel, and they slipped from his fingers and fell back to the floor. He repeatedly tried to pick them up, but they fell through his fingers every time.

The cop grinned and put his hand around Liza's throat, squeezing steadily until her face was purple and her tongue lolled from her mouth.

He sat up sweating, his breathing ragged. It wasn't the only time he'd had the dream this week; in another version, the gun had a rusty trigger that would not pull no matter how hard he tried.

He supposed Freud could have a field day analyzing those dreams. Even though Matt had never taken psychology, he knew the dreams were caused by his anxiety, by a fear that the gun would fail or he would fail when the moment of truth came.

He had counted meals since he had been in jail, and deduced eight days had passed. This morning he left his breakfast untouched, a mix of runny scrambled eggs and burned wheat toast.

Liza remained dormant on the bed, the silence in the block punctuated by her groans as her suffering grew worse. He feared she didn't have much time left, and hoped gangrene wasn't setting into the wound. It seemed less and less likely that she would be able to assist him when the time came to make an escape.

The day passed without much fanfare, with no way to tell time for there was no window in the block.

When he guessed it was getting close to evening, he looked down the hallway to make sure no one was watching and took the revolver out from under the mattress. He tucked it in his waist at the small of his back, the metal digging hard into his flesh. He pulled his shirt tail over the gun. It wasn't exactly comfortable, but it was the only place he could conceal it and have relatively quick access to the gun.

Shortly after he had concealed the gun, the red-haired cop strolled down the hallway, a Remington shotgun tucked under his arm.

Wonderful.

He was hoping the cop would have only his sidearm and would have to draw it from the holster, but he obviously felt he needed to be heavily armed.

Why not just bring a goddamn bazooka while you're at it?

He breezed past Liza's cell and stood in front of Matt's, exactly what wasn't supposed to happen. Liza must have been too out of it to get up and try and coerce the cop into opening her cell first.

"On your feet. Let's go."

"Where we going? Can I drive?"

"Turn around so I can cuff you."

"Oh, all right."

Matt stood and turned his back to the cop, his arms hanging at his sides. His shirttail covered the revolver. Behind him, keys jingled as the cop prepared to open the cell door.

One for the money . . .

He lifted the shirt and pulled the gun from his waistband. Matt spun around, feeling like his feet were stuck in drying concrete, even though the motion only took a second.

When he turned around, the cop was leveling the shotgun to fire; the son of a bitch was quick, you had to give him that.

Matt fired first, catching him in the shoulder, then again in the chest. The shotgun roared, and Matt dove for the bunk, the skin on his hand flayed off as the buckshot skimmed him and slammed into the wall. Instinctively, he clutched at his wounded hand, dropping the revolver in the process.

It bounced once and blooped through the bars like an errant ground ball.

Oh, fuck.

Hand stinging, he rolled off the bunk and spotted the jailer's five keys on a ring lying an arm's length away outside the bars. The cop was on his back, blood pooling under him, but still stirring.

The shotgun lay next to him on the floor, directly in front of Liza's cell.

Matt kneeled by the bars, pressing himself up as tight as he could while sticking his arm through the opening, grasping for the keys. They were two inches out of his reach.

He squeezed up tighter until cold steel dug his collarbone, sending excruciating pain up his neck. An inch away. A goddamn inch!

Lord, please give me another inch.

His gaze flicked to the side, where the revolver had landed. It was three feet away, and it might as well have been three miles, because there was no chance of reaching it.

The cop rolled onto his side, his shirt dark with blood.

Matt got his middle finger on the key ring and slid it toward him a hair closer to the bars.

Matt was dimly aware of movement out of the corner of his left eye, and it took him a second to register: Liza slid off her bunk and was crawling on her hands and knees, holding her wounded hand in close to her body.

"Bastard," he said to the keys, as if that would inspire them to move closer to his fingers.

The cop was up on one knee, patting around on the ground like a man hunting for a lost contact lens.

The cop was looking for the shotgun, but unable to find it even though it was only a foot away from him. The wound must have put him in shock and momentarily disoriented him so even a simple task such as locating an object was difficult. It wouldn't last much longer, for he was bound to find the gun.

Liza reached the bars at the front of the cell and groped through with her good hand, finding the shotgun and yanking it by the barrel. Her actions seemed to jar the cop out of his state of shock, and he turned, looking surprised that the gun was still there.

"Give me that damn shotgun," he said.

Liza turned the gun so the barrel was away from her, and got it halfway through the bars.

In the meantime, Matt stretched himself until he thought his shoulder would pop from the socket.

"Motherfucking keys!"

With a final stretch, he hooked his fingertip around the key ring and dragged them toward the bars. Drawing them inside the cell, he stood up and began trying the keys in the lock.

The first attempt yielded nothing.

Liza sat on her rear end, the gun almost through the bars, when the cop grabbed the other end of the weapon.

Liza put her feet against the bars for leverage, the stock tucked under her armpit, hanging on for dear life. She looked at the weapon and realized her advantage. She pulled the trigger and the shotgun boomed. The shot grazed Clarence's arm, but he still tugged.

Then her grip slipped. Matt knew he had to get the door open. Finally, the fourth key clicked home and he opened the door just as the cop ripped the shotgun away from Liza.

Rafferty's cell phone rang. It was Linda.

"Report of shots fired at the elementary school."

"On my way," Rafferty said, and hung up.

Rafferty raced to Saint Mark's, his lights on but his sirens off. He pulled up in front of the main doors wondering if his watchdog had found intruders.

Father Mike Hannah was waiting for him. Father Mike was the vice principal, and he had called from the neighboring rectory to report noises.

He wore a trench coat thrown over flannel pajamas and had on a pair of black penny loafers. Rafferty could see the milky tops of his feet for he wore no socks. The wind whipped up and messed the priest's thinning gray hair.

Rafferty climbed the front steps.

"Hello, Chief Rafferty."

"Can you open the door?"

"Yes," he said, producing a ring with at least twenty keys on it.

Rafferty stood close to him, getting a whiff of his sour breath, the breath of sleep.

Father Mike unlocked the front door.

"No alarm system," Rafferty said.

"Unfortunately. Not in the budget. Do you want me to go in with you?"

"No. There could be dangerous people running around. Wait out here. Will I need any of those keys?"

"No. You should be able to circle around the new wing and then back without any problem."

Rafferty switched on his flashlight, the beam cutting into the gloom inside the door. He stepped into the main foyer and trained the light on the trophy case, where a film of dust coated the mock gold and silver prizes.

The doors to his right led to the old wing and the gymnasium, and those were surely locked. He would take the old priest's advice and make his way down the new wing of the school, then circle around. For reasons known only to the architects, the entrance to the new wing did not have doors, so anyone who got into the building through the main entrance could travel down the new wing freely.

He hoped he wouldn't need Father Mike to open any doors, for truth be told, the old man gave him the willies. Being around anyone associated with a god made him nervous.

Making his way down the wing, he passed the third grade classrooms and made a right, then passed the fourth grade rooms until reaching a stairwell near the art room.

At the top of the stairs, he shined the beam into the gloom and proceeded into the old wing, drawing his revolver and sweeping back and forth with it.

He stopped at a dusting of white powder spread on the floor. Crouching down, he ran his finger through it and rubbed his fingers together. At first he had no clue what it was, then he saw the fire extinguisher on the wall. He shined the light on it, revealing residue at the tip of the hose.

To confirm his suspicions, he took the fire extinguisher off of its bracket, pulled the pin and squeezed the lever. Foam whooshed out, definitely the same substance that was on the floor.

Someone's been up here playing with fire.

A faint burnt smell lingered in the hallway. It was coming from upstairs, and he didn't need his eyes to tell him what his nose already knew; they had set his watchdog on fire.

He started up the stairs, knowing he would find the charred creature, either dead or dying from its wounds.

What had probably happened was they had found it (or it had found them), and they decided on using fire to roast it alive. Although he lost his watchdog, at least he knew that Jill and Pierce had been here. But they didn't know that Rafferty was aware of them, and that could give him the element of surprise. The best fucking weapon ever invented.

He found the piano on the landing near the roof door and shoved it aside. The blackened, twisted corpse lay on the ground, and he put his hand on it. Still warm to the touch. There were two jagged holes in its head where bullets had torn through, obviously the source of the gunfire that Father Ed had heard.

Rafferty shuddered at the thought of being burned alive. It was the only thing that his race feared, for they had no natural enemies, but fire touched on something primal in them. The place deep down that was strung tight like piano wire, waiting for someone to pluck it and send shivers through the body.

He could bring a whole army to the school right now and sniff them of their hiding place, but that would ruin all his plans. He had a very special ceremony planned and he was intent on carrying it out. So confident was he that they would fall right into his hands, he dismissed the idea of finding Jill and Harry immediately. They would be his in time.

He rolled the piano back in place, leaving the body as he had found it. Better to let his little mice think the bad old tomcat was never here at all.

He left the building to find the priest waiting for him, his coat clenched in a liver-spotted fist, trying to keep out the damp air.

"Find anything?" Father Mike asked.

"Nope. Your ears are playing tricks on you. Why don't you go home and get some sleep?"

"Okay. You know best, Chief."

He smiled, showing yellowed teeth, but the look on his face told Rafferty he knew something happened in that school.

"I'll send an officer over in the morning to make another sweep, okay?"

"That would be nice, Chief."

Rafferty descended the steps and got into his patrol car, leaving the priest walking away, shaking his head and muttering to himself.

Matt slid the door open as the cop fumbled with the shotgun. Matt lunged and plowed into the cop. The guy was solidly built—and it was like hitting a side of beef. Still, the cop was half sitting up, and the blow was enough to knock him on his back.

Now on top of the cop, Matt brought his forearm down and slammed it into the redhead's forehead. All he got for his trouble was a sore arm.

The son of a bitch's skull must be two inches thick.

The cop's hand shot up and gripped Matt around the throat, Matt letting out a choking sound. Even wounded, the officer was incredibly strong. He began to squeeze. It was like having a damn boa constrictor around your neck.

When he was in the Rangers and training regularly,

Matt could bench-press two hundred and eighty pounds—and he was no weakling. But when he clawed at the cop's hand, trying to free himself, it was like attempting to break an iron shackle.

The room was starting to blur and spin all at once.

He reached down and grabbed the cop's lower lip, yanking on it as hard as possible.

"Cocksucker!" Clarence's grip let up just enough for Matt to slap his arm and roll away, wheezing for air. His throat felt raw and bruised, as if he had just swallowed a glass of Tabasco sauce.

He decided there was no way he could go hand-to-hand with the cop, for the beast inside him was active and providing much of that strength. If he were to get out of here alive, he would need to grab the shotgun.

As he started for the gun, the door from the squad room flew open and all six-five of Ed Rafferty filled the door frame. Matt spun around to see Rafferty standing there with a look of surprise on his face, as if he had just walked in on someone sitting on the john.

Rafferty had his revolver at his side, out of the holster. He paused, taken by surprise, and Matt used this to his advantage. He stooped down, picked up the shotgun, pumped it and fired at Rafferty. The chief saw it coming and dove out of the way, the blast splattering wood chips from the door frame all over the floor.

Matt was reaching for the key stuck in his cell door when a bullet whizzed past him and ripped open the mattress, shooting feathers into the air. That smelly old thing deserved to be put out of its misery.

Not wanting to end up like the mattress, and sure that Rafferty's next shot wouldn't miss, he eyed the door in the center of the block, the one leading to the garage. He turned to duck out into the garage. The red-haired cop pawed at his leg in an attempt to stop him, but it was obvious the bullet wounds had taken their toll. Matt kicked him away. Clarence ceased moving, eyes fixed on the ceiling.

The revolver appeared around the door frame, Rafferty intent on firing blind and hitting something.

As Matt pushed through Rafferty's cannon went off, ripping past him by inches. Once inside the garage, he turned quickly and pointed the barrel at the door, expecting Rafferty to come through at any second.

He was an easy target out in the open, so he crouched behind the rear end of the unmarked beige car, still parked in the garage.

Thirty seconds went by. Forty-five. A minute.

Was Rafferty circling around to sneak up on him? He looked toward the garage doors and back to the door to the cells, trying to watch both at once.

No Rafferty.

The police chief was probably waiting for him inside the hallway; Matt dreaded the thought of leaving himself exposed, but he had to go in and get Liza out of the cell. There would be no leaving her behind, Rafferty or no Rafferty.

Staying low to the ground, he moved across the garage and listened at the door. There was silence on the other side, and he imagined Rafferty crouched on the other side of the entrance, the massive revolver waiting to blast anything that came through the door.

He pumped the shotgun, guessing that he had two shells left to work with.

Approaching the door, he held the shotgun in his left hand, out and away from his body. He would open the door with the right, stick the barrel in the door and fire blindly on an angle. Liza's cell was straight ahead, and he felt confident the angle he took would keep the shot away from her.

If he were lucky, he would catch Rafferty right inside the doorway and blow a hole in him.

Ripping the door open, he jammed the barrel inside and fired, the gun bucking in his hand. It flew from his hand and landed next to the concrete steps leading up to the cell block. If Rafferty were behind the door, and Matt didn't hit him, he would be dead in a matter of seconds, for he was now unarmed and exposed.

Wrist throbbing, he picked up the gun and pumped it, the door wide open.

The garage and the hallway were silent, save for the sound of his breathing.

Rafferty was gone and Liza's cell door was wide open.

Outside, tires squealed on the blacktop and he knew he had been duped. He ran to the garage doors and peered out the window to see a Lincoln police cruiser speeding out of the lot with Ed Rafferty at the wheel.

Approaching the hallway, Matt aimed the gun, ready for someone to charge him, or gunfire to erupt, but nothing happened. The only person in the cell block was the dead cop. Rafferty no doubt had Liza in the backseat.

Inside the hallway, he rolled the dead cop on his side, unbuckled his gun belt, and put it on, tightening the buckle to the last notch. He wore it low on his hips the way Jesse James might have worn his six shooters back in the Old West.

In his haste, Rafferty had left the keys in Liza's cell door, and Matt pulled them out and stuck them in his pocket. Then he entered the squad room, expecting to find reinforcements, but finding only empty chairs and desks. If there were any other cops at the station, they surely would have come running when they heard shots fired in the hallway.

The squad room was filled with standard issue gray desks and office chairs kept together with duct tape strapped over their wounded seats and backs. A white cup with a streak of dried coffee running down the side sat on the desk to his left, surrounded by a stack of pink and yellow forms. *Only thing worse than cold coffee is warm beer*, he thought, for no apparent reason.

He wanted to find the room where they kept the big toys, more weapons like the shotgun, and more important, the ammunition for them. There was a door with frosted glass panes next to the receptionist desk that he tried and found locked.

He pulled the key ring from his pocket, and the third key opened the door. Past the door was a narrow hallway, the walls painted yellow, two doors on the left and one on the right almost near the end.

He was about to start down the hallway when he heard a soft mewling sound. It was coming from underneath the receptionist's desk. He hadn't noticed before, but someone's lumpy, purple-clad rear end stuck out from underneath the cutout in the desk. The legs were in white support hose, and the shoes were chunky and black.

"It's okay. You can come out," Matt said reassuringly.

"Please don't shoot me."

"I'm not going to shoot you."

"Promise?" A sniffle.

"Promise. Come on out."

The woman shuffled backward, her purple skirt riding up. She stood up, never taking her gaze off the shotgun.

"Relax. I won't hurt you."

"But I heard shooting."

"I know. Listen, ma'am . . ."

"Linda."

"Okay, Linda. Do yourself a favor. Go home, pack some bags and get out of town. Something awful is about to happen and anyone who isn't on Chief Rafferty's side is going to get hurt. Understand?"

"What do you mean?"

"I don't have time to explain. Just get out. And if you have family here, tell them to leave too. Pronto."

"But—"

"No buts. Get going."

Linda opened the desk drawer, took out a black handbag roughly the size of Alaska, then shuffled quickly down the hallway and went out the front door. Matt hoped she would take his advice and leave town.

He proceeded down the opposite hallway, one leading deeper into the station. Matt unlocked the door at the end with the fifth key on the ring. It was the room he wanted, and he had hit it on the first guess.

He flicked the switch and the lights hummed to life, revealing racks of shotguns, assault rifles, tear gas launchers, Kevlar vests and riot gear. Scanning the room, he spotted what he was looking for; boxes of shotgun shells that were useable in the twelve-gauge he was carrying.

Opening one of the boxes, he removed the shells and slid them into a bandolier hanging on the wall. He reloaded the shotgun, and draped the bandolier across his chest, Pancho Villa–style. Then he left the room, wishing he had time to grab more goodies.

He opened the garage door, climbed into the sedan and started it up. Then he sped across the lot for Saint Mark's Elementary.

He parked one block over. Hoping no one would see him, he got out, carrying the shotgun, and jogged up the driveway of a red Cape Cod style house. Its backyard butted up against the rear of the school, with only a fence and three feet of concrete separating the two.

He stubbed his toe on a turtle-shaped sandbox crossing the yard, but kept going, hopping the fence at the rear of the property. His wrist flared a bit, but he tried to block it out, along with all the other aches and pains he had acquired since returning to Lincoln.

He slipped between the garage and the school building so that no one could see him from the house, then ducked and checked the frosted basement windows. He rattled them to see if they were open, but neither would budge.

Going in one of the doors was unthinkable; Rafferty surely had guards posted at the doors, and even if he didn't the chance of being spotted was too great. So he opted to smash a window.

He lowered himself down into the basement of the school, dragging the shotgun in after him.

A rusted boiler took up most of the room, with pipes and gauges jutting from the monster. Cobwebs covered its surface, giving the boiler a seedy, dangerous look, as if it could pull an unsuspecting child near and deliver a blistering burn.

He started across the room, searching for a door (and unconsciously giving the boiler a wide berth) and ducking to avoid the pipes crisscrossing beneath the ceiling. Many a maintenance man must've uttered a curse after banging his head.

Matt squinted in to the gloom and saw an opening. The heavy steel door that guarded the boiler room was wide open. Why the hell would someone leave the door to a dangerous room like this wide open?

It occurred to him that something might have opened the door and gooseflesh broke out on his arms. What if one of them was down here, looking for intruders? Perhaps Rafferty went through and opened all the doors, allowing his creatures to roam the school and seek out any unwanted visitors.

He raised the shotgun, gripping it until his knuckles were white.

"Get ahold of yourself," he said. Being this tense in a combat situation could get you killed. He was liable to blow a hole in his own foot being this wired up, but he couldn't help it.

Slipping into the hallway outside the boiler room, he

caught a smell that reminded him of rotten eggs. And something else beneath it.

The corridor extended fifty feet to his right, and the smell wafted strongly down the hallway. He could hear wet sniffing coming from that direction, the sound of a predator scenting prey.

Had it smelled him already?

There was a yellow door at the other end of the corridor, and he backed up toward it, taking a glance at the boiler room door and noticing the metal handle was twisted like Play-Doh. It had been in this room, perhaps moments before he'd broken in. If he had gone in sooner, he might have been ripped apart as soon as he broke the window.

Thank the Lord for small favors.

He moved quicker, backpedaling toward the yellow door until he bumped into it. Keeping the shotgun pointed at the other end of the hallway, he reached behind his back and fumbled with the handle.

Please in the name of all that is holy do not be locked.

The door opened as the thing charged down the hallway, chuffing and growling.

Matt slid through the door and backed up as fast as he could, banging against something, a table. There were several tables set up in rows, with metal chairs. A spiked flagpole with the Stars and Stripes draped from it stood near the door, and next to that another flagpole with a green-and-gold flag on it. He realized he was in the cafeteria.

A second later, the door blew off its hinges as the creature crashed through. Matt fired, the flash illuminating his foe's face for an instant, revealing the sickly yellow eyes, bared teeth and dripping saliva. Even hunched down, it was big, maybe seven feet at full height.

It skidded past him, overturning a table.

He pumped the shotgun and readied to fire, but it

was on him too quickly, batting the gun away. The shotgun flew from his hands and landed at the monser's feet.

Sensing it had him, the thing backed up, picked up the shotgun, and flung it across the floor. There was no reaching it now.

He reached for the sidearm in the gun belt, but the thing got a grip on his shirt and flung him toppling over a metal chair.

If anything else were in the building, they were sure to hear the clatter in the cafeteria and send reinforcements.

Scrambling to his feet, he had just enough time to dive out of the way as it leapt at him, claws outstretched. Again it tried for him and he somersaulted out of the way, and it flew over top of him.

Matt bolted for the other end of the cafeteria, the beast in pursuit, wet breaths coming from its nostrils, anticipating a kill. He spotted the flagpole with its spearlike tip. It was maybe five feet behind him, and there would be no time to draw the gun from the holster, turn and fire.

He would have to improvise.

He slowed as he reached the wall.

When he was almost to the wall, he reached out for the flag stand, pulled it horizontal and braced the base of it against the wall. It tried to stop, but couldn't. The tip of the flagpole caught it in the throat and ripped out the back of its neck.

Thick dark blood splashed onto Matt's arm as the creature flailed at its throat, the flag stand sticking out from it at an angle. It fell to the ground, limbs twitching.

Matt took out the pistol and stepped around the body, giving it six feet of clearance, expecting it to spring back to life. When he was satisfied it was really dead, he took one last look at the creature and left the cafeteria.

CHAPTER 34

People had begun to file into the gym about half an hour ago, and the room buzzed with the murmur of conversation.

Jill and Harry crouched behind the file cabinets on the balcony, crammed into a corner, both of them kneeling. Jill's kneecaps started singing after about ten minutes and she hoped they wouldn't have to stay in this position much longer. Harry looked equally uncomfortable, like a salmon packed into a sardine can.

"What do you think's happening?" Jill said.

"Waiting for Rafferty, maybe."

Just then the volume rose, the crowd whooping and hollering as something riled them up.

Jill couldn't resist any longer, and she slid out from behind the cabinet. Crawling to the balcony wall, she peered over.

She wondered if Rafferty had found the creature that she and Harry killed. They hadn't heard anyone rummaging around the school, but that didn't mean anything; it was a large building and someone could have been walking around the wings without them hearing.

Harry joined her at the edge of the balcony after squeezing out of their hiding spot, huffing and puffing from the exertion.

The gym was cloaked in shadows, the only illumination coming from the emergency lights mounted on the walls. Jill estimated the crowd at about two hundred, less than what they anticipated, but still a formidable number. The crowd faced the stage, some of them craning their necks or standing on tiptoe in order to get a better look.

She looked toward the stage to see what the fuss was about, and her stomach knotted instantly. Now she knew why they had been hollering before.

"Oh God," she whispered.

"Sweet Lord," Harry said.

Ed Rafferty stood on the stage, and next to him was Liza. She had been fastened to an X-shaped cross, her ankles and wrists secured to the cross with rope. Her head hung down, and Jill wondered if she wasn't already dead.

Rafferty surveyed the crowd, hands tucked into his pockets, rocking back and forth on his heels like a man who is truly satisfied with himself.

There were two other empty crosses on the stage, no doubt reserved for her and Harry.

"I'll kill him." Harry tried to stand, but Jill clamped onto his shoulder.

"What are you doing?" she said.

"I'm gonna take this rifle and put a new hole in his head."

"You can't do that," she said.

"Don't tell me what I can or can't do."

"Slow down, Harry. Take a few deep breaths."

He looked at her like a man who's been cut off in traffic and is ready to run the other driver off the road.

"I know you're angry, but stop and think."

He exhaled a few quick breaths and then his face relaxed, the tension lines and wrinkles smoothing. "You're right. We have to stick to the plan."

"We'll get her out, okay?"

"All right."

"Where do you think Matt is?" Jill said.

"Maybe he got away," Harry said, although Jill suspected Harry had the same thought she did: Rafferty had killed him.

She had to reject that type of thinking if she wanted to keep going and survive this ordeal. If she had to, she would will him to be alive.

"Are you ready?" Harry said.

"As ready as I'll ever be."

They had counted on Matt being able to use the revolver and free himself and Liza, leaving Harry and Jill to light the school ablaze and destroy Them. Now, they had to worry about Liza.

"How will we get her out?" Jill said. "Do you think Matt's still alive?"

"I honestly don't know, Jill. I'm sorry." Harry reached down, picked up the transmitter, and handed it to her.

"What are you going to do?"

"I'm gonna try for the stage. You light this place up. I'm hoping they'll panic when they see the flames."

"They'll rip you to pieces."

"I can't leave her down there. Better that I go trying to save her than leave here a coward."

"Harry—"

"No arguments. I'm doing this."

Jill saw from the look in his eyes that she wouldn't be able to change his mind. She sighed and nodded; that was all she could do, short of shooting him in the leg.

"Light up the door to the gym after I go through. Bring a few of those cocktails down to toss into the gym. Then get your ass up to the balcony and start lobbing firebombs. If it gets really bad, get out of here and set off the explosives."

They dug two Molotov cocktails out of the box and Jill traded the M-16 for the shotgun. Harry would have better luck with an automatic weapon, as he would need to fire quickly and often.

They crept low to the ground, keeping below the balcony wall, and sneaked down the stairs to the gymnasium door. It was closed, to her relief, which would provide them some cover.

Harry opened the janitor's closet and slid the gas cans out. Then he took out his Zippo and flipped it open, the flame waving back and forth hypnotically.

"I'll open the door. Lob two of those high in the air and then shut the door. Light the gasoline and get upstairs."

"How will you get out?"

"There's that door behind the stage that leads to a service corridor near the cafeteria. I'm going to try for it. Ready?"

She nodded her head and he lit the rags. Harry flipped the Zippo lighter closed and gave it to her.

Harry opened the door and broke into a run, drawing confused looks from the crowd near the door. Many of them turned to watch, but were so stunned to see a fat guy with a rifle in their midst that nobody moved.

Jill stepped into the doorway and pitched the first cocktail softball style into the air, then the second. They rose, hung in the air, then dropped and shattered.

A high-pitched squeal arose from the crowd and someone yelled, "Fire! Fire!" as the crowd parted in the center, flames flickering in the dark gym. The crowd began to swirl and break, like a mosh pit, trying to escape the two areas of the floor that were now in flames.

From the stage, she heard Ed Rafferty yell, "What the fuck! Now! Start it now!" Rafferty yelled.

A change came over the crowd, twisting, spasming, gripping at their backs as if in horrible pain. Some fell to their knees and threw their heads back, howling. Others went straight to the floor, writhing like snakes. A middle-aged balding guy in a suit raised his hand in front of his face and watched it as the bones lengthened beneath the skin. All around Jill could hear popping and soft crunching and she realized with disgust that it was the sound of bones and joints rearranging themselves.

Not wanting to see anymore, she slammed the door and dragged the cans to the foot of the stairs. After unscrewing the caps, she heaved one, then the other onto the bottom step and them kicked them over, spilling the gasoline. It lapped across the floor and spread under the gym door.

She climbed to the landing and flipped the top of the Zippo. Then she tossed it into the puddle of gasoline and it lit with a whoosh, the wave of heat warming her face. Turning, she was ready to head to the balcony when she heard something coming down from upstairs.

Something big.

Son of a bitch.

Rafferty still had the old woman tied up, and that was in his favor, but if he didn't get the situation in the gym under control, half of them would be roasted alive before anything could get started.

The fat one named Harry was rushing the stage, an automatic weapon gripped in his hands. Best think fast, Ed.

His people would be transformed shortly, and when they were finished, they could surround Harry and tear him to shreds if he ordered it. But that wasn't what he wanted. The fat bastard and the rest of them had to die slowly, the way Rafferty had planned it. They would be tied to the crosses, slit open from crotch to chest and have their entrails ripped out before their eyes. That was how it had to happen.

Rafferty surveyed the crowd and saw that two of his followers had completed the change and had spotted Harry. He yelled, "Wait!" but they couldn't hear him over the din in the gymnasium, so he removed his revolver and fired at one of them, winging it on the arm. The beast turned with fire in its eyes, ready to attack, until it saw who fired at it.

Rafferty met its gaze and motioned for it to come to the stage. With two quick strides, it was at the foot of the stage. Rafferty leaned down and said, "I want him alive."

It grunted and then spoke to another creature in a series of clicks and snarls. The two of them started for Harry, but he saw them coming and raised the rifle. Firing on them, he scored two headshots, reducing their brains to black jelly.

"Shit," Rafferty said.

Smoke clogged the air in the gym, and he could see plumes of it chugging under the door that led to the stairs. They'd obviously started a fire out there too, hoping to cut off the only escape route.

Harry was on the move again, his back to the wall, firing deadly bursts at the ones that had transformed and were leaping at him.

The creatures retreated from the center of the floor, now littered with burned corpses stacked on one another. The gasoline had spread, starting three smaller fires on the floor, and Rafferty knew he had to get them out of here before the whole Harvest was ruined. It was going up in flames, literally.

He fired a shot in the air. "Quiet!" he shouted. His voice echoed in the gym. His followers looked to the stage.

"Surround him," he said, pointing to Harry.

Six of them formed a half circle around Harry, and his gaze darted back and forth between them and Rafferty, waiting. He still had the weapon trained on them, although he could never hope to kill six at once, even with an automatic.

"Give it up, boy. You tried to change the deal on me," Rafferty said.

"You had no intention of keeping a deal with us," Harry retorted.

"Oh, but I do. Drop the gun, put your hands on your head and you'll be escorted up here. And then I let the old lady go. Hell, I'll even call an ambulance for her."

"You produce more bullshit than all the steers in Texas."

"Don't argue with me. You got ten seconds to drop that gun or I blow the little lady's brains out her left ear."

He had them either way. The fat one was surrounded, and Rafferty had just cranked up the leverage he already had by threatening the old woman. Jill would be found by one of his sentries, and then they would die as soon as he could get out of the building and away from the fire.

He was curious to see if Harry would be stupid and weak enough to drop the gun and surrender himself for the old woman. Rafferty found the whole thing quite amusing despite the smoke that was pouring under the main door and the ever-spreading flames.

There would be a way out of the gym for him, maybe

by climbing up to the balcony. If worse came to worse, he could charge through the flames in the hallway. If he survived, his body might heal and restore the damage done by flames.

To his delight, Harry dropped the gun and placed his hands on his head.

He had them.

There was a red door coated with glossy paint in the cafeteria wall, the word DANGER painted in white letters. Matt let his curiosity get the best of him and tugged on the steel handle, hoping that it would swing open.

He heard someone coming in the corridor from where he had just come.

He heard sniffing. Trying to smell him out again. And it was close, almost at the end of the hallway.

He had to get out of here quickly, so he knocked on the door, expecting the ring of metal but surprised when it was thick wood.

Backing up, he aimed the nine-millimeter at the lock and fired twice, shredding wood and turning the lock into a gnarled lump. Then he yanked on the handle, the door jiggling but refusing to open.

Try turning the handle, stupid.

He did, and with a hard pull, the door popped open.

As Matt slipped into the service corridor, his pursuer reached the end of the hallway outside the boiler room. Shutting the door behind him, he hoped for another way out of the service hallway.

He moved through the gloom; a cobweb kissed his cheek, and Matt brushed it away. Three gray electric boxes lined the wall, with thick white cables running out of their tops and up the wall.

Matt felt his way along the coarse concrete wall, expecting the beast to crash through the door at any second. His heartbeat sped up for a moment when he thought there was no way out of the corridor except the way he had come in.

But his hand found a cool, smooth surface, a door.

Leaning into it with his shoulder, he pushed, stumbled and went through the doorway. He shut the door behind him, glad to have two doors between him and the pursuer, however flimsy. The creature that was after him had most certainly found the body in the cafeteria and would be out for blood.

He was in a room three feet across with block walls. Three concrete steps led to another door directly in front of him.

Matt opened the door in front of him and stepped into haze, his eyes watering. He squinted and made out a green curtain ahead of him; he was behind the stage's rear curtain.

Rafferty's voice was audible from in front of the curtain and it sounded like he said, "Bring him here."

Did they have Harry or were they dragging some other poor soul up onto the stage for a sacrifice?

Feeling his way along the curtain, he found the seam in the middle and parted it slightly. Rafferty stood with his revolver pointed at someone strapped to an X-shaped cross and Matt realized it was Liza. There were two more of the crosses on the other side of Rafferty, meant for him and the others.

A crowd of creatures gathered at the far wall and moved backward in a rough semicircle, surrounding someone, herding them to the stage.

Through a gap in between two of them, Matt made out the squat frame of Harry.

The crowd on the gym floor began to squeal again, beating at one another, climbing over each other to avoid flames.

If Harry was down on the floor, then where was Jill? In better shape than Harry or Liza, he hoped.

Fire flashed in the center of the gym as one of them fell onto the flames, and the air began to smell like burning flesh. It was an alien smell, like hot metal and cooked meat mixed together.

If Matt was lucky, Rafferty was thinking that he was farther away, maybe trying to break into the school rather than lurking twenty feet from the police chief.

They had Harry almost to the stage steps when Matt decided to make a move and bust up Rafferty's party. He slid through the seam in the curtain with the pistol's barrel aimed squarely between Ed Rafferty's shoulder blades.

He fired three times, hitting Rafferty in the upper back, twirling him around, Rafferty clutching his chest and spinning off the edge of the stage. He looked like a bad actor hamming up a death scene.

In a perfect world the bullets would have killed Rafferty stone dead, but things were far from perfect. Hell, they weren't even normal, with abominations from God knew where congregating in an elementary school gym and preparing for a ritual slaughter.

The gunshots got the attention of the monstrosities surrounding Harry, and they looked at Matt, snarling deep in their throats.

Harry sensed opportunity and he lowered his shoulder and plowed ahead like a two-hundred-sixty-pound cannonball, knocking one of them off balance and breaking out of the circle.

Harry moved with surprising speed, taking the steps in one bound. It was amazing what a little fear and adrenaline pumped in your veins could do for your time in the ten-yard dash.

When he reached the top of the steps, one of them darted from the crowd and grabbed his pant leg, hooking its claws into the fabric. Harry jerked his leg and the jeans gave way. Harry shot forward, half of his pant leg gone, exposing a leg covered with thick gray hair.

The one that ripped his pants got up and Matt pumped two shots into its face and it rolled off the stage.

Harry ran to Liza and began to untie her bonds.

When she was untied, she fell into his arms and he joined Matt near the back of the stage.

"You saved my ass," Harry said.

"Don't get ahead of yourself."

Ed Rafferty, now transformed, climbed onto the stage, seven feet of muscle and fangs. Three others joined him.

"You got her?" Matt said.

"Yeah. Let's get the hell out of here."

"We're not leaving without Jill."

"First we get out of the gym," Harry said.

Rafferty and the others started forward.

While Matt and Harry were busy in the gym, Jill was dealing with problems of her own.

She had started back up the stairs when she heard heavy footsteps on the upper level, then caught a whiff of something sour. She knew one of them was on its way down the stairs. Which was worse, the flames or the beast?

She thought about making a run for the lobby doors, but that was nixed as the creature stuck its head over the railing, grinning and drooling. When she looked into its eyes, Jill thought she might die then and there. For the first time death seemed real, for even at the cabin she had known they would live to fight another day.

This was different. She was face-to-face with one of them, and the menace was all the more real being this close.

It moved rabbit quick, blocking the doors to the lobby. She backed downstairs, getting as close to the fire as she dared without setting herself ablaze. The smoke raked her lungs and she coughed.

It crouched, staring at her, cocking its head to one side, then the other, as if sizing her up.

It looked at the fire, then back at her. It backed up, then moved forward, then back again.

Afraid of the fire, but for how long?

The flames leapt over the bottom step, forcing her one step closer to the creature; she couldn't hold her position much longer if she didn't want to be burned to a crisp. Sweat poured down her back and a rivulet of it ran down her neck, chilling her despite the heat.

She had to think of something quick.

"Come on, you son of a bitch. If you want me, come get me."

Saying that to the creature felt a little like tapping an angry bull on the snout with a stick, but she had to do something to get things moving.

It growled, crouched low and worked its claws, clenching and unclenching.

"Come on!"

That was all the encouragement it needed. It pushed off the top step, almost instantly on top of her. She was a hair quicker, and flattened herself against the steps as it flew over her and rammed into the door, falling into the flames.

Pulling herself up with the railing, she climbed the stairs in a hurry as the thing shrieked behind her, the flames blistering its flesh. She knew it wasn't dead and would likely pursue her up the stairs.

She opened the balcony door and slammed it behind her, the pursuer roaring up the stairs and smashing into the door, full of pure idiot anger. She hurried to the far end of the balcony and grabbed the shotgun.

It kicked the door so hard it flew off the hinges and fell over the edge of the balcony. She aimed the shotgun and braced herself against the file cabinets, knowing that the shotgun would have one hell of a kick.

It charged and she fired, the gun digging into her shoulder. The blast hit the flaming creature in the face, and it staggered to the side and went over the edge, flaming and howling.

Her shoulder felt as if she had been mule-kicked, but there was no time to dwell on the pain. She had to find Liza and Harry and get the hell out of here before more of them came looking for her.

Looking over the edge of the balcony, she got a little taste of what hell might look like: a flaming pit filled with demons. Her Molotov cocktails had started fires in three locations, and the beasts flailed and pushed against each other to avoid the flames. One of them tried climbing the opposite balcony.

The gym stank of putrid flesh, and clouds of smoke rose from the crowd, swirling around the ceiling and blotting out the already dim emergency lights.

She coughed, realizing that they wouldn't last much longer in here with all the smoke.

Looking to the stage, she saw Harry and Matt backing up as a group of demons advanced, Harry with Liza in his arms.

She took another Zippo out of the bag then pulled a Molotov cocktail from the box.

Lighting the rag, she lobbed it over the side, and it looked like a flaming meteor falling from the heavens. She didn't wait for it to hit the ground before lighting the next one and tossing it over.

CHAPTER 35

"Go, Harry!"

Harry backed up into the rear curtain and slid through.

Matt scanned the creatures on the stage, looking for a subtle twitch or sign that would indicate a charge was coming. He could slow down maybe two of them with the automatic, but if they all came at once, he wouldn't have a chance. The only thing in his favor was their arrogance, for they were sure they had him and could pick him off at their leisure.

A flicker of light caught his eye, then another. Glass shattered and a high-pitched wail rose from the crowd.

Another fireball hit the floor, lighting up the gym and sending the creatures rushing to get out of the way as the flames searched them out.

Rafferty and the beasts on the stage turned to see what the commotion was, and Matt took the opportunity to slip through the curtain and out the back stage door, closing it behind him. Jill had just saved their hides. At least for the moment.

Harry stood in the hallway with Liza in his arms.

"How is she?"

"Barely breathing."

They passed through the hallway and service corridor, winding up in the cafeteria.

In his haste to escape the gym, Matt had forgotten about the unseen intruder that he had heard on his way to the stage. Now, when he glanced to the left, he saw it—a malevolent shape in the darkness. Its eyes glowed hotly.

"Go that way. There's a boiler room where I came in. I smashed out the window."

Matt took a clip from the gun belt and slammed it home. He had one more left after this one.

Harry started for the door that would take him to the boiler room. The creature sniffed the air, tracking its prey. The eyes moved back and forth, and Matt thought that this was what it would be like to be caught on train tracks at night, facing a locomotive. Only this locomotive had teeth and claws.

He backed up and aimed at the eyes, aware that more of them could come crashing through the door at any second.

It came for him, and he fired, the flash from the barrel lighting up the darkness, the monster slamming chairs out of the way.

Matt held the trigger down, the gun bucking in his hand, spitting shells at the still-charging creature. The gun clicked empty as it hit him. It was like getting run over by a Buick.

The gun slid away and it knelt on him, pinning his arms to his sides.

He struggled to move, but it only dug its knees deeper into his flesh.

It opened its mouth, ready to kill, and he closed his eyes, hoping for a quick death.

Smoke bellowed up from the gym floor as Jill lobbed the second-to-last Molotov cocktail over the balcony. She had tried to spread her volleys all over the floor, and it had paid off, as a good third of the crowd was on fire, thrashing and burning.

There was a thud as the gym door was battered open and they spilled into the stairwells, no longer afraid of the flames in the hallway now that the gym was an inferno.

After launching the second-last firebomb, she slung the duffel bag over her shoulder, not wanting to lose the transmitter. There was one more cocktail left plus the Zippo, and she shoved them in the bag just in case.

Then she picked up the shotgun and decided that since Matt and Harry had ducked out the back, it was time for her to get on her horse and ride.

If she stayed any longer on the balcony, she would be cut off.

She started for the door as one of them popped its head over the balcony wall. It must have leapt up, grabbed purchase on the bottom of the balcony and scrambled up to the top.

It reached an arm over, then a leg, intent on climbing over the lip. She wasted no time, pumping the shotgun, getting three feet from its head and firing. Its head exploded like a melon with an M-80 inside it. The headless body fell over the side and landed on one of its flaming brethren.

She tried to leave again, but the balcony door flew open and another one of them stepped out, hissing at her. Plumes of smoke rose from its skin and she could smell the scorched hair on its hide.

She pumped the weapon, ready to fire, when she was spun around from behind.

This one towered over her, and she knew it was Ed Rafferty coming to take her.

The cold floor pressed against the back of Matt's skull.

He heard quick, heavy footsteps on the cafeteria floor and the grip on his arms loosened.

Opening his eyes, he saw Harry standing next to it, landing punches against its skull and shouting "Mother-fucker!" over and over.

He must have pissed it off, for it thrust itself off of Matt and landed on Harry, who punched at it, landing haymakers that would have left a human bloodied and bruised. Instead, Harry's fists bounced off as if he were pounding on a basketball.

Matt scrambled for his gun, but he was too late.

The thing raised its arm and brought it down, bury-ing its claws in the side of Harry's neck, blood spurting as his jugular gave way.

It shook Harry violently, looking like a man trying to remove a piece of tape from his finger. Matt moved up behind the beast, pointed his automatic six inches from the back of the skull and fired six rounds into the head.

The abomination jerked as blood and bone sprayed from its forehead. Its claws tore from Harry's neck, ef-fectively tearing Harry's throat open and finishing him for good. The creature whipped to see who had put the bullets in its brain, and Matt fired three more into its face for good measure.

It fell to the ground and ceased to move.

Matt knelt at Harry's side and cradled his head in his arms. His neck and shirt looked as if someone had dipped him in India ink, but Matt knew it was the darkness making it appear black. The blood would be a scorching shade of red in the light.

Harry's eyes were open, the stare of the dead, and his mouth hung slack.

"Aw shit, Harry."

Hot tears came to his eyes and he fought back the urge to vomit, reminding himself that there were still several hundred of Them running around.

Matt said an "Our Father," the only prayer that came to mind, then closed Harry's eyes. Then he ripped the American Flag from the flagpole that he had used to kill the other beast, and draped it over Harry's body. Matt hoped the other creatures wouldn't find Harry's body; if they did, they would surely consume it. The man deserved more dignity than that.

Matt proceeded to the hallway outside the boiler room and found out why Harry had attacked so recklessly. Liza's body rested on the floor, her arms crossed, hands folded as if in prayer. The infection and the time in the damp, cold cell had taken its toll on her. Without Liza, maybe Harry figured there wasn't much to live for, or perhaps he wanted to join her. Whatever his reasoning, he had given his life to save Matt.

He would owe Harry Pierce for the rest of his life.

He said another "Our Father" for Liza and slipped into the boiler room. Winding his way around the boiler, he reached the window and pulled himself up, grateful now for the pull-ups he had done in the Army.

He got to his feet, hopped the fence and ran through the yard, then cut through the parking lot to the side of the school. Jill was still in there somewhere and he was ready to go back to get her, fire or no fire.

He slid along the wall until he reached the front of the building. A host of demons erupted from the doors, some of them on fire, others with skin burned down to the bone.

Lights came on in the houses across from the scho.

God, please shut your lights off. It'll attract them like moths to the flame.

An elderly man stuck his head out his front door, and one of the creatures immediately charged after him. It took off across the street, moving with terrifying speed to smash through the door. Matt could hear thin screams for mercy that would not come.

Focus on Jill. You can't help those people, he thought.

Matt backed up, realizing that the front door would not be an option. Then he heard a woman's voice, frantic, yelling, "Let me go! **Let me** go, you son of a bitch!"

Jill.

He bolted around the corner and was knocked flat as one of them came around the corner.

Looking up, he could see the Rafferty-thing with his arm hooked around Jill's waist, grinning as if to say, "Lookie what I got."

Matt gripped the gun and raised it, but Rafferty thwarted him by wrapping his hand around Jill's throat. She would be dead with one squeeze.

Jill still had the duffel bag slung over her shoulder, and she gripped the strap hard. Taking it off her shoulder, she swung the bag back and tossed it so that it skidded on the pavement and landed in front of Matt.

"Detonator," she choked out. "In the bag."

He unzipped the bag and found a white cylindrical radio transmitter. Keeping the gun aimed at Rafferty with one hand, he removed the transmitter with the other. In his haste to escape the school, Rafferty either hadn't noticed the bag on Jill's shoulder or hadn't cared it was there. Whatever the reason, it was a godsend. Then he fished out a Zippo lighter and a Molotov cocktail rolling on the bottom of the bag.

Rafferty spotted the firebomb and the lighter, his amber eyes narrowed in suspicion, and released Jill to lunge at Matt. Matt set the Molotov and lighter down as fast as he could, and flipped the switch on the detonator.

There was nothing for a second, then a low blast erupted from the school's guts, as if the hammer of the gods had struck at the foundation. The ground shook, and all three of them were thrown to the pavement. The school shook, fire licked from a basement window, glass whizzed through the air; a piece sliced Matt's cheek open, and bits of stone and brick flew overhead.

The ones that had been at the front of the school picked themselves up from the ground as more of their brethren stormed from the front doors, some of them missing limbs, one completely decapitated but still moving. One dragged itself out on its belly, the once powerful legs smashed and twisted.

Rafferty took off across the school parking lot with his arm wrapped around Jill.

Matt got up and, looking around, shouted to the neighborhood in general: "Get back in your houses! Lock your doors!"

A woman in a pink housecoat got pinned to the ground, her fuzzy slippers visible as her legs thrashed in an effort to free herself.

Have to get to Rafferty, Matt thought.

He scooped up the Molotov and the automatic, and ran back to the unmarked car. He started it up and peeled out of the parking lot. Rafferty was likely headed back to the police station, a logical choice. He could hole up there, maybe switch back into his regular form, thinking Matt couldn't touch him there. He was wrong.

Matt pulled into the police station lot. He grabbed the automatic and the Molotov cocktail off the seat and jumped out of the car. The garage door stood open, as it had when he left. Light glowed from the open cell block door.

Rafferty rounded the corner, Jill in his arm. She thrashed against him, attempted to punch him. *That's my girl*, Matt thought.

He spotted Matt and stopped. He cocked his head and gave a grin, showing off those teeth again. Matt felt strangely calm. He had seen them enough now where the initial shock of their appearance didn't bother him.

Rafferty proceeded to the open garage. He flung Jill to the ground, then turned around and, with a clawed finger, beckoned Matt to come closer.

Matt watched the muscles in Rafferty's legs. They flexed, tensed. He was lowering himself into a crouch.

Now.

Matt dropped into a shooter's stance, and before Rafferty could spring, he held the trigger down. Rafferty started forward, but the force of fifteen slugs from the automatic tore into his hide, dropping him three feet before his intended prey. He rolled on his back. Black blood trickled down its face; one of the slugs had blown out his eyeball.

Matt looked down at him. "You killed my family. Now you have to burn."

He lit the rag on the cocktail. It caught fire, and he raised it over his head. The creature looked up at him with dim awareness. Backing up, he smashed the cocktail on the ground next to Rafferty. Rafferty rolled, squealing like a dying pig. He lashed at Matt. Matt backed up and watched Rafferty's vain attempt to claw at him.

In a moment he stopped, a blackened monstrosity.

Matt looked to the garage. Jill was up on her feet, the front of her shirt smeared with oil from the fall to the garage floor. She looked tired and ragged and beautiful.

"Is he . . . ?"

Matt nodded. "Come here."

Jill started toward him. As she came out of the garage,

he heard the pop of gunshots and saw the front of her shirt erupt in a spray of red. She fell to her knees, a pleading look on her face.

The red-haired cop stood in the garage, a revolver clutched in his hand. He grinned at Matt. "Did you really think you'd win?" he said, and collapsed on the ground.

The automatic slipped from Matt's hand. He looked at Jill's body and screamed. And screamed.

He went to Jill and rolled her over, hoping for some sign of life. She flopped over on to the concrete. The bullets had shredded the front of her shirt. The blood had spread in a star-like pattern. It was futile, but he touched the side of her neck. She had no pulse.

With the back of his hand, he stroked her cheek. He looked at the police station, at the red-haired cop lying spread eagled in the garage. They had done it to him again. Taken it away. Right in front of his face.

He slid his arms under Jill and carefully picked her up. He walked to the unmarked car and opened the rear driver's side door. Then he laid her on the back-seat. After shutting the door, he looked down at his shirt and hands. They were smeared with her blood. He didn't wipe it off.

He had left the automatic on the pavement. Scooping it up, he strode toward the open garage. He could smell the stink of Rafferty's burning corpse. As he passed the red-haired cop he spotted a gas can. Gas can. That was what he needed.

He picked up the can and flipped the top open. Then he spattered the dead cop's body with gasoline. He went through the cell block and squad room, dumping gas on anything he thought would burn.

After grabbing a road flare from the supply room, he

walked back out and looked at the garage. The dead cop's fingers twitched. There would be no resurrection this time.

He lit the flare and it hissed. Matt tossed it in to the the pooled gasoline in the garage. The flames crept across the floor, up and over the cop's legs.

He'd never thought it would end like this—he'd hoped to ride out of Lincoln with Jill.

He got in the car, pulled out of the lot. The flames had caught, and now they shot out of the garage door as if from a dragon's mouth. In the distance, sirens sounded. He glanced in his rearview mirror and watched the smoke rise and curl into the sky.

As he reached the edge of town, he passed Folsom Furniture. He tried not to think about Jill's body in the backseat. He tried instead to remember sitting on her porch sipping lemonade, dinner at Morotto's, the night of sweat and passion in her apartment. And what could have been.

He drove ten miles, into the village of York. As he rolled past the rows of drugstores, plazas, and bars that lined York's main drag, he thought: *They have no idea.* All these people, scampering in and out, buying hair dye and condoms, picking up dry cleaning, drinking a cold one in a dank bar. They had no idea what was happening down the road in Lincoln.

He spotted the municipal building, a brick structure with tall white columns in front. He pulled up to the driveway for the lot and saw the red-and-white police cars in the lot. This was the right place.

He swung the car into a spot and killed the engine.

Entering the front door, he walked down a long hallway to a window cut out of the wall. A heavyset man in a police uniform stood with his elbows on a counter. Through the glass he said, "Help you, sir?"

"I need to talk to a cop."

The guy glanced at Matt's shirt, and Matt looked down. He was covered with Jill's blood.

"You hurt?"

Matt shook his head.

"I'll get the lieutenant."

Matt took a seat in one of the wooden chairs that lined the wall. A few moments later, a trim-looking cop in a crisp white shirt walked out of an office door. He approached Matt as if Matt were a ticking bomb that might detonate.

"How can we help you?"

"There's a dead woman in the back of my car. It's a brown sedan, you'll see it. And you need to send someone into Lincoln. All hell's breaking loose."

He spent the next few hours in a haze, as if things around him were part of a play or television program and he was just observing. After the York police checked out the car and found Jill's body in the back, the lieutenant, whose name was Campbell, sent a patrol car.

They kept Matt in a seat next to one of the desks, unsure of what to do with him yet. He'd told them he hadn't killed Jill, that one of the cops in Lincoln did it. Soon cops were scurrying around the squad room. He caught a glimpse of one bolting out the door with a shotgun in hand.

Apparently someone had gotten on the horn with the Feds, because a tall, thin man with a gray brush-cut entered the room. He wore a dark blue suit and a red tie. "Matthew Crowe?"

"That's me," Matt replied woodenly.

"Agent Adam Haynes."

"Who are you with?"

"Not important, but I'll need you to come with me."
He brushed aside his suit coat to reveal a sidearm in a
holster.

"Not till you tell me who the hell you are."

One of the cops in the squad room, a balding guy
with a goatee, said, "You'd better go with him, Mr. Crowe."

"Not until I know where he's from."

Agent Haynes gripped him by the arm. He lowered
his voice. "Let's just say we know all about what happened in Lincoln. Our people are taking care of it. Now
come with me—this involves national security and even
though you are a valuable witness, I will not hesitate to
hurt you. Got it?"

Matt pulled his arm away. "Fine."

Haynes latched back onto Matt's arm and led him
past the dispatcher's window and outside. As he stepped
outside Matt looked up and saw a dull green helicopter
zip over the municipal building.

Haynes led him to the curb, where a dark blue van
waited. It was windowless on the sides except for the
passenger. He half expected to be driven to a wooded
area, where the last thing he would feel would be the
cold steel of a gun barrel against his skull.

As they approached the van, a second man in a gray
suit jogged around and opened the sliding door on the
side. Haynes moved in closer and nudged him and Matt
got a whiff of the man's cologne and the garlic on his
breath.

Matt slid onto a bench seat. He was vaguely aware of
someone behind him and he turned around to see a
third agent, this one in mirrored sunglasses, sitting as
still as the Thinker.

"Turn around," the agent said.

Matt did, and he felt fabric draped over his eyes and
then heard the *thwipp* of it being tied into a knot
around the back of his head. Great. Blindfolded.

He heard the van doors slam and the engine start, and soon the van rolled forward.

"I don't suppose I get to know where we're going," he said.

"Sorry, chief," Haynes said.

They drove for a few hours, Matt lurching back and forth with the bumps in the road. From behind him, he heard the low rhythmic breathing of the agent in the rear. The van slowed, then stopped. Someone killed the engine. From the front seat, he heard fabric against fabric. Haynes turning around?

"Were you up at that cabin? The one Pierce owned?"

"How'd you find out about that? Drug and torture someone?"

Haynes snorted out a laugh. "Big evil government agents, right? No, the fire department in Pottsville called the cops when they found one of those things' bodies. The cops didn't know what to make of it, so they called the Bureau boys in, who called us."

"And who is 'us'?" Matt said. This guy was starting to piss him off.

"Classified, my friend. We just missed Pierce, tracked him down to a hotel and then lost the scent. We were more concerned with the baddies we found up at the cabin. I'm hoping you can shed some more light on what happened in that little town of yours, Mr. Crowe. The media's dying to get in there, but we scared the socks off of them, told them there'd be jail time if this thing went public."

"How about taking this blindfold off?"

"In a minute."

* * *

The accommodations were comfortable, if a little Spartan. The walls were painted government gray, but they had provided him with a bed, a table and television, and all the books and magazines he wanted. Over the next week, he talked to one dark-suited agent after another; a psychiatrist; a doctor, who performed a complete physical; and two brass with stars on their fatigues. He had shared everything, from the story of Rafferty killing his family to all the events in Lincoln through the Harvest. Most of them listened and nodded, and Matt guessed they had seen the evidence firsthand because no one came in and gave him a happy shot in the arm.

Now, he sat on the bed. The door opened and Agent Haynes strolled in, pulled up a chair and sat down. Matt still didn't know which agency the guy was from, and he doubted Haynes would ever tell him.

"They're doing an autopsy on one of them, you know."

"Let me guess—classified, right?"

"Yeah," Haynes said. "But the medical guys are having a field day with it from what I hear."

"When am I getting out of here?"

Haynes shrugged. "We'll see. Can we get you anything else?"

Matt shook his head.

"You should at least feel safe in here after what you went through."

"I don't know if I ever will."

"Matt," Haynes said. "This place is locked up tight. There's enough firepower on the base to level a city."

So it is a base, he thought.

"You should rest easy," Haynes said. "We're going to hunt them down."

"Agent Haynes?"

"Yeah?"

"You going on this hunting trip?"

"We've got troops for that."

"Don't be surprised when they end up in body bags."